TWO ACTION-PACKED WESTERNS AT ONE LOW PRICE!

CANAVAN'S TRAIL

Canavan saw Sheriff Ben Hughes come bolting out of his office. The lawman stopped at the curb and fired. Canavan couldn't see the target, only the answering flash of a gun somewhere in the street. Hughes staggered.

A dark, shadowy figure lurched across the walk some fifty feet from where Canavan was standing and suddenly pitched out from the curb and fell headlong in the gutter.

Loosening his own gun in his holster, Canavan shot a look in Hughes' direction. The sheriff was down on his hands and knees. Canavan clawed for his gun and fired twice at the shadow that ran down the street.

BROTHERS OF THE RANGE

"I'll probably regret this the rest of my life," Mary Rowan said to her son Pete. "But I'm going to see to it that you get safely away."

She held the rifle on him. "Thanks for your help, Ma," the young man said bitterly.

"I'm willing to help you escape only because your father would have wanted me to do it—even though it's against my principles. Walk ahead of me, Pete, and don't try any tricks. I might forget you're your father's son and shoot you down just like you did that jailer!"

CANAVAN'S TRAIL/ BROTHERS OF THE RANGE

BURT and BUDD ARTHUR

LEISURE BOOKS   NEW YORK CITY

A LEISURE BOOK®

August 1992

Published by

Dorchester Publishing Co., Inc.
276 Fifth Avenue
New York, NY 10001

Printed in the United States of America.

CANAVAN'S TRAIL

One

Sprawled out on the flat of his back, Canavan lay diagonally across the made-up bed in his hotel room with his big hands clasped behind his head and his booted feet resting on the uncovered floor. His gunbelt with the smoothworn butt of his Colt jutting out of the cutaway holster hung from a bedpost. His saddlebags with his hat perched on top of them occupied the room's only chair, a hard, straightbacked thing that stood next to the bureau which held an age-yellowed doily and a lamp with a turned-down light burning in it. A step or so beyond the bureau was the wash stand with its customary basin and water pitcher. A small, folded towel lay next to the pitcher. When the lamplight flickered a bit, Canavan took his gaze from the ceiling with its criss-crossing cracks and focused it on the lamp. After a moment the light steadied and burned evenly again. With a wearied sigh he hauled himself up from the bed, yawned and stretched mightily, rising up on his toes, rubbed his nose with the back of his hand and hitched up his belt. He sauntered over to the window and ran up the shade. It got away from him somehow and shot upward and flapped wildly a couple of times around the roller and, gradually slowing itself, finally stopped altogether.

Standing at the window with his thumbs hooked in his belt, his critical expression reflecting his awareness that both the upper and lower panes were dirt-smudged and rain-furrowed, he stared down moodily into the crookedly laid out street that comprised the town. There was no signpost to reveal its name to newcomers. He hadn't bothered to ask when he had ridden in at sundown, tired and hungry and anxious to sleep in a bed for a change instead of rolling up in a blanket somewhere on the hardpacked rangeland. He had seen so many towns exactly like this one that they had long begun to look alike to him. The only thing that was different about them were their names. Most of them had come into being as wayside stagecoach stations that had mushroomed into settlements and finally into full-fledged towns. There were hundreds of them throughout the west. Laid out in like fashion, all of them had narrow, planked walks, low wooden curbs and wheel-rutted gutters that rain turned into quagmires. Shabby, weatherbeaten frame buildings that were badly in need of repair and painting stood shoulder-to-shoulder on both sides of the street. Some of them sagged so because they were able to lean on one another to keep from collapsing.

As his hard eyes ranged over the street, he noticed that many of the stores had turned out their lights and shuttered their windows, leaving vast stretches of darkness that were broken only here and there by blazing lamplight that burned defiantly against the deepening darkness. There were two good-sized saloons down the street, a couple of doors apart from one another. The bright lamplight that spanned the walk and reached out to the gutter came from them. That they attracted customers and business was attested to by the solidly packed ranks of horses that were tied up at the hitch rails in front of both places. Apparently too there was enough business to warrant the existence of two such establishments. Loud voices and coarse laughter and the tinkle of piano keys drifted streetward from both of them.

It was only about nine o'clock, he judged. Yet in the short span of some two and a half hours since his arrival there four times the sound of brawling had brought him to the window and on two of the four occasions gunplay had resulted. He wondered if that indicated a break-down of the law, the presence of a cowed sheriff who made no attempt to maintain it, or if it meant that there was no sheriff. But because he had long decided to adopt a purely disinterested attitude that left no room for anyone else's problems, he gave no more thought to anything save getting himself someting to eat. He caught up his hat and brushing back his hair with one hand, clapped on the hat with the other hand. He lifted his gunbelt off the bedpost and buckled it on around him, thong-tied the holster around his right thigh and left the room. Minutes later he was striding down the street in search of a restaurant. He found one shortly. But its doors were locked and the light in the window turned out to be a night light that had been left burning. He spied a lunchroom diagonally across the way, halted briefly at the low curb to permit a mounted man to jog past, then he crossed over. But when he came up to the place and peered in through the window he saw that it too was closed. At the far rear of the lunchroom was a turned-down light similar to but not quite as bright as the one in the restaurant. Disappointedly he stepped back from the window, turned and retraced his steps across the street to the hotel and trudged up the rickety stairs to his room.

He took off his hat and laid it on top of his saddlebags. He was about to unbuckle and take off his gunbelt when he heard a muffled scream somewhere along the landing, heard a door open and heard it carom off a chair or a wall as it was flung back. He walked about halfway to his own door when he heard sobbing, then running footsteps that came toward his room. Quickly then he went on to the door and opened it. Just as he was about to poke his head out, a sobbing girl clad in a flowered kimono burst in upon him. He glimpsed an expanse of uncovered chest and the swell of firm young breasts straining against a ribboned and eyeletted camisole. Instinctively he put out his hands to ward her off. But she broke through them and thumped against his body and even though he curled his big hands around her arms to push her away, she managed to withstand them. There were uneven bootsteps outside and a burly man with a mop of mussed hair, beady, bloodshot eyes and a growth of black, stubbly beard on his pock-marked face lurched into the doorway. He swayed a little from side to side. Saliva oozed out of a corner of his mouth; he wiped it away with the soiled, turnedback cuff of his undershirt sleeve. He thrust out a hairy, thickwristed and dirty fingernailed hand for the girl.

"All right, you," he said gruffly to Canavan. "Leggo o' her. She belongs to me."

The girl broke away from Canavan, easily avoided the burly man's lunge for her, and whirled around behind Canavan.

"I don't belong to him or anyone else," she cried. "I was in my room changing my dress when I happened to turn around and saw him standing in the doorway. How he got in without me hearing him, I don't know. The way he gaped at me, that—that filthy beast!"

"Lousy young trollop," the man said darkly. "You

go callin' me names and I'll slap your ears off." Then he said to Canavan: "Her boss said he'd fixed it up for me with her. He must've because she left the door open for me. But soon's she saw me, she put up a holler." Then again to the girl: "Come on, I said. You got my dough. Now I aim to get what I paid for."

"I don't want your money," she cried at him. "It's where you put it. On the bureau. Go and get it and go back to Rogers and tell him if he thinks he owns me, I don't want to work for him any longer."

The stubbly-faced man lurched across the threshold. He stopped instantly, a little unsteadily though, when Canavan moved in front of him, barring his way.

"Oh," he said. "So that's the way it's gonna be, huh?"

"That's right," Canavan told him evenly. "This is my room and I don't want you stinkin' it up for me. So you'd better haul yourself outta here."

The burly man glared at him for a long moment. Then he pulled back his right fist. But Canavan who was watching him alertly was ready for him when he swung. He blocked the rather clumsily and wildly thrown punch with his left arm and exploded his own right fist squarely in the middle of the bristly face. The full power of Canavan's muscular two-hundred-pound body was behind the pulverizing blow. It sent the man careening backward out of the room. His buckling legs carried him across the narrow landing. He crashed into the banister rail. It splintered under the impact. But it held though. Canvan heard the girl gasp when the man toppled over the rail and plummeted downward and disappeared from sight. An instant later Canavan heard his body thump on the stairs, heard him cry out as he rolled down the few remaining steps to the bottom. Bolting out of the room and peering down over the rail,

Canavan saw the man drag himself up to his feet, and clutching his right arm to him with his left, stumble out.

Slowly Canavan turned around. Holding her kimono tightly in place around her, the girl was still standing where she had been before. Their eyes met. As he halted in the open doorway, he said: "You can go back to your room now. I don't think he'll be around again to bother you. Leastways not for a while. Way he was holding his arm when he staggered out, I kinda think he musta broken it."

"I don't know what I would have done if it hadn't been for you."

He made no response to that.

"I don't even know your name," she said.

"Does it matter? Chances are we'll never see each other again."

"Mean you're leaving town?"

"At dawn tomorrow."

"Going home?"

He shook his head. "Wherever I hang my hat is home."

"Oh!" she said.

"I'm heading for California."

"I've heard it's beautiful country out there."

"It is."

"Then you've been there before?"

He nodded and she said wistfully: "Wish I were going there."

"What's to stop you?" he countered. "The stage'll take you to the railroad and you c'n go the rest o' the way by train."

"That the way you're going?"

"No. I'm going the cheap way. On my horse. It'll take me a mite longer that way. But that's all right. California'll still be there."

10

"Wonder how much it would cost me by stage and train?"

"Haven't any idea."

"I was just wondering. No more than that though because whatever it would cost, it'd be more than I can afford. So I guess California's out for me," she said with sudden bitterness. Then with startling suddenness her tone and manner changed. She smiled, and her rouged, parted lips revealed clean, white, and even teeth, and she went on, "Maybe one 'o these days when I've had my fill of this flea-bitten town, I'll point myself westward and start walking. And like you, it won't matter any how long it takes me to get where I'm headed. Just so long as I get there."

"Hope you're good at walking," he remarked with a smile.

They stood facing each other in silence after that, each eyeing and appraising the other. He had already taken note of the fact that she was pretty. She was about twenty-three, he judged. While he wondered how long she had been working in a saloon, he decided that it wasn't exactly new to her. It was a tough life, and the recognizable signs of her calling were there. There was a bold, challenging, tempting look in her eyes, and a studied and deliberate sensuous way in which she held her kimono around her. It accentuated every curve in her body. Then too she had learned how to stand in front of a man, thrusting out her breasts in order to whet his appetite for her. And finally, the cheap rouge that she used so lavishly on her cheeks had already begun to take its effect. It left tiny pinpoint holes in the skin. Perhaps the average man might not have noticed. But Canavan did. He had seen so many others like her in his long years of knocking around the cattle country that there was no need for her to tell him anything about herself.

11

In turn she found herself eyeing him interestedly. He was a big man, an inch or two over six feet, she told herself. Actually he was taller than that, six feet four. His shoulders were broad and he was as flat-bellied as a boy. Big men, she knew, tended to put on weight around their stomachs once they lost their youth. But he hadn't. He would prove to be the exception, she decided. She had already taken approving notice of his red hair, and more particularly, of his even features. He was not handsome. But he was good looking in a man's way, and she liked what she saw. And the manner in which he had handled and disposed of the burly, dirty-looking man who had slipped into her room impressed her. She hadn't met many like Canavan—in fact very few, and it made her wonder. When her curiosity overcame her, she asked: "You a lawman, a marshal or something?"

"What made you think that?"

"Well, are you or aren't you?"

"I was a Texas Ranger for about nine years."

"I thought so," she said. "There's something about you, the mark of a lawman on you."

"Mean it stands out on me?"

"Only in the way you handle yourself. You have confidence, and you know how to use your fists. That comes from experience, doesn't it?"

"I suppose so."

He backed out of the doorway to permit her to pass. She flashed him a smile as she glided out.

"Bye," she said over her shoulder. "And thanks again."

"Bye," he responded. "Good luck."

She halted briefly and looked back at him. "Thanks," she acknowledged. "I'll need it."

He followed her with his eyes. When she reached her room, three doors up the landing from his and the one

12

nearest the stairs, she went in and closed the door behind her. He stood motionlessly, listening, waiting to hear the key turn in the lock. When he heard her lock the door, he stepped into his own room and swung the door shut.

As he unbuckled his gunbelt, he thought to himself: "Wouldn't't've had to ask her twice to come along with me. Bet she'da taken me up on it right off. And that woulda been all I need, to tie up with somebody like her. That wouldn't be just asking for trouble. Woulda been beggin' for it."

He was up at five the next morning. With his saddlebags riding across his left shoulder and his rifle, reclaimed from under the bed, clutched in his right hand, he emerged from the hotel and stood for a while on the walk fronting it and ranged his critical gaze over the deserted street. In the thin pre-dawn light the town looked its shabbiest. He sauntered across the street. He was waiting in front of the lunchroom when its proprietor, a lean, round-shouldered and tired-looking man in his late forties or early fifties, appeared.

He eyed Canavan almost respectfully, and asked a little grumpily: "S'matter, mister? Don't you like to sleep?"

"Sure. But when I'm hungry I want to eat."

The man grunted, unlocked the door and led the way inside. He headed for the rear and disappeared briefly. When he reappeared some minutes later he had removed his hat and coat and had donned a long, soiled apron that flapped around his ankles. Canavan had draped his saddlebags over a stool at the counter and was straddling the one next to it with his rifle propped up between the two stools and leaning against the counter.

"Coffee'll be ready in about ten minutes," the proprietor announced. "What d'you wanna eat?"

"Double order o' hot cakes, some bacon an' coffee."

"Comin' up."

Canavan eyed the man. "You mad at something," he asked, "or is that the way you always look?"

"What's there to be bright an' cheerful about?" the lunchroom owner demanded. "Lousy, two-bit town, I wish t'hell I could clear outta here and go somewhere's else. Only that takes dough and I don't have it. Leastways not enough for what I'd like to do. So with nothing to look forward to, what's there to be bright an' chipper about?"

Canavan had no ready answer for him. The man turned and trudged away, pushed through a swinging half-door that led to the kitchen.

For a time Canavan sat hunched over the edge of the counter on his folded arms. When he heard the approaching crunch of wagon wheels and the dull clop of horses' hoofs, he turned his head and looked out to the street and saw the early morning stage come rumbling into view and brake to a stop in front of the hotel. He got up from his stool and stood in the doorway, saw the driver climb down from his high seat and tramp inside. After a couple of minutes Canavan retraced his steps to his stool and straddled it again. Time passed. When he began to get impatient, he jerked around toward the kitchen, and just as he was about to call out and ask how his breakfast was coming along, the proprietor emerged, backing out through the swinging door, and brought him a heaped up plate of hot cakes and a smaller plateful of crisp, sizzling bacon, and put them down in front of him.

"Ah," Canavan said, moving in a little closer to the counter. "Looks good and smells even better."

Tarnished silverware was forthcoming as was a cup of steaming hot coffee.

"Sugar an' milk?"

"Nope," Canavan replied. "Like my coffee just the way it is. What time's that general store open?"

"Oughta be open now."

Even though Canavan didn't ask him to do it, the disgruntled man tramped to the window, and craning his neck, peered downstreet.

"Yeah, she's open," he announced as he turned around.

Some fifteen minutes later Canavan left the lunch-room, crossed the street, and marched past the general store and turned down the alley that led to the stable. When he reappeared shortly after he was leading his saddled horse, a sleek and light-footed mare whose previous owner had misnamed her Willie. His blanket roll that he had left in the stable was strapped on behind the saddle. His rifle was pushed down into the boot while his saddlebags were slung over the mare's back. Up the street they went. Halting in front of the general store, Canavan tied Willie to the hitch rail, and stepping up on the walk, crossed it and went inside. When he came out again he had a small but well-filled gunny sack with a drawstring at the top of it riding his shoulder. Willie eyed the sack wonderingly, perhaps with some misgivings too, when Canavan hung it from the horn. He climbed up on her, backed her away from the rail, and shifting himself into a somewhat more comfortable position in the saddle, rode up the street. As he neared the hotel he noticed that the stage had gone. He noticed too that the town had finally awakened from its sleep, and was preparing to face the new day. Evidence of it was the appearance of several of the townspeople, a handful of men who were going to work, and a couple of women with marketing baskets clutched in their hands. The men glanced at him as he came abreast of them. The women did not. Willie quickened her pace of her own accord and began to lope. A couple of times she

15

looked around at the gunny sack that was thumping against her side, and snorted, voicing her disapproval of it. But Canavan ignored her. So grumbling deep down in her throat she loped on.

They were nearing the corner with the open road ahead of them when a rifle cracked spitefully, startling the mare. A bullet whined past her head and tore into the wooden curb beyond her. Instantly Canavan twisted around, his gun flashing in his hand at the same time, seeking the rifleman. He caught a glimpse of a rifle barrel poked out at him from an alley. Then he spotted a burly figure with a heavily bandaged right arm peer out at him and he knew the identity of his assailant. He pegged a shot at the man. The bullet struck the far side wall of a frame building that flanked the alley and must have spewed gouged-out splinters at the rifleman forcing him to beat a hasty retreat for now there was no sign of him. When Canavan jerked the reins, the mare bounded away with him. Moments later they had left the town behind them and were racing away westwardly over the open road that spread away before them. Pulling up and bringing the mare to a stiff-legged, sliding stop, Canavan looked back. The burly man was standing on the walk with his lowered rifle in his left hand, and like some passersby who had stopped and turned around to follow his gaze, looked long and hard at Canavan who was not out of rifle range. Squaring around and holstering his gun, Canavan nudged Willie with his knees and the mare trotted away only to break into a lope almost immediately afterward. But when she again sought to quicken her pace, Canavan pulled back on the reins, slowing her. She snorted protestingly and fought for her head. When Canavan refused to ease up on the reins, she renewed her deep-throated grumbling. When he reached down and patted her, she stopped her grumbling and whinnied happily and loped along.

16

Two

Following the freshly cut wheel ruts, Canavan knew that the stage couldn't have gotten too far ahead of him even though it had pulled out probably some twenty minutes before he had. So he expected to sight it shortly. He spotted it suddenly, sooner than he had expected, when he rounded a bend in the road. Drumming along at a steady pace, the loping mare gradually narrowed the distance between them, a little more than half a mile, Canavan judged. Willie finally overtook the lumbering vehicle, came up behind it and swerved around it in order to pass it. As they came abreast of it, a woman's rouged face appeared at one of the open windows.

She smiled and called out cheerily: "Hey, Ranger!"

Canavan recognized her at once. It was the girl from the saloon. He grinned back at her and waved his hand, rode past her, exchanged a half-salute with the driver, forged ahead of the stage and pulled into the middle of the road. Even though the girl meant nothing to him it was only natural that her unexpected appearance should make him wonder about her.

"Last night she didn't have the dough," he thought aloud to himself. "But this morning she's got it. Wonder if she had to roll some drunk in order to swing the trip. Wouldn't put it past her.''

He gave no further thought to her. Willie had already begun to increase the distance between the stage and themselves. The miles continued to fall away behind them. At noon he pulled off the road, guided the mare up a slight embankment, halted her when he came upon a good spot for a fire and swung down from her. Minutes later he was boiling water for coffee. He munched three biscuits of a good-sized bagful that he had bought at the general store and washed them down with two cups of coffee.

He was just about to mount and resume his journey when the stage came rumbling up into view. He waited at the side of the road till it came up to him, and again the girl and he waved to each other. Again he followed the stage. This time though he held the mare down, refusing to let her put on a spurt and get ahead of it. When the mare took to grumbling, he spoke sharply to her and she subsided.

Throughout the long afternoon Canavan permitted the stage to lead the way. Then at about five o'clock when the long-fingered shadows of approaching evening began to reach out over the land and drape a filmy veil over it, there was a sudden crash ahead of him. He looked up instantly. The stage had toppled over and lay on its side with its free wheels still spinning.

He lashed Willie with the loose ends of the reins and sent her pounding up the road. He brought her to a sliding stop at the side of the stage and flung himself off the quivering mare. The stage's right front wheel had come off somehow, plunging the top-heavy vehicle to the ground. Canavan spotted the wheel; it had rolled across the roadway and caromed off some thick brush that flanked the road and toppled over. The four horses that had been hauling the stage were still standing in the

18

traces, their sides heaving and their eyes ranging about wonderingly. One of them whinnied when he saw Canavan. But the latter ignored him. He was concerned only for the girl.

He scurried around the stage to the other side of it, yanked the door open and peered inside. She lay on her knees in a huddled, doubled-over position with her head bowed against the far side door. He reached in, got his arms under her and carefully lifted her out. There was no blood on her face, so he decided that she had struck her head on something and had been knocked unconscious.

Turning with her in his arms, he carried her off to the side of the road, knelt down with her and gently eased her down into the thin grass that carpeted the area. Quickly he returned to Willie, dug in his saddlebags for his canteen, opened it as he hurried back to the girl, and wetting his bandana, swabbed her face and pressed the bandana to her wrists, eased back on his haunches and peered closely at her.

When she moaned and stirred, he was relieved. When she opened her eyes and focused them on him, he said: "Don't move. Stay put while I go see about the driver."

He came back to her after a couple of minutes and bent over her again. Her eyes held on him and probed his grim face.

"He all right?" she asked him.

"He's dead," he told her simply and she caught her breath. "Broke his neck," he added. "Now what about you? Anything hurt you?"

"My head," she replied, and raised her right hand to her head and touched it gingerly. When he bent closer over her and used his big fingers to part her hair over the spot she had indicated, she asked: "See anything there? Any blood?"

"No," he said. "Just a good-sized bump. Musta hit your head on the door or maybe on the roof and knocked yourself out. But you'll be all right."

"That's nice," she said a little sarcastically, and demanded: "What am I supposed to do now? Just wait around for another stage to come along? Suppose it doesn't show up for say a couple o' days? They'll find me laying here with a bump on my head and the rest o' me dead of starvation."

"Don't go getting ahead o' yourself," he said. "Gimme a chance to think and figure out what to do with you."

Her eyes burned.

"While you're doing your thinking, how about getting me up on my feet? Or will that interfere with your thinking?"

He ignored her sarcasm. "Have anything to eat today aside from your breakfast," he asked.

"Didn't have any breakfast," she answered crossly. "There wasn't enough time."

"Then the first thing I'd better do is fix you something to eat."

"Yeah? Like what?"

He frowned, his expression reflecting his annoyance with her. He made no attempt to conceal his feelings when he said curtly: "I don't haul a restaurant around with me. So you won't be getting steak with all the trimmings. You'll have to be satisfied with what I've got."

"All right," she shot back at him. "No reason for you to act up with me. I didn't ask for this to happen. When you get right down to it, if you hadn'ta got me all worked up about California, I supposed I'da beefed some but I still woulda been satisfied to stay put where I was and with what I had going for me. So you see, you're really to blame for this."

"I am, huh?"

"'Course. What's more, Mister Whatever-your-name-is—"

"You talk too much," he said, stopping her with an impatient gesture. "So for a change, I think you'd better listen and listen good. You've got a temper and a nasty tongue, and I don't like either o' them. Even so I'm willing to do what I can for you because you're in a bad spot. But I'd do the same for anybody, even a dog. You keep runnin' off at the mouth with me and I'll leave you flat. So you'd better watch it."

She made no reply. He got his hands under her armpits and sat her up.

"How's that?" he asked her. "All right?"

"Yes. But I'm a little woozy though," she said, curling her hands around his wrists and clinging to him.

"Think maybe you oughta lay back awhile longer?"

"No. I'd rather sit up. You go ahead with what you were going to do." She took her hands from his wrists. As he stood up, she asked: "Got a bottle with you? I could do with a shot."

"'Fraid you'll have to do without it."

"Thought every man carried a bottle in his saddlebag. But you have to be the exception. You have to be different. Figures though, doesn't it, that it'd be your kind that I'd get mixed up with? Funny though. Thought I had you figured back there in the hotel. Guess I was all wrong about you. Maybe that happened because I've never had 'ny dealings with characters like you."

"That makes us even. I've never had 'ny dealings with steerers and drunk rollers. Although I've seen enough o' them in my travels. But they don't rate very high in my book. So I've steered clear o' them. Last night you said you didn't have enough dough to carry

21

you all the way out to California. But alluva sudden you're in the chips. What'd you do, roll some drunk after you went back to work?"

Her eyes blazed. "None o' your damned business!" she flung back at him.

He turned on his heel and strode away. She followed him with narrowed, angry eyes. She watched him set to work building a fire. He returned to the idling mare to haul the coffeepot and a small frying pan out of his saddlebag and dig in the gunny sack for a couple of paper-wrapped things. He knelt on one knee, his back turned to her, as he worked over the fire. When the fragrance of freshly brewed coffee reached her, she raised her head and breathed it in.

When she smelled the panful of bacon that he was frying, she forgot she was angry with him, and called out: "That smells awf'lly good!"

He looked around at her over his shoulder. "Then you won't mind that it isn't steak?"

"I won't mind at all!"

Minutes later he brought her a tin plate that was covered with criss-crossed strips of sizzling bacon, two biscuits that he had warmed up for her, and a cup of coffee.

"Sorry, but I don't have any tools. Think you can manage with your fingers?"

"Oh, sure!"

He squatted down in the grass opposite her and watched her eat. She looked up when she felt his eyes on her and said: "You're quite a hand with a skillet. And this bacon is out o' this world." She lifted the tin coffee-cup and sipped some of its contents. "Where'd you learn to make coffee like this?" she asked.

"From a Chinam'n," he told her.

"He must've been quite a cook."

"He was."

"Aren't you going to eat?"

"Yeah, sure. Just waited to see that you were makin' out all right."

"I'm making out just fine."

He got to his feet, turned and marched back to the fire. He rejoined her shortly with another tin plate of bacon and a cup of coffee for himself, eased himself down again and sat crosslegged in the same place he had occupied before.

She watched him eat for a while, then she said: "Something I want to tell you."

"Why? You don't have to, you know. You don't have to account to me for anything."

"I know. But I want you to know this anyway."

"All right. If it's that important to you."

"I didn't roll anybody last night. When I told Rogers that I was quitting and heading for California, he surprised me by paying for the whole week even though there were still three days to go. Then on top o' that, he threw in an extra ten spot. That's how I was able to swing the stage fare."

"Uh-huh," he said.

"I figured I'd take the stage to Hopewell, the county seat. The railroad comes through there," she continued. "Get me a job in one of the saloons and stay put there for a couple o' weeks or even a little longer, all depending on how much I'm able to put away. Once I've got me some kind of a stake, I'll quit and take the train west."

He made no response to that.

"I wanted you to know," she said simply, "so you wouldn't go on thinking the worst of me."

He nodded and asked: "Have enough, or d'you want some more?"

23

"I wouldn't know where to put any more. I ate like this was my last meal."

"How's your head feel?"

"Still hurts. But I feel better here," and she indicated her stomach. "So I guess I'll live."

He removed the tinware. She saw him rinse out the coffeepot and wash out the frying pan, the plates and the cups, dry them with a piece of striped cloth that she decided must have been part of a shirt, and stow them away in one of his saddlebags. He stamped out the fire and kicked dirt over it, smothering it completely. He disappeared briefly around the front of the stage, backed the horses out of the traces and tied all four of them to the rear wheel. He led Willie a little inland from the road and tied her up behind some of the brush, unstrapped his blanket roll and yanked his rifle out of the saddleboot and carried them away with him. He found a spot that was fairly thickly grassed, flipped open the blanket and spread it out and laid his rifle in the middle of it. He trudged back to the stage, rummaged around inside of it and backed away from it with a folded sheet of canvas and a lantern. He made a light in the lantern. The darkness had settled over the land and the lantern, swinging from his hand, burned yellowishly against the night.

He put down the lantern in front of the girl, knelt and helped her to her feet. She bowed her head against his chest for a moment or so.

"Think you can make it over to the blanket?" he asked.

"I—I don't know. I'm a little dizzy. But I'm willing to try if you'll stay close to me."

"No, no sense to that," he said, handing her the lantern. "Hang on to it so I c'n see where I'm going."

He lifted her in his arms and carried her over to where

24

he had spread out the blanket, knelt with her in about the middle of it and gently eased her down.

"Lay back," he instructed her, and she obeyed.

He fumbled around till he found the low-knotted ends of the laces of her high shoes. "You don't have to do that," she said, but he proceeded to unlace and remove her shoes.

He reached across her and drew the other half of the blanket over her, and said: "Sleepin' out in the open can't begin to compare with sleepin' in a bed. But when you can't have a bed, you have to settle for the next best thing." She made no reply and he went on. "I know it's kinda early for you to be turnin' in. But you oughta be tired enough to sleep anyway. So give it a try."

He climbed to his feet, caught up the lantern and marched off with it. She followed him with her eyes. The distorting night light made him look even taller and more broad-shouldered than he was. When he disappeared in the darkness, she slumped down again. It was ridiculous, she thought to herself. She would never tell it to anyone because she knew she wouldn't be believed. He had come to her assistance the night before, and now he was taking care of her even to the point of taking off her shoes. Yet neither of them knew the other's name. And when he finished whatever he had gone off to do, she was sure that he intended to get in under the blanket with her. Up since dawn, it had been a long and tiring day for her. In addition the blow that she had received made her head throb. It subsided only when she closed her eyes. But because she was determined to stay awake, she opened them again. Despite her resolve, the steadily deepening darkness and the silence that had draped itself over the open countryside proved overpowering and she surrendered to them, closed her eyes and fell asleep. Proof of her weariness was the deep sigh that came from her.

She awoke with a start when there was movement close by her and she heard something heavy drop in the grass. She raised up again when she saw a tall figure that she recognized. "Oh!"

"I wake you up?" Canavan asked.

"It's all right," she assured him. "I was only dozing."

"So used to being alone, 'fraid I forgot you were here and dumped my saddle without thinking. I'm sorry."

"Forget it. Oh, meant to ask you this before. What'd you do about the driver? Leave him laying out there in the road?"

"No. Found the lantern and some canvas under the seat inside the stage and rolled him up in the tarp and laid him in the grass at the side o' the road."

She couldn't see the light from the lantern and took that to mean that he had blown it out. He seated himself on the blanket and tugged at his boots and finally got them off, lifted the blanket and drew it up over him, and turned himself on his side with his back to her.

"If I snore," he said over his shoulder, "just give me a poke. G'night."

"G'night," she responded.

She lay rigidly for a while, refusing to doze off again till she was certain that he was asleep. A couple of times she felt herself dropping off and doggedly forced herself to stay awake. She turned toward him and looked in his direction, raising herself up on her elbow to peer at him. He appeared to have fallen asleep but she couldn't tell for certain even though she could hear his measured breathing. She found herself wondering about him, wondered what he was really like, wondered if he had ever been married, and if he had, what kind of a woman he had chosen for his wife, and finally what had become of her that had turned him into a footloose wanderer.

Remembering what he had said about steerers and drunk rollers, she smiled a little scornfully to answer, and thought: "Maybe she wasn't as straight-laced as he was and when she couldn't stand him any longer, walked out on him. Maybe that soured him on all women and explains why he's footloose. Wonder if that's it?"

He stirred once and she stopped her conjecturing and held her gaze on him. But then he lay quietly. Sleep overtook her again shortly after that.

It was morning when she awoke, again with a start. It took her a minute to remember where she was and how she had gotten there. Then she saw that she was alone. The blanket had been drawn up closer around her. She couldn't recall having done that, and decided that he had done it when he had awakened. There was an uncomfortable chill in the air despite a warming sun overhead. She forced herself up into a sitting position and hastily made a grab for the blanket and pulled it up around her and huddled in it. She was agreeably surprised to find that movement of her head did not cause it to throb. She raised her eyes when a tall figure topped the tiny upgrade that led inland from the road. As he neared her she saw that he was carrying a cup of coffee.

"Think this oughta help you stand the chill," he said and handed it to her.

She sipped it and looked up again.

"Good and hot," she said. "I can feel it all the way down to my toes. Thanks."

"Just a part o' the service."

"You keep it up and you'll spoil me for sure."

He smiled. "Sleep all right?"

"Woke up a couple o' times," she replied. "But went right back to sleep each time. So all in all, I'd say I had a pretty good night."

"Take your time with that coffee. I've got some

27

things to do," he said and turned to go but stopped and looked back at her and asked: "How's your head feel?"

"All right."

"No more dizziness?"

"No sign of it so far."

"Good," he said, and tramped away.

Minutes later when he rejoined her he found her on her feet, looking down at herself critically. Her dress was badly wrinkled and so was the short jacket she wore over it. She raised her eyes to meet his.

"I'm a mess," she said unhappily. "I feel like one and I'm sure I look like one."

"I wouldn't say that. Outside o' lookin' a little wrinkled and your hair needing a mite o' fixing, I think you look fine. Oh, that box that got dumped off the top o' the stage, one made outta some kind o' cloth with flowers in it, that yours?"

"Yes. My clothes are in it."

"Want it?"

"Please. I'd like to change into another dress."

"I'll get it for you. When you're ready to have your breakfast, lemme know."

She had changed her dress and combed her hair and had even rouged her face and lips and applied cologne. When she came close to Canavan, he made a wry face.

"What's the matter?" she wanted to know.

"You have to use all that stuff even when you aren't working? Y'know you were in my room only about ten minutes. But when I got up this morning I could still smell that—that cologne. And that stuff you use on your face, don't you know what it's doin' to your skin?"

She looked annoyed.

"It's a good thing I'm not married to you," she retorted.

28

"You c'n say that again."

"You'd have me looking like an old frump."

"You've got a nice face. So why d'you have to use all that paint and make yourself look like a Comanche on the warpath and smell like his squaw?"

Tight-lipped, with her eyes burning, she said angrily: "Why don't you leave me here and go on your way? Maybe the next man who comes along won't be so fussy when he sees and smells me? Maybe he'll like me just the way I am? I've known a lot of men who've liked me and who would've taken me in a minute."

"I wouldn't do that to a dog," he answered. "Leave him to shift for himself out here in the middle o' nowhere. So I can't do that to you either. C'mon now, squat, so's we c'n eat and get going again."

She was angry with him, but she did not permit her hurt feelings to make her do anything foolish like declining his offer of breakfast. They ate in silence. She avoided his eyes, looked away when he looked at her. When the coffeepot, the plates and the cups had been washed, dried and put away, and the fire had been smothered, and the idling mare had been saddled, Canavan's rifle was pushed down into the boot. He folded his blanket into a thick pad and laid it across Willie's back behind the saddle. He climbed up and at his insistence the girl handed him the box, and holding it in front of him he freed his left hand, and said as he reached down: "Lift your dress. You can't ride side-saddle 'less you wanna get bounced off."

When she raised her dress about even with the tops of her shoes, he frowned and said curtly: "Lift it higher. I've seen women's legs before, and I don't think yours c'n be any different from theirs. What's more, if you didn't show enough o' yourself when you were workin' in that Rogers' saloon, he'da fired you a long time ago

29

instead o' keepin' you on.''

He gave her no opportunity to answer. The moment she raised her dress high enough to permit her to straddle Willie, he caught her under her left arm and hoisted her onto the mare's back. She squirmed about in an effort to smooth out her dress under her, and finally settled herself comfortably.

''What d'you say? All set?'' Canavan asked her.

''Yes!''

''Now comes the part you're really gonna love,'' he said, squaring around. ''I don't wanna lose you. So you'd better put your arms around me and hang on.''

She obeyed, curled her arms around his waist only to draw them back and get a firm grip on his pants belt. He made no comment, but simply nudged Willie with his knees, and the mare plodded away with them and shortly broke into a jog.

Three

There was no conversation between them. Apparently their silence must have puzzled the mare for she looked around at them several times rather wonderingly in the course of the long hours that followed. At about ten-thirty Canavan halted her in order to give her a breather and a chance to blow herself. While she stood a little spread-legged, Canavan helped the girl get down and then dismounted. He glanced at the girl. She stood with her back turned to him, looking back at the road over which they had come.

When the mare pawed the ground with her hoof, a sign that she was ready to go on again, Canavan patted her and climbed up on her. The girl came forward. Wordlessly he pointed to her box. She lifted it and he bent and took it from her. Again he settled it in front of him, and as before, reached down for her and with a slight heave of his left shoulder and a tightening of his left arm, swung her up behind him. He waited patiently for her to tell him when she was ready; when there was no word from her, he said over his shoulder: "Lemme know when you're all set."

"I'm all set now," she snapped.

"Thanks," he said dryly.

"You're welcome," she retorted.

Willie trotted away with them. Again neither Canavan nor the girl made any effort to talk. It was shortly after twelve when they made their second stop, this time for their midday meal. It consisted of generously heaped plates of hot cakes and coffee. They sat opposite each other and ate in silence. When Canavan was finished, he simply rose and stalked off. He was rinsing out the coffeepot when the girl brought him her plate and cup and sauntered away again. Ten minutes later they were again on the move.

At three o'clock they made their third stop. Again it was for the benefit of the mare, and only incidentally for them. Canavan stamped up and down and twisted his body from side to side as he sought to rid his thighs and back of the stiffness that had developed in them. He shot a look at his silent companion. She was standing in the middle of the road ranging her hand-shaded gaze over the open country southward.

"Y'oughta work your arms and legs a bit," he told her, "or you'll find yourself stiffened up."

She ignored him as though she hadn't heard him. He shrugged and held his tongue after that. He stood at Willie's head and patted her. In turn the mare whinnied softly and nuzzled him. After a while Canavan swung himself up into the saddle, and without looking around at the girl, said: "Let's go."

They were riding along about an hour or so later when the girl suddenly broke her silence. "Hope we don't have to spend another night sleeping out here."

Apparently the long ride had mellowed her. Canavan was tempted to say something about it, but decided against it. Instead he said: "Stage makes it to Hopewell in one day, doesn't it?"

"That's what I understood the driver to say."

"Then we will too."

"We aren't going very fast."

"I know. I've been holding Willie down because I didn't want to make it any tougher on you than I had to. You've been getting enough jouncing around."

She made no response to that. But after a brief silence, she asked: "What does 'JC' stand for?"

He knew where she had spotted his initials. They were pin-scratched in the metal heelplate of his gun.

"For my name," he replied. "For John Canavan."

"Oh," she said. "My name's Kowalski. Jenny Kowalski."

"Kowalski?" he repeated. "That's Polish, isn't it?"

"That's right. And Canavan—what's that, Irish?"

"Uh-huh."

"I thought you looked Irish. And that was even before I knew for sure."

"What'll you do if you don't find a job, or if you have to wait till one opens up for you?"

"Hopewell's a big town and there oughta be a lot o' saloons there. So there oughta be plenty o' jobs. And if there aren't and I don't hit it, I haven't gone hungry yet or without a place to sleep."

"Uh-huh," he said again.

They rode on in silence after that. It was evening when they sighted Hopewell, and just about seven o'clock when they wheeled into town and rode down what appeared to be the main street. Since it was the county seat it proved to be what Canavan expected, a good-sized town with fairly wide and intersecting streets. What surprised him though was the fact that save for the hotel which he spotted almost at once and a couple of rather widely separated stores whose

33

flickering lights were still burning against the gradually descending night, the rest of what he could see of the town was darkened and shuttered. What surprised him even more was the absence of glaring light and the usual sounds that he had come to associate with saloons. He made no mention of it, but chose instead to wait till Jenny noticed it.

She did shortly when she said: "Funny thing. But this is supposed to be a big, live town. But where are the saloons? Never heard o' them being anywhere else 'cept on the main street, and this looks to be it. Only I don't see a sign of even one."

"Maybe they have off nights," he suggested, "when they close at sundown."

"If they do, that's a new one on me. Far as I know, saloons never close."

"Well, don't go worrying about it just yet. Wait'll we get to the hotel. Then you can ask the clerk, or whoever else is around."

He reined in directly in front of the hotel, helped Jenny get down, then he dismounted. Carrying her box, he followed her into a cubicle of a dimly lit lobby. There was a spectacled, bald-headed man behind the counter that served as a desk, and another man who was leaning over it, talking with him.

When Jenny came up to the counter, the clerk nodded and said: "Evening, ma'am," while the other man straightened up and stepped back. Fairly tall and rather lean, he wore a star pinned to his shirtfront. He glanced mechanically at Canavan who had put down the box, then he looked at him a second time. He moved around Jenny and lifted his eyes to Canavan. "Think I know you," he said.

"Could be," Canavan answered, hitching up his gunbelt. "I've been places."

"So have I. Only we were both in the same place, say

ten, maybe even twelve years ago. It was down on the border. I don't remember your name, only that you were a Ranger and a heckuva man with your hands and your gun. I was a marshal then. My name's Hughes. Ben Hughes. Wanna take it from there?"

"Yeah, sure. We were both after the same man. Think his name was Harvey," Canavan offered with a grin.

"That's right."

"But being that you were a gover'ment man, you had first call on him. Think he was wanted for murder."

"Right again. He'd held up and robbed a mail car and killed the clerk in charge."

"We trailed him to a gambling joint and went in together after him and had to fight our way out've the place after we grabbed him and tried to take him out."

"Uh-huh," Hughes said, nodding. "Nothing the matter with your memory. Anyway, somebody threw a knife at me. I ducked but it caught me in the shoulder. You put a slug right smack in the middle of the knife thrower. A Mex he was. You half carried, half dragged me outta the place while I was still hangin' on to Harvey."

Canavan held out his big right hand; the local lawman grabbed it and pumped it vigorously.

"You're Irish and you've got an Irish name," he said. "And I've forgotten it and I'm ashamed o' myself."

"It's Canavan."

"Red Canavan," Hughes said instantly. "And I'm sure glad to see you again. If it hadn't been for you, I'da never made it outta there alive."

"Excuse me," Jenny said and both men looked at her. She addressed herself to Ben Hughes. "Canavan tells me all the saloons in town have closed. That right?"

Hughes nodded. "Town council decided we could get

along fine without the saloons and the women they had workin' in them. Being that the council hired me and pays me my wages, when they told me to close th'm up, I did just that. The saloonkeepers knew better'n to try and buck the law. So they loaded their stock and their women into their wagons and pulled out. Couple o' th'm headed west, the others went off in other directions.

"That's nice," Jenny said sarcastically. "So because some old pussyfooters with one foot in the grave objected to letting others enjoy themselves, they turned what I'd heard tell was a good, live town into a cemetery."

The sheriff smiled and said evenly: "We didn't shut down everything. We let a couple o' beer parlors stay open. If anybody wants booze instead o' beer and can't get along without it, there's no law that says he can't pull outta here and go somewhere's else. One thing I c'n tell you though, ma'am. Shuttin' down the saloons has made life for me and for our womenfolks a heckuva lot easier."

"I'm so glad," she said with a touch of anger in her voice.

She flashed him a hard, lip-curled look and turned her back on him. Canavan saw the bald-headed man hold out a key to her, and saw her snatch it out of his hand. The three men followed her with their eyes as she headed for a flight of uncovered stairs just beyond the lobby, and watched her go up.

When she topped the stairs and disappeared from view, Hughes said: "Can't please everybody, huh?"

"Waste o' time and effort to try," Canavan said.

When they heard a door on the upper floor open and then shut, Hughes remarked: "Kinda think the lady's mad."

"If she is she'll get over it."

"How long you gonna be around, Red?"

"Till tomorrow morning."

Hughes looked disappointed. "You hafta pull out that soon?"

"I'm heading for California," Canavan explained, "and that's a long ways off."

"I know."

"And being that I'm going, I wanna keep going and get there. Don't wanna make a career outta the trip."

"Will you stop by and have breakfast with me?"

"Yeah, sure, Ben."

"I'll look for you."

"Any place still open where I c'n get me some supper?"

"The Greek's. That's 'way down the street. Look, Red, you go put your horse away. I'll stop and tell Nick that you're a friend o' mine and to stay open awhile longer and that you'll be in say in what, half 'n hour or so?"

"That'll be fine."

The sheriff hitched up his pants belt, seemed to be debating something with himself, and finally asked: "Mind me asking your something, Red?"

"Mean you're wondering about the girl, and how she comes to be with me?"

"Yeah. But now that I think of it, it's none o' my business, and I shouldn't've asked. So forget it. See you tomorrow."

Canavan smiled. "It isn't anything like what you think, Ben. So there isn't any reason why I shouldn't tell you."

Without going into too much detail, Canavan told Hughes how Jenny and he had become acquainted. The sheriff listened attentively, and when Canavan finished, he simply said: "The stage company office is down the street too. Suppose I stop in there and tell Pete Horner who runs the line what happened and leave it to him to do what has to be done about the driver and the busted-down stage?"

"I'd be obliged to you, Ben."

"G'wan," Hughes retorted. "It's damned little I'm doing in return for what you did for me." He nudged Jenny's box with his boot toe. "This thing yours, Red?"

"No. Belongs to the girl. To Jenny."

Hughes turned to the bald-headed man and said: "Bick, be a good feller and tote this thing upstairs to the lady."

"Right, Sheriff," Bick responded. He looked at Canavan. "You want a room for tonight too, mister?"

"Yeah."

"I put the lady in number four. Number six is right next door. I'll hold that one for you."

"Thanks."

Canavan and Hughes left the hotel together. They stopped on the walk in front, briefly, for a last word before they parted for the night.

"Stable's up the street, Red."

They shook hands again. Then Hughes strode off down the street while Canavan crossed the walk to the curb, climbed up on Willie, wheeled her and headed up the street to the stable. Ten minutes later when he re-entered the hotel with his saddlebags draped over his shoulder and carrying his rifle, Bick handed him a key. Canavan trudged up the stairs, turned on the landing and stopped when he came to Jenny's room. There was a large white-lettered "4" on the door. He knocked and waited.

"Yeah?" he heard Jenny ask grumpily.

"It's me, Jenny. Canavan."

The floorboards creaked under her step. She opened the door. She was wearing the same kimono that she had worn the time she had burst in upon him. Turned-down lamplight somewhere behind her silhouetted her figure.

"Yeah?" she repeated.

"Hungry?"

"I suppose so."

"Gimme say five minutes to get cleaned up and we'll go get us something to eat."

"Mean there's a place still open in this graveyard?"

"Down the street. The man who runs it, a Greek named Nick, is waiting for us."

"I'll be ready when you are."

"Five minutes," he repeated.

She made no reply, simply stepped back and closed the door.

It was just about five minutes later when he returned for her, knocked again on her door and waited.

"It's open," she answered. "Come on in."

He opened the door and poked his head in. Jennie was standing in front of her bureau, peering into the looking glass at the top of it while she tried to hook up her dress at the back.

"Musta been outta my head when I let myself get talked into buying this thing," she muttered. "All o' my other dresses hook up the front. So I had to go and buy this one so's I'd have something else to aggravate me." He moved into the open doorway and halted there and watched her futile efforts to hook up her dress. She turned her head and looked at him and said crossly: "If you expect to eat tonight, you'd better come over here and see if you can hook me up."

As he advanced into the room he took off his hat,

dropped it in the chair that stood nearby, moved behind her and carefully hooked up the dress.

"All right?" she asked.

"Yep. All hooked up, and you look very nice in it."

"Thanks." Her box stood open against the opposite wall. She turned and took a jacket from it, turned again and held it out to him and said simply: "Please."

He took it from her, held it for her and helped her into it, turned and picked up his hat, clapped it on his head, walked to the open doorway, and half-turning, waited for her. She fussed briefly with her hair and came across the room. Standing in front of him she said: "Hope you've noticed that I didn't put on any o' what you called my warpaint. And no cologne either."

He smiled but made no comment. He pushed back against the doorjamb to permit her to pass, followed her out of the room and yanked the door shut. She handed him her key. He locked the door and returned the key to her and saw her put it in her jacket pocket. He followed her down the stairs. The lobby was deserted. They emerged from the hotel and marched down the street, Canavan's bootheels thumping rhythmically on the planked walk. The night was clear, the air crisp and clean-smelling.

"I had it all figured that this was gonna be the place for me," Canavan heard Jenny say, and he shot a look at her. "Wouldn'ta taken me any time at all to've gotten enough money together to pay the train fare, and there woulda been a little left over for a stake. Just my luck though that they took it into their fool heads to shut down the saloons. Y'know something, Canavan? That's the way it's been with me all my life. Every time I've made plans, something's always come up to spoil th'm for me."

"Y'know, there are a lot o'stores here in Hopewell,

and all kinds o' th'm too. Have you given a thought to getting yourself a job in one o' th'm?''

She stopped in her tracks. Fortunately Canavan was still looking at her. He jerked to a stop too.

"Aw, c'mon now," she said. "You oughta know better than that. Only kind o'work I've ever done has been in a saloon. Can you picture me working behind a counter selling something like ribbons or maybe yard goods?"

"How d'you know you wouldn't be able to make a go of it when you haven't tried?" he countered.

"I know what I can do and what I can't," she insisted.

"And I think you c'n do just about anything you set your mind to," he told her. "What d'you think o' that?"

"I don't think anything of it. You're trying to sweet-talk me into doing something that I know I'm not cut out for, and it's no go."

They walked on. A signboard that hung from a length of iron pipe that jutted out from the flat roof of a small building across the street and swung to and fro above the walk caught Canavan's eye. It bore a one-word legend: SHERIFF. Despite a curtain that spanned the lower half of the window and a shade that was drawn down to meet it but overlapped it and hung an inch or so below it, Canavan glimpsed turned-down lamplight in Hughes' office.

Jenny ranged her gaze after Canavan's, and said: "I don't think I like him."

"I do."

"Wanna know something, Mister Ranger? There were a couple o' times after you hauled me outta that stage when I didn't like you either. But you let me know right off that you didn't like my kind, so that made us

41

even. And what you did for me, you said you'd have done for anybody, even a dog. Case it means anything to you, although I don't think it does, I didn't feel flattered. No matter what you think o' me, I think I oughta rate a little higher than a dog."

"Of course you do, Jenny. A lot higher too. And I'm sorry I said that. That must be the place."

He took her by the arm and guided her across the walk to the Greek's place, stepped ahead of her, opened the door for her and followed her inside. It wasn't much of a restaurant, probably no more than a cut above a lunchroom. The absence of a counter and some stools constituted the only difference between them. A short, stocky, aproned man with a shock of iron-gray hair, metal-rimmed spectacles and a thick mustache with turned up ends appeared before them as Canavan closed the door.

That he was expecting Canavan was evidenced by the fact he simply pointed to a nearby table, one of some seven that crowded his establishment's floor space. "Sheriff say you don't have no sopper. So what you wanna eat? You like a nice steak maybe?"

Canavan laid his hat in the chair next to him. "Yeah," he said. "A steak'll be fine."

"For the lady too?"

"For the lady too," Canavan repeated. "And all the trimmings."

The Greek made no response. He simply trudged away to the rear. They sat in silence for a while, Jenny with her hands clasped and resting on the edge of the table and her eyes downcast. Suddenly she looked up at him and asked: "You got a wife somewhere?"

Canavan shook his head.

"But you did have one once, didn't you?"

"Uh-huh," he said, but he volunteered nothing beyond that.

"She walked out on you?"

"Nobody walked out on anybody."

"Then what happened to your wife?"

"She died in a fire."

"Oh, how awful!" Jenny exclaimed, and she shuddered. "Tell me about her."

"What d'you wanna know?"

"What was she like?"

"About your height, Jenny, brown hair and brown eyes."

"Pretty?"

"Very pretty."

"Go on."

"She was everything a man could ask for in a wife."

"Where were you when it happened?"

"I was away on an assignment at the time."

"Was it an accident?"

"No. She was visiting a cousin of hers. He'd refused to join in with some other cattlemen who wanted to drive some nesters out of the area. They got sore at him and late one night crept up to his house and set fire to it. When his wife, Beth, and he tried to break out, they were shot down.

"Was that your wife's name, Beth?"

"Yes."

"What happened to those cattlemen?"

"There were five o' th'm. I tracked th'm down, all of them, and I killed all five. That's why I had to quit the Rangers. For taking the law into my own hands."

She made no comment. Again she lowered her eyes and took to studying her hands.

"I suppose you'll be leaving here tomorrow," she

43

said after a brief silence.

"Right after breakfast."

"Think I oughta go back and ask Rogers to take me on again?"

"I'm afraid you'll have to decide that for yourself. You'd rather do that than try to find something to do here?"

"No, but I might have to. And that worries me. I'm afraid that if I go back, that'll be the end of California for me. And I want so to go there."

"Then don't go back."

She raised her eyes and seemed to be staring off into empty space beyond him.

"If I stay here and I do as you think I oughta, get me a job in one o' the stores even though I won't like it or be happy with it. . ."

"It's either that, like it or not, or Rogers. 'Course I know you won't get the kind o' money here that you were getting in a saloon and that it'll take you a lot longer to put away enough money to take you to California. Still—"

There was a sudden, startling roar of gunfire outside and Canavan sat upright. He started to get up from his chair when the stocky restaurant owner came running from the rear. He rushed past Canavan to the door, flung it open and stepped out on the walk, and looked up the street.

Twisting around, Canavan called to him: "What is it, Nick? Y'see anything?"

There was another burst of gunfire. Canavan pushed back from the table, leaped to his feet, whirled around and ran out. He skidded to a stop at Nick's side.

"The stage company," the latter told him, and pointed up the street.

"Y'mean it's a holdup?"

"Sure a holdup. There's the sheriff."

Canavan, shifting his gaze, saw Ben Hughes come bolting out of his office.

Hughes' gun was in his hand. He stopped momentarily at the curb and fired. Canavan couldn't see his target, only the answering flash of a gun somewhere up the street. Hughes staggered. A dark, shadowy figure lurhced across the walk some fifty feet up from where Canavan and Nick were standing, and suddenly pitched out from the curb and fell headlong in the gutter. Quickly Canavan shot a look in Hughes' direction. The sheriff was down on his hands and knees. As Canavan, loosening his own gun in his holster, dashed across the street to Hughes' side, the lawman sank down on his face and belly.

Four

Ben Hughes with his right arm outflung and his gun still gripped in his hand lay half in the gutter and half on the walk. Leaping over the curb, Canavan dropped to one knee at the sheriff's side. Just as he was about to bend over him movement diagonally across the street followed by the rush of booted feet attracted his attention, and he looked up instantly and saw first one shadowy figure and then a second one burst out of a darkened store and race up the street.

Canavan clawed for his gun and came up with it and fired twice. One of the running men, and by now the second one had overtaken his companion, stumbled, tripped over something, either a loose plank or his own feet, and fell. Canavan's third shot missed the first man who skidded on the walk and darted into an alley and disappeared. But in another moment there was a flurry of hoofbeats, and the man reappeared, not yet mounted but struggling to haul himself up into the saddle while his horse pranced about. He accomplished it finally, but only after he had kicked the skittish animal viciously, forcing him to stop his antics. The snorting horse carried him out to the gutter. As his rider wheeled him, Canavan fired again.

His bullet found its mark, causing the man to sag brokenly in the saddle. He toppled into the dirt. He fell heavily, landing on his shoulder and turned over on his belly. Propping himself up on his left elbow, he managed to draw his gun and level it. He pegged a shot at Canavan. But his aim was poor. Fired too high, the bullet struck and shattered a windowpane somewhere off to the left of Canavan. It fell in with a dust raising crash. Tinkling bits and slivers of glass spewed out over the walk.

Canavan replied. Again his bullet found his target. The fallen man slumped down on his face. One of his legs threshed convulsively, but only briefly. After a moment or so he lay still.

Canavan, who had been watching the man alertly with his gun, then became aware of lamplight flaming in windows on both sides of the street. Some of the windows were run up and heads were poked out. Most of the curious were men. In most instances they withdrew their heads shortly only to come hurrying out of their houses rifle or pistol-armed, some of them only half-dressed and several of them carrying lighted lanterns in addition to their weapons. As they poured into the street, other men came from other directions, and all converged upon the scene of the shooting.

A handful of them formed an uneven circle around the man who had stumbled and fallen on the walk, more of them gathered around the latter's companion who lay in the gutter. He was dragged over on his back and lantern light was played over him and shone in his face. Apparently he was a stranger for those who had a close look at him and failed to recognize him simply turned their backs on him and joined the other townsmen who were already standing around Hughes.

A lone man carrying a lighted lantern bent over the

holdup man who had exchanged shots with the sheriff only to fall with him. After a close look at him, the townsman came erect again and trudged across the street.

Lantern light revealed a small pool of blood under Hughes. Some of the blood had already run together with the dirt, puddling it. Carefully avoiding stepping in it, four men lifted Hughes and laid him on his back on the walk. Apparently someone living close by who had witnessed the shooting of the sheriff had lost no time in summoning the doctor, for now a coatless man carrying a small bag and followed by a limping townsman came hurrying up.

Those who were standing around Hughes moved apart so that the doctor could get to him. Bending over him and then kneeling at his side, the doctor motioned and lantern light was quickly played over the unconscious lawman. The doctor opened Hughes' shirt and his undershirt, baring his chest. Both shirts were bloodsoaked, his chest blood-smeared.

"Y'think he's dead, Doc?" someone asked.

The doctor was using his stethoscope on Hughes.

"If he's dead, it's a damned shame," someone else said. "A damned good man and one helluva good sheriff."

"Y'can say that again," a third man added. "And we're gonna have to look far an' wide to find another one like him."

"That's right," a man standing next to him said.

The doctor hung his stethoscope around his neck and got up. All eyes were on him.

"He's still alive," he announced, "so he's got a chance."

A murmur of relief swept through the crowd of on-lookers.

"But I can't do anything for him out here," the doctor continued. "Some of you carry him over to my office. But go easy with him. He's probably hemorrhaging now and careless handling of him may make things even worse."

Willing hands lifted the obviously well-liked Hughes, and with the doctor leading the way, the unconscious lawman was carried off around the corner. Those who stayed behind sent questioning glances at Canavan but he ignored them. Then a hand who had been standing on the fringe of the crowd sauntered over to Canavan, smiled and said: "You're a right handy man with your gun. Good thing you were around or those two holdup men would've got away."

Canavan look at him. The man was Bick.

"Oh," he said. "H'llo."

"I was standing in front o' the hotel gettin' a breath o' fresh air," Bick told him, "when those holdup men broke in on Pete Horner." Canavan's eyes followed Bick's when the latter looked across the street in the direction of the stage company's office. Now there was a light burning in it, and Canavan could see several men inside the place and others idling on the walk in front of it. "They musta gunned Pete down and grabbed up whatever cash they could lay their hands on, shot out the light and started to run for their horses. They'd left th'm in an alley a couple o' doors up from Horner's place. I saw the sheriff come outta his office on the run and shoot at one feller, a lookout I guess he was, who fired back at him. Then as he and Ben fell, I saw you come hustlin' across the street from the Greek's and take over for Ben. That was a nice thing for you to do, and a heckuva risky one too, and I thought the town council oughta know about it. So when I bumped into Al Lennart, he's the head man of the council, I button-holed him and told him about you and what you'd done. I think the town owes you something."

He smiled again and marched across the street. Canavan was following him with his eyes when there was a pluck at his sleeve. He turned his head. The girl was standing behind him.

"Jenny," he said. " 'Fraid I kinda forgot about you. Sorry."

"You needn't be. You had more important things to 'tend to. You all right?"

"Yeah, sure."

"How about the sheriff? He get hit bad?"

"Bad enough. Caught a slug in his chest."

"Think he'll make it?"

"I sure hope so."

"He's your friend. So I hope so too."

He took her by the arm and led her to the corner to avoid having her pass too closely by the dead men and those who were standing around them. He could feel the onlookers' eyes following them and wondered if any of them had heard what Bick had said to him. Nick saw them coming, turned and hurried back inside.

As they stepped up on the walk, Jenny said: "People seein' you taking me by the arm will start talking once they know about me. Aren't you afraid o' what I'll do to your reputation?"

"Nope."

As they reentered the restaurant Canavan drew his gun and reloaded it and holstered it again. He followed Jenny to the table that they had occupied earlier. Seating themselves, Canavan hunched over the table on his folded arms.

"We were talking about you goin' back to Rogers' place or stayin' on here," he began. He heard the street door open. When he saw Jenny raise her eyes and look past him, he asked: "S'matter?"

"A man," she replied low-voiced. "I think he's coming over here."

"All right. Let him come."

He did not turn his head when he heard approaching bootsteps and gave no sign at all when the man halted at their table. It was only when the latter said, "Excuse me," that Canavan lifted his gaze to him.

The man took off his hat, smiled at Jenny and said to Canavan: "My name's Lennart. I'm head o' the town council. Since you aren't eating yet, mind if I speak my piece and get done with it so's I don't interfere with what you're gonna eat when Nick gets to serving it?"

"Go ahead."

"You'll excuse me, ma'am?"

Jenny flashed him a smile. "Of course."

"Pull up a chair," Canavan suggested to him.

Lennart reached for the nearest chair, swung it around, and seated himself in it with his hat in his hands. He was about average in height but rather heavily built, his neatly combed hair gray in streaks through a healthy looking head of black.

"First off," he began, addressing himself to Canavan, "I think I ought tell you what I know about you. Your name's Canavan, you used to be a lawman, you're headed for California, and you and Ben Hughes are old friends." When Canavan nodded, Lennart continued. "Town owes you something for what you did tonight." He dug in his jacket pocket and produced a crinkly new fifty dollar bill and laid it on the table. "We'd like you to buy yourself something with this and call it a present from the people of Hopewell, a token of our appreciation. You'll be needing a couple o' pack horses on your trip west so the horses those three stickup men rode in on are yours. I've had them taken down to the stable and they're keepin' your horse company."

"That's mighty generous of you," Canavan said. "But there wasn't any call for you to do anything in return for what I did tonight. Most of it was for Ben. The rest, guess having been a lawman for such a long time, when I see something happening, I just naturally have to take a hand in stoppin' it."

When Canavan sought to push the bill back to him, Lennart stopped him.

"No," he insisted. "That's yours."

"All right," Canavan said. "If that's the way you want it."

"It is."

"Thanks."

Lennart nodded. "Now think it'd be possible for you to lay over for a spell and carry on for Ben till he's up and around again and able to take over himself? We'd be only to glad to pay you same's we've been payin' him. 'Course we're gonna go on payin' him while he's laid up. We wouldn't think o' doing otherwise. Ben's done a top job for us and we appreciate it and him. What d'you think?"

"I'll wanna stay over for a while anyway," Canavan told him. "Because I'll wanna know how Ben's makin' out."

"Then it's a deal?" Lennart asked eagerly.

"Long's it doesn't mean that I have to lay over too long."

"I understand."

Lennart stood up, swung the chair around, and held out his hand. Canavan got up too and shook hands with him.

"Thank you, ma'am," Lennart said to Jenny.

He put on his hat and went striding out. As the door

closed behind him, Canavan picked up the bill, studied it, looked up at Jenny and said: "Well, what d'you know about that?"

"You deserve it. You earned it and more. You laid your life on the line for them and I'm glad they appreciate it." She smiled. "Y'know something? That's the first time anybody's ever trusted me the way he did, like I was somebody, like I was a lady. And I kinda liked it. 'Course," she added quickly, "I realize he treated me with such respect because of you. Even so—"

She stopped when Canavan folded the bill in two and pushed it across the table into her hands. She stared at it and flushed and finally lifted wide eyes to him. "What's that for?"

"I think that oughta cover your train fare to California and leave you enough to keep you eating for a while after you get there. So forget about Rogers and everything else and dig into your steak when it gets here and enjoy it."

She was still staring at him a moment later when Nick brought them their steaks.

"Ah," Canavan said after he had cut into his and had chewed a small piece. "That's good." When there was no response from Jenny, he looked up. She hadn't touched her steak. She sat headbowed. When he saw a tear trickle down her cheek, he put down his knife and fork. "Hey, what is it? What's the matter? What are you cryin' for?"

She didn't answer. He leaned over the table, put a big finger under her chin and raised her head. There were more tears in her eyes.

"You're the first man, in fact the first anybody who's ever given me anything," she told him. "I owe you so much already without this, and you keep givin' me more."

"You don't owe me a thing. Here," he said, and he produced a clean, neatly folded bandana and held it out to her. She took it. Without unfolding it, she dabbed at her eyes with it, dried her tears and handed it back to him. As he pocketed it, he said: "Now go to work on that steak. Don't let it get cold."

She obeyed, began to ply her knife, but stopped shortly and meeting his eyes, "It isn't right. You aren't responsible for me or for what happens to me," she said.

"Eat," he commanded.

"You aren't that flush that you c'n hand over a fifty just like that."

"No, I'm not flush. But I'm not hurting for anything either, and that includes cash. G'wan now. Eat."

She didn't answer, simply proceeded to eat as he had directed. But she ate in silence.

Nick came to their table and said: "Got it nice opple pie. You like some?"

"Yes," Canavan told him. "And coffee."

"For the lady too?"

"For the lady too," Canavan repeated gravely.

Nick looked at Jenny. "Steak is good, lady?"

"Very good," she answered.

Obviously satisfied, Nick turned and plodded away. He returned shortly with their coffee and two generous cuts of pie, and again left them alone.

Half an hour later when they left the Greek's and started up the street Canavan was quick to note that the bodies of the dead men had been removed and that the lamps that had been lighted after the attempted holdup were still burning, holding off the darkness. There were little knots of men still standing about here and there, a sign that the excitement that had awakened them and brought them out to the street had aroused them to such a pitch that they had no desire to go back to bed. Appraising eyes were lifted to Jenny and Canavan as they marched along.

As they neared a group that was standing on the walk in front of the stage company's office, Al Lennart, detaching himself from the others, stepped forward, lifted his hat to Jenny and said to Canavan: "Hate to have to tell you this, Canavan. But Ben Hughes is dead. Never came to and died on Doc Morris' table. Knowing the Doc the way I do, I c'n tell you he musta done everything he could to save Ben. But it was no go. I'm sorry."

"So am I."

"We'll be burying Ben and Pete Horner tomorrow morning say around nine. Horner was the feller who ran the stage line office here."

"I know. Hughes told me about him."

"He had less a chance than Ben did. When those three skunks busted in on him, they blasted him to bits," Lennart continued. Then he added in a lighter tone: "Meantime I'll be getting in touch with a couple o' good men I've heard of who might be able to handle Ben's job. Soon's I hear anything worthwhile, I'll let you know so's you'll be able to figure on when you c'n head out."

"Right."

"You c'n move into Ben's place any time you like. I think you'll find he kept it nice an' clean. That's the kind o' man he was."

"Think I'd rather stay put in the hotel."

Lennart shrugged. "Up to you."

Canavan and Jenny walked on.

"I'm sorry about that man Hughes," Jenny said shortly.

"They're gonna have t'do a lot o' lookin' around

before they come up with another man like him."

Bick was behind the counter working on a long column of scribbled figures on a page in a worn ledger, a stub of a pencil gripped between his teeth, when they entered the hotel. He looked up when he heard their step. He took the pencil out of his mouth. "You hear about the sheriff?" he asked.

Canavan nodded. "Lennart just told me. Oh, and thanks for giving me such a buildup to him."

Bick smiled and returned to his figures as they headed for the stairs. He looked up again as they made their way up, followed them briefly with his eyes, and began to add the figures as they topped the stairs and turned on the landing. They halted when they came to Jenny's room.

"Shoulda asked Bick about the trains," Canavan said. "No point in you hangin' around here any longer'n necessary being that you're all set to go."

"I didn't know you were in such a sweat to get rid o' me," Jenny said with a little smile parting her lips.

"I'm not."

"Aw, c'mon now! If I let myself believe that, the next thing you'll pull on me will be how much you know you're gonna miss me when I'm gone."

He shrugged wordlessly.

"I wish you liked me. Even a little. Instead o' just putting up with me."

"How d'you know I don't like you?" he demanded. She was taken back by his sharp tone. "You don't know it but I didn't like the idea of you even thinkin' of goin' back to work for Rogers. No more'n I did of leavin' you here and knowing how unhappy you'd be doing something you had no liking for. I'd already made up my mind to stake you to a ticket and something extra to keep you going once you got out to California. 'Course

56

having Lennart come through with that fifty dollars made it easy for me. So y'see you don't know all the answers. Must be the kind you've gotten used to dealing with in those lousy saloons has got you thinking that everybody's the same. You couldn't be more wrong.''

She moved closer to him. Her hands came up and gripped his arms. Suddenly she was pressing herself against him with her arms climbing upward and curling themselves around his neck. She brought his head down and kissed him hard on the mouth. The pressure of her supple young body against his and her kiss rekindled something deep down inside of him. His arms came up to encircle her and crush her to him. But something stopped him and he drew his arms down.

"That was nice," he said. "But what was it for?"

"Does there have t'be a reason for everything? Maybe I just felt like doing it. Or maybe it was my way o' saying thanks.''

He didn't say anything. She bowed her head against his chest and whispered: "Something's happened to me, John. All of a sudden I find I've lost my nerve. And it's because o' you.'' He held her off at arms' length and peered into her face, plainly puzzled by what she had said. "I've come to look to you to do whatever's to be done. And without you to turn to, once I get on that train, I'm gonna feel lost. Sure I want to get out to California. But I'm afraid I'm not going to feel up to takin' on a lot o' strangers. Up until you came along, nothing ever fazed me. Now I've got a kind o' sinking feeling deep down inside o' me. Let me go out there with you, John. Please.''

"But I'm tied down here. You know that. Leastways, till Lennart finds himself a new man for the sheriff's job.''

"I know, and I don't care. I can wait till you're ready

57

to go. And I'll promise you this. I won't do anything to embarrass you or make you ashamed o' me. I handled myself like a lady tonight, didn't I, in front o' that Lennart? Well, that's the way I intend to—''

She stopped when they heard a voice downstairs that both of them recognized as Lennart's.

"No, you don't have to call him, Bick. Just tell me what room he's in and I'll go up myself. Got something important to talk to him about."

"It's No. 6, Al," they heard Bick say.

"We'll go into this later," Canavan told Jenny, and they parted, she going into her room and he into his.

He had just struck a light in the lamp when he heard Lennart's step outside his room, then his knock on the door. Canavan delayed answering it for a moment or two, then he strode to the door and opened it.

"Hello again," the heavily built councilman said with a wry grin. "Got something to discuss with you if you've got a minute and a mind to listen."

"I've got both," Canavan replied and backed with the door and closed it again after his visitor.

The latter stepped inside, took off his hat and put it on the bureau.

"I've been talking with the other members of the council," he began, "and they think that instead o' us lookin' around for somebody else to pin Hughes' star on that we might be missing a good bet by not makin' you a real good offer to get you to forget about California and stay put here. You wanna hear more, or is it California and nothing else but?"

"'Fraid that's what it is.''

Lennart looked disappointed.

"Well," he said, "if that's the way it is with you, then I don't suppose there's any point in goin' on with things. 'Less of course you wanna sleep on it and let me know for sure tomorrow morning before I go gettin' in touch with some others who might be interested in the job. Y'know, things have a way of looking different after you've had a chance to sleep on th'm. We're willing to sweeten the pay to sixty-five bucks a month to keep you here. That's the story.''

Canavan smiled. "I've worked for a heckuva lot less.''

"Uh-huh. That's why I figured this might be something you wouldn't wanna pass up."

Lennart took his hat from the bureau and put it on, nodded to Canavan, turned and walked to the door. "G'night.''

"G'night," Canavan responded.

He followed Lennart to the door and closed it after him. He stood motionlessly for a time, listening to the councilman's fading footsteps. When he was satisfied that Lennart had gone, he left his room and tapped lightly with his fingertips on Jenny's door. There was no answer. Instead the door was opened very quietly. As he stepped inside he noticed that the light in the lamp that stood where his did, on the bureau, had been turned down to its very lowest. He noticed too that the window shade had been drawn to the sill. Jenny closed the door and stood backed against it. As he turned to her, she said: "I was standing behind the door and listening."

"He wanted to know if I'd be willing to forget about California and stay on if they raised the ante," he told her.

"Oh?"

"I turned him down. But because he asked me to I agreed to sleep on it and let him know tomorrow. But my answer won't be any different then."

"I hope you aren't turning him down because o' me."

"I don't want the job. I quit bein' a lawman a long time ago, and I wanna stay quit." When she made no comment, he continued. "I'll give him a reasonable length o' time to get himself a new sheriff. Say a week or so. But if he hasn't tied on to somebody by that time, that'll be it. We'll go on our way."

"Whenever you say the word, I'll be ready to go. Oh, unhook me, will you please?"

She turned herself around. He unhooked her dress and stepped back from her and she turned to him again.

"I tried unhooking it myself. But I couldn't make it."

"Ever drive a wagon?" he asked her.

"A wagon?" she repeated. "Yeah, sure. But that was a long time ago. When I was a kid. But why d'you ask? We gonna go by wagon?"

"If I c'n make a deal for one with the stableman. Oughta be a lot more comfortable living and sleeping in a wagon."

"And how it oughta. I don't think much of sleeping out in the open."

"And it'll be a lot better if we run into rain."

"That's right. Hey, you think of everything, don't you?"

"Let's say I try to. Well, time to turn in. It's been a long day for both of us. I'm kinda beat and you must be too. Oh, don't forget to lock your door."

Half-turning she took the key out of the door and handed it to him. He looked at her wonderingly.

"You lock it," she said. "From the outside. Case I'm still asleep when you're ready for breakfast, and chances are I'll still be pounding my ear by then bein' that I'm not used to gettin' up early, come in and wake me. You mind?"

"No, 'course not."

"All right with you if I call you Johnny? John sounds kinda stiff to me."

He smiled. "Johnny'll be fine."

"G'night," she said and offered him her lips.

He kissed her lightly. "G'night, Jenny."

"Thanks for everything."

"Forget it."

"Johnny. . ."

"Yeah?" he asked with his hand on the doorknob.

"If we don't hit it off right, it won't be because I won't have tried. Fact is, I aim to try harder to please you than I've ever tried doing anything before."

"I'm sure we'll get along just fine. So don't worry about it."

She moved back from the door. He opened it and went out and drew it shut. When she heard the key grate and turn in the lock, she sauntered away from the door, taking off her dress at the same time.

Five

Canavan awoke at dawn the next morning. Turning on his side and leaning out of his bed, he raised a corner of the threadbare window shade and peered out. The thinning night shadows had already begun to lift and dissolve, revealing the street in all its shabbiness. It was hushed and deserted, its shops still shuttered and locked up tight. A gust of wind that came sweeping into town from the open prairie flung dust and dead, curled up leaves over the narrow walk opposite the hotel, and then changing direction veered away to about the middle of the gutter, half-turned a second time and raced up the street and fled out of town. The sky, Canavan noticed, when he raised his gaze briefly, was empty and grayish. He let go of the shade and it dropped back in place over the window, shutting out the dawn light. However some thin rays of light sifted into the room through the cracks in the shade.

It was far too early, he knew, for Jenny to be awake or for him to wake her. So he slumped down again on his back and stared up at the ceiling. He spied a cobweb in a far corner of the room where the right-angling walls and the ceiling came together. But he forgot about it when he suddenly thought he heard sounds of movement in Jenny's room. He kicked off the covers, swung his long legs over the side of the bed and stood up on his bare feet and winced because the uncovered floor was cold. He pressed his ear to the wall between the two rooms and listened. But he couldn't hear anything. After a minute or so, deciding that he must have imagined it, he returned to his bed, drew up the covers and lay back again.

His thoughts went back to the previous night, particularly to Jenny rather than to any of the other happenings. He had been thinking about her when sleep had overtaken him. Now that he was fully awake, he began to wonder if he had let himself in for trouble by letting her persuade him to take her along with him. Yet how could he have avoided agreeing to it? He couldn't have refused her without being cruel, and even though she wasn't the kind of woman to whom he would have been attracted under ordinary circumstances, he had no desire to hurt her. Despite her saloon-acquired worldliness, once the hard crust had been stripped away, she was just an average woman with an average woman's weaknesses and an unconcealed desired for a strong man to serve as a buffer between her and the world.

Something that she had said came back to him and bothered him. While he wasn't certain of her exact words, as he recalled it, it was something to the effect that she would try harder to please him than anything she had ever tried doing before. No woman would ever say anything like that, he told himself, unless she had something in mind, and quite obviously what Jenny had in mind had to do with marriage. Then he recalled something else that she had said. That was just before he had left her. If they didn't hit it off right, it wouldn't be because she hadn't tried. Both things confirmed his fears. She was going to do her best to make herself the kind of woman he would want for his wife.

"Well, if that's it, and it figures it must be, then it sure looks to me like I've let myself in for a helluva lot more'n I bargained for when I hauled her outta that busted down stage," he thought to himself. "Now the only trouble is that I don't know of any way o' backin' outta the deal without hurting her. All I'd have to do is up an' tell her that I've changed my mind about takin' her with me. That'd be one helluva slap in the face for her. Just goes to show you how a man c'n get himself in something way over his head by tryin' to do somebody a good turn."

Again he kicked off the covers and, making a wry face in anticipation of stepping onto the cold floor, made a lunge for his clothes and brought them back to the bed with him, and sitting in the very middle of it, proceeded to get into them. He filled the basin with water from the pitcher and poked a big finger into it. It was cold, and the thought of washing and shaving with it was anything but appealing. For a moment he considered tramping downstairs and getting Bick to rustle up some hot water for him. But sensing that it was too early for Bick to be up and about, he abandoned the idea.

Some fifteen minutes later, still chilled by the cold water, he locked the door to his room and moved on to Jenny's. He put his ear to the door. But there was no sound of any kind from within her room. He tapped lightly a couple of times on the door. When there was no response, he frowned, inserted the key in the lock and turned it and opened the door the barest bit, and peered in. She lay huddled up, with the covers drawn up so high about her that only the very top of her head was visible.

"Jenny," he whispered.

She didn't answer. She didn't move either. He glided inside on tiptoe, debating with himself whether to touch her and wake her as she had instructed him to, or to let her sleep.

"Come right down to it," he thought to himself, "there isn't any reason for her to get up this early just because I'm up."

Noiselessly he backed out, closing the door quietly and returned to his own room. In one of the bureau drawers he found a piece of paper and in still another drawer a stub of a pencil and proceeded to write her a note.

I'll be over at the office. When you're ready to eat, come over.

Once again he tiptoed into her room and ranged his eyes around it, looking for a good place to leave the note. When he failed to find the kind of place that suited his purpose, he backed out again, locked the door from the outside, got down on his knees and laying the key on top of the note, managed to slip both things under the door. Then he turned and went down the stairs. The tiny lobby was deserted, the desk, behind which he had gotten used to seeing Bick posted, unmanned.

"Must be poundin' his ear same's Jenny is," he muttered to himself as he passed it and strode out.

Halting on the walk in front of the hotel, he sent his gaze over the street. It was still hushed and deserted. He lifted his eyes. There was a tiny, flickering glimmer of candlelight in the dawn sky. But as he watched, it began to spread. It grew stronger and burned steadily and soon the entire sky was filled with brightening light, a sign that it was day. A brisk wind came spinning into town. But it was empty-handed and left nothing behind it as it flashed up the street.

When Canavan heard slow, almost measured,

scuffing bootsteps, he looked in their direction. The slope-shouldered figure of the unhappy lunchroom owner came into view and Canavan held his gaze on him as he came steadily closer, and watched him unlock his door and step inside. Moments later Canavan saw the night light at the rear of the place go out. He sauntered across the street and entered the lunchroom.

The owner poked his head out of the kitchen. "You're the feller who doesn't like to sleep," he grunted.

"Only when I'm hungry," Canavan responded, straddling a stool, thumbing his hat up from his forehead and hunching over the lip of the counter on his folded arms.

"What d'you wanna eat?"

"Oh, some coffee and a couple o' buns oughta do me for now."

"Gimme ten minutes."

"You've got th'm," Canavan said.

He sat motionlessly for half a minute or so, then hoisting himself up from the stool, hitched up his pants and sauntered over to the open doorway. Halting astride the worn metal threshold strip, he stood there, gazing about him. Now there were signs of activity and proof that the town had finally awakened. A couple of aproned storekeepers who had already unlocked their doors and removed the shutters from their windows were sweeping off the dust and leaf-strewn walk that fronted their establishments. Canavan heard a window run up somewhere up the street. Then from the opposite direction came the shrill voice of a woman. A dog barked and a man ordered the dog to be quiet. The dog obeyed. There was a brief silence. Then Canavan heard the woman's voice a second time. The man yelled something back at her, and this time the woman held her tongue. Canavan grinned fleetingly. A man came striding down the opposite side of the street. Canavan leveled a long look at him and recognized him as he came closer. It was Al Lennart. Canavan stepped out on the walk and waited. When Lennart neared the hotel and glanced across the street and saw Canavan idling in front of the lunchroom, he angled over, stepped up on the walk, and gave Canavan a nod. "Morning."

"Morning," Canavan responded.

"I was gonna leave this for you with Bick," the councilman said. "But when I saw you standing here. . ." He didn't finish but fished in his pants pocket and finally produced a key that he handed to Canavan. "That's your office key. You'll find Hughes' star layin' on the desk. Put it on like a good feller so folks around will know that the law's on the job and that you're it."

"Right," Canavan said, and put the key in his shirt pocket.

"What'd you decide?"

"Sorry to disappoint you, but it's still California for me soon's you come up with somebody to take over the job."

"I was afraid that that'd be your answer," Lennart said, managing a wry smile. "But I kept hoping anyway that you'd take us up on our offer and stay put. And while I'm disappointed, I can't rightly say I blame you. California's new and big, and judging by what I've heard tell, it's rich country too. So you oughta do all right there for yourself."

"I sure hope so."

"Soon's the funeral's over, I'll get busy sending out some letters. While I don't expect to come up with anybody as good as you or Ben Hughes, long as one o' th'm looks like he might be able to do a passable job for us, we'll have to settle for him." When there was no comment from Canavan, Lennart said: "See you in church."

"Yeah, sure. You mind telling me where it is?"

"'Round the corner from the Greek's. Funeral's set for nine o'clock. Try to make it a mite earlier than that so's things can get started on time. Reverend Mayberry doesn't like to be kept waiting."

Lennart marched off and Canavan slowly returned to the lunchroom doorway. After a few minutes, just when he was about to retrace his steps to his stool, the grinding spin of wagon wheels and the measured thump of horses' hoofs made him look up the street. A stagecoach came rumbling into town. Behind it came a second one. Both pulled up at the curb in front of a shop whose window bore the word BARBER in large letters. There was something else below that in much smaller letters that Canavan had to crane his neck and look hard at it before he was able to make out the words "Undertaker."

An aproned man emerged from the shop and talked briefly with the drivers of the two stages who had already climbed down from their perches. Then the three converged upon the second stage. The door to it was opened and held back. Canavan saw a canvas-wrapped body lifted out. It was the body, he told himself, of the driver of Jenny's stage. The three men carried the dead man into the shop. As the door to it closed behind them, Canavan returned to his stool. He was washing down the last of three buns with a second cup of coffee when he heard a light step. He glanced in the direction of the open door. The newcomer was Jenny.

"Good morning," he said, getting to his feet. "I was just having a little something to hold me till you were ready for breakfast."

"I'm ready now."

He gulped down the rest of the coffee. "Mind if we eat here?"

"No, 'course not."

He helped her seat herself on the stool next to his, took off his hat and put it on still another stool.

"Why didn't you wake me?" she asked Canavan.

"It was so early and you were fast asleep, so I figured I'd give you say an hour more, then if you didn't get up, I'd go back upstairs and wake you."

"I look all right?"

He drew back a little and looked at her. "You look fine," he told her.

"Even without my warpaint?"

He grinned at her. "Even better without," he replied.

"I chucked it together with that cologne you didn't like."

"Oh?"

"I wanna get rid of just about everything I've got with me," she continued, "and get me a couple o' plain little dresses that hook up the front and that can stand hard wear. And a pair o' plain shoes."

He nodded. "Get 'em outta that fifty."

"Nope," she said with a shake of her head. "I've got enough o' my own dough to get me what I need and to keep me going till we pull outta here." She smiled and added: "Then I'll be living offa you."

"You'll earn your keep."

"I aim to," she said gravely. "One of the first things you're gonna do once we get going is teach me how to cook. That's a woman's job and I aim to do that along with whatever else there will be for me to do. Oh, before I forget this," and she put her hand in her jacket pocket, produced the fifty dollar bill and handed it to him. "I won't need it."

He shrugged. "All right," he said and pocketed the bill. "But if you run short I want you to tell me so I c'n give you some. Understand?"

"Haven't anyone else to turn to, or anyone else I'd want to turn to. So if I need 'nything, I'll let you know quick."

"That's what I want you to do."

"What time's the funeral?" Jenny asked.

"Nine. Don't think it's eight yet. So we've got plenty o' time."

The angular lunchroom owner came out of the kitchen., "What c'n I fix for you, lady," he asked Jenny.

"I'd like a fried egg, please, and some coffee."

"And you, mister?"

"I'll have the same," Canavan answered.

Half an hour later they left the lunchroom. As they neared the sheriff's office, Canavan said: "Have to stop at the office for a minute. Lennart wants me to wear Ben's star."

Jenny waited outside while Canavan unlocked the door and went in. Minutes later with Hughes' star pinned to the flap of his shirtpocket, he opened the door intending to call Jenny and have her come inside so that she might see how neat and orderly Hughes had maintained the office and his living quarters.

He stopped abruptly in the half-opened doorway and watched a beefy man attired in city-tailored clothes and carrying a small cloth-covered valise come rushing across the street with a glad cry of "Hey, Jenny!" and throw both arms around her. She struggled to free herself. But the man laughed and held her tight, saying, "You used t'be glad to see me whenever I hit Rogers' place."

"Let go o' me, you—you fat slob!" Canavan heard

her rage at the man who looked like a drummer.

Canavan poked him in the back with a big finger.

"Let go of her," he said evenly.

"It's all right, partner. She's an old girlfriend o' mine. And in her own way I know she's glad to see me."

Jenny kicked him in the shin and he released her for a moment. "Hey, what's the idea? That hurt!" he said and reached for her a second time.

Canavan curled a muscular arm around the man's neck and tightening his arm, dragged him away, and with a mighty heave sent him careening across the walk. Stumbling and tripping over his own feet, he fell in the gutter on his backside and stared wide-eyed into Canavan's face when the latter bent down in front of him.

"There's a stage up the street," Canavan told him. "Go ask the driver when he's due to pull out so's you c'n be on it."

"What's idea?" the man, suddenly red-faced, sputtered. "I didn't do anything."

"I know. But just to make sure you don't do it again, be on that stage when it heads out."

"But I've got business here," the man protested. "What's more I've got friends here. So you can't run me out just like that."

Canavan pointed to his star. "Wanna bet?"

"Oh, the law, huh?" the man said. "All right, Sheriff. I'll go find out about that stage right away."

"Now that's what I call using your head," Canavan said. He gave the man a hand and hauled him to his feet. "Better dust off the seat o' your pants. You've got some o' the gutter sticking to it."

He watched the man hurry across the street in the direction of the idling stages and saw him slap himself on the backside with his right hand in an effort to rid himself of the dirt that his encounter with the gutter had attached to him. As he neared the first stage Canavan saw one of the drivers come out of the barber shop. The drummer and the driver stopped to talk.

Turning and stepping up on the walk, Canavan said to Jenny: "There's a looking glass on the wall in the office. You can straighten your hat in there."

He moved past her to the half-opened door, held it wide and followed her inside and mutely pointed to the looking glass. Standing tight-lipped and a little flushed in front of it, she straightened her hat and smoothed down her dress. "I'm sorry for what happened. I didn't mean to make a scene."

"It wasn't your fault," Canavan said.

"I know. But I'm still sorry it happened. Those people who were watching from across the street, I can imagine what they must have been thinking."

"They can think anything they like long's I don't hear them say anything. Let's go."

He followed her outside. Again she waited on the walk, this time while he locked the door. He had ignored the townspeople who had been standing across the way before. Now he stopped and looked hard at them. Apparently they understood the look he gave them for they moved so suddenly and so awkwardly that they collided with one another. It was plain that many of them had heard of his exploits the previous night. And this time all of them had seen him manhandle the hapless drummer. They had no desire to have him manhandle them.

As they scurried away, Canavan took Jenny by the arm and led her to the corner, crossed the street with her and passed the Greek's place. Rounding the next corner they slowed their step when they saw a number of people crowding the walk in front of a building that

Canavan took to be the church. Closer at hand though was a small group of men who were talking quietly among themselves. Lennart was one of the group.

As Canavan and Jenny neared them, Lennart lifted his hat to Jenny and smiled. "Morning, Ma'am."

Jenny responded with a smile and a murmured "Good morning."

A couple of the other men touched their hats to her too. Most of those who were idling directly in front of the church were bonnetted women. Some of them eyed Jenny critically and she stared back at them stonily. Others smiled at her politely as Canavan led her past them and into the church. They seated themselves in the last row. The church was about half-filled, Canavan noticed, as he sat on the hard bench. There was a general turning of heads, most of them women's, and Canavan, glancing at Jenny out of a corner of his eye, saw her flush.

"Take it easy," he told her in a low voice. "Don't let them get you."

"Old biddies," he heard her say. "Word gets around fast, doesn't it? By the time we get outta here every woman will hear what happened and soon's they get home their neighbors'll hear about it and the first thing I know even the kids will be giving me dirty looks."

Both turned and looked when there were heavy bootsteps behind them. Four men carrying a plain wooden coffin filed down the aisle and placed it upon two wooden horses. They trudged out but returned shortly with a second coffin, and this one too was lowered onto a pair of horses. The people who had been waiting outside trooped in and soon the church filled up. The minister, a thin, pinch-faced individual, appeared and the service began. It was surprisingly brief.

When the service was over and the coffins were

carried out, Canavan nudged Jenny. "Let's go."

She rose without a word when he did. Together they walked out. An open wagon that had its body, wheels and shafts painted black held the coffin. Canavan glanced at Jenny a couple of times as they neared the corner and rounded it. She was tight-mouthed and silent. They passed the Greek's and turned up the street. Still she held her tongue.

As they came directly opposite his newly acquired office, she finally said: "You've got a job to do. So you'd better go do it. I'm going back to the hotel."

"And do what there, just sit and then sit some more, and let those gossipy women force you to hide? What about having something to eat later on?"

"I'll let you know then. Right now the thought of eating anything sickens me."

He made no attempt to leave her, and if she was aware of it, she didn't say anything. When they entered the hotel, the tiny lobby and the counter were deserted. Jenny leaned over the counter and studied the board on the back wall that held the room keys. Canavan pointed wordlessly to a white-painted "4" on the board and Jenny lifted the key off the nail above the numeral. He followed her up the stairs and turned after her on the shadowy landing and waited patiently while she unlocked her door and trooped inside at her heels. He closed the door and backed against it. She took off her hat and put it on the bureau, removed her jacket and tossed it on the box that held her clothes, perched herself on the edge of the box and finally looked up at him.

"It's no good, Johnny," she said. "It's no good and it won't work. So I'm not going with you." When he made no answer, she went on. "Everywhere we go, there'll always be a chance o' me running into somebody who used to come into Rogers' place and who'll remember me from there. It'll be embarrassing for you and there's liable to be trouble, and you're the last one I'd ever want to hurt. You've been too good to me for that. You've treated me like I was, well, a somebody, and while I've liked that and even enjoyed it, somebody could pop up most anywhere and we'd have what happened today all over again. And I don't want that. If I'm alone and it happens, that's one thing. But when it happens when I'm with you, I feel ashamed, even dirty because you're decent and clean and I'm fresh out've a saloon. So if you'll find out for me if there's a stage outta here tonight headed east—"

"Nope," Canavan said curtly. "I'm not gonna do anything o' the kind because you aren't going anywhere except west and with me when I'm ready to go. Now get this straight, Jenny. If anybody has the right to back out, it's me. Not you. I didn't invite you to come along with me. You invited yourself. It was all right with me then and it's still all right with me now. So I don't wanna hear 'nymore outta you about you changing your mind and quitting on me."

"I was only thinking of you, Johnny," she answered, averting her eyes. "I wanted to save you from the embarrassment that's sure to come every time somebody reco'nizes me and from the way people look at me once they know I used to work in a saloon."

"I think I'm man enough to handle anyone and anything that c'n come up," he retorted. "So don't you go worrying about me."

"All right," she said.

In a gentler tone than he had used before, he said: "You said you need a couple o' dresses and shoes, and maybe you'll think o' some other good things you want too once you're in the store. You're gonna get th'm now, and anybody who even looks sideways at you is gonna wish he hadn't because I'm gonna trail along with you and they'll get it good from me. It's warm out. So you won't need your hat or your jacket. Soon's we get you fixed up, I'll go get started earning my wages. C'mon.''

He stepped back from the door, opened it and held it wide, turned his head and looked at her.

"Well?" he asked her. "Time's a-wasting, y'know."

She got up slowly. Slowly too she came across the room to him. There were tears in her eyes. He frowned, took out his bandana and held it out to her. She took it, dried her tears and returned the bandana to him.

He removed the key and followed her out, closed and locked the door, and put the key in his pocket. Together they went down the landing, trooped downstairs, and passed through the deserted lobby out to the street.

"Which way?" he wanted to know.

"Up the street, I think."

Side by side, they walked up the street. When they came to a double-windowed store, they stopped, and Jenny peered in through the open door, turned and nodded to him, and led the way inside. There was a wooden rack of dresses opposite the door. Jenny headed for it and began to look through the dresses while Canavan drifted away from the door and leaned against the counter.

A man, average-sized and rather thin-faced, obviously the proprietor, came from the rear, looked at Jenny, frowned and said coldly: "I don't think any o' those will suit you. Why don't you try one o' the places across the way like Schwab's? The women from the saloons uster go there because Mrs. Schwab uster stock the low cut, frilly things they went for."

"Mean you'd rather not sell me?" Jenny asked.

"That's the general idea," the storekeeper answered bluntly.

"If you see anything you like, take it, Jenny," Canavan said, and the storekeeper who hadn't noticed him standing quietly off to a side jerked his head around and crimson-faced, stared at him with wide, fearful eyes.

"If our righteous friend objects, I'll shove the rack down his throat and make him eat it."

The man gulped and swallowed hard. "Don't get me wrong, mister," he said, swallowing again. "'Course I don't object to the little lady's lookin' at what I've got and pickin' out whatever strikes her fancy. Heck, that's what I'm in business for."

"Hmm," Canavan said.

Jenny selected three dresses, and turning to Canavan, held each one up in front of her so that he might see them. Each time he nodded and each time Jenny laid the approved selection across the storekeeper's arm.

The latter laughed a little hollowly. "Gotta hand it to the little lady, mister. She sure knows what's nice." Then he turned to Jenny. "Anything else you want? Maybe you'd like to take a look around?"

"I need a pair of shoes," Jenny answered. "Oh, and a couple of petticoats."

"Yes, ma'am. You mind coming this way?"

Fifteen minutes later, with the dresses draped over Jenny's arm and Canavan carrying a paper-wrapped package that contained her other purchases, they turned to go. The storekeeper followed them to the door.

"Been a pleasure waitin' on you, little lady," he said. "If there's anything else you need, I sure hope you'll come in and let me show you what I've got. I keep a pretty full stock, you know."

As they came to the open doorway to the hotel,

Canavan slowed his step a little and grinned. "After you, little lady."

Jennie stopped, turned, and gave him a hard look. "If he'da called me that just once more," she said, "I think I woulda screamed."

"And I woulda wrapped the rack around his neck. Go ahead Jenny. Wanna get you and your things upstairs so's I c'n go to work."

"And I'll just lay around and get fat."

"If you do, I'll hitch you to the wagon in place o' one o' the horses and let you help haul it for a couple o' hours. Betcha that'll thin you out."

She smiled and led the way through the lobby and up the stairs to her room.

Six

Canavan's first day as Hopewell's sheriff had passed uneventfully. Now it was evening, a minute or so after eight, and Jenny, wearing one of her new dresses, and he were having their supper at the Greek's. Two young men sauntered in, glanced at Canavan but looked interestedly at Jenny who promptly averted their eyes. They seated themselves at a corner table from which they eyed her without Canavan being aware of it. One of them, a stocky, brawny towhead of about twenty or twenty-two, said low-voiced: "She's just my style, Ollie. I could go for her."

His companion, brown-haired and about average-sized, and perhaps a year or two older, grinned. "Never saw a pretty girl who wasn't your style, Howie, or one you couldn't go for."

"This one's different."

"So what?"

"I've gotta find out about her."

"Meaning you're gonna make a play for her?"

"That's the idea," Howie answered. As he saw Nick come toward their table from the kitchen, he said: "Maybe this feller c'n tell me."

Nick halted at their table. "What you wanna eat?"

"Who's the girl?" Howie asked.

The Greek shook his head.

"Mean you don't know?" Howie pressed him.

"No. Him," Nick said, turning slightly and indicating Canavan with a nod. "Him sheriff. Him bad man with gun. Him kill two men last night when they try rob stage company."

"Hell with him," Howie said. "I wanna know about the girl."

"Maybe you wanna go ask sheriff?"

"Don't be so smart," Howie answered curtly.

"What you wanna eat?"

"Looks to me like they're nearly finished," Ollie said.

"They have their coffee yet?" Howie asked Nick.

Nick shook his head.

"Just bring us some apple pie an' coffee."

"Opple pie an' coffee," Nick repeated and trudged back to the kitchen.

The mustached Greek served Canavan and Jenny coffee and pie and followed with the youths' order.

"Let's get done," Howie said. "Wanna get out before they do so's we c'n see where the girl goes."

"Hope we ain't goin' out've our way lookin' for trouble," Ollie said. "I don't like tanglin' with the law, 'specially when the law's so blamed big and handy with his gun."

"I've tangled with even bigger characters than this one," Howie answered, "and made out all right with th'm."

"I know. I was there. Only they were drunks who couldn't hardly stand up, let alone fight back."

"Get done, willya?"

They gulped down their coffee and crammed big

forkfuls of pie into their mouths. Then they got up, grabbed their hats, slapped some coins on the table, and strode out. They found that save for two places, the hotel and Canavan's office whose lights were still burning, the rest of the street was shrouded in deepening darkness.

They took refuge in an alley just beyond the Greek's place and waited. It was so gloomily dark in the alley, neither of them could see the other. Howie peered out guardedly and hastily withdrew his head when he saw Canavan and Jenny coming up the street. When he saw them pass, he peered out again, saw them halt on the walk in front of the hotel and talk briefly. When he saw Canavan turn and cut across the deserted street and head for his office, Howie said to his companion: "Let's go."

"Know where the girl went?"

"Into the hotel."

"And the sheriff?"

"He's in his office. So he's outta the way. So you c'n quit worrying. C'mon."

At Howie's insistence they slipped out of the alley and walking casually and unhurriedly to avoid attracting attention to themselves even though there was no one about, they sauntered into the hotel.

Bick who was behind the counter looked up and nodded. "Evening."

"Evening," the two youths answered.

The towheaded Howie leaned over the counter.

"I'm tryin' to catch up with an old girlfriend o' mine," he told Bick in a confidential tone. "'Less I'm mistaken, I think I saw her comin' in here."

"Oh?" Bick said.

The youth described her.

"Uh-huh," Bick said, nodding. "You've got a

mighty sharp eye, young feller.''

"Only one trouble," Howie continued, hunching over on his folded arms. "I dunno what name she's goin' by here. Y'see, she ran away from her husband, a bastid who used to beat hell out of her every time he got a load on and that was just about every day. He's been trailing her ever since. Helluva nice girl and like everyone else who knows her, I'm doggoned sorry for her. Maybe she's runnin' short o' dough. If she is, I'd like to give her some.''

"If you wanna leave it here with me, I'll see that she gets it.''

Howie pretended to consider Bick's offer. He looked disappointed and finally said: "Now don't get me wrong, Mac. Don't want you to think I don't trust you or anything like that. Only I wanna surprise her.''

"Tell me your name," Bick said, "and I'll go ask her if she knows you. If she does, I'll ask her to come downstairs. That's fair enough, isn't it?''

Howie dug in his pants pocket and produced a handful of crumpled up bills, took a five-dollar bill from among them and laid it on the counter, pocketed the other bills, grinned boyishly at Bick and said: "Duplicate keys must cost you anywhere's from a nickel to a dime. I'm willing to pay five bucks for it, giving you a clear profit of four bucks and ninety or ninety-five cents. What do you say? Is it a deal?''

Bick looked at the bill as Howie smoothed it out, then he raised his eyes to meet Howie's.

"Sorry, partner," he said with a shake of his head. "But it's no deal. I'm willing to call her down here if she knows you. But that's it.''

Howie's smile and his friendliness vanished. He glanced at Ollie who was standing quietly a couple of steps away. "Keep our friend here company, Ollie. Only keep him covered.''

82

Reluctantly it seemed to Bick, Ollie drew his gun and held it on him.

"Trot out a key to the lady's room, Mac," Howie ordered Bick, "and hurry it."

Bick didn't say anything. He partly opened the drawer under the counter, glanced at the gun that he kept in there together with a box of duplicate keys, put the box on the counter and opened it, and poked around among the keys with his fingers till he found the one that he was looking for, raised his eyes to Howie and held it out to him. "Here y'are. Room 109."

Howie snatched it out of Bick's hand, picked up his five-dollar bill and shoved it into his pocket, turned and headed for the stairs. Ollie turned and followed him with troubled eyes. Unconsciously he lowered his gun. It gave Bick the opportunity he sought.

As Howie topped the stairs and turned on the landing and disappeared from sight, Ollie shook his head and slowly turned around. He stared with wide eyes when he saw the leveled gun in Bick's hand and the muzzle gaping at him hungrily. He gulped and swallowed hard.

"Be smart, young feller," Bick told him quietly, "and put your gun on the counter and get the hell outta here. That's if you wanna go on living. 'Course if you don't. . ."

Bick didn't finish. There was no need. He could see the look of fright in Ollie's eyes, so he knew the cowed youth would obey him. Ollie promptly confirmed his belief. He laid his gun on the counter, stepped back, and started for the doorway when Canavan suddenly appeared in front of him. Recognizing Canavan, and obviously awed by his size, he panicked and hastily backed off from him. Canavan eyed him, then taking his gaze from him for an instant, shot a look at Bick. When he saw the gun in the latter's hand, he looked concerned.

Bick said quickly: "His sidekick's upstairs lookin' for the girl's room."

"Oh?"

"Claims he knows her. But I don't believe him."

"He know where to find her?"

"No. I gave him the key to 109. It won't fit because we've changed the lock. Didn't know what to do 'cept stall him."

"I'll wait for him down here," Canavan said. "You," he said, turning to Ollie, "get down behind the counter with Bick and stay put there. If he lets out one single peep, Bick, wallop him over the head, and good."

Ollie was alive and above everything else he wanted to stay that way. So he needed no urging to obey Canavan. Moving faster than he had ever moved before, he whirled around the counter and dropped down behind it even before Bick did. It took Bick a couple of seconds to grab Ollie's gun off the counter before he dropped to his knees next to the crouching youth.

Loosening his gun in his cutaway holster, Canavan crossed the lobby to the counter, squared himself around and leaned back against it with his elbows resting on the edge of it and the fingers of his hands dangling. There were heavy, scuffing bootsteps overhead. They came rapidly toward the stairs.

Canavan did not turn his gaze on the stairs till he judged Howie to be about halfway down. Then he turned to the youth and said: "Oh! Thought you were the desk clerk. You see 'nything of him?"

Howie frowned. "He was here a minute ago," he replied gruffly.

"Wonder where he went?"

"I wouldn't know," the frustrated youth said.

He came off the stairs, hitched up his pants rather angrily as he came abreast of Canavan, stalked past him and headed for the street. He was within a stride of the open doorway when Canavan came erect and at the same time called: "Hold it a minute, young feller."

Howie stopped, looked back over his thick shoulder, and asked grumpily: "Yeah?"

"What were you doin' upstairs?"

"Lookin' for somebody."

"Like who?"

"For a feller I thought I recognized comin' in here."

"Find him?"

"It wasn't him. It was somebody else who looked something like him."

"You're a liar," Canavan said evenly and Howie bristled. "Unbuckle your gun belt and let it fall."

"Why?"

"Because I said so."

Howie stared hard at him. Then his lip curled a little and he said: "You characters are all alike. Somebody pins a piece o' tin on you and right off you think who the hell you are. You don't mean anything to me, and you don't scare me none."

"Unbuckle your gunbelt and let it fall," Canavan repeated.

Howie grinned evilly. "Maybe you'd like to try an' make me," he said tauntingly.

Canavan took a step toward him. Howie clawed for his gun, came up with it and spun around to shoot. But Canavan who had outdrawn him, outgunned him too. His Colt thundered, and Howie cried out, dropped his gun and clutched his right wrist to him with his left hand. Blood spurted from his wrist and burst through his fingers, drenching them, and ran down the front of him, staining his shirt and pants and puddling his boot-toes.

"You bastid!" he raged at Canavan. "I'll kill you for this!"

He bent over suddenly and sought to pick up his gun

with his bloodied left hand when Canavan leaped at him, applied his right foot to Howie's backside and sent him sprawling on his face. With the same foot, Canavan kicked the youth's gun away. It went slithering across the lobby floor and caroming off the bottom step of the stairway. Pushing himself up from the floor with his left hand and leaving a bloody imprint of his flexed fingers that spanned two boards, Howie got up only to have Canavan fling him around and slam him into the side wall.

"All right, Bick! You c'n come out now!"

Bick promptly stood up. Canavan who had just picked up Howie's gun, shoved it down inside his pants belt. "Be a good feller, Bick, and go fetch the doctor."

"Yeah, sure. Oh, what d'you want me to do with this young feller back here with me?"

"Let him come outta there. I'll keep an eye on him too."

"All right, bucko," Bick said to Ollie. "Up on your feet."

Herding the cowed youth ahead of him at gunpoint, Bick brought him out from behind the counter. Then he retraced his steps, opened the drawer and put his gun away and laid Ollie's next to it. He reached for the opened box of keys, closed it, and put that in the drawer too, and slammed the drawer shut.

As he emerged again, Canavan turned to Ollie and, pointing to the wall opposite the counter, said: "Sit down on the floor against the wall." Ollie hastened to obey. Turning to Howie whose face was contorted with pain, Canavan told him: "Down on the floor next to your partner."

Howie glared at him. "Like I told you before, you bastid," he said thickly, "if it's the last thing I ever do, I'll get you for this."

Canavan leveled a long look at him. "You run off at the mouth. If you don't close it and keep it closed, I'll do it for you. Now get over there."

Howie glowered, but made no attempt to move. Canavan, obviously out of patience with him, caught him by his left arm and with a powerful heave sent him stumbling across the floor. He sprawled over Ollie's feet and fell heavily on his left shoulder, turning himself instinctively to protect his injured arm.

"Goddamn you and your stinkin' big feet!" he yelled at Ollie, livid with rage.

Practically pouncing upon him from behind, Canavan grabbed him by his pants belt and dragged him up, turned him and slammed him into the wall and pushed him down on his backside. Howie shot a look at Ollie who flushed and hastily averted his eyes.

"You yeller-bellied bastid," Howie gritted at him. "How'n hell did I ever let myself get tied up with the likes o' you? You hàven't got the guts of a louse. Wanna tell you something, and you'd better hear me good. Stay the hell away from me, or I'll beat your head off."

"Nice, friendly feller, isn't he?" Bick said to Canavan as the latter moved back from his two prisoners.

"Yeah," Canavan answered. "Only where he'll be spending the next couple o'years, he won't have anything to say about who gets put next to him, or about anything else. Go ahead, willya, Bick?"

"On my way," Bick said, and hurried out.

Backed again against the counter with his thumbs hooked in his gunbelt, Canavan was watching his prisoners when he suddenly became aware of wide eyes holding on him. He glanced at the doorway. It was filled to overflowing with townsmen, most of them armed with rifles. The carrying echo of gunfire and their over-powering curiosity to know what had caused the shoot-ing was responsible for their sudden appearance there, he told himself.

There was movement behind them, some pushing and shoving and Canavan heard a familiar voice say, "Lemme through, boys. Lemme through." Al Lennart, rifle-armed like some of the townsmen, shouldered his way through the men crowding the doorway. He stopped a step or two inside the lobby, looked at Canavan, then at the two youths, and again at Canavan. "I dunno what they did, or even what they tried to do. But from the looks of that one," and he jerked his head in Howie's direction, the latter still clutching his injured wrist with his blood-drenched left hand, "I c'n see what you did to him."

"They were looking for trouble and they found it," Canavan said. "Only more than they could handle."

"Uh-huh," Lennart said. "Judge Martin'll be back in a couple o' days and you c'n bring them up before him. Then the marshal who covers this area and who comes through here every five or six weeks is about due, and you can turn them over to him. He'll see to it that they find their way into prison."

"I'd like to see that everything's all right upstairs. You mind keepin' an eye on them for a minute or so?"

"Go right ahead," Lennart told him.

"I sent Bick to fetch the doctor. He oughta be along any minute now."

"Uh-huh," Lennart said again.

Canavan trudged up the stairs. Jenny unlocked and opened her door in answer to his knock and his call. "It's me, Jenny."

"Why didn't you tell me those two young squirts were makin' eyes at you in the Greek's when we were having our supper?'' he wanted to know.

"I didn't pay 'ny attention to them," she replied. "Besides, I didn't want to start 'nything and bring on another scene like I did this morning with that fat drummer. One was enough for today."

"Next time you let me worry about makin' a scene."

"All right, Johnny."

"I wouldn'ta known anything about it if it hadn't been for the Greek. He didn't like the looks o' those two smart alecks, 'specially the light-haired one who has a big mouth. Soon's Nick locked up, he came over to the office and told me. Thought I oughta know. That's what brought me hustlin' over here. To see that you were all right. The big-mouthed one told Bick he knew you and came upstairs lookin' for you. I was waiting for him when he came down. He sassed me and went for his gun only I beat him to the draw. I coulda killed him. Instead I put a bullet through his gunwrist. It'll never be of much use to him again. Now he'll have to learn to do things left-handed."

She had held her gaze on him throughout his recital of what had happened. When she made no comment, he continued. "Lennart's downstairs keepin' his eye on the pair. I sent Bick for the doctor. He's probably here now fixin' up big mouth's wrist."

She looked troubled. "Y'see, Johnny? Why I didn't want to go on with this and why I'd finally made up my mind to go back to Rogers and forget about California? Like I told you, everywhere we go—"

"No," he said firmly. "This was different. It wasn't because somebody's recognized you like that drummer did. This was a case of two young punks who thought they could find you after I left you and make time with you. And that kind o' thing could've happened anywhere."

"I wish we could get away from here. I don't like this place."

"Don't think I do either. I'm sorry I agreed to stay on, but I promised. But it won't be too long before we pull outta here. I won't let it be. I'll hound Lennart till he grabs the first man who comes along, so's we'll be free to go."

"You have to go back to your office?"

"Yeah, sure. Gotta lock up those two punks. Got a couple o' cells in the cellar under the office. But soon's it gets to be ten o'clock, that'll be it for me. I'll call it a day and lock up. You tired? You wanna get to bed?"

She shook her head. "No. I'll wait till you get back."

"Lock your door," he instructed her.

"No, you do it, and take the key with you."

She took the key out of the lock and gave it to him.

"Watch yourself with those two, Johnny. Those young uns can be awf'lly tricky."

"Don't worry about me. I've hooked up with their kind before. So I know how to deal with th'm." He gave her a reassuring smile and put his hand on the doorknob. "I won't be any longer'n I have to."

As he turned the knob to open the door, she put her hand on his, stopping him. He turned questioning eyes on her. "S'matter?"

"Nothing," she said and took her hand away. "Go do what you have to and come back here."

He gave her a wondering look. She turned away from him. "What's bothering you, Jenny?"

"Nothing," she flung at him over her shoulder. "Go do what you have to."

He was motionless for a moment. Then he closed and locked the door. Pocketing the key, he went downstairs. Lennart and two townsmen, all of them with their rifles on the two youths, were backed against the counter while Bick, who had returned, was behind it. The doctor with his opened kit on the floor was kneeling at Howie's side and bandaging his right wrist. Everyone except the doctor looked around at Canavan.

"Howie glared at him. "Lousy bastid," he fairly spat at Canavan. "Why didn't you kill me instead o' crippling me?"

"Maybe I shoulda," Canavan answered. "I coulda easy enough. That woulda been one sure way of shutting your mouth."

The doctor had finished his bandaging. Now he fashioned a sling out of a piece of white cloth, secured the ends of it behind Howie's neck and gently eased the youth's arm into it. He closed his bag and stood up. Turning to Lennart, he said: "Think I'd better have a look at that arm daily for the next couple of days.

Lennart indicated Canavan with a nod and the doctor looked at him.

"You can see him any time you like," Canavan said simply.

The doctor grunted, picked up his bag, and turned to go. The men who were still crowding the doorway moved as he came toward them, opening a path for him, and he went out. Promptly, though, the path closed again.

"All right," Canavan said to Ollie and Howie. "Up on your feet."

Ollie got up at once, by himself. Howie seemed to experience some difficulty, so Canavan gave him a hand and hauled him to his feet, ignoring the hard look the youth gave him.

"Sheriff," Bick said and beckoned. Canavan leaned over the counter and listened to Bick's account of what had happened prior to Canavan's sudden return to the hotel. "That's it," Bick said. "Thought you oughta know."

Canavan nodded. "You took an awful chance with

these two smark alecks. Glad I got here in time to make sure that nothing happened to you."

Bick grinned. "So am I."

Turning around again, Canavan said: "All right, you two. Let's go."

"Just a minute now," Howie said. "Just what are you takin' us in for? What'd we do aside from makin' the mistake of comin' into this lousy town?"

"If you don't know, and if you can't figure it out for yourself, then I'm sorry for you because you're even more stupid than I thought," Canavan replied. "So you wait till you come up in court. The judge'll be only too glad to tell you."

"And how he will!" Lennart chimed in. "He's old and crotchety, and if there's anything he hates it's a smart aleck. He'll give you everything the law says he c'n, and then just for good measure, he'll add a little on his own."

"Let's go," Canavan said, as he herded his prisoners ahead of him.

The path that had opened earlier for the doctor opened again, a little wider this time to permit the two youths and their captor to make their way out to the street. Canavan guided them across the darkened street and into his office. Lennart followed them and, closing the door behind him, stood backed against it with his rifle cradled in his arms.

Thumbing his hat up from his forehead, Canavan seated himself at his desk, picked up a stub of a pencil, and reached for a blank piece of paper. "You," he said to Ollie. "What's your name, how old are you and where d'you come from?"

"Ollie Phelps, I'm twenty-three and I hail from Kansas," was the reply.

"Whereabouts in Kansas?"

"Rocky Pass."

Canavan noted the information on the paper and lifted his eyes to Howie.

"All right," he said briskly. "Let's have it. Name, age, and where you come from."

"I'm not tellin' you a damned thing," Howie said spitefully.

"If that's the way you want it, it's all right with me," Canavan answered calmly. "Only I hope you don't get too hungry before you change your mind about talking because you're not gonna get anything to eat or drink till then."

He rose and opened the door that led to the sheriff's living quarters, crossed the room to still another door, opened that one, and went down a short flight of stairs, his bootheels thumping on the steps. When he returned a couple of minutes later, he held the connecting door wide and said curtly: "C'mon."

Ollie moved without delay, Howie a little reluctantly. Lennart following them with his eyes, saw them with Canavan dogging their bootsteps go down the stairs. He heard an iron door open and slam shut and heard a key grate in the lock. The same procedure was repeated a moment later. Then Canavan reappeared, closed the connecting door behind him and put a big iron key in the top desk drawer.

"That's that," he announced.

Lennart nodded, turned and stepping back, opened the street door and sauntered out. Canavan turned out the light in the lamp that hung from a short piece of chain from a rafter directly above his desk, followed Lennart out to the street, and yanked the door shut and locked it.

"Guess I c'n go turn in now," Lennart said, hoisting his rifle and slinging it across his shoulder.

Canavan nodded. "Thanks for your help."

"G'wan," Lennart retorted, leading the way across the street. "All I did was stick my nose in where it wasn't needed. Far as I could see you had everything under control. So the last thing you needed was help from anybody and that included me. Y'know, just watchin' you, the way you did things, I learned something that's gonna make it tough on the man who takes over from you. I know what to expect from him. So he'll have to measure up, or we'll keep lookin' around for somebody to replace him."

"I sure hope you get somebody real soon," Canavan said. "I'm getting itchier every day to get going."

"Uh-huh. Well, let's see what tomorrow brings us. Maybe somebody who's had experience and who's lookin' for a lawman's job will come wandering in."

"I'd like that to happen."

"Doesn't cost 'nything to hope, y'know."

"I know, and I'm hoping right along with you."

They stepped up on the walk in front of the hotel. The doorway was empty. The townsmen, their curiosity satisfied, had returned to their homes.

"See you tomorrow, Canavan."

"Right."

The lobby floor was wet, proof that Bick had mopped it, removing traces of the blood that Howie had left behind him. The lobby itself was deserted and the counter unmanned. Just as Lennart would do shortly, Bick had already turned in. Canavan tramped up the stairs, halted in front of Jenny's room, fished in his pocket for her key, found it and unlocked her door. He poked his head in. The lamp on Jenny's bureau showed only the barest bit of light burning in it, leaving most of the room in shadowy darkness. She hadn't waited for him to return. She had gone to bed. She lay on her side, her back turned to the door. He glided in, quietly closed the door, and tiptoed across the uncovered floor. He frowned when a board creaked under his foot. He came up to the bed, bent over and peered closely at Jenny.

"Jenny," he breathed at her.

Without opening her eyes she mumbled: "Go 'way. I'm tired and I wanna sleep."

"All right," he said, straightening up. "I'll see you tomorrow."

"That'll be nice," she said sarcastically. "I c'n hardly wait."

He frowned again. "S'matter with you? What's eating you?"

"I told you I'm tired and I wanna sleep, didn't I?"

He made no response. He turned on his heel and went striding out. He yanked the door shut behind him, locked it, and, kneeling in front of it, pushed the key under the door.

Seven

It was the next day, the time about noon. Considerably more thoughtful-looking than usual, but with an air of impatience about him, Canavan was idling in the open doorway of his office. While he kept shifting his gaze about over the street, most of the time it was focused on the window in Jenny's room. The fact that the shade was fully drawn meant that she was still asleep. It irked him because this was one morning when he had hoped that she would get up at a reasonably early hour. They had things to discuss and matters to settle between them, and the sooner they got to them and talked them out, the better he would like it. Her unexplained, and as far as he was concerned uncalled for, change in manner the previous night had given him cause for concern. While he was annoyed with her, and disappointed in her too, he did not deny himself that he would be even more disappointed if she decided at the last moment not to accompany him to California.

"I'd be lyin' to myself if I tried to make myself believe that I don't want her or need her when I know damned well that I do," he thought to himself. "So even though she isn't the kind o' girl I'd go after ordinarily, and the fact that she's quick tempered and she's got a sharp tongue, I'm willing to make allowances. Only thing that makes me leery about her is her on-again, off-again moods. That's why I think we'd better do us some plain talking and settle things between us once an' for all. If she's gonna go on gettin' her back up every little while, the deal between us is off.'' Suddenly he saw the shade over her window go up. ''She must be dressed,'' he said half-aloud. ''So she oughta be coming out any minute now.''

He fixed his gaze on the hotel doorway. Several long minutes passed before she appeared. She emerged, crossed the walk to the curb, and waited there till a buckboard with a man and a bonneted woman riding in it rumbled by. Then, lifting her full skirts, she crossed the street, and, again raising her skirts, stepped up on the walk. She halted and looked at Canavan, obviously waiting for him to join her. A couple of townspeople, a woman going down the street and a man heading in the opposite direction, glanced at her as they came abreast of her. She ignored them. Canavan stepped outside, yanked the door shut, and strode over to her. There was no exchange of greetings.

''You mind eating in here?'' he asked, nodding in the direction of the lunchroom which was just beyond them.

She turned her head. ''Up to you.''

''Handier to the office.''

''Then by all means let's eat here.''

He followed her into the lunchroom, helped her seat herself on one of the stools, straddled the one next to hers, and put his hat on the stool next to him.

''I'm sorry about last night, Johnny,'' she said.

''So am I. You mind telling me what got you so het up at me?''

''It wasn't you. It was me. I was outta sorts.'' When

he made no comment, she continued. "I haven't anything to do with myself and that's not good. I lay around waiting for you to get back—and with nothing to do but think, I get the craziest ideas. It's stupid of me, I know. But I can't help it. Do you honestly think we'll ever get away from here? I've put all my hopes in California, and in you, but somehow I get the feeling that it'll never be. That it isn't meant to be. That in the end you'll stay put here, and I'll wind up back in Rogers' place. So I get feeling low. And when I take it out on you, even though I don't mean to, I feel twice as bad. Maybe you oughta let me go back where I came from, and you stay put here, or go on your way alone? It'll be easier on you either way without having me around to make trouble for you. What d'you think, Johnny? Be honest with me." Before he could answer, she said low-voiced: "We're getting company. Lennart and another man."

Canavan who had just hunched over the edge of the counter on his folded arms, straightened up, and turned his head toward the door. Lennart, followed by a tall, lean, sun-bronzed man who wore his gun the way Canavan did, low-slung and thong-tied around his right thigh, came up to him. Lennart smiled at Jenny and lifted his hat to her while the man with him took off his hat and held it in his hands.

"Canavan, I'd like you to know Dan Peeples."

Canavan who had already gotten to his feet shook hands with the newcomer.

"Dan's just quit sheriffing over at High Mount," Lennart said. "After eight years there, he thinks he c'n do with a change o' people and scenery. He's ready to take over from you right now, or whenever you say the word."

Canavan grinned. "Right now's good with me."

He unpinned his star and handed it to Lennart who pinned it to the flap of Peeples' shirt pocket.

"So you're your own man again," Lennart said to Canavan. "How soon d'you figure you'll be pulling out?"

"Soon's I made a deal with the stableman for one o' his spare wagons," Canavan replied.

"Uh-huh. Will you come over to the office after a while and help me get Dan started?"

"Yeah, sure," Canavan said. "Say in about an hour or so?"

"Fine," Lennart answered. "We'll be looking for you."

Peeples followed him out. Canavan seated himself again, looked at Jenny, and asked: "Well? What've you got to say now?"

"I'm awf'lly glad, Johnny. But at the same time I'm ashamed of myself for letting myself think those foolish things. I should have known better."

"Forget it. What d'you wanna eat?"

"Funny thing. But when we came in here, I wasn't at all hungry. Now, all of a sudden, I'm starved."

"Once I know we've got a wagon, I'll go get stocked up on grub and everything else we might need. Meantime if there's anything you might want, get it while the getting's good. We won't be hitting any towns, y'know. We'll be keeping to the open country."

"You planning to pull out today?"

"'Course. Why wait around and lose time when he c'n be putting distance between us and Hopewell? So soon's we finish eating, get yourself packed up. My stuff's ready. All I have to do is grab it. I'll see Bick and get squared away with him for both of us."

"I'll be ready to go when you are."

At three that afternoon, with the mare, Willie, tied to

the tailgate of their wagon, and protesting nasally because she felt that Canavan was neglecting her by driving the wagon when he should have been riding her, they left Hopewell and took the road west.

"Nothing to it," Canavan said to Jenny. "Just play out the lines so that the horses won't fight you when they wanna run. Same time though see that you have a good grip on the lines in case you think they're running too fast and you wanna slow th'm down. Wanna give it a try?"

"Yes."

He passed her the reins and she got a secure grip on them. She watched the horses continue their pace without breaking stride and looked at Canavan. "They don't even know I'm doing the driving now."

"No." She drove on and after a while, he said: "Pull up so's I c'n get down."

She obeyed, bringing the team and the wagon to a full stop. One of the horses looked around at her.

Canavan climbed down, and shifting his holster a little bit, disappeared around the back of the wagon. He reappeared shortly astride Willie and ranged up alongside of Jenny. "All right. Go ahead," he said.

She jerked the reins and the horses trotted away. "I like that Lennart man, Johnny," she said, "and Bick too."

"Both o' th'm are good men in my book. Lennart gave me a whole week's wages even though I didn't have anywhere near that much coming to me. Twenty-five bucks and one o' the horses went to the stableman for the wagon and the harness. So actually it wasn't anything out've my pocket that swung the deal for us."

"Uh-huh," she said, easing up a little on the lines. The horses, obviously eager to run, promptly quickened their pace. "Lennart gave me such a warm handshake and wished us all the best, and Bick made such a to-do outta saying goodbye to me, they made me feel good all over. Oh, what about those two smart alecks? What happens to them now?''

"I gave Peeples the story on them. Soon's that judge gets back, Peeples will bring them up before him.''

"I see. Hey, how am I doing?''

"Fine. Like you've been driving a team all your life.''

She laughed lightly. He eyed her. She was brighter than he had ever seen her before. She was happy that at long last they were on their way.

"How long d'we keep going?'' she wanted to know.

"Till around sundown. Then we'll make camp and have us something to eat, and after a while we'll turn in. Wanna get us an early start tomorrow morning. Cover more ground before noon than y'do in the afternoon. By then the sun gets hot and the horses, having been on the go for hours, feel it, so you don't make any time worth talking about. So it's how far you get by noon that really counts.''

"Oh,'' she said. "How long d'you figure it'll take us to get to California?''

"Somewhere's around four weeks. Depends of course on the weather. If we get bogged down by rain and mud, it'll take even longer.''

There was little conversation between them after that. Time and distance dropped away from them. Save for the jingle of the harness, the creak of the wagon, the cutting spin of the big wheels and the rhythmic beat of the horses' hoofs, silence hung over the open country. It was as though they were the only ones abroad in that vast expanse of prairie land. Once though when they came within a mile or so of a house from whose chimney smoke was lifting lazily into the late afternoon sky, Jenny couldn't take her eyes from it. Canavan noticed but made no comment.

"People living alone out here in the middle of no-where," he heard her say, and he raised his eyes to her. "Wonder how they like it?" When he offered no opinion, she continued. "I suppose they must like it or they wouldn't stay put. Right?"

"Right."

"'Course if they get along, they don't need 'nybody else. With the man working the place and keeping busy at it all day and the woman just as busy with her chores, time oughtn't hang heavy on their hands. And if they have a couple o' kids, watching them grow up oughta help make life interesting for th'm."

"It isn't an easy life, Jenny. Fact is, it's a hard life."

"What kind isn't?" she countered.

He made no attempt to answer her question. Instead he asked: "Think you'd like that kind o' life? Don't you think you'd get fed up with it after a while and want out of it?"

She thought about it briefly before she replied.

"Nope," she said frankly. "I kinda think I'd like it. I've had enough excitement to last me a long, long time. So I think I'd like a change. The kind o' life those people over there must live. What about you, Johnny?"

"Well, like you, I've had my share of excitement, and I don't need any more. I'd like to have a place of my own again. Only I wouldn't want it out here, away from the rest o' the world. I'd like it fairly close to a town, and the smaller the town the better I'd like it. And with nice, decent, friendly people in it."

"Uh-huh," she said. "And what about the kids?"

He grinned at her. "I like kids, and all kinds o' th'm too. Fact is, I'd always hoped I'd have a flock o' th'm. Something of my folks musta rubbed off on me because they had six."

"And mine had one. Me."

He ranged his gaze around and looked skyward. Longfingered shadows were beginning to drape themselves over the prairie.

She looked about. "We've been jawin' away like a couple o' good fellers. So we didn't notice it was getting dark. Leastways, I didn't."

"Yeah, be evening soon," Canavan said. "Think we'll make camp right here. "Pull up, Jenny, and turn inland."

Again she followed his instructions, slowed the team to a walk, and followed him up a slight embankment and on some twenty or thirty feet beyond. She halted the horses when he wheeled around and held up his hand.

"Pull back hard on the handbrake," he called to her, "and loop the lines around it and slip-knot th'm."

"Right," she said, did as he told her to. "Anything else?"

"Nope. That's it."

She stood up and waited. He dismounted and came to her, held up his arms for her and she came to him, curling both arms around his neck. He lifted her clear of the front left wheel and turned with her. But instead of letting him set her down on the ground, she clung to him and kissed him hard on the mouth.

"Now don't ask me what that was for," she said. "I kissed you because I wanted to. That a good enough reason?"

He grinned at her. "I can't think of a better one."

With her arms still encircling his neck and their faces but an inch or two apart, she said: "Y'know something? Outside o' that one peck you gave me the night Lennart came upstairs to proposition you to stay on in Hopewell, you've never kissed me just like that, or even made

103

'ny move to. You afraid o' me, Johnny? Afraid you're liable to catch something from me if you let yourself go with me?''

"No, 'course not.''

"Are you afraid I'll think you're taking advantage of me and that I'll let out a big holler?''

"Nope.''

"Then what is it?'' she pressed him. "Is it on account o' Beth? If it is, then you oughta know you can't go on the rest o' your life makin' out she's still alive and waiting for you to come back to her when she's been dead an' gone for years.''

"Beth hasn't anything to do with it.''

"Then what has?'' she asked him. "Wait up now. I know what you think o' women who work in saloons. Is it because o' that, that I was one o' th'm and you can't let yourself forget that, that you're willing to help me get to California, but that's all, and that that's why you've been keeping your distance from me?''

"You know how fond I am of you, Jenny.''

"Being fond o' me is fine for a starter. But can't you do a little better than that? If you'd let yourself go, you might be surprised to find yourself feeling about me the way I do about you. Y'know, when I talked you into agreeing to take me out to California with you, all I wanted was to get out there. Then I'd go off on my own. But things have changed since then. Leastways they have with me. Maybe I shouldn't tell you this. But I'm hoping that by the time we get there, you'll be so used to having me around, you won't wanna let me go. That you'll wanna keep me around for always.''

"Could be. Now lemme ask your something.''

"Go ahead. Ask me anything you like.''

"When you say that things have changed with you since then, what's that supposed to mean? You tryin' to tell me you're in love with me?"

"What d'you think, you big ox?" she demanded. "Who's been taking care o' me and lookin' out for me ever since you hauled me outta that busted-down stage? Or if you wanna go back to the day before that, to that time in the hotel when that scurvy lookin' bum came barging in on me when I was changing my dress, who'd I come running to and who saved me from him? And who was willing to stake me to a ticket to California and do something extra to keep me going when I got there when there wasn't any call for you to do that like I was your responsibility? And who's always treated me like I was a somebody, and who kept me going whenever I got feeling low and sorry for myself? You, that's who. 'Course I love you, you big redheaded ox. After all you've done for me, even if I hadn'ta wanted to fall for you, d'you think I coulda stopped myself? I'd have had to be made o' stone instead o' flesh an' blood."

There was a sudden, startling sound of whimpering somewhere beyond them yet close by in the rapidly deepening shadows. Then there was movement in the lush grass that carpeted the area.

"What's that?" Jenny breathed at Canavan.

"I dunno. But I'm gonna find out. Look, you get up in the wagon and stay put there till I get back." He turned with her, again lifted her clear of the wheel and helped her reach the driver's seat. "Climb down inside," he told her. "There are a couple o' lanterns under the seat. Gimme one o' th'm."

She followed his instructions, swung around over the seat and climbed down into the body of the wagon, and disappeared. But she reappeared almost at once.

"Here," she said in a low, guarded voice. "But be careful, Johnny."

She passed him a lantern. He knelt down with it next

to the wagon. She heard a match strike, and presently saw light flame in the grass. Peering out she saw him put the lighted lantern on the ground a dozen feet or so from the wagon and saw him move hastily away from it and crouch down in the grass. He would be out of the circle of light that the lantern cast off and safely within the shadows while whoever was coming toward the wagon would be in the light. The whimpering was a little louder as it came closer and so was the movement in the grass. Then she heard Canavan's voice.

"Well, hello there, young lady. You looking for someone?"

Craning her neck, Jenny stared with widening eyes when she saw the figure of a little girl come into view, and saw Canavan on his knees in front of her.

"We've got company, Jenny," she heard him call. "Come on out here and have a look."

"Coming," she answered. Hastily she hoisted herself up on the seat and swung herself over it. Moments later she was kneeling at Canavan's side and looking wonderingly at the little girl who was sniffling and in turn looking wide-eyed at them. "Where's your mother, honey?" Jenny asked.

"She's still sleeping," was the reply. "I couldn't wake her up. When it got dark, I got frightened and I didn't know what to do."

"You poor darling," Jenny said and held out her arms to her. The child came to her quite willingly and Jenny comforted her. "We'll take you back to your mother. But don't cry. There's nothing to be scared of now."

"Will you wake Mama up and tell her I'm awful hungry?"

"Yes, honey," Jenny assured her. Then turning to

106

Canavan she asked: "Johnny, think you can. . .?"

"I'll get her something she can eat while we're taking her back," he said, getting up on his feet.

He strode back to the wagon. When he returned some minutes later, Jenny was sitting in the grass wth the little girl in her lap. Jenny lifted her eyes to him.

"Her name is Dora May Cole," she told him gravely. "But Mama calls her Dolly."

"Uh-huh," Canavan said. "Here y'are, Dora May." He held out something to the child. "A nice, fresh sugar bun and it's all for you."

"Thank you," she said with surprising graciousness. She took the bun from him and bit into it and promptly added: "This is good. Can I have another one?"

Canavan knelt down again and laughed. "Soon's you finish the one you're eating now."

The first bun was quickly devoured. The child was eating the second one when Canavan helped Jenny to her feet. But she refused to put the little girl down and insisted upon carrying her. With Canavan holding the lantern high and leading the way, they started off in the direction in which Dora May had come. It took him fully half an hour before he spied the rounded, upper structure of a full-sized Conestoga looming up in the night light. Halting in front of it and ignoring the whinnies of a team of horses that were standing in the traces, Canavan, with the lantern swinging from his hand and the turned-up light playing over the high step, hauled himself up to the driver's seat and called out: "Mrs. Cole!"

There was no response, no sound either from inside the big wagon.

Maneuvering himself over the wide seat, Canavan climbed down into the wagon. Raising the lantern, he played the light over its interior and contents. It was loaded with furniture, big, heavy pieces as well as many smaller ones. A narrow aisle that was flanked by furniture and ran the length of the wagon held his eye for in it, stretched out on the flat of her back on a doubled-over blanket, lay a fully dressed woman. Canavan knelt at her side. "Mrs. Cole."

Holding the lantern just above her so that the light shone on her face, he watched her closely for a couple of moments, and finally bent low over her. Then slowly, grim-looking, he eased back on his haunches, and presently stood up, made his way forward again to the driver's seat, tugged at the canvas curtain that hung behind the seat and freeing it, let it drop. Minutes later he was standing at Jenny's side. She leveled anxious eyes at him.

"I think we'd better let her sleep on," he said, more for the child's benefit than for Jenny's, "and not try to wake her tonight. She must be very tired. Tomorrow morning right after breakfast we'll come back here. All right?"

Jenny answered for Dora May as well as for herself.

"I think that's a very good idea," she said. "Dora May can sleep in our wagon tonight. Would you like that, honey?" she asked the child.

"I—I guess so," was the somewhat hesitant reply. "If you think Mama will think it's all right."

"Oh, I'm sure she will," Jenny assured her. Then turning to Canavan, she asked: "We go back now?"

"In a minute. Wanna unhitch the horses and tie th'm up to the wagon. Give th'm a little more freedom and a little more room to move around in."

While Jenny held the lantern, Canavan unharnessed the horses and tied each to a big wheel. Then taking the lantern from Jenny, he said: "If she gets too much for you, lemme know and I'll spell you."

"My arm's a little tired now. If you'd like to take her for a while. . ."

He handed the lantern back to her and held out his arms to Dora May.

"How about a ride on my shoulders?" he asked her. When she leaned toward him, he lifted her, turned her and seated her astride his shoulders, and turning his head, asked her: "How's that, all right? Comf'table?"

"Oh, yes!" Dora May answered quickly. "This is fun."

This time Jenny took the lead, holding the lantern aloft so that Canavan, trudging along at her heels, could see where he was going. Once or twice he sagged deliberately and promptly came erect, jouncing the child, and she laughed. The darkness, continuing to deepen, lay over the far-flung land like an obscuring blanket. They went on in silence after that, till Jenny happened to turn and look back. Then she said in a guarded tone: "She's asleep, Johnny."

He stopped and reached up and eased the child off his shoulders and, cradling her in his arms, tramped on after Jenny. When they came up to their wagon, Jenny climbed up and Canavan handed her the little girl, then while Jenny waited with her, he hoisted himself up too, swung over the seat and dropped down into the wagon. Jenny heard him moving about and wondered what he was doing, and just as she was about to turn her head and call to him, he reappeared and held up his arms for Dora May. Following his instructions, Jenny managed to ease herself down into the wagon too.

"I've opened my bedroll," he told Jenny. "Lay her in that after you get her things off."

While he held the child, Jenny undressed her, and while she laid Dory May in the bedroll and covered her up, Canavan busied himself at the rear of the wagon. When he rejoined her, he said: "Laid out the mattress and the blanket we're gonna use. You hungry?"

"No, not very. Fact is, a cup o' coffee would do me fine. Y'got any more o' those sugar buns left? You know, for Dora May when she wakes up."

"Got a whole bagful. All that lunchroom feller had. Think he said there were twenty-six all told."

"Think I could go one o' them with the coffee."

Some twenty minutes later, as they were sitting cross-legged in the grass near the wagon with the lantern on the ground just beyond them, drinking the freshly boiled coffee and each munching a bun, Jenny put down her cup. "Poor kid. She doesn't know what she's in for without her mother to take care o' her and look out for her. I know what it's like, and you c'n take my word for it it's lousy. What are we gonna do about her, Johnny?"

"Can't leave her here and with nobody around for us to turn her over to, looks to me like the only thing we can do is lug her along with us."

"Uh-huh," she said, raising her cup to her lips.

"Tomorrow morning I'll bury her mother. We'll take the horses. Y'never know what c'n happen to the ones we've got and it's nice to know we've got a couple o' spares just in case. But we'll leave the wagon. Anybody who comes along and wants it and the stuff in it c'n have it."

They finished drinking their coffee in silence. When he took her cup from her and got up, she arose too and said:

"I'm kinda beat, Johnny. So if it's all right with you, I think I'll go turn in."

"Go ahead. Got a few things to do before I c'n turn in. But it shouldn't take me long."

"Careful when you climb up so's you don't wake Dora May."

"I'll watch it."

She turned toward the wagon, stopped and said over her shoulder: "Chances are I'll be asleep by the time you're set to turn in. So I'd better say goodnight to you now."

He put down the cups and came to her, gripped her by the arms, bent his head and kissed her full on the lips.

"G'night, Jenny," he said, releasing her.

"G'night, Johnny," she responded. "That was nice. Like you really meant it."

"I did mean it."

"That makes it even nicer."

The cups and the coffeepot had been rinsed out, the fire stamped out and covered with scooped-up dirt, Willie unsaddled and tied to a rear wheel on one side of the wagon and the team unhitched and tied to a wheel on the other side when Canavan finally hauled himself up into the wagon. Turning down the lantern light till only the barest glow burned in it, he removed his boots, tiptoed around the sleeping child and made his way to where Jenny lay blanketed on the mattress. Her dress, he noticed, lay on top of two large gunny sacks of foodstuffs. He turned out the light and put the lantern on the floor, and laid his rolled-up gunbelt next to it and within easy reach. He took off his shirt and draped it over a sack of potatoes and started to take off his pants. He stopped and looked thoughtfully in Jenny's direction. As though he were a young bridegroom about to get into bed for the first time with his newly acquired bride, he seemed hesitant and shy. But then he pulled off his pants and slung them across his shirt, lifted the blanket

111

and quietly got in under it.

"Johnny," Jenny whispered, startling him.

He jerked his head around to her.

"S'matter?" he asked her. "Thought you were asleep."

"I waited for you to come to bed so's I could ask you something."

"Oh? What is it?"

"I don't want Dora May to hear me. Can't you move a little closer to me?" He moved himself closer to her. "That's better," she said. "Johnny, can't we keep her?"

"Y'sure you want her? Mean a lot o' work for you taking care of a sprout like her, y'know."

"I know, and I'm willing. But it's up to you."

"If you want her that bad, we'll keep her."

"Thanks, Johnny."

"For what? She's a cute kid, so I'll enjoy her as much as you will."

For a while after that they lay quietly, probably no more than six inches apart. A couple of times he started to move even closer to her. But each time he stopped himself, and each time he promptly berated himself. There was an invisible barrier between them that he couldn't seem to surmount despite his longing for her. It was Johnny who helped bridge the space between them when she moved even closer to him so that their shoulders touched.

"Funny, isn't it, how things happen?" she whispered.

"How d'you mean?"

"For years you were a loner. Then you met up with me, did me as good turn and followed that up by just about saving my life. So I paid you back by latching on to you." She moved again, this time so that her head was against his shoulder with the fragrance of her hair lifting into his face. "Now that we're gonna keep Dora May, you've got yourself a family. Funny, isn't it? Proves you never know what's gonna happen next."

Before he could answer, Willie suddenly whinnied, and Canavan lay motionlessly, listening intently. When the mare snorted and whinnied again, louder this time than before, Canavan told Jenny: "Stay put. Something's goin' on outside and I'd better go see what it is."

"You hafta?" Jenny wanted to know a little crossly.

He didn't answer, but simply kicked off the cover, reached for his pants and drew them on, pulled on his boots, fumbled around for his gunbelt and drew his gun. He tiptoed to the rear of the wagon, quietly untied the drop curtain, lifted a corner of it and stole a guarded look outside. Despite the obscuring and somewhat distorting darkness, he managed to make out the figures of two men, one of them mounted, the other one on foot. The latter was trying to untie Willie. When she snorted and shied away from him and rearing up, suddenly lashed out at him with her fore hoofs, he backed off in alarm.

"Aw, c'mon, willya, Mack?" Canavan heard the mounted man say. "We're wastin' time here. You lookin' to get us caught?"

"How long d'you think that plug o' yours is gonna carry the two of us?" the man named Mack retorted. "I want a horse o' my own and this one looks like the kind I've always wanted. So I aim to have her."

Again he sought to grab Willie's bridle, and again she lashed out at him.

Quietly Canavan climbed over the tailgate and ease himself down to the ground. Inching his way around the back of the wagon, he stepped out boldly with his gun leveled. "Reach, you buzzards, or I'll shoot," he said evenly.

113

The mounted man flung his horse around, lashed him and sent him pounding away. Canavan ignored him and held his gaze on his companion. The man cursed and backed off a step or two. When his right arm jerked, a sign that he was going for his gun, Canavan shot him. The man gasped when the bullet, fired at such close range, slammed into him, robbed him of his breath. He sagged and fell against the wagon and crumpled up in the grass in a broken heap.

Eight

It was some ten minutes later when Canavan climbed back into the wagon. As he eased himself over the tailgate and stepped down on the floor, the lantern flamed, lighting up the interior of the wagon. Jenny, who was wearing her kimona over her nightdress, hastily lowered the light, twisted around and caught up a rifle that lay across the heaped-up blanket on the mattress.

"Oh!" she said when she saw him. There was relief in her voice. "You all right?"

"Yeah, sure," he answered. "Where'd you get that," he asked, pointing to the rifle, "and what were you gonna do with it?"

"I was gonna go see what was keeping you. I remembered seeing a couple o' rifles laying under the seat when I fished out that lantern for you. So I grabbed up one o' th'm. That shooting I heard—"

"There was only one shot. Some highbinder was trying to untie Willie and make off with her."

"And you chased him away."

"No. I had to put a slug in him." He held out his hand for the rifle. She gave it to him and he propped it up in the corner of the wagon where the tailgate and the

115

side wall of the wagon came together at right angles to each other. "I dragged him away from the wagon and dumped him in some tall grass. Didn't want you or Dora May to see him layin' right outside when you came out for breakfast. Then I had to calm down Willie."

"I'm glad that's all there was to it. You're gonna hafta be awf'lly careful from now on. You can't afford to take chances. You've got responsibilities, y'know."

He grinned at her. "Y'mean I've got me a family to look out for?"

She smiled back at him apologetically and said: "I'm afraid so, Johnny. I know you weren't lookin' to be saddled with one. But you are. Aren't you sorry you ever took up with me?"

"Nope. G'wan back to bed."

"What are you gonna do?"

"Go back to bed too."

When he rejoined her under the blanket and reached out for her to bring her into his arms, she whispered: "Wait, Johnny. You doing this because it's what you want, or because you think it's what I want you to do?"

"It's what I want."

He was up again at dawn and, carrying his boots, managed to climb out of the wagon without waking either Jenny or Dora May. There was only the barest bit of light in the sky. The air was dampish and uncomfortably chilly. Suddenly remembering that he needed a shovel for the unpleasant task that awaited him, he climbed up again and groped around under the seat till he found what he was looking for.

It was forty minutes later when he returned, driving the dead woman's team ahead of him with the lines and the shovel gripped in his left hand and a cloth-covered box similar to Jenny's on his right shoulder. The spare horses were unhitched and tied to the tailgate, the shovel with bits of sweet-smelling, freshly turned earth clinging to it was propped up against the wagon while the box that held Dora May's clothes rested on the wide seat of the wagon. He had just finished building a fire and was about to boil water for coffee when the drop curtain behind the seat was pushed aside and Jenny poked her head out at him.

"Johnny!" she called.

He strode over to the wagon and lifted his eyes to her. "Dory May and I could use some hot water."

"Gimme a couple o' minutes and you c'n have it."

Jenny withdrew her head and the curtain dropped back in place and hung motionlessly. The hot water was forthcoming shortly, poured into a second pot from the coffeepot. Then more water was boiled. When coffee was spooned into it, the beans promptly dissolved and almost at once a rich, tempting fragrance began to lift and fill the early morning air. The light in the sky, Canavan had already noticed had brightened while the damp chill that had greeted him when he had climbed down earlier was gone. It would be a pleasant day, he told himself after another skyward glance.

"Oughta be able to make time today," he muttered. "Gotta take advantage of every good day that comes along because there'll be plenty o' bad ones in b'tween."

"Johnny!"

Again he strode over to the wagon. The box had been removed. As before, Jenny's head was poked out at him.

"Yeah?" he asked her.

"Dora May's papa is in heaven," she told him gravely. "I've told her that her mama's gone there too, to join him, and that from now on Dora May's gonna be our little girl.''

''Right.''

''She's ready for breakfast. Will you take her, please?''

''Yeah, sure,'' he replied and hauled himself up to the seat and held out his arms to the child when Jenny lifted her onto it. ''My,'' he said, ''aren't we lucky to have such a pretty little girl for our own?''

Dora May managed a wan little smile. However her eyes showed that she had been crying. He lifted her off the seat, settled her securely within the hollow of his left arm, and climbed down with her. He carried her over to the fire and seated her on his saddle that he had dragged out from under the wagon and had brought over for her to sit on. When Jenny hoisted herself up from the body of the wagon and onto the seat, Canavan hurried over and held up his arms to her. She came to him and he lifted her clear of the right front wheel and set her down on the ground.

As she smoothed down her dress over her hips, she said: ''I liked being kissed goodnight. Think I'd like being kissed good morning, too.''

''Oh, you would, huh?'' he said with a grin and kissed her. ''You one o' those, what d'they call 'em, creatures of habit?''

''Uh-huh. And when it's such a nice habit, I'm all for it. You mind?''

''Nope. Fact is, I like it too.''

When he held out his hand to her, she took it and squeezed it, and let him lead her over to the fire. Dora May moved and made room for her too on the saddle.

''Don't you think she's a good size for four an' a half?'' Jenny asked Canavan.

''Uh-huh. And about as pretty a young un as any I've

ever seen. She'll be a real heart breaker when she grows up."

"I think so too. But I don't think I'll look that far ahead just yet. Oh, and she drinks coffee when there isn't any milk."

Canavan filled two cups and handed one to Jenny, the other one to Dora May and then brought each of them a bun. He filled a third cup for himself and eased himself down in the grass with it and sat cross-legged and lifted it to his lips. Suddenly Willie whinnied and Canavan and Jenny looked up, the latter apprehensively.

"Somebody coming?" she asked.

He nodded, put down his cup and got to his feet. He stood motionlessly for a moment or so, then he turned and looked in a northwesterly direction. Jenny stood up too and ranged her gaze after his. But after a moment or so, when she could neither see nor hear anything to confirm Willie's warning, he said: "There they are, Jenny. See th'm?"

She stared with wide eyes that refused to believe what she saw. Seemingly out of nowhere came a band of horsemen. She couldn't understand why she hadn't spotted them when he had. He reached out and caught her hand and drew her back behind him. She looked concerned when she saw him loosen the gun in his holster. The oncoming horsemen, a dozen of them, were tightly bunched together. When the man who rode at their head flung up his hand, there was a general reining in and a dozen horses were brought to a halt in front of Canavan.

"Posse," he said side-mouthed to Jenny in an effort to assure her that there was nothing to fear. "And he's a lawman. A marshal."

"Oh," Jenny said, and wondered how he knew till

119

she suddenly spied a silver star pinned to the leader's shirtpocket.

"Morning," the latter said, and added "ma'am" when he saw Jenny peer out at him from behind Canavan. He touched his hat to her. Slacking a bit in the saddle, he asked: "You folks see 'ny strangers around?"

"Yeah," Canavan answered. "Two o' th'm and they were riding double on a plug that didn't look like he had it in him to carry even one o' them."

"That sounds like the pair we're looking for," the marshal said, and murmur ran through the mounted men grouped around him. "Which way were they headed?"

"One o' th'm was named Mack only he isn't headed anywhere. He's layin' in the grass back there a piece," Canavan told him.

The marshal, a rangy, sun-bronzed man of about forty, gave him a curious look and nudged his horse in the indicated direction. When they came abreast of the wagon, the lawman glanced at Willie, then at the two horses that were tied to the tailgate. He pulled up abruptly some twenty feet beyond the wagon, dismounted rather stiffly, a sign of long, unbroken hours in the saddle, and bent over. He straightened up shortly, swung himself up on his horse, wheeled him and came trotting back and reined in at Canavan's side.

"That's one o' th'm, all right," he announced. "Joe Mack. What happened to his sidekick?"

"I wasn't concerned about him," Canavan explained. "Only with Mack who was tryin' to untie my horse and make off with her. The other one hightailed it southward and I didn't try to stop him."

"Think he has too much of a jump on us for us to

catch up wtih him?''

"If he was ridin' a good horse, you wouldn't stand a chance. But that nag he's on couldn't take him too far. So you oughta be able to catch up with him if you keep ridin' and lookin'.''

"Uh-huh,'' the marshal said, settling himself in the saddle. "Oh—if you wanna collect, you'll have to make it to town.''

"Collect what?''

"The reward. There's a hundred bucks a piece offered for those two buzzards, dead or alive.'' He grinned a little at Canavan. "Bet it isn't every day you earn yourself a hundred, is it?'' He turned to the waiting horsemen, ran his eye over them, and finally focusing it on one of them, a thin, rather sad-faced, droopy mustached man, said: "You, Lafe Berry. You look kinda beat. Supposin' you ride back to town with these folks and show them where they c'n find the judge?''

"You goin' after Ellis?''

"'Course.''

"What about my cut o' the reward money when you get him?''

"You'll get it,'' the marshal replied. "Let's go.''

Berry backed his horse away from the others who with the marshal again at their head drummed away to the south. Berry dismounted and dropped the reins at his horse's feet and sauntered forward. He glanced at Dora May, looked at her a second time, then looked at Jenny and remarked: "That's a right pert lookin' young un you've got there, ma'am.''

"Thank you,'' Jenny answered with a pleased smile. "We think so too.''

Berry looked down at the coffeepot and lifted his eyes to Canavan. "C'n you spare some o' that?''

121

"Yeah, sure. Take a minute or so to get it heated up."

The mustached posseman bent over, touched the top of the pot and then the side, came erect again and said simply: "She's fine just the way she is."

Canavan made no response. He emptied his cup into the grass, rinsed it out with water from an oversized canteen, filled it with coffee and handed it to Berry. "What'd those two, Mack and the other feller do? They kill somebody?" he asked.

Berry took a swallow of coffee and wiped his mouth and mustache with the back of his bony hand. "Jumped the sheriff and killed him with his own gun."

"I see."

Berry took another mouthful of coffee, swallowed and said: "That's good coffee. Your missus does a good job o' fixin' it. Most women make it too weak, so that it's more like soup than coffee. And when a man makes a to-do about it they make it so strong, it's the nearest thing to sheep dip."

Jenny had turned and walked off toward the wagon. "Johnny," she called.

Canavan joined her. "Yeah?"

"Think you shoulda said something to the marshal about Dora May and her mother?"

"Don't think it would have meant anything to him. He was interested only in Mack and the one who high-tailed it. When we get to see that judge Berry's takin' us to, I'll mention it to him."

"Uh-huh. I was just wondering. Now there's something else. I don't like taking credit for something I didn't do. So if you wanna keep peace in this family, first chance you get you'd better show me how to make coffee the way you do. I like getting compliments. But only when I deserve 'em.''

"Yes, ma'am," Canavan said, saluted her, and trudged back to Berry's side.

"Hope you don't mind, mister," the latter said, "but you were kinda busy. So I helped myself to s'more coffee instead o' waiting to ask if it was all right."

" 'Course it was all right."

Berry downed his second cupful, smacked his lips and handed his cup back to Canavan.

"It's quite a piece back to town," he said. "Soon's you're ready to go, supposin' I give you a hand gettin' hitched up?''

"Swell. Gimme a couple o' minutes to get organized. Then we'll hitch up."

Ten minutes later, with Jenny in the driver's seat and Dora May inside the wagon, they were ready to roll. With Canavan astride Willie and riding alongside the wagon, and Berry leading the way, they headed for town. The morning hours went by slowly. The trip itself was quite uneventful with nothing but the plod of the horses' hoofs, the swish of the wheels and the dismal creak of the harness to break the silence of the prairie. The sun was hot and wilting, and it was necessary every so often to stop and let the horses blow themselves.

Then, shortly after noon, Berry who was riding some twenty or thirty feet in advance of the wagon, suddenly twisted around, pointed and yelled: "There she is! Less'n a mile away!"

Half an hour later they followed Berry down a slight decline—at the head of which a signpost that bore the name PIERSON in faded letters lay crookedly in a rock-filled hole—and into a small, sun-drenched and deserted-looking town.

Berry pulled up, wheeled his horse and waited till

Canavan and the wagon came up to him. He shifted himself in the saddle, and said: "T'aint more'n a hole in the wall, I know. But it's a pretty decent place to live and the people are right friendly. And that's a heckuva lot more'n I c'n say for a lot o' bigger an' richer towns that I've been in."

"What's the name o' the judge we're gonna see?"

Berry grinned. "Same's the name o' the town," he replied. "The Piersons built it and own most of it. That is, whatever's worth owning. Like the bank, the general store and so on. Wanna tell you about the judge before you take him on. Don't let him scare you any. He looks kinda wild bein' that he's got a big mop o' white hair that nobody ever remembers seein' cut or combed and it stands out on every side of his head. But he's a good man. Square as they come. Maybe a mite straight-laced. Oh, yeah, one thing more about him. He hollers a lot and he's got the voice for it. But he doesn't mean it the way it sounds."

Canavan nodded. "I've met up with others like that. And I don't scare easy. Where'll we find the judge?"

"Down the street a ways," Berry answered, wheeled around and trotted off.

"All right, Jenny," Canavan said.

She jerked the lines and the sweat-coated horses plodded on after Berry. The latter swerved in to the low curb after a bit and pulled up in front of a store whose dirt-smudged window bore nothing on it to distinguish it from several others like it. He dismounted and dropped the reins at his horse's feet, turned and waited till the wagon braked to a stop behind his horse.

Canavan swung down, tied Willie to a front wheel, looked up at Jenny and told her: "Loop the lines around the brake and get down inside with Dora May. I won't be long. Leastways, no longer'n I have to be. But long's you're outta the sun—"

Berry interrupted him. "What d'you say, partner?"

Canavan followed him across the planked walk and into the store. The back door was open and a surprisingly pleasant and refreshing breeze was dancing in. A man with a huge head of unruly white hair was sitting behind a big desk thumbing through some papers. He did not look up.

"Be with you directly," he grunted.

There were several straightbacked chairs backed against the side walls.

"Sit down if you want to."

Berry looked at Canavan who shook his head and said: "Feels good to stand for a change."

"Yeah, does at that. 'Specially after so much ridin' on a skinny backside like mine."

The white-haired man squared back in his chair and looked up.

"Oh," he said when he saw Berry. "What's your problem, Lafe?"

"Haven't got 'ny, Judge," the latter replied, thumbing his sweat-stained hat up from his forehead. "This feller," and he nodded at Canavan, "he's here to collect his hundred bucks for killin' that Joe Mack. Marshal told me to bring him in to you."

"I see," the judge said, eyeing Canavan. "What about Mack's companion?"

"Marshal and the rest o' the men are after him. They'll get him. He," and again he indicated Canavan, "he told the marshall which way to go to catch up with Ellis."

The judge nodded. "Good, Lafe. You can go. I'll take care of our friend here."

125

Berry patted Canavan on the back, settled his hat on his head and trudged out. As the door closed behind him, the judge who had been ranging an interested and appraising eye over Canavan, said: "Based on the fact that you killed Mack, you must know how to handle your gun as well as yourself. Have you ever considered working for the law?"

"I've done more than that. I've been a lawman. Texas Ranger."

"Oh? And what are you doing now?"

"On my way to California."

"California, fiddlesticks! What's so wonderful about California?"

Canavan smiled. "Just about everything."

The judge frowned and retorted: "Propaganda. You'll find that out for yourself when you get out there, if you're gullible enough to believe what you hear about it, and go there."

"I've been there," Canavan said quietly.

Pierson's frown deepened, and Canavan, remembering what Lafe Berry had told him, thought to himself: "Here we go. He'll let out a holler that'll lift the roof off."

But to his surprise there was no outburst. Instead the judge asked in a moderate tone:

"Got a family?"

Canavan was glad he hadn't been asked if he were worried.

"Uh-huh," he answered.

"How many children?"

"One."

"How old?"

"Four an' a half."

"You owe it to your family to settle here," Pierson

said authoritatively. "You'll have to look far and wide to find a better place than this to plant your roots and raise your child." When Canavan made no response, the judge added bluntly: "You won't have to go job hunting. I can offer you one right now. The sheriff's job. Pay's good too, forty-five dollars a month. Interested?"

"Nope. Just quit one that paid me more and that woulda been anteed up to sixty-five a month if I'da been willing to stay on."

"Hmm," the judge said, still frowning. "Got a job waiting for you out there?"

"Nope. And I don't want one either. I was raised on a ranch and spent a lot o' years learning about cattle. So when I get to California I'll look for a small place for my own and stick to workin' and buildin' it, and I'll leave it to somebody else to uphold the law."

Pierson gave him a hard, reproachful look, jerked open the middle drawer in the desk and produced a well-filled manila envelope, took some bank notes out of it, counted out ten ten-dollar bills and pushed them across the desk. "Count it. I wouldn't want to cheat you," he said curtly.

"There's a hundred there. I counted it with you." Canavan picked up the bills, folded them in half and put them in his pocket. "Thanks," he said, and turned to go.

"Mean you're going to pass up what might easily prove to be the best opportunity you'll ever be offered?"

"'Fraid I'll have to be the best judge o' what's best for me."

"You're a fool, and an ingrate. Get out!"

Canavan held his tongue. He opened the door and

went out, and slammed the door shut. There was instant reaction to it, a yell of protest from inside. He grinned as he walked off. Lafe Berry was waiting for him at the curb.

"Get your dough?" he asked.

"Yeah, sure. But that wasn't all I got."

"What d'you mean?"

"He offered me the sheriff's job and when I turned him down he got put out with me, called me a fool and told me to get out. So I got."

"Only hollering I heard was just now. When you came out."

Canavan grinned again. "I wanted to hear him holler. So I gave him a chance to let loose. I slammed the door."

"Oh," Berry said.

"He kinda surprised me though. 'Specially after what you'd told me to expect out've him. I thought he'd start hollering sooner'n he did. Trouble with him is he's spoiled. Wants to have his own way. Got everybody kowtowing to him, and when somebody who won't knuckle down to him comes along, he acts like a spoiled brat."

"Aw, he ain't that bad."

"You c'n have him, Berry. I don't want him," Canavan said. He pushed his hand into his pocket, fished out a ten-dollar bill and handed it to the mustached posseman who looked at it and at Canavan a little wonderingly. "That's for you in case they don't catch up with that Ellis feller. Wouldn't want you to lose out on your share of the reward money. G'wan, put it in your pocket."

"Well, now," Berry said, pocketing the bill. "That's right nice o' you, partner, and I sure appreciate it. But there wasn't any call for you to do that, y'know."

"I didn't gun down that Joe Mack for the reward," Canavan pointed out. "Anyway, I'm still ahead ninety bucks, and that's fine with me. There some place around where we c'n get a bit to eat?"

"Yeah, sure. Y'see that place down the street on the other side with the sign 'Eat' over the doorway?" Canavan turned and looked in the indicated direction. "It's only a lunchroom. But it's clean and the grub's good, and far's I'm c'ncerned that's all that matters."

"I'll go along with you on that."

"If you wanna get your horses outta the sun before it fries th'm, drive your wagon into the alley 'longside the lunchroom."

"Uh-huh," Canavan said, nodding. "How about you joining us?"

"Thanks. But I've got some things that need tending to. So if it's all the same to you. . ."

"Whatever you say, Berry."

They shook hands gravely and parted, the latter climbing up on his horse, backing him away from the curb and trotting him up the street while Canavan untied Willie, led her around the wagon to the rear and tied her to the tailgate. The Cole horse nearest her promptly looked up interestedly and sought to nuzzle her. She snorted protestingly and the surprised horse hastily moved away from her.

Canavan hauled himself up to the driver's seat and said: "Jenny."

"Yes?"

"Gonna get us something to eat. Think Dora May would like a bite and a glass o' nice, cold milk?"

"I'm sure she would," Jenny answered quickly. "You would, wouldn't you, honey?"

"Oh, yes!" Canavan heard the child answer.

He unwound the lines and released the brake and

drove down the street, the sun-wilted horses plodding along heavily and wearily, and wheeled into the alley next to the lunchroom. It was shady in there. In addition a light breeze was blowing through the alley. The horses whinnied happily. Canavan reached down and took Dora May from Jenny and made his way down with her, and helped Jenny to the ground. Then, emerging from the alley, they filed into the lunchroom.

Nine

"Take your time eating," Canavan instructed Jenny and Dora May. "Wanna kill as much time as we can. Besides giving the horses a chance to cool th'mselves out, the more time we take, the less time the sun'll have at them and at us."

He had already noticed that the back door was open and had already become aware of a pleasant little breeze sifting into the place. So the table he selected stood squarely in the path of the breeze. Dora May was seated between Jenny and Canavan.

"Nice an' comf'table in here, isn't it, honey?" Jenny asked the child.

"Yes, ma'am," the child answered. "It was kinda hot in the wagon."

"Before you get up in it," Canavan told her, "I'll tie back the front an' back curtains so's you c'n get some air in there."

So they took their time ordering, and took even more time eating. It was almost an hour and a half later when they finally pushed back from the table, got up and headed for the door. As they left the lunchroom, with Dora May clinging tightly to Jenny's hand, and turned

131

into the alley, Canavan stopped abruptly and put out a restraining hand. Jenny stopped too and looked questioningly at him. When he motioned for her to back out of the alley and she saw him loosen his gun, she paled a bit but hastily obeyed, pulling Dora May back with her.

Silently Canavan made his way to the front of the wagon, stood motionlessly for a moment with his hand on his gun butt. Then he commanded: "All right. Come outta there or I'll shoot."

There was no answer, no sound either from inside the wagon. Drawing his gun, Canavan sidled along the wagon to within inches of the rear of it. A minute passed, two minutes, three, and then he heard the faint squeak of a floorboard. Guardedly a hatless man poked his head out for a quick look around. Then hoisting one leg over the tailgate he proceeded to climb out. Shifting his gun to his left hand, Canavan suddenly lunged, got a grip on the man's belt, dragged him down to the ground and ignoring the frantic punches that his captive sought to throw at him, slugged him twice and pinned him down by planting his knee on his chest.

"How many more in the wagon?" he demanded.

"One," the man wheezed at him.

Canavan relieved him of his gun, stuck it down inside his pants' belt, and warned him: "One peep outta you and it'll be your last. Understand?"

The man gulped and swallowed hard.

"Now call your sidekick an' tell him to come out so's you c'n get outta here."

Canavan put the fire-blackened muzzle of his gun to the man's temple.

"Now," he hissed at him. "Not loud. Kinda quiet-like."

"Curly, c'mon, willyuh? Wanna get away from

here," Canavan's captive called to his companion.

There was a moment-long delay before the latter answered. "All clear, Zeke?"

"Yeah, sure."

"What was that noise I heard before?"

"Took a header when I was climbin' down."

A man's booted foot and pants leg straddled the tailgate. As before, Canavan reached up. He got a fistful of Curly's shirt and with a sudden yank, dragged him down. He fell heavily, with a body-jarring thud. When Canavan stepped on his right hand, almost grinding it into the ground, Curly cried out. Ignoring it, Canavan bent and tore the gun out of his holster, and with a heave of his shoulder flung it away, far down the alley. Then stepping back and holding his gun on the thwarted pair, he ordered them to empty their pockets. A scant handful of small coins, a key, a pocket knife and a soiled and crumpled-up bandana constituted their personal belongings.

Canavan's lip curled. "Pick up those things," he commanded, "and stand up."

Zeke obeyed without delay. His battered face attested to the power of Canavan's punches. His nose and lips were puffy. A cut under his left eye was oozing blood. Curly, clutching his crushed hand to himself, made no attempt to get up. Canavan grabbed him by his shirt-front and dragged him up. Holstering his gun, Canavan tore open Zeke's shirt. Satisfied that he had not taken anything from the wagon that he might have concealed on his person, Canavan pushed him away and ripped open Curly's shirt. He ran his hands over Curly and again stepped back.

"Let's go," he said simply.

"Wait a minute, Mac," Curly said. "We didn't take

anything. So what are you fixin' to do with us?"

"You fellers come from around here?"

"Uh-huh."

Canavan frowned. "I'm gonna give you a break you don't deserve," he said after a moment's thought. "I'll probably be sorry for it and wish I'd brought you into Judge Pierson's instead o' letting you go. G'wan now, get outta here before I change my mind."

The two men needed no urging. They bolted out of the alley and fled up the street.

Jenny, with Dora May almost hidden behind her, was standing on the walk backed against the lunchroom window. She lifted worried eyes to Canavan who smiled at her and said: "They didn't take anything. And rather than get involved with that judge on account o' them, I let th'm go."

"Oh," she said, and she looked and sounded relieved. "You say anything to that judge about Dora May?"

He shook his head.

"No. Didn't get a chance to. He got sore at me because he offered me the sheriff's job and I turned him down, 'specially after he went to the trouble of telling me what a wonderful place this is to bring up a kid. When I told him we were heading for California, that was all he hadda hear. He gave me the hundred, called me a fool for passing up what he was sure was the best opportunity I'd ever be offered, and told me to get out. So I got."

"Let's get away from here, Johnny."

"I'm willing, believe me. C'mon." He led them back into the alley, had them wait till he had climbed up and tied back the front and rear curtains, took Dora May from Jenny, and put her in the wagon. Then he jumped down and helped Jenny mount to the driver's seat. At his insistence she unwound the lines and released the handbrake. "Just sit tight," he told her. "I'll back you out to the street."

He backed the horses and the wagon out of the alley and into the street, untied Willie and hauled himself up into the saddle.

"All right," he said to Jenny, pulling up alongside the wagon. "Take it easy till we get outta town. Then you c'n ease up a little on the reins."

Just then a man who came striding diagonally across the street, apparently headed for the lunchroom, stopped and said to Canavan: "See you're still here. I hope that means you've been reconsidering my offer."

"Sorry to disappoint you, Judge," Canavan replied. "But the fact that we're still around only means we've just finished having a bite to eat. Now we're heading out."

Judge Pierson frowned. "You, young woman," he said, lifting his gaze to Jenny and addressing her. "Has he told you of what I've offered him?"

"Yeah, sure," Jenny said. "He's told me."

"And that I've pointed out to him that this is an ideal place in which to raise your child?"

"Far's I c'n see, it's anything but ideal. When we were coming outta that lunchroom," and she nodded in its direction," two o' your high-class citizens, two o' the scurviest looking characters I've ever laid eyes on, were up in our wagon looking for something to steal. Let's go, Johnny."

"Just a minute," Pierson commanded, holding up both of his hands. He turned again to Canavan. "Where are they? What have you done with them?"

"They didn't take anything," Canavan answered. "So I let th'm go."

135

"Let them go?" the judge repeated in shocked tones. "Don't you realize that that is encouraging them to commit more crimes? Don't you realize—?"

Jenny had already gotten the wagon under way. Hastily Pierson leaped aside. Canavan guided the mare around him and loped off after Jenny.

"Confound it!" he heard the judge yell in a voice that carried the length of the street and brought several wide-eyed people to doorways of apparently deserted stores to see what had shattered the silence that lay over the town. "I haven't finished with you! Come back here!"

The fleet mare's hoofs drummed rhythmically but only briefly as she overtook the wagon and ranged up alongside. Slowing her to a fast trot to match the wagon horses' pace, Canavan looked at Jenny and grinned at her.

"I don't think the judge likes either one of us now," he told her. "First it was only me for turning him down, and I don't think most people do that to him. Then you upped and talked back to him, and that soured him on you."

"I shoulda kept my big mouth shut. I shoulda left it to you to do the talking for us."

"Any time you've got something to say, you say it."

"No," she insisted. "It isn't the woman's place to do the talking. It's up to the man. I'll remember that next time."

Minutes later they had left the town behind them and were rumbling over the westward road that lay ruler-straight before them. Jenny eased up a bit on the lines. But the horses showed no desire to quicken their pace, and Jenny made no attempt to urge them on.

"Y'know something, Johnny?" she called to

Canavan. "D'you remember that house we passed standing all by its lonesome out in the middle o' nowhere? Remember me sayin' that that was for me? I meant it then and now I mean it even more. Kinda think I've lost my taste for living in town."

"That's being anti-social, y'know. Wanting to get away from other people."

"If that's what that means, what you just said, then I guess that's what I am. Must be I've soured on people and that I've about had my fill o' th'm. All I want now is a place for just us."

"I'm afraid that what you've got now, the wagon, will have to do you for a long time to come."

"That's all right," she responded. "I'm willing to wait till we have something better."

He gave her a curious look. But he did not pursue the matter beyond that point.

Later on that day when they made camp, he handed her a small roll of bills. "Put that away, Jenny. On you. Not in a box where somebody c'n find it. There's ninety bucks outta the hundred that the judge gave me, and Lennart's fifty. Hundred an' forty all told."

"H'm, hundred an' forty, huh?" she said. "That's more'n I've ever had in my life. But how come you're giving it to me to hold?"

"Who else c'n I give it to? Dora May?"

"You're makin' me fell like we're married, giving me your money."

"Mean you don't like the feeling?"

"I didn't say that, did I?"

"No, you didn't. I just wondered. That's why I asked." Then he added gravely: "Y'know before we started out you told me you hope I get so used to having you around, that by the time we hit California I won't

137

wanna let you go, and that I'll wanna keep you around for always."

"Yeah," she said. "I remember saying that."

"If that happens," he continued as gravely as before, "I'm afraid I won't have 'ny alternative. To make you an honest woman I'll have to marry you."

"That'll be real big of you."

"Mean you wouldn't want me to?"

"I ever say anything about me wanting you to marry me?" she demanded.

"No, not that I c'n recall. Leastways, not right out."

"You know I didn't, not right out or any other way. I didn't say it before we started out, or after, and I'm not saying it now either. What's more I never will."

"But supposing I want to?"

"You won't and I don't want you to do me any favors."

She turned away abruptly. He called after her but she stalked off. He followed her briefly with his eyes, finally shook his head, and after a moment or so set about preparing their supper. He was kneeling and bending over the fire shortly after that when someone came up behind him and plucked at his sleeve. When he turned his head he found it was Dora May.

"Want something?"

"No," she replied. "She's crying."

"Huh? Who's crying? Oh, you mean Jenny?"

"Yes," she said, nodding. "Did you make her cry?"

"If I did, I didn't mean to. I don't like to make anyone cry, 'specially Jenny or you." He came erect. "I'll be right back, Dora May. Don't go any closer to the fire."

"I won't."

He patted her gently on the head, hitched up his pants

and headed for the wagon in search of Jenny. He found her shortly, sitting hunched over in the grass a dozen feet beyond the wagon, with her knees drawn up, her arms encircling her head and resting on her knees. She was still sobbing.

He thumbed his hat up from his forehead, knelt down in front of her and sought to take her in his arms. She twisted away from him.

"Go 'way," she told him. "Leave me alone."

"No," he said. "I was only fooling. Teasing you. Thought you knew that."

"No, you weren't," she flared up at him. "You meant it. But that's all right with me. When we get to California, the first town we hit, you c'n drop us off there, Dora May and me. We'll make out by ourselves."

"She's just as much mine as she is yours."

"Doesn't matter. She belongs with me. I can look out for her better than you can."

He eased back on his haunches. "Alluva sudden you've gotten awf'lly touchy, y'know? Now why don't you stop this silly acting up and c'mon back? Dora May got worried when she saw you crying and came an' told me. That's why I came lookin' for you. If you keep her waiting much longer instead o' letting her know right off that you're all right, she'll worry even more. And who knows what kind of ideas kids like her c'n get in their heads?"

When he produced a new bandana and leaned toward her she did not resist. Gently he dried her eyes and her cheeks, even a single teardrop that had come to rest on the very tip of her nose. He pocketed the bandana, got up and helped her to her feet.

But when he put his arms around her and tried to kiss her, she pushed him off, saying: "Don't. I don't want

139

you to kiss me. That's another o' your favors I c'n do without."

He made no response. He simply released her and stepped back from her and followed her back past the wagon. Dora May was standing where he had left her, staring down at the fire, apparently fascinated by the crackling flames. When she heard them coming, she looked around. Jenny stopped and dropped to her knees and held out her arms and the child ran to her and Jenny caught her in her arms and held her tight. Canavan trudged on to the fire and resumed his preparations for supper.

Twenty minutes or so later when they were seated around the fire eating their meal, Dora May and Jenny again sitting together on Canavan's saddle while he sat cross-legged in the grass, Willie suddenly whinnied and both Jenny and Canavan looked up. When Canavan put down his tin plate and got to his feet, Jenny looked troubled.

"Sit tight," he told her, "while I go have a look."

He strode off briskly with his hand resting on the butt of his gun. As he rounded the wagon, Willie whinnied a second time. He moved up to her and patted her gently.

"S'matter, girl?"

This time though, instead of responding to him as she usually did by nuzzling him, she tossed her head, snorted and even shied away from him, and he eyed her wonderingly.

Suddenly he heard a strange voice, a man's voice, and he turned quickly and peered out from behind the back of the wagon. Fortunately it hadn't yet gotten too dark, so he was able to see quite clearly. Standing around the fire were two men, both of them shabbily dressed and stubbly-faced, and both had their hands on their holstered guns as they ranged their gaze around, obviously looking for him. One of them was stocky and barrel-chested, his companion about average in height and build. But the latter, Canavan was quick to notice—and it angered him—was eyeing Jenny with more than just normal interest.

"Asked you something, lady," Canavan heard the stocky man say, "and I'm still waiting for 'n answer. You an' your kid makin' it out here by yourselves and without a man, or—"

"Who are you and what do you want?" Jenny demanded, getting to her feet and moving squarely in front of Dora May.

"That's a saddle she's sittin' on, Jess," the taller man pointed out. "She couldn'ta hauled that over here by herself. Had t'be a man who did it for her. So he must be around here somewhere's. Grab the kid, Jess, just in case he shows up before we're ready to go. Meantime I'll go have a look at their horses an' see if they're any better'n ours."

He moved around the fire, apparently heading for the wagon. He stopped in front of Jenny and smiled. "Well, now! You're even nicer lookin' closer up than I thought. When I think of how lonely I've been at night with nobody 'cept him," and he jerked his head in Jess' direction, "to keep me company, I realize what I've been missing. Gonna be real nice having you around to cheer me up and give me a new interest in life."

"I won't go for that, Wick," Jess said. "We've got enough trouble as it is without addin' any more."

"When I ask your permission to do anything," Wick retorted over his shoulder, "then you c'n speak your piece. But not till than. We're takin' her with us, and if you don't like it, you know what you c'n do."

Noiselessly Canavan glided along the side of the wagon and crouched behind the horses that were still standing in the traces. It was Jess who was the first to spot him as he moved a step away from the horses, straightening up at the same time with his gun half-drawn.

"Wick!" Jess yelled, and clawed for his gun.

Canavan's Colt thundered and the stocky man gasped and dropped his gun. Doubling over with his thick arms curled around his middle, he suddenly pitched forward and fell heavily on his face, just missing the fire. Wick then turned toward Canavan and went for his gun only to freeze when he saw the muzzle of Canavan's pistol gaping at him. Slowly, as Canavan advanced toward him, his hand came away from his gun, and he moved backward a couple of steps.

"You scurvy, mangy bum," Canavan raged at him. "So you'd like to have her around to kinda cheer you up, huh?"

He leaped at Wick, battering him, pistol-whipping him in the face and head and forcing him backward under a vicious rain of blows. Blood burst from his cut face and Jenny gasped and turned her back and clutched Dora May to her.

When Wick's legs began to buckle under him and he began to totter drunkenly, Canavan, holstering his gun, grabbed him by his shirtfront and beat him with his free hand. It was only when he ran out of breath and became arm-weary that he stopped slugging Wick and flung him away. Wick fell brokenly. Canavan stood over him for a moment, bent and ripped the gun out of Wick's holster, picked up Jess' gun too, trudged back to the wagon with the two guns and tossed them up on the wide seat.

He was still heaving from his exertions when he rejoined Jenny.

"How d'you like that for gall?" he demanded of her. "That lousy slob! You an' Dora May get up in the wagon. Those two don't do anything to this spot 'cept stink it up. So we'll go find us another."

He followed them back to the wagon, helped Jenny climb up and hauled himself up after her with Dora May in his arms. He put the child on the seat and helped Jenny get down into the body of the wagon and handed her Dora May. Jumping down, he picked up their supper plates and scraped them clean into the fire, causing it to sputter. He flung scooped-up dirt over it, smothering it.

Settling himself on the seat then, he released the brake, flicked the ends of the lines over the horses' heads, stirring them into reluctant movement, and drove westward. Some minutes later he pulled the team to a stop, braked the wagon, and turning, called Jenny.

"Yes?" she answered.

"Found us a swell spot," he told her. "Right next to a stream. I'll water the horses and then fix us something to eat. Wanna gimme Dora May, then I'll help you get down? Oh, better let me have a couple o' lanterns. We're gonna need th'm. It's pretty dark, y'know."

It took him more than forty minutes to get things "set", as he put it. He had just announced that supper was ready when he groaned. "Damnation!"

Jenny looked hard at him. "S'matter?"

"Left my saddle back there."

"Oh? Do you have t'go after it tonight? Can't we pick it up tomorrow morning before we go on our way?"

"Yeah, guess it'll keep over night."

He trudged back to the wagon and returned with two wooden boxes on which Jenny and Dora May perched themselves. Suppertime passed uneventfully. Then it

143

was time for Dora May to be put to bed.

"Bedtime, honey," Jenny told her.

The child got up from her box.

"Goodnight," Dora May repeated.

"I think you c'n do better than that," Jenny said, bent and whispered something to her. "All right?"

"Yes, ma'am."

Dutifully the child came to Canavan and kissed his cheek.

"Thank you," he said. "That was very nice. Now can I kiss you?"

"Yes. If you want to."

"I want to very much." He kissed her cheek. "Good night, Dora May. Happy dreams."

Clinging to Jenny's hand while Canavan trooped after them with one of the lighted lanterns, the child led them to the wagon. Handing the lantern to Jenny, Canavan helped her climb up and watched her maneuver herself over the seat and down into the wagon. Then he followed with Dora May.

He was sitting on one of the boxes within the cast-off rays of the second lantern, staring down into the fire, watching it burn itself out when he heard Jenny call him in a guarded voice.

"Gonna sit up all night?" she asked.

"Be along d'rectly," he told her.

He stamped out the fire and took care of the plates, cups and coffeepot and two frying pans that he had used, and with the lantern swinging from his hand, hoisted himself up into the wagon. He blew out the light and took off his boots, untied the front curtain and let it drop, carefully made his way around the sleeping child, noticing the while that the lantern that he had given Jenny stood on the floor at the rear, with the light in it turned down to its lowest. The back curtain, he saw, had been untied and hung in place, shutting out the night. He undressed himself and eased himself down on the mattress, drew up the cover and turned himself on his side with his back to Jenny.

"Johnny," she whispered, and he turned his head. "Isn't she the cutest thing?"

"Couldn't be any cuter."

"Never thought I could be so crazy about any kid, 'less maybe it was my own. But she does something to me. I have the hardest time of it keepin' myself from hugging an' kissing her every time I look at her."

"She ever say 'nything about her mother? She must miss her."

" 'Course she misses her. And she speaks of her a lot. Mostly when I'm undressing her and getting her ready for bed. When she says her prayers, she always asks God to be good to her mama an' papa because they were always so good to her. And she asks God to be good to us for takin' care of her."

He made no comment. Jenny was silent for a brief time, then she whispered: "When you get mad, you really do a job of it, don't you? The way you went after that man Wick, I thought you were gonna kill him. I didn't know you could get that mad."

"Takes a lot to get me going."

"I mean that much to you, that you woulda killed him for wanting me?"

"Best way I c'n answer that, Jenny, is to tell you something that I wasn't gonna tell you, leastways not just yet. But I guess I might as well."

"I'm listening."

"I had it planned, once I'd finished my business with that Judge Pierson, to have him marry us." He felt her raise up, prop herself up on her elbows, apparently to look hard at him despite her awareness that the deep darkness in the wagon would have made it impossible for her to have seen her own hand in front of her face. "I told you what happened, how he just about kicked me out've his office. So you know why I didn't get to it."

"Wait, now," she commanded. "I wanna get this straight. Y'mean you were really gonna marry me?" she asked in a hushed voice that reflected her disbelief.

"Uh-huh. Really."

"Even though you know you don't have to?"

"Uh-huh," he said again. "Even though."

"You really want to?" she pressed him. "Or is it because you think it'd be the nice thing to do?"

"Look, you tryin' to talk me out of it?"

"I'm not tryin' to do anything, talk you out of it or into it. I just want you to be sure you know what you're doing so you won't be sorry afterwards."

"I'm so sure it's what I want that the next town we hit, whoever's around who has the right to do the job for us, we'll get hitched." Then he added: "Takes two to make a bargain. So you have to be willing to have me. That goes without saying."

She didn't answer. She eased herself down again and lay on her side with her back to him. When he felt her body heave, he knew she was crying. He turned to her, reached out for her and turned her around to him and held her in his arms.

"What's the matter?" he asked her in a whisper. "What are you cryin' for?"

"You're a man. You wouldn't understand."

"Y'mean it's something that only women understand? G'wan, I don't believe that."

"I'm crying because I'm happy. Now tell me that doesn't make sense to you."

"It doesn't. But if it makes sense to you, go ahead an' cry. I'm happy. But if it's all right with you, I won't cry."

"I don't expect you to."

"You finished cryin'?"

"Why?"

"How c'n I kiss you when you're still blubbering?"

"I didn't know you wanted to." She raised her head. "I'm not blubbering now."

Despite the darkness he had no difficulty finding her willing lips with his.

Ten

The days that followed were uneventful. The good weather continued and they were able to make steady and substantial progress. In an effort to use fresh horses, Canavan alternated his original pair with those that he had taken from Mrs. Cole's wagon. The far-flung range seemed to be deserted. There was no sign of life, human or animal, anywhere about them that they could see, and the only sounds that could be heard were of their own making.

But it was an eerie silence that blanketed the land, and while it had no effect on Canavan or little Dora May, it was disquieting to Jenny. She slept poorly, got up a dozen times during the night, and several times when her rising woke Canavan, he found her peering out guardedly from behind a lifted corner of either the back curtain or the front one. Each time she insisted that she had heard something that sounded to her like stealthy bootsteps. Canavan tried to assure her that there was nothing to fear, adding that Willie's sense of hearing was far keener than hers or his, that if there had been anyone about, the mare would have heard it and sounded an alarm. Reluctantly she conceded that she might have imagined it.

Each time he brought her back to bed and she snuggled up close to him. But half an hour later he would feel her ease herself out of his arms and get up again. Every now and then she claimed she had gotten up to see that Dora May was all right. Then during the day he kept watching her and he would find her looking back or standing up, ranging a quick look over the prairie. He made no comment. But he noticed that lack of rest and sleep had begun to take its toll on her; she was sluggish in her movements, short-tempered and appeared to have lost her appetite.

A light, gentle rain began to fall on the night of the fifth day. About midnight when they were asleep, Jenny's exhaustion having finally overcome her, a violent storm burst upon them. The thunder echoed over the hushed range like the roar of distant cannons. The flashes of lightning and the repeated claps of thunder woke the three of them and so unnerved the horses that they struggled frantically to break their tethering lines. The animals milled about in their fright, trampled and kicked one another, and made such a to-do that Canavan was forced to get dressed and go out to them and move about them in an effort to calm them down.

The rain then came pelting down and the accompanying wind tore at the wagon's canvas covering with such fury that it finally succeeded in ripping it off, subjecting Jenny and the child to a severe drenching before Canavan was able to retrieve the canvas and hoist it up over them. Ignoring the driving rain and the howling wind, he managed to secure the canvas.

Wringing wet, he surveyed the interior of the wagon with a critical eye and a sad shake of his head. Twice the light in the lantern that he had lit was blown out, and each time his wet hands made the matches he fished out of his pocket worthless, and he had to scrounge around for dry ones. It was nearly dawn by the time the storm finally abated. The rain gradually stopped and the wind slacked off till it was little more than a breeze.

Jenny and Dora May had taken refuge under the driver's seat and had dozed off. Wearily Canavan stripped off his soggy clothes, dried himself with an old towel that had somehow managed to escape the effects of the rain, donned some old clothes that he had planned to discard, and climbed down from the wagon. The rangeland was a sea of mud, and the wheels of the wagon mired in it. He hunted around till he found a couple of small, flat rocks, uprooted them from the muck, and made a base of them for a fire. He returned to the wagon for a small box that he broke into pieces and set it afire to boil water for coffee. With a couple of cupfuls in his stomach he felt better. Again he returned to the wagon, this time for two lariats that he pressed into service as washlines, looping one end of each around an iron stave that helped support the canvas covering atop the wagon and knotting the other end around the trunk of a droopy-branched tree that stood some twenty feet away. Just about everything, and that included his wet clothes, that he was able to haul out of the wagon without waking Jenny or Dora May was hung out to dry.

At about eight-thirty, a warming, cheerful sun burned off the clouds. Brushing against the two cloth-covered boxes that held Jenny's and Dora May's clothes, he found that while the cloth had received a thorough drenching, the contents of the boxes were quite dry.

It was about the middle of the morning when Jenny awoke. Hearing her move about in the wagon, Canavan brought her a cup of hot coffee.

"Hey," she said when she saw the bright sunshine outside. "What time is it?"

"Must be somewhere's around ten-thirty. Slept all right for a change, huh?"

"And how I did! And Dora May's still pounding her ear. Poor kid, she was scared to death. How bad did we get it?"

"Bad," Canavan replied. "Gonna have to find us a town so's we c'n stock up again. Most of our grub's ruined, water-soaked. Only good thing the storm did for us was fill our water barrel right smack to the top. Outside o' that, it just about put us outta business."

Dora May woke up shortly after that and Jenny interrupted her own getting deessed to put the child in dry clothes. The bedroll and their nightclothes were soon hung on the washline, then Canavan helped the two get down. He stripped off the canvas covering and spread it out in the grass so that the sun could dry it as well as the inside of the wagon.

"Hate to lose a whole day," he told Jenny when the three of them were breakfasting on the last of the buns. Only Dora May made a wry face when she bit into the bun that Jenny handed her and found it was soggy. But when neither of her elders voiced any complaint, she made none either, and ate her bun quietly. "Like I started to say," Canavan began again, "while I hate to lose a whole day, I think we'd better lay over till tomorrow and give the sun a chance to dry us out."

Jenny nodded.

"Besides," he added, "when the ground's so soft, the horses won't find it easy going."

The sun cooperated fully. However at sundown, when Canavan climbed up into the wagon and found the floorboards damp, he hauled out a sheet of canvas and spread it out over the floor as a protective base for the bedroll and the mattress.

Since it had been a long and tiring day for all of them,

everyone was ready to turn in at a rather early hour. The next day proved to be another bright and sunny one and, after an early cup of coffee, they resumed their journey. From time to time throughout the day Canavan ranged ahead of the wagon seeking high ground from which he might spot a town. Unwilling to leave Jenny and Dora May alone for too long, he drummed back every little while to see that they were all right and to give them the assurance of his nearness.

Late in the afternoon when he was about to abandon his efforts, and he was about to wheel around and ride back, Willie whinnied and he promptly twisted around and cast a quick look over the prairie. Coming toward him from about half a mile away was a wagon train with rifle-armed horsemen riding its flanks and half a dozen others at the head of it.

"Comp'ny coming, Jenny!" he called to her as he came loping back.

She pulled back instantly on the lines, halting the wagon, and asked apprehensively: "Trouble?"

He reined in alongside the heaving horses. "Nope. Wagon train headed east," he answered, and turning, pointed to it.

She stood up and followed his pointing finger with her eyes. "Couple o' men coming this way, Johnny," she said.

He wheeled Willie around.

"What d'you suppose they want of us?" she asked.

He offered no opinion. "I'll go meet th'm and find out."

He drummed away to meet the oncoming mounted men. There were two of them, and he came together with them shortly, nodded to them and slacked a little in the saddle. One of the two men said: "When we spotted your wagon, mister, we thought we oughta stop you and warn you that you might be running into trouble."

"Oh? What kind o' trouble? Highbinders?"

"Uh-huh. Gang o' men, about twenty o' th'm, showed up yesterday. The scurviest lookin' crew you ever saw. When they saw the size of our outfit—we've got forty-three wagons and forty-five men and all o' th'm right handy with a gun—they kinda veered off. We've been keepin' a sharp eye out for th'm. But I don't look for them to come around again. They won't wanna tangle with us. We're too strong for th'm. What they go after are small outfits. I kinda think it might be a good idea for you to swing north so's to avoid th'm. Y'know? By the way, I'm Cy Fairly, and this," turning to his companion, "is Mike Cousins. Mike's our scout."

"My name's Canavan, and I sure appreciate you tippin' me off."

"Forget it," Fairly said. "Wish you were goin' our way. Then you could pull your wagon in with ours."

"You pass any towns?"

"Not the last week or so. Fact is, we've been steerin' clear o' th'm and stickin' close to our route. Why d'you ask? Runnin' short o' grub?"

"That storm just about ruined what we had."

"Got enough water?"

"Yeah, sure."

"We might be able to spare you some meat an' flour an' coffee, if they'll help you out. Leastways till you're able to get a real stockin' up."

"I'd be obliged to you for whatever you can spare."

Fairly's train had ground to a halt, and Canavan, lifting a quick look to it could see its people eyeing the lone wagon that stood diagonally opposite it about fifty feet away.

"Suppose you bring your wagon over to our lead wagon?" Fairly suggested.

"Right," Canavan answered.

He parted from the two horsemen, wheeled Willie and loped back to his own wagon. Jenny held her gaze on him as he came riding up to her. He smiled. "Don't look so worried. They don't want anything of us. Instead they wanna help us which proves what kind o' people they are. They offered to fix us up with whatever they c'n spare like meat, flour an' coffee to hold us till we hit a town, and I took th'm up on it."

"Oh," Jenny said.

"Wanna follow me over to their lead wagon?"

" 'Course," she responded.

Trotting the mare across the intervening space to the halted train, Canavan led the way and Jenny followed him, and pulled up when he did. She could see the people aboard the strung-out wagons focusing their eyes on her and she flushed.

Canavan swung down from Willie and was joined by Fairly and Cousins. They talked together briefly, then Canavan followed Cousins away. A handful of women who had already climbed down from their wagons, apparently glad for the opportunity to stretch their legs came sauntering over and stopped just short of Jenny, lifted their eyes to her and smiled. Fairly came up and touched his hat to her.

"Glad to be o' some help to you people, Mrs. Canavan," he said. "Wouldn't you like to get down a minute? Sittin' up there and driving must be kinda tiring after a while."

When he held up his arms to her, she moved across the seat and let him help her climb down.

"Mary," he said over his shoulder, and a slim, graying woman came to his side. "You wanna keep Mrs. Canavan comp'ny while I go see how Mike's takin' care o' her husband?"

154

"Of course, Cy," was the reply. As Fairly, hitching up his pants and shifting his holstered gun to a more comfortable position, trudged off, his wife asked Jenny: "Where are you headed for, dear? California?"

Before Jenny could answer, the other women crowded forward around Mary Fairly. One of them said: "My, isn't she pretty!"

"She is indeed," Mrs. Fairly said. "Mrs. Canavan, this is Mrs. Macklin," and indicated each of the others with a nod as she introduced them. "Mrs. Halstead, Mrs. Costa and Mrs. McDole."

Jenny exchanged a smile and a murmured, "How d'you do?" with each woman.

She was too busy being lionized by the train women to notice the transfer of foodstuffs from Fairly's wagon to Canavan's. It was only when the two men shook hands that the friendly talk among the uneven circle of women stopped.

"Mind you now," Jenny heard Fairly say to Canavan, "keep a sharp eye out. And don't forget when you get to Sacramento to look up my brother Tom. He'll be only too glad to help you get located."

Canavan nodded and thanked Fairly. Then he turned to Jenny. "Time for us to get rolling."

"Oh," she said, and her voice mirrored her disappointment.

As Canavan helped her climb up to the driver's seat, Mrs. Fairly said: "Sorry we couldn't get a look at your little girl. She must be very lovely."

Jenny, settling herself on the seat and unwinding the lines from around the handbrake, flashed her a smile. "She is."

"She's taking a nap," Canavan added.

"So your wife said."

Jenny had just released the handbrake when

155

Canavan, astride Willie, looked up at her and nodded. She jerked the reins and the horses plodded away, lurching the wagon into movement behind them. There were cries of "Goodbye" and both responded to them. Then pulling ahead of the wagon, Canavan headed northward. Twisting around and looking up at Jenny, he thought she seemed to be a little puzzled. So he reined in and waited till the wagon came abreast of him and he moved up alongside of it.

But before he could explain why they were changing direction, Jenny said: "We were heading west before, weren't we?"

"Uh-huh, and now we're heading north."

"All right for me to ask why?"

" 'Course. Fairly says there's a gang o' highbinders, bushwhackers, or plain bad men if you like that better, on the loose an' I wanna avoid th'm."

"I see," she said.

"There's hill country northward," he continued, "and Mike Cousins, Fairly's scout, thinks we'll be safer working our way through the hills where we c'n always find cover than down here on the open range where we wouldn't stand a chance if we got jumped."

She was silent for a moment, then she said: "Heard somebody once say that those gangs usu'lly hole up in the hills and—"

"That's right," he said, interrupting her. "They hole up there because they know the law won't go up there after them. Take an army o' men to flush a gang outta the hills and the law never has that many."

"And they come riding down only when they're looking to do some raiding."

"Right again. But being that this gang's down here on the prowl, I figure this is the best time for us to get into the hills and push through and come out the other side while the gang's away and busy. Understand?"

"Yes," she replied. "It'll be getting dark pretty soon. We gonna stop an' make camp, or are we gonna keep going?"

"Keep going long's we can. Closer we get to the hills, the better I'll like it. Then first thing tomorrow morning, the minute it begins to get light, we'll get going again."

He trotted away and Jenny followed him, easing up on the lines in an effort to encourage the horses to quicken their pace. They showed no desire to take advantage of what she offered them. Time passed and the shadows that had already reached out to span the prairie lengthened and deepened. But Canavan ignored them, evidence that he had no intention of stopping till he was forced to. Several times Jenny saw him stand up in the stirrups and quickly look around, then sink down again and ride on. When they came to a thinly grassed incline, the horses slowed their pace, and Jenny flicked the loose ends of the reins over their heads. They responded by manfully toiling upward. When they topped the incline and the ground leveled off, she was surprised to find it barren, hardpacked and strewn with stone and shale that crumbled under the grind of the wheels. But the horses' ironshod hoofs and the iron-rimmed wheels produced an echoing metallic clatter that she was certain could be heard for miles around. Riding some twenty feet in advance of the wagon, Canavan kept looking back at Jenny and the toiling team. A couple of times when he thought the horses were beginning to lag, he beckoned vigorously and again Jenny used the ends of the lines to urge them on. Finally he reined in and waited and when the wagon came up to him, he held up his hand and Jenny promptly pulled back on the lines, halting the heaving horses. It was evening by then and visibility was rapidly decreasing.

"See there?" Canavan asked Jenny, turning and pointing northward.

"What is it?" she wanted to know.

"The hills," he told her patiently.

She looked hard in the direction in which he was pointing. At first she couldn't see anything and was about to say so. Suddenly though she saw it, the barely discernible outline of some low-lying hills. "Oh, yes," she said. "I see them now."

"No more'n about a mile away."

"Yeah, but it's getting so dark, in another couple o' minutes you won't be able to see your hand in front o' your face. Don't tell me you're aimin' to . . ."

"I'd like to give it a try."

There was no answer from Jenny.

"We'll give the horses a couple o' minutes to blow themselves. Then we'll see if they're up to it."

"You're the boss," she said.

He frowned. He hadn't liked the grumpy way in which she'd said that. But rather than call her on it and make a to-do when he realized she was tired and concerned about what could happen to them if they fell into the clutches of the bushwhackers, he remarked: "Haven't heard a peep out've Dora May all afternoon. She all right?"

"Yeah, sure." Leaning down into the body of the wagon, Jenny asked loud enough for him to hear: "You still playing with your doll, honey?" Canavan heard the child's voice, but he couldn't tell what she had said. Jenny squared around. "Dora May says she's doing fine. Kinda hungry though."

"Tell her it won't be long now, no more'n say half 'n hour before we eat. Got some nice cold meat and some cake that I know she's gonna like."

Again Jenny turned, this time to repeat Canavan's words to Dora May. "Next town we come to, we're gonna have to get Dora May a new doll. One she's got now is just about coming apart," she told him.

"We'll get her the best they've got." Straightening up in the saddle and wheeling Willie, he said: "All right, Jenny. Let's go."

Willie responded to Canavan's knee-nudge and trotted away with him. Lightly Jenny slapped the horses with the reins and they snorted protestingly, a sign of their unwillingness to go on. She jerked the lines, perhaps a little harder than she had intended. Reluctantly the horses obeyed her, grumbling deep down in their throats as they moved after Canavan. They started off jerkily, so the wagon swayed and then lurched forward. The big wheels rolled over the rough ground, crushing shale into powder and driving the stones deeper into the dirt. On and on the wagon went with the horses straining in the traces. It was only then that Jenny realized that they were going uphill.

Suddenly from somewhere off in the dark distance beyond them came the startling echoes of gunfire. Grimly Canavan told himself that the raiders had found a victim.

"Johnny!" Jenny cried. "Wasn't that shooting?"

"Sounded like it," he answered over his shoulder.

"Think it coulda been those—what'd you call th'm—bushwhackers?"

"I'm afraid so."

"God, I hope it wasn't the Fairlys that they hit!" she said emotionally. "They're such nice, friendly people."

"I don't think it coulda been them. Their outfit's too big an' too strong for any gang to jump."

"Then it coulda been a smaller one."

"Yeah, that's the kind the bushwhackers go after."

Again Jenny applied the reins, only this time she really lashed the horses. Doubly anxious now to put distance between the raiders who would be returning to their hideout in the hills once they had killed off their victims and had finished looting their wagons, her fears refused to permit any lagging or stopping.

"Go on, go on!" she cried to the horses, and lashed them again.

Wheeling Willie around, Canavan waited, and when the struggling horses came abreast of him, he brought the mare up close to the nearest horse and grabbed the reins.

"Loop the reins around the brake, but easy though," he instructed her. "I'll lead the horses. You get down in the wagon and light one o' the lanterns only keep it down on the floor and don't turn it up any higher'n you have to. Then look around in that stuff that I got from Fairly till you find the meat, cut off some small hunks and you an' Dora May eat. You'll find a knife under the seat. It's in a leather holder. Got that?"

"Yes," she answered. "But what about you?"

"I'll eat later on. Go ahead now. Only hold on when you climb down. Don't want you takin' a spill. And make sure the back curtain's down. Don't want the light to be spotted."

It was just about a minute later when he heard Jenny's voice.

"I'm down, Johnny, and I've lit one o' the lanterns. But you watch y'self, y'hear?"

He didn't answer. He was occupied with the struggling horses as they fought their way up the hills. The upgrade grew steadily steeper the higher they climbed.

Their heaving and panting became louder and several times one of them lost his footing and slipped to his knees. Fortunately though the team continued to forge its way upward.

Twice Canavan halted the horses in order to give them a minute-long breather. And each time that he led them on it was with mixed feelings of hope and misgivings. If they could make it the rest of the way, once they entered the hills, the going would be easier, he told himself. The outline of the hills was gone now, having melted away into the darkness. So he couldn't tell how much farther they had to go. But he was sure it couldn't be very far. Once they reached fairly level ground, he would switch horses, he decided, replacing the exhausted pair with the two that were tied to the tailgate.

It was fifteen minutes later when they came off the upgrade and onto what he judged was a level stretch of ground. Again he halted the hauling horses, unhitched them and led them around the wagon to the rear, untied the fresh team and brought it forward and backed it into the traces and hitched it up, returned to the rear to tie up the waiting pair and hoisted himself up again on Willie's back.

"Johnny!" he heard Jenny call and he turned in the saddle.

"Yeah?"

"Something the matter?"

"Stopped so's I could switch horses. You an' Dora May doin' all right?"

"Yeah, sure. You gonna keep going?"

"Yep. Wanna give the fresh team a chance to earn its keep."

"I'm ready to take over the driving again," Jenny offered.

"No, I think you'd better stay put and take it easy."

"It isn't fair leaving it to you to do everything. You must be pretty well beat as well as starved out. So how about it? How about giving me a chance to earn my keep too?"

"You've done more'n your share already, Jenny. Besides by takin' care o' yourself an' Dora May, you're relievin' me of that worry. So like I said, stay put."

She was silent for a moment. Then she said: "Awf'lly dark out, isn't it? How c'n you see where you're going?"

"Oh, it isn't that bad. Or maybe I'm more used to the darkness than you."

"I suppose so. "You hear 'nymore shooting?"

"Nope. Just that one time."

"Think that's a good sign?"

"Could be that one blast drove off the raiders."

"I sure hope that's what it means."

He turned away, brought Willie up close to the nearest wagon horse, got a good grip on the lines, then gave it a yank and the horses moved with him. On and on they went, and Canavan was aware of a brisk breeze sweeping down upon him. Then suddenly there was no breeze, and he looked up wonderingly. He could see a limited span of the sky but he couldn't see anything on either side of him. Then he noticed that the trail that he had been following had disappeared and that it was even darker than it had been before. Then his leg brushed something that was solid and smooth. He raised his eyes.

Towering high above him and losing itself in the darkness was a canyon wall, and he sensed at once that they were going through a pass. It was a narrow one, just about wide enough for a single wagon to make it through safely. The water barrel that was lashed on to the side of the wagon scraped the wall.

On through the pass they went with Canavan wondering how far it ran and what he would find at the end of it. It was difficult to judge distance in the deep darkness but after a while he guessed that they had spanned a hundred feet of the pass, then still another hundred, and the end of it was not yet in sight. Time and distance continued to fall away behind them. Finally though the wall that had begun to taper off dropped away altogether and they emerged into the open and again Canavan felt the rush of clean, brisk air.

It was lighter now too and when he looked skyward he found a bright moon directly overhead. Rays of silvery light glinted on sun-bleached, white-faced boulders that rose up on both sides of the trail. The ground, he was quick to notice, was fairly level though rough and stony. The grinding wheels and the horses' hoofs produced an echoing clatter. Then they began to go down a gentle slope and quite suddenly there was thinning grass underfoot.

Down and down they went as the grass thickened and muffled the churning wheels and the plodding hoofs. Canavan knew that they had broken out of the hills and had entered a valley.

That their luck had persisted and that it had enabled them to avoid running into the raiders was something to be grateful for, and he was. But he insisted upon believing that if fate had intervened in their behalf and had spared them, it had to be because of Dora May rather than because of them. Fate, he maintained, in an effort to make up to the child for the loss of her parents, would continue to safeguard them if for no other reason than that Dora May had need of them. He wasn't at all certain that Jenny would be willing to accept his belief. But it didn't matter. He believed it and he would continue to believe it.

Eleven

After a couple of days they turned to the southwest again and then westward. The weeks that followed were uneventful with each day the same as the one before it. As though they were crossing a virgin land they saw no signs whatsoever of others abroad in that vast prairieland. The weather was good and they took full advantage of it, putting as much distance between each day's sunup and sundown as the laboring horses permitted.

"Wonder where we are?" Jenny asked one morning when she awoke and peered out from behind the front drop curtain.

"Your guess is as good as mine," Canavan answered as he kicked off the blanket and reached for his pants. "All I c'n tell you is what I've been telling you every time you've asked. We're makin' time and knockin' off miles every day and that c'n mean only one thing, that we must be getting closer to California all the time."

"All the same though, wouldn't it be nice to know where we are, or at least have some idea?"

" 'Course it would. Way I figure it we oughta be in Colorado, the southern part of it."

"That doesn't tell me much. What comes after Colorado?"

"Utah. Then Nevada and after that California."

"Utah?" she repeated thoughtfully. "Isn't that Mormon country?"

"Uh-huh," he answered, tucking in his shirttail.

"Hey," she said, turning around to him. "How would you like to be a Mormon with a flock o' wives?"

"Thanks but no thanks."

"G'wan," she retorted. "Don't give me that. You could pick yourself different kinds, like a different kind for every day in the week and the nicest lookin' one for Saturdays an' Sundays. What a time you could have!"

"Far as I've been able to find out, man who c'n handle one wife has a full time job on his hands."

"How come they don't have some place where a woman c'n have more'n one husband?"

"Mean you'd like that?"

"I didn't say that. All I did was ask."

"Write a letter to Congress. Maybe somebody there will think the idea's worth trying and he'll get a law passed allowing women to have as many husbands as they like."

"That's what I get for wondering out loud."

"Now you've got me worried."

"I have? What about?"

"You gonna be satisfied with just one husband?"

"Try me and find out."

"Nope," he said with a shake of his head. "I'll wanna know for sure before I marry you."

"Suppose I say 'yes' when the time comes and I change my mind afterward?"

He grinned at her. "Maybe I won't care then. Maybe I'll be glad to get rid of you."

166

"You ever get to feeling that way about me, Johnny Canavan, and—"

"Yeah?" he teased her. "And what?"

"I don't know," she confessed. "But I think it'd just about finish me. I wouldn't be any good to anybody, me more'n anybody else. Guess all I'd want to do then would be to hide, curl up an' die."

He came across the creaky wagon floor, tiptoeing to avoid disturbing Dora May who was still asleep.

"When I marry you," he said to Jenny in a guarded tone, "it'll be for keeps."

"I wouldn't want it any other way," she said earnestly.

He took her face in his hands and kissed her on the lips. "How about you fixin' breakfast this morning?" he suggested.

"Gee, y'think I c'n do it?"

" 'Course. You've been watchin' me all this past week. Just take your time and you'll do all right," he assured her.

"I'll get dressed right away."

"And I'll go get a fire started."

"I'll want some hot water."

"Gimme five minutes and you c'n have it."

More days passed, as uneventfully as those that had preceded them. Then quite suddenly, and more startlingly than it would have been if it hadn't been for the long spell of silence to which they had become accustomed, the report of gunfire came echoing across the prairie.

Instantly Canavan who was loping along some twenty or thirty feet ahead of the wagon, reined in, wheeled around and dashed back. Promptly Jenny pulled back hard on the lines, halting the wagon team.

"I heard it," she said as Canavan came up to her. The color had already begun to drain out of her face. "Think it means another raid?"

"I'm afraid so," he said. He dismounted and climbed up into the wagon, filled his pockets with shells for his rifle and made his way down again. Hoisting himself up on Willie's back, he told Jenny: "We're gonna head north again. Maybe we c'n circle wide around wherever it is that that shooting's comin' from."

She nodded wordlessly.

He rode northward and Jenny followed him. Mile after mile that was punctuated by distant gunfire slipped away behind them. When he quickened the mare's pace, Jenny lashed the wagon horses and drove faster. There were more and more bursts of gunfire that carried across the range, and Canavan wore a grim look as he continued to lead the way. From time to time he stood up in the stirrups and peered intently in a westward and then southwestward direction. He felt a little less worried when he failed to spot anything. But just as he sank down in the saddle after a last look there was the grass-muffled thumping beat of horses' hoofs and he spied four mounted men coming toward them at a swift gallop from about half a mile away. He pulled up at one but beckoned Jenny on and the wagon came abreast of him.

"Four men comin' this way," he said. "Now don't panic. I think I c'n hold them off. Keep headin' north and don't stop or even slow down. Y'hear? I'll follow you soon's I can. Just watch yourself and don't go worryin' about me. I think you know I c'n take care o' myself. Go ahead, Jenny."

"I'm goin'," she answered. "Only be careful, Johnny."

"I'm not lookin' to die just yet," he said lightly.

She flicked the reins over the horses' backs and they responded and the wagon lumbered away. Yanking his rifle out of the boot, he hand-held it across the saddle as he followed Jenny at a trot. The wagon, in full flight now, soon got far ahead of him and as he watched it continue to lengthen the gap between them, he nodded approvingly.

Looking back over his shoulder he watched the oncoming horsemen narrow the distance between him and themselves. He held his hard eyes on the man who rode in advance of his companions and when he suddenly raised his rifle and fired, the man toppled off his horse and crashed to the ground. He fired a second time and his bullet struck squarely, sending one of the others' horses plunging to his knees and catapulting his rider over his head. Obviously stunned, the man lay motionlessly in the grass. The wounded horse threshed about wildly for a minute or so, then his body seemed to relax and then, like the man who had been riding him, he too lay still.

Easing himself around, Canavan sent the fleet mare loping away. When he looked back the two surviving horsemen were lashing their mounts as they sought to overtake him. Both men fired at him, but their shots fell far short of him. Reining in briefly and waiting for his pursuers to come a little closer, he fired again and his eyes gleamed when he saw a third man sag brokenly in the saddle and fall off his horse. The fourth man fired again at Canavan but this time his bullet went wide. Bringing his horse to a sliding stop, he wheeled around, and abandoning his felled companions and further pursuit, rode off in a westerly direction. Reloading his rifle and shoving it down in the boot, Canavan drummed away after Jenny.

He overtook her after a spirited run and ranged up alongside the wagon, slowing Willie at the same time.

"You all right?" she asked him, pulling back a little on the lines and slowing the team to match the mare's pace.

"Yeah, sure," he replied. "Don't have to worry any about those four. I got two o' th'm, spilled the third one, and saw the fourth man turn around and ride off."

She looked relieved. "We still gonna keep headin' north?"

"Yeah, sure. That feller that turned tail will tell the rest o' the gang and if they decide to come after us, I wanna give th'm as hard a time to catch up with us as I can."

"Uh-huh. You gonna lead the way again like before, or d'you want me to go on ahead?"

"Go on same's you were. I'll follow you only I'll kinda hang back a little and keep an eye out for uninvited company."

She smiled a bit and drove on. Canavan did not ride after her right away. Instead he sat Willie motionlessly for a time, ignoring her whinnying, a sign of her eagerness to rejoin the wagon horses, and looked southward and then shifting his gaze, looked westward.

A couple of times he stood up in the stirrups for an even better view of the range. When he seemed satisfied that there was no sign of renewed pursuit, he sank down in the saddle, swung Willie around and trotted her northward. The mare wanted to run; twice she sought to lengthen her stride. Each time Canavan checked her and ignoring her snorting, forced her to trot.

When he spotted the wagon idling a hundred yards or so ahead of him, Canavan gave the mare her head and she bounded away with him. He pulled her up short when they came abreast of Jenny.

"Horses were beginning to slow themselves," she explained to Canavan. "So I figured I oughta give th'm a breather."

"Uh-huh," he said.

Ten minutes later the horses appeared to be sufficiently rested and ready to go on again. When the wagon lurched after them, Canavan wheeled into position some fifteen feet behind it. Time passed slowly. Eventually the day wore away. But because he was unwilling to chance being overtaken while it was still light, Canavan instructed Jenny to keep going. It was only when darkness forced them to stop that he conceded and called to Jenny to pull up.

Without a fire, supper was limited to some cold meat. When Canavan announced his intention to stay up, Jenny quickly informed him that she wouldn't turn in either. It was only when he insisted that she go to bed and promised to wake her at once if he heard anything that she finally agreed to lie down. She wouldn't be able to sleep, she maintained, knowing that he was still awake. So, fully clothed except for her shoes, she stretched out on the mattress. But she was tired and despite her insistence that she would only doze, she fell into a tight sleep.

Looking in on her a half an hour after he had helped her climb up into the wagon, Canavan gently drew up the blanket around her, saw to it too that Dora May was well covered up, hauled out a heavy jacket and quietly left the wagon.

There was a rapidly stiffening breeze blowing, and it was a cold one. He quickly donned the jacket and buttoned it up, whipped up the collar around his neck, and, with his rifle slung over his shoulder, he kept watch.

After a while he decided to switch horses, so he replaced the tired team with the pair of fresh ones, backed them into the traces and hitched them up. He did not unsaddle Willie. She too would be ready to move at a moment's notice.

He sauntered about, stopping every little while and standing motionlessly, listening for sounds of horses and men. But he heard nothing except the usual night sounds.

At the first sign of light in the drab dawn sky he climbed up into the wagon and reluctantly shook Jenny awake. At his insistence, because the air was damp and raw, Jenny wrapped their blanket around herself before she took her place on the seat and prepared to drive off. When they got under way again and he led her in a southwesterly direction, she did not question the wisdom of returning to their orignal route. His judgment had been faultless, so she saw no reason to doubt it now. Obviously he was satisfied that they had left the raiders behind them. So she was satisfied too.

At about eight, when the sun completed the job of burning off the dampness and the chill, she shed the blanket, bunched it up and half-turning, dropped it behind and below the seat. He had taken off his heavy jacket half an hour before and had tossed it up to her. Now the blanket lay on top of the jacket. At nine Dora May awoke and Jenny called to him. Wheeling around, he came trotting back to Jenny's side.

"Any chance o' getting a cup o' coffee?" she asked him.

"Yeah, I think so. What d'you hear from Dora May?"

"So far, only that she's awake."

"How d'you suppose some hot cakes, bacon an' coffee'll sound to her?" he asked gravely.

"I don't think she'll mind if I answer for her. Sounds swell. I didn't do any washin' up, y'know. And I'm sure Dora May's face and hands c'n do with some soap an' water."

"Gimme a little time to get a fire going. Five minutes after that you c'n have your hot water."

"I was gonna fix breakfast this morning if you thought we could have a fire."

"And I was gonna let you. But you've got other things to do. So I'll let you off this time and do the fixin' myself."

"You're an angel, Johnny. Is it any wonder that I love you?"

He grinned at her. "G'wan. Don't gimme any o' that. It's the Irish who are supposed to dish out the mullarkey. Not the Polish."

"Maybe some o' the Irish in you has rubbed off on me," she answered. She braked the wagon and looped the reins around the brake, turned and eased herself over the seat and disappeared inside the wagon.

He was still grinning when he dismounted and tied Willie to one of the wagon's front wheels. Then he set about finding a suitable spot for a fire.

It was shortly after ten when they resumed their journey. Again a great silence hung over the open country. Then just before the sun moved into position directly overhead with its unspoken announcement that it was noon, they turned westward. It was just before two o'clock when they made their second stop. Their midday meal which consisted of cold meat took but fifteen minutes, and they pushed on again. It was about four when the wagon horses began to labor and Jenny promptly called Canavan's attention to it. Dismounting, he unhitched them and substituted a rested team.

As he stepped up to the waiting mare and prepared to mount her, Jenny who had been looking on quietly, asked him: "Switching horses this late in the day mean you're gonna keep going for a while after it gets dark?"

"That's the general idea," he replied. "You add up the extra miles we knock off every day after sundown and you'll be surprised to find how many days' travelling time they come to. Let's go, Jenny."

It was late afternoon and then dusk and still Canavan kept pressing on, challenging the oncoming darkness and daring the night to deprive him of those extra miles he sought to put behind them. Loping away in search of some high ground and leaving it to Jenny to catch up to him, he rode up a grassy incline, halted Willie at its very crest and gave her an opportunity to blow herself while he ranged a long look over the prairie.

Despite the cushioning and muffling grass that carpeted the prairie he was able to make out the pounding beat of massed hoofs and the churning roll of many wagon wheels. Movement to the east attracted his attention and as he leveled his gaze at it a wagon train that was still on the move in spite of the approaching nightfall came into view. It was a good-sized train with its wagons drawn up in a double row with mounted men of whom he could see some six or seven riding its flanks.

"Feller who's bossing that outfit knows his business," he thought to himself. "With outriders to hold off raiders and the wagons doubled up and all set to circle up at a minute's notice, the gang that tries to jump that train will find it's bitten off a helluva bigger bite than it can chew. Damned little chance for anybody to break through without being blasted to hell an' gone."

174

The outriders ranged up and down the entire line of wagons, apparently urging lagging drivers to speed up and close any gaps that existed between them and the wagons directly ahead of them. The train came closer all the time, and as Canavan watched, the lead wagons came abreast of him and rolled past him.

He swung Willie around and rode down the slope and trotted her back to meet Jenny. Suddenly his keen ears caught the drum of approaching horses and he jerked his head and around instantly and looked northward. He sucked in his breath and stared with wide, troubled eyes when he spotted a band of tightly bunched together horsemen heading in Jenny's direction at a swift gallop. He sent Willie racing to meet her, and when he came close enough to her, he pointed northward.

"Raiders!" he shouted. "head for that wagon train!"

As proof that she understood and that she had no intention of panicking, she swerved southward. She drove the horses toward the train at a furious though somewhat uneven gallop with the wagon lurching from side to side when its wheels rolled over half-buried rocks. Yanking out his rifle, Canavan flung two shots into the raider's ranks, causing one man to sag brokenly in the saddle and plunging another's horse to the ground.

The wounded animal cried out in pain and rolled over a couple of times from side to side and finally rolled over his thrown rider, crushing him under him. Again Canavan pegged two shots at the raiders. He missed with one shot, but steadying himself succeeded in targeting a victim for his next shot, tumbling a man off his mount.

The riderless horse skidded to a rather uncertain stop,

and turning, collided head-on with another mounted man. The two horses and the horseman went down in a tangle of threshing legs and flashing hoofs. Again Canavan fired, but again he missed. Shoving his rifle down into the boot, he drew his Colt and snapped a couple of shots at the raiders, then without pausing to see the effect of his fire, he dashed after Jenny.

As he neared the train he saw that it had ground to a halt, and saw too that several of the outriders as well as men on foot were pouring gunfire into the already thinned out raiders' ranks. Overtaking Jenny, he pulled up when she did after giving him a couple of anxious moments when he was afraid she was going to pile into one of the halted wagons. Fortunately she was able to stop in time to avoid crashing into it.

Breathing a deep sigh of relief, he dismounted. Horsemen from the train flashed past him and he followed them with his eyes, lifted his gaze beyond them and saw four raiders, apparently the only survivors of the band, wheel around and ride off. Shot down men and horses were strewn about, some of them lying in grotesque positions. A fatally wounded horse, obviously already overtaken by death, lay on its side with its legs thrusting straight out and stiffening. A dozen feet away was a raider who was down on his knees with his body hunched over and his bowed head nudging the ground, his hands hanging limply at his sides, but with his backside higher than the rest of him.

Just as Canavan was about to shift his gaze, the man slumped over and sprawled out on his back.

Armed riflemen and returning mounted men converged upon Jenny and Canavan. She turned and lifted Dora May onto the seat with her. When willing hands reached up for them, Jenny passed the child to a stalwart, bearded man who handed her to Canavan.

Then Jenny was helped down from the wagon and she held out her arms to Dora May. The child leaned toward her and Jenny took her from Canavan and held her tight.

A tall, rangy man with a deeply lined and weatherbeaten face and gray hair showing in his sideburns pushed through the other men to Jenny's side, chucked Dora May under the chin, and asked Jenny: "You all right, ma'am?"

She flashed him a smile. "Yes, thank you."

"Good." He turned to Canavan. "That was a real close one, mister."

"Too close," Canavan replied wryly. "We'da been goners if you people hadn'ta come along when you did."

The man smiled and said: "That's one gang o' bushwhackers less for us to worry about. But they weren't as smart as they shoulda been, followin' you right down into the muzzles of our guns. 'Course it could be that they didn't see us till it was too late for them to pull up and turn tail. I'm wagon master. Name's Tom Bonner."

"Mine's Canavan."

The two men gripped hands.

"You headin' for California?" Bonner asked. "If you are, and if you an' your missus have had enough of tryin' to make it across the prairie by yourselves and you'd like the protection we c'n give you, pull your wagon into line wherever you find an empty space. Oh, it'll cost you twenty-five bucks to join up with us."

"Fair enough," Canavan acknowledged.

"Forgot to say that that's what it'll cost you if you've got your own grub. If you haven't—"

"Haven't got enough left to make it worth talking about."

"Then it'll cost you more. But that part o' the deal we c'n figure out later on. We'll keep tabs an' let you know later on, say when we're nearing California, what it comes to and you c'n square up before you leave us."

"Want the twenty-five now?"

Bonner grinned. "Uh-huh. It's not that I don't trust you or any o' my other people. I do. It's just that I find it's a heckuva lot easier on me doing a cash-in-advance business. Saves me from burning the midnight oil, keepin' books and makin' out bills and handing 'em out and then having to hound people to pay me what they owe me. Keep just one little book that tells me how much I've taken in and how much I've laid out. So I'll take my dough now."

Canavan dug in his pants pocket and hauled out a fistful of crumpled bills. From among them he drew out a couple of tens and a signle five-dollar bill, and started to smooth them out only to have the wagon master stop him.

"They're fine just the way they are, Canavan. I don't care what they look like or what shape they're in. What's more, I'll take a whole barrelful just like yours and I'll be only too glad to do the smoothing out myself and it won't matter even one little bit how long it takes me."

Canavan handed him the bills and Bonner stuffed them in his pocket.

"Now suppose you pull your wagon into line so's we c'n move on? Don't wanna make camp where there are a lot o' dead men and horses layin' around. They don't smell too good and they don't add anything to the scenery. Besides I don't think our women an' kids would like lookin' at them."

Canavan nodded and turned away.

"When we get circled up," Bonner added and

Canavan looked back at him over his shoulder, "bring your family over to my wagon for supper. I'll tell the cook to fix some extra."

As Canavan squared around again he collided with the big bearded man who was obviously waiting for him for he had moved in front of him deliberately, blocking his path. Both put out their hands, Canavan doing it instinctively, to hold off the other.

"Only keep you a minute, partner," the big man said. "But I heard you say your names Canavan. You come from Texas, say around Amarillo way?"

"That's right. Why? Why d'you ask?"

"Last I heard from my brother, he was still riding for a big outfit around Amarillo and the man who owned it was named Canavan."

"John Canavan's my father."

"And Arlie Watts is my brother."

"I know Arlie. Haven't seen him though in some time now."

"That makes two of us. I'm Steve Watts."

"And I was named for my father."

The bearded man laughed and thrust out his big right hand. Canavan shook it.

"Small world, huh?" Watts asked, chuckling and pumping Canavan's hand vigorously. "Arlie swears by your old man, Canavan. Fact is, he treats Arlie like he's one o' the family, like he's one o' his sons. First chance I get, I'll get off a letter to Arlie so's he can tell your folks who I met up with."

"Fine," Canavan said, nodding. "You do that."

"Oh, something that Arlie wrote in one o' his letters just came to me. One o' you Canavans joined the Rangers, right?"

"Right. And I was the one. But that was a long time ago."

"I'd sure like having you for a neighbor, Canavan. How about you pullin' your wagon into line next to mine?"

"Wanna lead the way?"

Minutes after Canavan had driven his wagon into the space that the burly Watts had led him to, the train ground forward again. Half a mile farther westward the order to pull up and circle up was relayed down the line. While Jenny and Dora May were in the wagon getting cleaned up, Canavan idled, leaned back against the right front wheel. It was there that Tom Bonner found him when he came riding around.

The wagon master reined in front of him. "See you've found a place for yourself," he said.

"Steve Watts led me to it. And I want to ask you something, Bonner."

"Ask away."

"Somebody once told me that in the eyes o' the law wagon masters have just about the same authority that ship captains do. That right?"

"Whoever told you that told you right."

"You ever marry any people?"

"Yeah, sure. Any number o' times. But who are you askin' for?"

"Being that I don't know any o' the people in the train 'cept Watts and being that he's been married for more'n fifteen years now, it figures that I must be askin' for me, doesn't it?"

Bonner looked hard at him. "Y'mean you and . . .?"

Canavan nodded. "That's right. Jenny an' me. You have to know how come we aren't married?"

"Nope," Bonner said evenly. "None o' my business. All I ask o' my people and that includes you now is that they keep the peace an' do their best to get along with the others. When d'you want me to do it?"

"Some time tonight. When there's nobody around. I don't want a crowd around to embarrass Jenny."

"Everybody usu'lly turns in around ten o'clock. That is, everybody 'cept those who are due to stand guard. That's something you'll have to do too, Canavan, along with the others. But that only means about once every six nights."

Canavan nodded again. "That's all right. Just lemme know when it's my turn and I'll be ready."

"Know where my wagon is?"

"Lead wagon, I suppose, huh?"

"No, that's the supply wagon. Mine's the one behind it. Supper oughta be ready in about half 'n hour."

"We'll be there," Canavan told him, "and we'll bring our appetites."

Bonner grinned and responded: "Lee Sing's a good cook. If you don't act like you're enjoying his cooking, you'll make him very unhappy."

"I c'n tell right now that we're gonna like everything he dishes out to us."

"That's the kind o' spirit that makes friends," the wagon master said, backed his horse and trotted him away.

It was some twenty minutes later when Jenny announced that Dora May and she were ready to be helped down from the wagon. Quickly Canavan responded, climbing up first to carry down Dora May, then he helped Jenny get down. While he looked on gravely, Jenny and Dora May, hand-in-hand, stood before him.

"Well?" Jenny wanted to know. "How d'we look?"

"Fine," he replied. "I don't usu'lly go in for bragging, but I think my womenfolks are just about the best lookin' anywhere. That a new dress you've got on, Jenny?"

"Uh-huh. One I've been saving for a special time.

181

Not that tonight's anything different from any other night. But I put it on anyway."

"Looks fine."

With Dora May walking between them, they headed for Bonner's wagon. Tom Bonner was waiting for them. Lee Sing, a short, pudgy, round-faced Chinaman, greeted them with a broad, toothy smile and even added a bow to Dora May. He made a to-do out of helping the child seat herself on a towel-covered box.

Bonner who stood by quietly looking on smiled at Jenny. "Can't let Lee outdo me. Don't remember the last time I had such lovely ladies at my table. Pleasure to have you here, ma'am." Turning to Dora May, he added: "You too, little lady."

Supper was a huge success. Lee Sing was generously complimented and beamed. When it was over and Jenny arose, Dora May did too.

"Thank you, Mr. Bonner," Jenny said. "And thank you again, Lee Sing."

"Our pleasure, ma'am," Bonner acknowledged. Then turning to Canavan who had just gotten to his feet, he said: "I'll be looking for you at ten."

"Right," Canavan answered.

As they headed back to their own wagon, Canavan remarked: "Be dark by the time you get Dora May tucked in."

Instead of answering, Jenny asked: "What are you and that Bonner man going to do at ten?"

"You're included in that too."

"That's nice. Then it should be all right for me to ask what we're going to do at ten, shouldn't it?"

He smiled, and leaning toward her, told her in a guarded whisper: "We're going to get married."

She stopped in her tracks and looked hard at him.

"You—you really want that?"

" 'Course I do. You asked me that once before and I told you the same thing then. Remember?"

"Yes. But that was then and this is now."

"Doesn't matter. I still feel the same way. That's why I asked Bonner if he could do the job for us. When he said he could and I told him we wanted it done when there wasn't anybody around, he set it for ten because that's when everybody's us'ully bedded down."

"I see."

"You don't sound very happy about it."

"You've never told me anything about your folks. They must be rich and important, judging by what that man, that Steve Watts said. Anyway, it got me to thinking. I'm a nobody and I come from very ordinary people. So I haven't got a thing to offer you. Why even this dress I'm wearing and the shoes I'm standing in, you bought them for me. And that goes for just about everything else I've got. If you hadn'ta bought them, I just wouldn't have a thing. What d'you want me for, Johnny? You could do lots better for yourself."

"I want you because I love you," he told her quietly. "And I know you love me. And if all you've got to offer me is you, I'll still be doing all right for myself. So being that I'm satisfied, you should be satisfied too."

"I don't like to keep asking you this, but are you sure? I don't want you to be sorry afterwards."

"I never felt so sure about anything in my life."

"All right, Johnny. I want to marry you more than anything in the world."

As he straightened up, Dora May looked up at her. "You crying, Jenny?" the girl asked.

"Yes, honey. I'm crying because I'm happy."

"Oh," the child said, obviously satisfied and relieved. She turned to Canavan, lifted her eyes to him. "Don't you want to hold my hand like Jenny does when we're walking?"

He looked down at her. Suddenly he knelt down.

"It's late, you know, and you must be tired," he told her, taking her hand in both of his. "Wouldn't you like to ride the rest of the way on my shoulders?"

"Oh, I'd like that!"

"Then up you go!"

He lifted her, settled her comfortably across his broad shoulders and, holding her hands in his, turned to Jenny. "All right?"

"Yes," she responded brightly.

Then, with her arm through his and Dora May laughing when he jounced her up and down, they marched on.

BROTHERS OF THE RANGE

ONE

When old John Rowan died, his three husky sons carried him up the dew-wet grassy side of a flowering slope and laid him to rest in a grave that they had hollowed out for him at the very top of it. Rearing itself skyward a couple of hundred feet from the Rowan ranch house, the slope dominated and commanded a broad view of the Rowan property that spread away in every direction as far as the eye could see. Mary Rowan, the old man's forty-six-year-old widow, twenty-four years his junior, and stepmother of his sons, had selected the site. Wild flowers of every kind studded the slope and bathed it with rich, heady perfume while soft, caressing breezes that drifted lazily over the ranchland below it, lifted and played over the slope, stirring the grass and flowers into musical whispers. Because it towered over the rest of the Square-R, the Rowan brand that had long been recognized as symbolic of the old man's integrity, Mary secretly nurtured the hope that the sun would be able to reach him and burn the rheumatism that had hobbled him so badly out of his tired old body. Finally, from the window of the rear upper floor bedroom that John and she had shared for nearly twenty years, she would always have a clear view of his resting place.

After a brief burial ceremony over which Mary presided, reading the simple service from a worn old Bible, she stepped back and stood quietly looking on as the freshly turned, sweet smelling dirt was shoveled down upon the box that held John Rowan's remains. When the last spadeful had been patted down smoothly over the mound, the Rowans stood with heads bowed around it for a minute. When Mary finally looked up and nodded, the Rowans shouldered their shovels with tiny clods of dirty still clinging to them and followed the slender, straightbacked, black clad figure of their step-mother back to the house.

The presence of death had draped a mantle of respect-ful silence over it. Yet in the background one could hear though only faintly the hushed echoes of voices and footsteps. In the spacious and always orderly kitchen that smelled of soap and water and of the savory good-ness of cooking and baking, Mary faced her stepsons, standing backed against the closed door with her hands behind her and curled around the doorknob.

"I've something to say to you," she began and they lifted their eyes to her. She shook her head when Matt who was twenty-five and the eldest, two years older than is twin brothers, Bill and Pete, started to bring a chair forward for her. Matt grunted, backed with it, put it down, spun it around and pushed it in close to the table with its checkered cloth and sugar bowl topping it and standing in the very middle of it. "It would be asking too much, I know, to expect any of you to be the man your father was. Even of you, Matt, even though you look so much like him. But because you three are John Rowan's sons, because you have his blood in you, I think I have the right to expect you to be good, decent, honorable men."

The three Rowans, standing around the table, Matt on one side of it, his brothers on the other side, shifted their weight from one leg to the other.

"I kept this from your father because I knew how it would have hurt him," she continued. "I'm told there's a rumor about that there's bad blood, that is, bad feeling, between you three, that now with your father

6

gone, it's liable to explode in violence. I want to know if there's any truth to it."

The twins averted their eyes. But Matt didn't. He met Mary's steady gaze and smiled back at her reassuringly.

"There's no truth to it, Ma," he told her. "It's just a lot of talk, and you ought to know better than to go putting any stock in talk. Folks who haven't anything better to do with themselves and their time like to talk even when they don't know what they're talking about. We're Rowans, Ma, and we're proud of it. So we don't aim to do anything to accommodate some flannel mouth who must be looking to stir up some excitement just because the town's dying on its feet and needs something to bring it back to life."

Mary's eyes shifted away from him, first to sandy-haired, blue-eyed Pete who looked even younger than his twin, then to brown-haired and brown-eyed Bill.

"Well, Bill?" she asked him. "Matt's had his say. Now I'd like to hear from you. Is it as Matt insists just talk that hasn't any truth to it?"

"That's right, Ma," Bill replied. "It's just talk."

"Then how do you suppose such a malicious rumor got started?" Mary pressed him.

He shrugged and said:

"Best way I can answer that, Ma, is this. We've had our differences, Matt, Pete and me. But what family hasn't had 'em one time or another? Point is we've never let them get outta hand and the way I see it, that's all that matters."

"That's what I was gonna say, Ma," Pete said, "when you got around to asking me."

"Satisfied, Ma?" Matt asked her. "You've asked us right out and we've answered you the same way."

"All right," Mary said evenly. "If that's all it is, just talk, we'll say no more about it. I'm taking each of you at your word and I'll hold each of you to it. Just see to it

7

that none of you ever does anything to bring shame to the Rowan name.''

Matt drew out the chair that he had offered her earlier, spun it around and straddled it, crossing his brawny forearms across the top of the backrest and leaned over them.

''About a year ago your father had Judge McCreary draw up some papers dividing the ranch in four equal parts,'' Mary continued. ''The division takes effect today. One quarter of the Square-R, the ground this house stands on, the barn, the corral and so on and enough additional acreage to make up the quarter is mine. The other three quarters go to you boys. You can decide among you which one each of you wants. There shouldn't be any trouble about it since they're all the same size and all worth the same, with the stream touching all four quarters so that all have easy access to water. So from this minute on each of you has his own land and each must shoulder the responsibilities that go with land owning.''

No one said anything for a moment.

''What about the stock?'' Pete wanted to know.

''You beat me to it, Pete,'' Bill said. ''That's what I was just gonna ask. Owning land is fine, Ma. I go along with what Pop used to say, that the best place to put your money is in land. But what good is it 'less you've got something to run on the land?''

Mary smiled and said:

''I'm coming to it. The stock and the horses, in fact everything on the ranch is to be divided the same way as the land. Equally.''

''Uh-huh,'' Bill said, nodding approvingly. ''That's more like it.''

''One last thing,'' Mary said. ''Your father left each of you a sum of money so that you'd have working capital. I think that's everything now.''

8

She shuttled her gaze from one to the other, apparently waiting for some sort of response. When there was none, she said:

"Judge McCreary has the deeds and the other things. He'll turn them over to you whenever you go to him." She thought for a moment, then she said: "Yes, I think that's everything. I don't think I've forgotten anything. But if I have, I'm sure the Judge will tell you."

She moved away from the door. Matt climbed to his feet. Again he spun the chair around, again too he shoved it in close to the table. The twins held their eyes on him, obviously waiting to follow his lead. When he started for the door, they moved after him. As he neared it, a stride or two ahead of them, Mary said:

"I wondered if any of you would be interested enough to ask what I plan to do. Apparently you aren't. However, I'll tell you anyway." They stopped and looked at her. "I've paid off the crew, that is all except Tom Spence, Lee Willis and Sam Potter. They're good, steady hands and they've worked for us a long time, longer than any of the others. The others are free now, so if you boys decide you can use them, any of them . . ."

She stopped and waited for one of them to speak.

Bill rubbed his chin thoughtfully and frowned a bit.

"I don't know, Ma," he said finally, and all eyes held on him. "I don't mean about the men. 'Course we'll want to take on some of them. I know I will and it figures that Matt and Pete'll need some hired hands too. But not till we've got something for them to do. So that can wait. Right now I'm thinking about you. Ma, I don't think that's such a good idea, you living here alone."

"She's just after telling us she won't be alone," Pete said to him. "With Spence, Willis and Potter . . ."

Bill interrupted him with:

"Alone in this house, I mean."

"Oh!" Pete said.

"Suppose," Bill said, half-turning to him. "Suppose she gets sick or something?"

"Yeah," Pete said, and he rubbed his chin thoughtfully as Bill had done moments before. "I didn't think of that."

"Now I'm sorry I said anything," Mary said with an unhappy shake of her head. "You boys will have enough problems of your own to deal with without having me add to them. If I should get sick, I'll send for the doctor. It's as simple as that, just what you boys would do if you were still living here. So please don't give it another thought."

"We won't be that far away that we won't be able to ride over every couple o' days," Pete pointed out, "and kinda see for ourselves how she's making out."

"That's right," Bill conceded, and he looked and sounded genuinely relieved.

"And if we see that she isn't getting along the way she should," Pete continued, "heck, between the three of us we oughta be able to work out something for her. But I don't think we oughta go worrying about things ahead of time. Time enough to do that when they happen. Besides, we won't be pulling outta here right away. Not for a couple o' weeks yet, maybe even longer than that. Gotta get ourselves set up first before we can even begin to think of moving over to our own spreads. Gotta have some kind of a house to live in, a barn, corral, a tool shed and . . ."

"Ma, you think it'd be all right, wouldn't look bad for us being that we just buried Pop, if we were to ride into town today?" Bill asked her.

"You aren't going in to celebrate, are you?"

"Celebrate?" he repeated, and stared at her blankly.

"Then I don't see any reason why you shouldn't go,"

10

she replied.

"Long's we know what's gonna be," Bill said to his brothers, "it might be a good idea for us to sorta begin making arrangements for things. Y'know? I mean start ordering the stuff we figure we'll need."

"Uh-huh," Pete said, nodding, and Mary, listening but offering no comment, shifted her gaze to him. "Takes time to get the stuff you need to build with. Then after you get it, it takes even more time to do the building. Even with somebody to help. I'll ride in with you, Bill."

"What about you, Matt?" Bill asked.

Matt who hadn't taken any part in the discussion nodded and went out and the twins trooped out after him. Mary heard the scuffing scrape of their boots as they marched down the gravel path that led to the barn, heard the fading murmur of their voices too. There was a brief silence, then she heard the thump of their horses' hoofs on the planked ramp as they rode out of the barn, heard the swiftening beat of hoofs as they loped away. The drumbeat died out quickly and a stillness spread itself over the place.

There were the usual chores to do about the house. But Mary could not bring herself to do anything. Fortunately she had made up the beds earlier that morning. She contented herself with that and decided that anything else that needed doing would have to wait till she felt equal to undertaking it. Slowly she crossed the kitchen to the table, drew out a chair and sank down in it, moved in closer to the table, and resting her folded arms on it hunched over them. Tears welled up in her eyes and rolled down her cheeks. She wiped them away with her hands. For a minute or so she sat upright in her chair. Then she sighed deeply, pushed back from the table, got up and slowly went upstairs.

TWO

The silence was even more oppressive on the upper floor that lay half in thin sunlight and half in shadows. It gave Mary an uneasy feeling. Despite the thick hall runner that ranged the full length of the landing from the stairs to the blank wall at the far end and cushioned her step, muffling it completely ordinarily, floorboards that had never squeaked before now groaned dismally underfoot. Her steps echoed and twice she stopped abruptly and looked back over her shoulder as though she felt that someone was following her. In the rear bedroom that was hers alone now, and standing at the curtained window, she peered out at the slope, and raising her gaze, at John Rowan's grave at the top of it. Again tears filled her eyes and overflowed and a great sob shook her. With her head bowed she wept, surrendering to the emotion that she had managed to hold in check save for the brief bit of sobbing at the kitchen table. After a couple of minutes she stopped her crying, turned away from the window and went out of the room.

Retracing her steps to the stairs, she stopped at each open door that she came to, pushed each door open wider, and looked in. The first room was Matt's, the second Bill's, and the one diagonally opposite his, Pete's. In each room a piece of clothing had been left lying about. In Matt's it was a shirt that he had draped around the back of a chair. In Bill's room and then in Pete's too, it was a pair of Levis that each of the twins had slung across his made-up bed. Ordinarily when she was doing her dusting and straightening up in the bedrooms, Mary hung away or put away whatever bits of clothing had been left out. This time though she did not touch anything. Slowly she backed out of Pete's doorway. Mechanically and apparently forgetting that she had started for the stairs, she turned, her expression indicating that she was deep in thought, and headed back to her own room.

Soon the boys would be gone and the few miles that would lay between them and her would grow. They would have their own problems to which they would have to devote their time and attention. Sooner or later they would marry and have families and their problems and responsibilities would increase. There would be more and more demands made upon their time and she would see less and less of them and finally nothing. But she had no quarrel with that. That was the expected, that was life, the way it was patterned, the way it had to be lived. Just as they would have to adjust themselves to the new life upon which they were embarking, she would have to readjust hers. Because they were young, their lives would be full ones, filled with new and excited happenings for every day would be a new adventure for them. She had lived forty-six years of her life while theirs were yet to be lived. She had had a good life with John Rowan. If theirs gave them as much happiness as hers had, she would feel that the Rowans were indeed singularly fortunate people. Undeniably with the boys gone her life would be empty and lonely. But again that was the expected turn that life took, that was what happened when children grew up and left the old home for new ones of their own making.

In her case though it was a little different than it was with other women because she was not the boys' mother. She had acquired her family through marriage with widower John Rowan. Since there were no blood ties between her and the boys, there was no obligation on their part, she told herself. As good as she had been to them in their childhood and then in their formative years, when she had happily seen to their needs and wants, there was a gap between them that couldn't be bridged. She supposed it was that way with all step-mothers who undertook to raise other women's children. When the Rowan boys had grown up and had turned more and more to their father and less and less to her, the gap had come into being and with the years had maintained itself. She had expected it and wisely she did not resent it, or at least, indicate her resentment. She would have been the first to insist that it did not mean that they thought any less of her than they had before. She would have been equally quick to point out that it was a natural transition. Having attained manhood and having suddenly found themselves closely associated with their father in working the Square-R, it was only natural that they should have transferred their attention to him because of their common interest.

She was suddenly aware that she was standing in the open doorway of her room. Something that peeked out at her from beneath the long, full folds of the bedspread caught her eye and made her bite her lip. They were John's old slippers.

The spacious closet that was backed against the side wall between the bed and the window held John's clothes as well as hers. She rounded the bed to the closet and opened it. The first thing she saw was an old jacket of his. She touched it gently, moved her hand inside of it. There was warmth in it, body warmth. Perhaps she should get rid of his things without delay. If she didn't, every time she went to the closet to get something of hers, his would be there too, and the sight of it, the feel of it, would bring back memories and make her even more miserable. She thought about it for a moment. But with a shake of her head, she closed the closet door and turned away. The old rocker with its pillowed and doilied headrest in which John had rocked away the last few weeks of his ebbing life still stood near the window, and she sank down in it. There was a familiar warmth to it, the body warmth that John had left in it. Lightly she ran her hands over the smooth, curved armrests. She could feel the same warmth on them too. She put her head back against the pillow. There was warmth in that also, in the very middle of it, where John's head had hollowed it out.

She was tired even though she hadn't done anything to tire her. Her eyes were heavy, so she closed them. After a bit, she told herself, she would get up and busy herself. It wouldn't do for her to indulge herself in self-pity. If she kept herself busy, she wouldn't have time to do that.

Her thoughts went back over the years, to the first time she had met the boys. That was twenty years ago, she told herself. Matt was five then, the twins three. She smiled a little to herself when she thought of them, picturing them as John had presented them to her in the Rowan kitchen the day she accepted him and his suggestion that she ride out to the ranch with him so that she might meet the family she was about to acquire. She could see them so clearly it was incredible, as though her first meeting with the Rowan boys had taken place that very morning instead of twenty years before. She could see every detail, their earnest young faces so vigorously scrubbed that they looked polished and shone, their hair in need of cutting but still wet and slicked back, their shirts so scrupulously clean and obviously new and unworn till then and a little too large for them. They stood together with Matt in the middle, with Pete clinging to his big brother's left hand Bill to his right. Despite John's repeated assurance that they would be cordial in their welcome, they looked up at her apprehensively and little Pete bit his lip to keep from crying.

She had accepted John's assurance without comment. She had expected the boys to look upon her as an intruder and they had. So she was neither surprised nor hurt. But she soon discovered that little boys were most reasonable and susceptible when they were hungry, and withe the first meal that she prepared for them, topping it off with a chocolate layer cake that made their eyes pop, she was able to break down some of their resistance to her. And as time passed and they came to know each other better, it was as though they had never had another mother. Amusing little incidents that marked their growing up came back to her and each brought a tiny flicker of a smile to her face. But then the smile faded out and so did the vision of her three young charges. She sighed a deep, wearied sigh. She squirmed a little and burrowed deeper in the comfortable depths of the old rocker. After a big of half-hearted struggling to stay awake, she forgot her resolve and surrendered and dozed off.

Word of John Rowan's death was a little late in reaching the Reverend Jeremy Goslin. However, when Goslin did learn that the town's most prominent citizen, by virtue of the generally accepted and never refuted belief that he was far and away its richest, had died, he borrowed a buckboard and a horse from the local stableman and set out for the Rowan place. Goslin refused to be stayed by the fact that neither the dead man nor any members of his family had ever attended his church since he had been installed at its head. Similarly he declined to be influenced by the fact that Rowan and he had never exchanged anything more than curt nods whenever they had met in town. The breach between them had originated some fifteen years before, when

Goslin had just taken over the church.

Finding the structure in a shabby and rundown condition, its treasury practically depleted, and being pretty much in the same straightened circumstances himself, he had lost no time in attempting to remedy the situation. When he was told that Rowan was the wealthiest man in the community, the reverend called upon him and without anything more than the bearest of formalities bluntly demanded of him a liberal donation in order to put both the church and himself on their feet.

It was the wrong approach, particularly for a stranger, to take with a rugged individual like John Rowan who had fought his way up from lonely, friendless and practically penniless pioneer to ownership of the biggest cattle domain in the township and county. A man who had successfully withstood the repeated assaults of nature and conspiring elements, rampaging Indians bent upon burning him out in their futile efforts to stem the westward surge of the white intruders, and rustlers who had sought to overrun his lands and make off with his budding herd of cattle was not likely to yield to a demand simply because it was thundered at him. Goslin made matters even worse for himself when sensing failure with the resolute cattleman he resorted to bullying and then threatening tactics. He wound up the victim of his own stupidity, bad temper and Rowan's aroused wrath on the shiny seat of his threadbare pants on the slightly warped floor of the Rowan front porch.

But now that Rowan was dead, the preacher was determined to see to it that the cattleman's heirs atoned for the sinful old man's failure to provide for him and the church. But he hadn't reckoned with Mary Rowan. Goslin who had always trampled and overawed everyone who had had the temerity to stand up to him knew about Mary. But he scoffed at the thought that she might resist and even withstand him. He had

17

disposed of most men with ease. He considered women beneath them, necessary to them, but of little importance beyond that. Mary, a pleasant-faced and quiet spoken, well set up woman of about average height and size, had just come downstairs from her room when she heard someone drive up. Stepping out on the porch she met Goslin coming up the steps, greeted him politely and invited him to sit.

Goslin made no pretense about his mission. That he hadn't come to offer his condolences was immediately clear.

"I have come to offer a church service for the deceased," he began stiffly, squaring back in his chair with his flat black hat in his bony-thighed lap, "and a grave for him in the churchyard cemetery."

"I'm afraid we shan't be able to take advantage of your kind offer, Reverend," Mary answered. "You see, we buried my husband this morning."

Goslin stared at her.

"Buried him already?"

"Yes."

"Without notifying me?" he demanded.

"It was my husband's wish that his funeral be private," Mary related evenly, "that attendance be confined to his immediate family, and that I should read a simple service for him. And last, that he be buried in familiar surroundings. So we laid him to rest in the very middle of the land he had loved so much and to which he had given so much of himself. I'm afraid, Reverend, he wouldn't have been able to sleep comfortably in a churchyard grave, in the company of strangers."

She might well have added that the tiny cemetery behind the church was known to be overrun with weeds and that grave markers had long been destroyed, knocked down or blown over and never replaced or restored. But she saw no point in mentioning it.

Jeremy Goslin was a gaunt, hollow-cheeked man who had done little or nothing to endear himself to his congregation. Because he was an impatient, intolerant, arrogant and bad tempered individual, wrongly cast in the role of preacher and spiritual leader, he had succeeded in alienating more worshippers than he had attracted to his church. Leaping to his feet, forgetting about his hat and dropping it, and startling her so that she jerked backward and stared wide-eyed at him, he denounced her for having abandoned her God and her church and for having failed in her responsibilities to her husband, her family and herself. Practically standing over her and thereby imprisoning her in her chair, and shaking his crooked, broken-nailed forefinger in her face, he blamed her for the Rowans' failure to attend church. It was her fault, he insisted, just as it was the fault of every wife and mother who permitted her family to forget its religious obligations. Men were apt to be lax about such things. Hence it became the duty of the wife and mother to see to it that church ties were maintained.

"Now, annd till further notice, I order you to appear in church every morning at nine so that I may pray with you and seek forgiveness for you," he thundered at her.

Pushing him off forcibly, Mary got to her feet.

"It was good of you to take so much time away from your other and certainly more important duties to call upon me, Reverend Goslin," Mary told him. "Now if you will excuse me, I have . . ."

But Goslin refused to be disposed of so easily, particularly in view of the fact that he had not yet completed his mission.

"By catering to the wishes of the deceased, you have made yourself a party to his childish modesty and immaturity," he boomed at her. "You owed it to him to disregard his wishes and give him his due, a public

19

funeral that everyone could attend. Instead you have deprived the townspeople of their rightful privilege, of an opportunity of paying him their last respects. Incidentally, did the deceased leave a will?''

"He did.''

The preacher's eyes brightened hopefully.

"Does it . . . does it contain a bequest for me?'' he asked eagerly.

When Mary's eyes burned, he made a begrudging correction, substituting church for himself.

"As far as I can recall,'' Mary replied, "there was no mention in it either of you or the church.''

Goslin stiffened again.

"Then I shall expect you to make amends for the . . . sinful omission,'' he said curtly.

"I'm sorry to disappoint you, Reverend,'' Mary said calmly. "But I don't intend to do anything about it. My husband never forgot anything. If he had intended to include the church or you in his bequests, he would have done so. The fact that he didn't speaks for itself.''

Goslin was so enraged, he snatched up his hat and clapped it on his head, stamped down the porch steps to the borrowed buckboard, hoisted himself up into it and lashing the startled and unoffending horse with the loose ends of the reins, and drove off.

THREE

It was some six weeks later. The boys had moved out of the old house almost three weeks before. Now it was shrouded in silence. Save for Mary's once-a-week entering to dust and cast an unhappy glance around, the doors to their vacated rooms were kept closed. When she came downstairs in the morning she seldom went up again till it was time for bed.

The first week the boys rode over to see her every day; Matt usually came in the morning to breakfast with her, the twins singly or together later on in the day. Quite sheepishly one morning Matt confessed that despite her instructions and a couple of demonstrations in the art of coffee-making, his coffee still couldn't come up to hers.

"And that isn't all, Ma," he continued, idling at the table over his third cup. "Had a hankering the other day for some hot cakes and bacon. So I fixed myself some. The cakes looked real good and I felt doggone proud of myself and wished you were there so you could see them for yourself. But when I picked one up and started nibbling on it, I got the shock of my life, Ma. On the level now, the blamed thing was as heavy as lead. If I'da dropped it on the floor, I'll bet it would've gone clear through to the cellar."

She laughed and said:

"Oh, Matt . . . really now!"

"That's the truth, Ma," he insisted. "So I pushed the cakes and the batter I hadn't used yet off to a side and fixed me some bacon. I tasted just one piece and that was enough for me. Madder'n a wet hen, I upped and heaved the whole business, cakes, batter, bacon, everything, right smack into the swill can. Ma, there's no use denying it. I'm a pretty lousy cook."

21

"What about your men, Matt? Who does the cooking for them?" Mary wanted to know.

"Eddie Wales. But he does his cooking down in the bunkhouse. I hung around there last night gabbin' with the boys till there wasn't any way outta it for Eddie 'cept to invite me to eat with them. I was so blamed hungry, I ate more than Eddie and the others all put together. I must have, Ma, because a couple of times I caught Eddie looking at me kinda funny." He grinned broadly. "But I didn't let that interfere with the business at hand. I went right on eating like . . . like, well, like it was going outta style and I wanted to get my belly full in case I didn't like whatever was gonna take its place showed up."

She offered no comment.

"This morning when I was coming down to the corral, Eddie came up to me," Matt continued. "Seems like somebody's told him that a Chinaman, a pot-bellied little character with a round, shiny face, had hit town and was looking for a job only he hadn't had any luck landing one. Now every Chinaman I've ever seen or heard tell of 'round these parts was a cook. So I had Eddie saddle up and head for town. I told him to find the Chinaman, and if he can cook, to hustle him out to my place."

"That's one way of solving your problem."

"If this Chinaman turns out right, I'll have him do the cooking for all of us, the boys too. That'll free Eddie for other work, and believe me, Ma, there's a-plenty of it."

"There's still another way of solving your problem, Matt. An even better way too."

Matt eyed her obliquely, and grinned again, wryly though.

"I know," he retorted. "And I've been wondering when you were gonna bring it up."

"It isn't meant for a man to live alone."

"Ma, the last thing I need right now is a wife. So if you don't mind . . ."

"A wife should be the first thing a man should acquire. Not the last. If every man waited till he was ready to take a wife, how many do you think would ever get around to actually doing it?"

He shot a look at the old clock on the wall.

"Hey, it's later than I thought," he said. "Got things to do, so I'd better get going." He gulped down the rest of his coffee, pushed back from the table and stood up. He wiped his mouth with the back of his big hand. "See you tomorrow, Ma."

He bent over suddenly and kissed her cheek, straightened up, turned and strode doorward; he lifted his hat off a wall peg near the door and clapped it on his head. He stood motionlessly at the door for a moment, back turned to her, apparently debating something with himself. Then just as she was about to ask, "What is it, Matt?" he looked around at her. "Ma, how is it for you living here alone?"

Relieved, she smiled and answered: "Oh, all right."

"Gets kinds lonesome though at times, doesn't it?" he pressed her.

"Yes, sometimes," she admitted. "But then I busy myself and that usually makes things easier. Matt, I wish you'd give some thought to that other matter."

"Yeah, sure. Ma, how would you like to come and live with me?" he asked eagerly, squaring around to her and thumbing his hat up from his forehead and letting it ride on the back of his head. "I've got me a real nice place and when I get finished fixing it up, I know you'll like it. Now don't get me wrong. I'm not asking you because for my dough you're the best cook anywhere. I still aim to take on that Chinaman if he can do the job. It's, well, it's just that I'd like having you close by. Then

23

I'd always know how you are because I'd be able to see for myself. This way I'm always worrying and wondering, and I don't feel easy about you till I get over here. What do you say, Ma?"

She was deeply touched and his concern for her made her eyes shine.

"It's kind of you to ask me, Matt, and I appreciate it. But this is my home. Thank you though for asking me."

"Will you think about it?"

"I don't have to, Matt," she said gently. "As I said, this is home to me. This is where my roots are, my memories, everything that I hold dear. This is where I spent the happiest years of my life. So this is where I want to stay."

He looked disappointed.

"But you can always change your mind, can't you?"

"Yes, I suppose so. And if I should . . ."

He seized upon her answer as an encouraging one, brightened and said:

"All you'll have to do, Ma, is have Spence drive you over. You won't even have to bother packing your stuff. I'll come and get it for you."

It was a long time since any of the boys had kissed her. The fact that it was Matt who had kissed her, Matt who had always been the least demonstrative of the three, pleased her greatly. Then his unexpected invitation to her to make her home with him added to her happiness. Tenderly she touched her cheek with her fingertips. It was with an unusually light heart that she finally arose and set about clearing away and washing the breakfast dishes.

Bill came late that afternoon. She looked surprised, a little disappointed too, when she saw that he was alone. He slung his hat up on one of the wall pegs and came sauntering up to the table. The grim look on his face, his tightened lips and the tiny twitch of his jaw muscles told

24

her that something was wrong. But she gave no sign that she was aware that he looked troubled. She knew that when he felt the urge to unburden himself she wouldn't have to pry it out of him. He would tell her of his own accord.

"Can I fix you something, Bill?" she asked as he drew out a chair and sank down in it.

He shook his head.

"Got something to tell you, Ma," he said. She made no response, simply seated herself in the same chair that she had occupied at breakfast that morning with Matt, sat back and waited for Bill to go on. "Ma, I'm gonna get married."

Her eyes widened, a reflection of her delight.

"Oh, how wonderful, Bill!" she said. The Fred Snows were their nearest neighbors and friends of long standing, and Ann, their pretty daughter, had long been the on-and-off object of the twins' interest and attention. Since she had no reason to think otherwise, she took it for granted that the bride-to-be was Ann. But she asked the question anyway. "Ann Snow, Bill?"

"Uh-huh," he said.

"She's a fine girl, Bill, and she'll make you a good wife," Mary told him. She stopped purposely, to give him an opportunity to add something. When he didn't, she went on with: "I think it's a wonderful thing for you. Not that it's any less wonderful for Ann too, mind you. You're both doing well for yourselves. Now I wish that Matt and Pete would follow in your steps. Be good for them. As I told Matt when he was here this morning, it isn't meant for man to live alone. By the way, Bill, have you seen Pete? He hasn't been here this week. I had hoped he might come with you. Now I'm concerned. I hope he's all right."

"I wouldn't know, Ma. I haven't seen him this week either. And I haven't seen Matt, so I haven't told him

25

about Ann and me. Telling Pete about us is what's bothering me, Ma. How he'll take it, I mean."

"You mean he's been seeing her again too?"

"Uh-huh. Began again right after we went off on our own."

"Oh?"

Bill moved in closer to the table, and hunched over it on his folded arms.

"I ran into Pete at the Snow place a couple of times," he related, "and I could tell he didn't like the idea of me being there. Before that we were seeing each other almost every day, Pete and me. I'd ride over to his place to see how he was doing or he'd come over to mine. Then it stopped. Now we don't see each other at all."

"Hm," Mary said and her expression mirrored her troubled thoughts.

"I admit he started calling on Ann first, and he probably felt that I was horning in on him," Bill continued. "But I liked Ann same's he did, and when I asked her if there was some kind of understanding between her and Pete, and she said there wasn't anything, that they were just good friends. I took that to mean the field was wide open to all comers, and I made my play for her. If she had picked him over me, Ma, I think I would've understood and I'd have taken it the only way . . ."

"And since she's accepted you over him, then he'll have to take it that way too. I'm sure he will, Bill. Once he's gotten over his disappointment. Has Ann set the date?"

"It's this coming Sunday, Ma."

"Goodness, that is soon, isn't it?"

The husky youth blushed a little, becomingly though, Mary thought.

"Long as Ann said she was willing, I couldn't see any point in waiting," he explained. "So we made it for this

26

Sunday morning. I'll come by for you about nine, Ma. Maybe a quarter of. Think you can be ready by then?"

"I'll be ready, Bill."

"Swell. Oh, one thing, Ma. We'll need the buckboard. So if you think of it the next time you're talking to Spence or one of the others, you might tell him to have it ready for us ahead o' time Sunday morning. I wanna be in church before Ann and her folks get there instead of them having to wait for us to show up."

"Of course."

As usual Matt came for breakfast the next morning. Mary had just finished setting the table when he entered the house. She greeted him with a smile and said:

"I wondered if you'd be here this morning."

"I'm still the world's lousiest cook, remember? Oh, you thought I'd be having breakfast as home, huh?"

"Has that Chinaman come to work for you?"

He shook his head.

"Nope," he said glumly. "Somebody else beat me to him."

"That's too bad, Matt. But there's always a chance that another one may come along."

He shrugged and asked: "Know anything I don't know?"

As he took his usual place at the table she repeated what Bill had told her.

"Uh-huh," Matt said, nodding. "So the son of a gun's getting himself hitched! If you pulled that, 'it isn't meant for man to live alone' stuff on him, Ma, he must've taken you right up on it. Now 'less I'm reading the signs all wrong, you want me to go see Pete and get things straightened out with him. Right?"

She smiled and nodded wordlessly.

He frowned a bit and rubbed his chin with the back of his hand.

"I dunno, Ma," he said after a brief, thoughtful

27

silence. "I'm kinda put out with Pete."

"Oh?" she said and she looked surprised. "Why?"

"Well, last time I rode over to his place, one day last week it was, Thursday or maybe it was Friday, not that it matters one way or another which day it was, he wasn't what I'd call delighted to see me. Fact is, he was anything but."

"I don't understand. You hadn't quarreled with him, had you?"

"Nope. Haven't been seeing enough of him for that. Anyway, he acted like I was a poor relation come to borrow some money from him."

"Perhaps he's finding that being completely on his own carries a far heavier load of responsibility than he bargained for?"

Matt offered no comment.

"I'd still like you to go and see him for me, Matt."

"All right, Ma. I'll ride over. Might be able to make it this afternoon. If not, then it'll be some time tomorrow."

"Thank you. Oh, would you like some coffee cake to take home with you? I made some extra."

Matt grinned at her.

"And how, I'd like it."

"Just one thing more before we have breakfast, Matt. If you get a chance after you've been to see Pete and you can spare the time . . ."

"I'll come by and let you know how I made out with him."

But for the first time in the many weeks since he had moved out, Matt did not appear at the old house for breakfast the next morning. Mary was a bit disappointed, but she was not overly concerned. Something of detaining or delaying importance must have arisen, she told herself, or he would have ridden over as usual. Hopefully she waited for him throughout the long morning and the even longer afternoon. Still confident

28

that he would be along as soon as he could get away from his own place, at any rate some time before the day ended, she was able to bridle her impatience. She was not quite so assured that everything was all right when evening came and then night and still there was no sign of him. When she finally tramped upstairs, two long, wearying hours past her usual bedtime, her face wore an unmistakable look of disappointment.

She was downstairs again shortly after dawn the next day, her drawn face reflecting the fact that she hadn't slept very restfully. When breakfast time came and went, her concern proved overpowering and she yielded to it. Whipping a shawl around her shoulders, she emerged from the back door, rounded the house and took the path down to the barn, topped the ramp to the rolled-back door and poked her head inside. There was no sign in there of any of the men. She withdrew her head and gathering her shawl a little closer around her because there was something of an uncomfortable chill in the brisk morning air; she hurried down to the bunk-house. The door to the long, squat structure stood open. Pushing it open a little wider, she called for Spence. When there was no response, no sound of anyone, she retraced her steps to the barn. Halting a second time atop the ramp, she debated with herself the advisability of substituting a coat for her shawl. After a bit, with something of an unconscious heave of her shoulders, a sign that she had decided not to take the time to make the change, she disappeared inside. From the shadowy depths of the towering old building came the echoing plod of ironshod hoofs on the wooden floor as the buckboard horses, yielding to Mary's persuasiveness, permitted her to back them out of their warm, comfortable stalls and hitch them up to the rig. Then some minutes later she drove out of the barn, down the sloping length of the ramp and wheeled away toward Pete Rowan's place.

29

FOUR

The long, ribbony span of road that led to town some eight miles away was deserted. It ran ruler-straight, tree-shaded in some spots and completely open in others, and then seemed to lose itself in the distance. Open fields flanked it on one side, the left; on the right was Rowan property with miles and miles of unbroken fence marking its southernmost boundary. Mechanically Mary's gaze ranged along the fence. She spied something, an animal of some sort, grazing inside the fence a couple of hundred feet ahead of her. As she neared it the form assembled into a horse. He looked up. When she came abreast of him, he poked his head through the bars and whinnied. In another moment though the buckboard had rumbled past him and had left him behind. Mary shot a wondering look behind her when she heard him trumpeting. He came galloping up along the fence, overtook the buckboard and ran along with it. Once or twice he forged ahead of it. Each time though, when he stole a backward and probably triumphant look and noted that he was outdistancing the buckboard, he slowed his pace and permitted it to overtake him and pull alongside. He kept abreast of it for some time, snorting and prancing and obviously trying to attract admiring attention to himself. But Mary was occupied with her thoughts, the horses concerned only with their task. Hence they disregarded him completely. Disappointed, and panting and heaving, unmistakable signs that his fast running and his antics had taken their toll of him, he fell behind the steadily moving buckboard. With a sudden spurt he sought to overtake it again. But his spurt was shortlived. He was unable to maintain it for more than a minute or so. Again he fell behind and this time he abandoned his efforts and pulled up. He stood quiveringly and followed the rapidly drawing away buckboad with his eyes. Then slowly he wheeled around and began to plod back to the spot he had left.

A couple of times along the way when Mary happened to raise her gaze beyond the fence, she glimpsed small bunches of grazing cattle. But she looked away again almost at once. Her grim expression mirrored the fact that she was thinking troubled thoughts and that now she was pretty certain that Pete had become involved in some kind of trouble. That, she told herself with an unconscious nod, explained Matt's failure to appear at the old house for breakfast on two successive mornings. To spare her, she added to herself.

Pete, she had been told, had cut away a ten-foot section of the road-fronting fence, had hinged one end and latched the other and had turned it into a gate that led to his place. She slowed the team to a trot and fixed her eyes on the fence so that there would be no chance of her overlooking and passing the improvised gateway.

So deeply absorbed by her thoughts, she hadn't noticed the approach of a rig drawn by a single horse. It was only when the creaky grind of the oncoming rig's wheels, body and shafts broke in upon her that she looked up. A man, she quickly noticed, was driving the rig. As the two vehicles came closer and continued to narrow the distance between them, she recognized the man. It was the Reverend Jeremy Goslin. They came together shortly, and when Goslin drew rein and held up his other hand, Mary halted her team. The reverend gave Mary a nod, whipped the reins around the rig's handbrake and climbed down and turning crossed the intervening space between them.

"I was on my way to call upon you," he told her.

Her eyebrows arched the barest bit. Obviously, she thought to herself, he was not one to permit a rebuff to discourage him. She prepared herself as best she could for a renewal of his demands for money.

"I have been devoting a great deal of thought to you," he went on. "Widowhood and the loss of a companion of many years must be most trying on a woman." She looked hard at him, wondering what he was leading up to. "Harder on a woman, I believe, than on a man. A man has his work and his friends to console him and help lessen his grief when he loses a loved one. Once he is over the initial shock, he is able to find new companionship far more easily than a woman for she must be discreet and keep herself aloof in her constant effort to protect her good name. Man may seek for a new mate wherever his fancy may lead him while woman must wait for man to seek her out." Mary could hardly believe her ears. This . . . this man was laying the groundwork for a proposal of marriage. "I think you need someone to . . . to look out for you and protect you and of course guide you in the handling of your interests. So I have decided to offer you my hand and myself in marriage."

"Thank you, Reverend Goslin," Mary replied. "Thank you for taking such an interest in me and my welfare and for your very flattering offer. However, I am well looked after and well protected by my three stalwart sons. As for what you call my interests, they too are well looked after by a most capable and completely trustworthy friend of long standing, Judge McCreary. And finally, my late husband was a man who towered above all other men and I doubt very much that I shall ever meet another one like him. I would never consider any man who did not in my opinion measure up to John Rowan. So I am quite certain that I shall never remarry. Now if you will excuse me, please, I must be on my way.''

Before Jeremy Goslin, rebuffed by her a second time, could collect himself and his shattered ego, and do something to stay her, Mary had driven on.

Topping the slight incline that led inland from the road, Mary slowed her team to a walk. A hundred feet or so beyond her the newly built cottage that was now Pete's home loomed up. The fresh paint on it gleamed and reflected the sunlight. Closer at hand was the framework of what would become a barn. She glanced at it in passing, mechanically though and focused her gaze on the cottage for it held far more interest for her. Suddenly she was aware of a saddled horse idling a little off to a side of the cottage. The animal lifted its head when it heard the thump of the approaching team's hoofs. The waiting horse whinnied and a tall, lean man came striding around the cottage from the rear. There was something of a swagger in his walk that made him look bandy-legged, the mark of a man who had spent much of is life in the saddle. Mary recognized him at once and leveled a wondering look at him. It was Sheriff Dan Quimby, a graying old-timer who had come into the area at about the same time that John Rowan had. He looked a little surprised when he saw Mary; she looked even more surprised to see him there, and a little troubled too. The buckboard rumbled up to the cottage and braked to a stop in front of it.

"Hello, Mary," Quimby said, touching his hat to her as he came up to the buckboard and halted at its side. "How are you?"

"Oh, all right, thank you, Dan," she answered, curling the lines around the handbrake. "What brings you out this way?"

33

"Just stopped by to see Pete."

"Oh?"

"Nothing special. Just passing by, so I stopped. Know where he might be?"

"He should be somewhere around here."

"He isn't though," Quimby said, thumbing his hat up from his forehead. His hatband was tight for it left a deep red line across his forehead from one temple to the other. He rubbed it with the back of his hand and smeared the line, crimsoning his forehead. "Rode all over the place looking for him. But I couldn't find him. Got himself a pretty good-sized spread here. Don't tell me he's trying to work it all by himself."

"Oh, no," Mary said quickly. "At least, I don't think so. I understood he had taken on two hands. Two of the men who used to work for us."

"Didn't see any sign o' them either. I had a look inside," the sheriff added, and he indicated the cottage behind him with a nod. "Door wasn't locked. So I went in and had a look around." Unconsciously he fingered the silver star that he wore pinned to the sagging pocket of his flannel shirt. It was tarnished around the edges. The legend SHERIFF across its face was practically obliterated. Only the last two letters, FF, were still readable. "How come Pete's house isn't even half finished, inside that is, while Matt's and Bill's are, right down to curtains on the windows?"

"I guess with some men, and I'm afraid Pete's one of them, a bed to sleep in, a table to eat at and a chair to sit in or hold his clothes, they make a home. Others want more. Others like Matt and Bill. But give Pete time and I'm sure he'll catch up with his brothers. He's probably devoting all his time and attention to what he considers are more important things. Is there anything you'd like me to tell Pete for you, Dan?"

Sheriff Quimby didn't answer. He rubbed his nose

with the back of his hand. Instantly Mary sensed that Quimby hadn't just chanced to be passing and that his call upon Pete was not a social call.

"You didn't just sto by to visit with Pete," she said quietly. "You came here looking for him." Then before Quimby could answer, she said severely: "Don't hold back on me, Dan Quimby. You'd better tell me what you want to see Pete about."

The lawman flushed a little under the eyes.

"It's a kinda personal matter you might say, Mary," he replied a bit lamely. "Something between Pete and me."

"I think you can do better than that. A lot better too."

Their eyes met and held for a long moment. Finally Quimby shrugged and said:

"All right, Mary. Pete's drinking. Drinking his head off too."

"Go on," she commanded with an authoritative gesture. "You didn't come all the way out here just to lecture him on the evils of drink. It's something more than that."

"Doggone it, Mary," Quimby blustered. "Don't the fact that the boy's father and I were old friends and the fact that I've known the boy ever since he was, well, nothing more'n a sprout give me the right to give him a talkin' to when I think he needs it?"

"Go on, Dan," she said again. "I'm listening."

He frowned. But then with what was obviously a helpless heave of his shoulders, he said:

"When a man gets to drinking the way Pete's been drinking and he runs off at the mouth, what he says is what's on his mind. Other times he might keep it to himself. But when he hits the bottle, it comes outta him. Spills right out too. I didn't want to worry you. That's why I kept hedging, trying to get around having to tell you. Mary, according to what I've been told, Pete's going after Bill.''

She caught her breath.

"When I heard about it, I went looking for him. But I musta missed him somewhere. Then thinking that he mighta come out here, I headed out here too. Now you know.''

"Has it . . . has it anything to do with Ann Snow?''

"Everything. The way I got it, Pete claims Bill stole his girl from him. So he's sworn he's gonna kill Bill, brother or no. That's why I'm looking for Pete. To see if I can talk some sense into him before he goes and does something he'll be sorry for afterward. When it's too late.''

Nearing Bill's new home and getting her first glimpse of it, Mary judged it to be larger than Pete's. The rumble of the buckboard's wheels and the beat of the horses' hoofs carried in the brisk air and the door to Bill's house opened a bit and a head that she recognized as Bill's was poked out for a quick look. The buckboard rolled past a sturdy but as yet unpainted barn with a small corral opposite it. In the corral, its bars gleaming with newness, half a dozen horses were idling about. All came trotting to the gate as the buckboard approached and swerved away and went on toward the house. The door opened wider and Bill emerged and stood waiting for Mary. The buckboard wheeled up to him, braked and ground to a halt. Bill, hitching up his Levis, sauntered over to it.

"Hello, Ma," he said.

"Hello, Bill," Mary responded.

"If it's about Pete, he hasn't been here."

"Oh, then you know he's looking for you!"

"Yeah, sure. Dan Quimby stopped by here earlier

and told me to be on the lookout for Pete. But I don't think he'll come after me here, Ma. I think he'll lay for me in town."

"You think that's where he is now?"

"If he isn't at his own place."

"He wasn't there twenty minutes ago."

"Then he must be in town."

"The sheriff didn't seem to think so. He said he had looked for him but hadn't been able to find him. That's what brought him out here."

Bill offered no comment.

"What are you going to do?" Mary asked him.

The husky youth's shoulders lifted.

"I'm not sure yet, Ma," he replied. "If he wasn't my brother, I wouldn't be here now. I'd be on my way to town as fast as I could get there; and when I cought up with him I'd shove his threats and his teeth too, right down his throat. But because he is my brother I'm staying out of his way, hoping he'll sober up and get over this. But brother or no, Ma, I know I won't be able to stay put here too long. When I get to the point where I have to do something or . . . or bust, I'm afraid there won't be any way out've it for me 'cept to go and do it."

"Hm," Mary said, and she looked even more troubled than she had before.

"Ordinarily, Ma," Bill continued and her anxious eyes held on his earnest young face. "Ordinarily this would be one of those things I'd have to face up to right off and get it over with. Or I'd have to run and hide. That's something I won't do for anybody. Run and hide, I mean. I wouldn't be able to live with myself if I did that. I wouldn't have any respect for myself and nobody else would have any for me either. So now . . ."

"Bill, will you do something for me, please?" Mary asked, interrupting him.

"'Course, Ma," and he eyed her questioningly.

"Will you go back to the old house and wait there for me till I get back from town?"

"What's the idea? Oh, you think that if Pete does decide to come after me that that'll be the last place he'll think of looking for me. Right?"

"Yes," Mary said simply.

"Meanwhile you'll head for town and try to talk some sense into him."

"I think I can do a lot more with him than anyone else can."

Bill shook his head.

"That's out, Ma," he said with finality. "I'm staying put here for now, and I don't want you to do anything 'cept go on back home. This is my business and I want to handle it myself and in my own way."

"Bill, please!"

"Sorry, Ma, but I've got to do things the way I think I oughta. I'm a man, full grown, and I've got to stand on my own two feet and that's exactly what I aim to do."

"If you won't think of yourself, then think of Ann!" Mary pleaded with him. "If anything should happen to you now with your wedding only a couple of days off, think what it would do to Ann."

"I am thinking of that, Ma, and of Ann too," he maintained.

"You can't be, Bill, if you're so willing to take a chance with your life when you don't have to!"

"All of a sudden, Ma," he said quietly, "I've come to that point I was talking about before, where I can't stay put here any longer and where I have to do something. I'm going to town tonight."

She drew back from him, squared around in the driver's seat, released the brake and drove away.

FIVE

It was late evening when Mary Rowen wheeled the buckboard into Ryerton. Slowing the prancing team to a trot, she drove down the long main street in which its businesses were centered. There was little activity and only a handful of people were about for it was suppertime. Most of the passersby were women, housewives. They were hurrying homeward, a couple of them clutching paper sacks, others with a marketing basket swinging from a toil-worn hand or wrist. It was a sign that they had discovered that they had neglected earlier to buy certain grocery items essential to their evening meal, necessitating a last minute scurrying out to the stores before they closed. They glanced mechanically at the oncoming buckboard and continued on their way. A drunken man weaving an erratic course up the street halted and bracing himself on stiff, spread legs peered headbent at the buckboard. After a moment he went on again, wobby-legged, careening crookedly across the planked walk, stumbling over his own feet, turned into a shadowy alley and disappeared in its depths. Most of the stores had already closed. The few that were still open to accommodate some late shoppers had already drawn their window blinds, and to discourage others from coming in had dimmed their lamps too. Soon the last customer would leave, the lights would go out, the doors would be locked, and the street would be hushed and as dark as the rapidly descending night itself. Only one place showed bright light and stood out boldly between the darkened stores that flanked it. It was Mike Campbell's saloon.

Located about midway down the street, its yellowish lights burned defiantly against the evening, streamed out over the planked walk in front of it and reached the low wooden curb. But it left the narrow, wheel-rutted, dirt and clay gutter in thin shadows.

Mary guided the team over toward the curb and drove along it. Here and there the iron rims on the wheels on the right side of the buckboard scraped against the curb. When she came abreast of the saloon, she stopped. She pulled back hard on the handbrake and wound the reins around it, got up on her feet, turned herself around and climbed down. Turning again on the walk she lifted her eyes to the saloon windows. They were dirt smudged and furrowed where rain a couple of days before had slanted down the panes. She frowned critically, drew her warm, hooded cloak a little closer around her, and squaring her shoulders, crossed the walk to the open doorway of the saloon.

A cloud of tobacco smoke that hung low over the place drifted streetward lazily and the stronger smell of malt, hops and beer reached out and enveloped her and she made a wry face. She blinked once or twice before she was able to peer through the haze of smoke and glary light. The hum of voices from the men at the bar, some ten or twelve of them, beat against her ears. Suddenly though it stopped. Every head turned in her direction, and wondering, surprised eyes stared at her. She stared back stonily. The bartender, a balding, sweaty-browed man, turned his gaze doorward too. He stared hard, even more wide-eyed than his customers, when he saw Mary standing in the doorway. Recognizing her at once and apparently sensing trouble, he flushed and hurriedly emerged from behind the bar, wiping his red hands on his long apron that flapped around his ankles.

"Evening, Ma'am," he said. "Something I can do for you?"

Mary leveled a hard look at him.

"My son, Pete," she said coldly. "Where is he?"

"Well, now, Ma'am," he began, and his flush deepened into a guilty crimson that even made his ears redden. He gulped and swallowed hard, painfully too, judging by the way he grimaced. "What . . . what makes you think he's here?"

"This is the only saloon in town," Mary retorted, and her sharp tone made the bartender wince. "Since he's been drinking, it stands to reason that this must be . . ."

She stopped abruptly. A big, burly, beefy man with a week's growth of beard on his heavy face stepped back from the bar, wiped his mouth with his shirt sleeve, and turning himself, lurched doorward. Mary's lips tightened and her eyes burned as she watched him come toward her. He came abreast of her, stopped and rocked a little unsteadily on his thick legs, and suddenly belched, almost in her face.

"Swine," she said furiously.

He belched again and laughed. Some of the other men at the bar laughed too. Mary's hand flashed upward and came swishing down again in a stinging, explosive slap in the man's face. He staggered backward, stumbling over his own feet. But he managed somehow to stop his careening, steadied himself with an effort, and squaring his thick shoulders, lumbered forward again. Someone came in behind Mary, stepped between her and the drunken man, pushed him off, and turning after him, watched him stumble out to the street. Mary stole a quick look at the man at her side. It was the sheriff.

"What are you doing here, Mary?" he asked her. "This is no place for you."

"I came to get Pete."

"Y'mean he's here?" Quimby didn't wait for an answer from her. He jerked around and looked hard at

41

the bartender. The latter was sweating profusely now. "What's the idea, Ed?" the sheriff demanded of him. "Why didn't you tell me he was here instead of letting me think he wasn't and then lettin' me go chasing myself all over the county looking for him?"

"He wasn't here then, Sheriff," the bartender protested. "Honest he wasn't. Or I woulda told you."

"Hm," Quimby said darkly, obviously unimpressed by the bartender's words.

Before the sheriff could say anything more or put out a restraining hand, Mary marched swiftly toward the rear. The men at the bar turned and backed against it as she neared them. She stared at them scornfully and passed them and they turned as one and followed her with their eyes. There was no one in the back room where tables with chairs pushed in close to them stood in measured rows. A portiere-draped doorway caught her eye, and she headed for it and pushed through it into a small private room. There was a single table in it and at the table backturned to her sat a hunched over man with his head bowing and nodding. Mary glided around the table and eased herself down into a chair directly across from him. She leaned over and nudged his arm.

"Pete," she said.

There was no movement, no response. She nudged him a second time and repeated his name. He stirred and slowly raised his head. His hair was mussed, his youthful face hair fuzzed and dirt streaked, his eyes heavy-lidded and red. Saliva oozed out of a corner of his mouth and ran down his chin. Mary looked at him disgustedly. He raised his hand and wiped it away.

"I've come to take you home, Pete," Mary told him.

It took him a moment or two before he was able to get his eyes properly focused.

"No," he mumbled. "Don't wanna go home. Don't wanna."

"I'll have no nonsense out of you, Pete Rowan," she said crossly. "I said you're going home with me, and you are. Come on. Get up on your feet."

"Don't wanna go home," he repeated.

Mary arose and moved around the table to his side.

"I'm glad your father isn't here to see you," she said to him in a low voice. "The shame of it would have killed him. Now get up and let's go home. I've had enough of this. Come on now."

She tugged at his arm; when she tried to drag him up out of his chair, he pushed her away.

"Lemme alone," he mumbled thick tongued.

"Weakling," she said scornfully. "That's what you are. A weakling. You're put out with Bill because Ann accepted him instead of you. You think there was something underhanded about it, don't you? You've said as much, haven't you, threatening to kill Bill because he stole your girl? If you were honest with yourself you'd know there wasn't anything underhanded about it at all. Bill didn't steal Ann away from you. She wasn't yours to begin with. She was never your girl. So instead of being put out with Bill, you should be put out with yourself because you're the one who didn't measure up while Bill did. Now get up."

This time she succeeded in hauling him up from his chair. The portiere was suddenly whisked aside and held back and Mary, raising her eyes, saw Bill standing in the doorway.

"Oh," she said. "Bill."

Pete was half bent over the table. Slowly he straightened up. With a sudden sweep of his arm he brushed Mary back, flung her back against the side wall, twisted around so clumsily that he nearly lost his balance and fell, and backing off from the doorway clawed with his right hand for his gun.

"Don't, Pete!" Mary screamed. "Don't!"

43

There was a deafening roar of gunfire, thunderous because of the narrow confines of the room. There was a gasp from outside the room. Mary stared. But she knew almost at once that it hadn't come from Bill because he had flung himself out of the doorway. She could see him standing off to a side with his own gun in his hand. He was looking over his shoulder at someone else. Mary's wide-eyed gaze followed Bill's and like his held on Sheriff Dan Quimby. Apparently the lawman had followed Bill through the saloon and back room, but then, as she reconstructed it, he had stopped short of the private room. He must have decided to wait outside, she told herself, preferring to give the Rowans an opportunity to straighten out the difficulty between them themselves rather than impose the law's will upon them.

Quimby was bent over a table, holding on to it with both hands. His bowed head jerked suddenly and his legs buckled under him and he crumpled, dragging the table down with him.

Mary's raised hand pressed hard against her mouth in an effort to stifle the cry that came surging to her lips. There was a rush of booted feet and she saw a handful of wide-eyed men with the bartender a stride ahead of them swarm into the back room. The bartender and Bill Rowan reached Quimby at about the same time, lifted the overturned table off the motionless figure that lay sprawled out on the floor and sent it slithering away. Both bent over Quimby. It was Bill who looked up first. He eased himself around on his haunches. Mary had come out to the doorway. Bill met her eyes.

"He's dead, Ma," he said simply. "Quimby's dead."

Matt and Bill had spent the night at the old house, Tom Spence having summoned Matt there at Mary's instance. Now it was the middle of the next morning and the Rowans, silent and grimly thoughtful looking, were sitting around the kitchen table. Matt sat up, squared back in his chair.

"Wonder what's keeping the judge?" he asked.

"Yeah," Bill said. "Thought he'd be here long before this."

"He'll be along," Mary assured them. "Either of you want anything to eat?"

Bill shook his head and Mary's gaze held on Matt.

"Matt?" she asked. "Hungry?"

"No," he replied. "My stomach's a little too jumpy right now for me to put anything in it."

Mary did not press the matter.

All three looked up at the same time when they heard the rumble of an approaching rig's wheels. Bill started to push back from the table. He stopped and sank down again in his chair when Matt, already on his feet, waved him back, and went striding across the room to the back door, opened it and poked his head out. There was a brief wait. Then there were footsteps outside. They heard Matt's voice, heard someone respond to his greeting, indistinctly though. Matt backed inside holding the door wide. A moment later the judge entered the house. White-haired and stocky Cornelius McCready had served on the bench for twenty years. Then he had retired and returned to the practice of law, limiting himself though to a mere handful of selected clients. The Rowans were among them. He shook his head when Matt held out his hand for his hat and put it in a chair that stood near the door.

Matt followed McCreary to the table. Nearing it, he stepped ahead of him and pulled out a chair for him, and the judge, wheezing a bit, sat down in it heavily. Matt rounded the table to his own chair.

"Well, Judge?" Mary demanded when she could no

longer hold her impatience in check.

"I'm sorry to say I've brought you more bad news, Mary," McCreary began, still a little out of breath.

"More?" Mary repeated.

"Yes."

"What more could there possibly be?"

The Rowans' eyes were fixed on the judge. He moved in closer to the table and leaned over it on his elbows, hunching up the checkered cloth that covered it in humpbacked waves.

"As you know," he said, "Dan Quimby was well liked by the townspeople."

"We liked him too," Mary said evenly. "So they aren't alone in their grief for him. And the fact that he met his death at the hands of a Rowan, even though it was completely accidental, makes us feel even worse."

McCreary nodded understandingly.

"By midnight last night," he went on, "feeling had begun to run pretty high in town."

"Why?" Mary wanted to know. "The shooting, that is the sheriff's unfortunate death was accident as I said before. Both Bill and I can testify to that. And everyone in that saloon, the bartender even more than the others, knows that Pete was too drunk to be held responsible for what happened when he drew his gun and fired. On top of that it was a wildly fired shot and not one deliberately aimed at anyone, certainly not at the sheriff." When the judge offered no comment, she added: "But that sudden outburst of feeling against Pete makes me wonder if there would have been any at all if it had been someone else. I wonder if Pete hadn't been a son of the richest man in the community if the townspeople who take a natural resentment to anyone who has more worldly goods than they have would have accepted Dan Quimby's death as unfortunate and made no more to-do about it?"

"Possibly," the judge conceded.

"Go on, please," Mary said, but she was still bristling indignantly.

"Quite a crowd had gathered in front of the sheriff's office," McCreary related. "Richie Weaver, Quimby's deputy, was afraid he wouldn't be able to cope with the situation if anything happened to incite the crowd."

Mary couldn't restrain herself.

"Huh," she said scornfully. "I'll venture to say that the loudest voices in the crowd belonged to those whom I saw in the saloon. They would be the righteous and indignant kind who would incite a crowd. Those . . . those worthless wastrels. Squandering their money on liquor instead of using it to take care of their families."

"Ma," Matt said, turning to her, reaching out and covering her hand with his. "No point in you working yourself up like that. The judge is only trying to tell us what happened. That doesn't mean he's giving those people in town right. So suppose we let him go on? All right?"

"Yes, of course. I'm sorry, Judge. Please go on."

McCreary nodded and went on again.

"Weaver decided it would be better for everyone concerned if Pete were removed from the scene. Accordingly he spirited Pete out the back way and took him to Rawlins and turned him over to the authorities there for safe keeping. Since Rawlins is the county seat and the authorities there are better equipped to deal with, well, violence, than we are, Weaver felt that he was doing the right thing."

There was no comment from anyone. The judge coughed lightly behind his upraised hand.

"This morning," he continued shortly, "oh, about an hour ago I'd say it was, Weaver burst in on me with some news that he had just gotten from Rawlins."

When he failed to go on, the three Rowans looked at

47

him wonderingly.

"What'd you stop for, Judge?" Matt asked him.

"Yeah," Bill added. "What was the news Richie'd got?"

"This morning at dawn Pete broke out of jail, shot down the jailer and fled."

Mary gasped.

"Oh, no!" she said, her tone reflecting horror and momentary disbelief.

The color had already drained out of her face leaving it ashen and thinly white and red streaked. Seated opposite her in the chair that Matt usually occupied at breakfast, Bill released his sucked-in breath in a low, drawn out whistle.

"Pete killed him?" Matt asked the judge.

"Yes," was the simple reply.

Matt shook his head, and turning to Bill asked him:

"Where d'you suppose he got hold of a gun?" Then before Bill could answer, a hazarded guess at best, Matt turned to McCreary and said: "According to Bill, he took Pete's gun away from him in the saloon and handed it over to Weaver himself. And I know doggone well that Richie wouldn't have given it back to him. So it figures that Pete must've got hold of another one from somebody else. Not that that matters, of course. Just got me to wondering for a minute."

"Pete probably took the jailer's gun from him when he overpowered him," the judge suggested. He lifted his elbows, smoothed out the rumpled tablecloth with his short-fingered, pudgy hands and sat back in his chair. "That's the situation as it stands now. Or as it did the last I heard."

There was a brief silence. Then Matt asked:

"Looks pretty bad for Pete, huh, Judge?"

McCreary would not commit himself. He shrugged wordlessly.

"There anything we can do?" Bill asked him.

"No, I don't think so, Bill. Fact is, I think you boys should stay right here and keep out of things. At least for the time being."

"Mean people might get ideas if we don't?"

"They might indeed," the judge said evenly. "In view of how feeling in town is running, why do anything to further antagonize people? If anyone should see you boys riding off, even to your own places, the first thing that would come to mind would be a suspicion that you know where Pete has taken refuge and that you're on your way to help him escape." He pushed back from the table and stood up. Matt and Bill arose too. "I'm on my way to Rawlins. If there are any further developments, any further information to pass on to you, I'll be back here. However, don't look for me before this evening. If there isn't anything to tell you, I'll hold off till tomorrow."

SIX

When the judge turned and walked to the door, Matt followed him, overtook him and again stepping ahead of him, picked up his hat and handed it to him, opened the door and held it wide, exchanged a grim, tight-lipped nod with him as he went out and closed the door after him. Turning, Matt backed against the door, his broad shoulders practically spanning its width, and stood slightly spread-legged with his big hands on his hips. Mary sat motionlessly at the table with her clasped hands on the very edge of it. Bill stood behind his chair, a deeply troubled frown riding his face. His head was bent a little and thrust forward, his hands poked finger-deep in the back pockets of his Levis, with his thumbs hooked over the outsides of the pockets.

"Oh, that foolish, foolish boy," Mary said with a shake of her head and Matt and Bill looked at her. "Quimby's death was bad enough. But because it was accidental, I'm sure the judge would have gotten him off. But this . . . this second killing. There couldn't have been anything accidental about that one. That was murder. They'll hang him for that one. He knows that. He must. So nothing will matter to him now. He'll kill others, anyone who stands in his way or who tries to stop him, because he knows the penalty for killing a dozen isn't any greater than it is for killing one. He knows they can only hang him once no matter how many more he kills."

There was no comment from Matt or Bill. With a deep, wearied sigh, Mary got up on her feet.

"I'm going upstairs," she announced in a strangely

dull and flat voice without looking at either of her step-sons. "I'm terribly tired. I . . . I think I'd better get some rest. I'd better be prepared for the next thing that happens, and I'm sure there will be something."

They followed her with their eyes, watched her go out of the room, heard her step on the stairs, heard it again on the landing overhead. It was only after they had heard her door close after her that Matt said:

"This thing has sure hit her hard."

"Yeah," Bill agreed. "It's taken a lot out of her, all right."

"Guess she didn't sleep much last night for worryin' about Pete. I could see it in her face when she came downstairs this morning. She looked like . . . like a real old woman."

Bill jerked his head around to Matt.

"How much sleeping did you do last night?" he wanted to know.

"Some. 'Course nothing like what I usu'lly do."

"I didn't sleep a wink."

"Kinda thought I heard you moving around in your room a couple o' times during the night."

"Oh, I tossed and I turned and after a while I gave it up and sat near the window looking out and wondering where Pete was."

Matt sauntered back to the table and sank down in the chair that Mary had been sitting in. He hunched forward over the table on his elbows and drummed on it with his fingertips, the tempo swelling, falling off and then picking up again. From time to time he raised his gaze and stole a look at his brother. He stopped drumming quite abruptly.

"Blaming yourself for what's happened," he said. "Aren't you?"

"Some," Bill conceded.

"And I've been wondering if some of it mightn't be

my fault.''

Bill looked hard at him.

"What'd you have to do with it, with what's happened?''

"I was thinking back. I used to ride herd on Pete, kept on top of him all the time and never let up on him. Now I wonder if that mightn't have had something to do with what's come over him lately and the way he's been acting?''

"I wouldn't know about that. But talking about the way you used to hound him, and me too for that matter, I'll bet you never had any idea how many times you came near having your head beat in. I can remember a couple o' times when we were both so blamed sore at you, we were all set to jump you and give it to you good.''

"But you didn't though.''

"No. But don't you go thinking it was because we were scared or anything.''

"Why didn't you do it, Bill? What stopped you?''

Bill shrugged. But he volunteered nothing beyond that. Wisely Matt did not press him. Instead he mused:

"And all the time I thought I was doing what was good for you two. More for him though than for you. He needed the prodding more than you did.''

Bill held his tongue.

"What are we gonna do, Bill?'' Matt asked him.

"Y'mean about Pete?''

"'Course. You know as well as I do that we aren't gonna sit by and let them catch him and string him up. Not just like that and without us doing something to help him.'' Matt watched his brother saunter about the room and halt shortly backturned to the table and facing the closed door. "Bill . . .''

Bill Rowan turned slowly.

"You're working on something,'' Matt said quietly.

"I can tell by the look on your face and from the way you're acting. I am too. But I'm not getting anywhere with it. So I'll forget it. Suppose you bring your idea out in the open and let the two of us kick it around? Two heads are supposed to be better'n one, you know. Maybe between the two of us we can make something outta the idea you're playin' around with. What do you say?"

Bill sauntered off again. He stopped and looked at Matt over his shoulder.

"You think he's hightailed it?"

"Nope."

"I don't think he has either. I think he's still around, and close by, too."

"All right. I'll go along with you on that, Bill. But where do we go from there?"

"I think he's holed up somewhere close by like I said, afraid to show himself by day because he must have enough sense to know the law's after him and that there must be posses out looking for him."

"So it figures the only time he'll come out will be at night."

"Right."

"Go on," Matt urged him. "I'm listening."

Bill came striding back to the table. He leaned over it, back bent, resting on his open-fingered hands.

"Matt, this whole fool business with Pete started when he got the idea I'd cut him out with Ann Snow," he said. "But it wasn't anything like that. You can ask Ann and she'll tell you I didn't do or say anything to sour her on Pete. She'll even tell you right out same's she told me that she liked him. But that was all. Only trouble is that Pete read the signs all wrong. He took Ann's liking him to mean she was in love with him. She wasn't though."

"Go on," Matt said again.

53

"Matt, I've got a crazy idea that when it gets good and dark he'll break outta wherever it is he's holed up and that he'll make a try to see Ann before he clears out."

"Uh-huh," Matt said and he squared back in his chair. "Ya mean just to see her, or do you think he might try to get her to go 'way with him?"

"The spot he's in, with a rope waiting for him, I wouldn't put it past him, knowing how desperate he must be, to try to force Ann to go with him."

"Hm," Matt said thoughtfully. "Then the thing for us to do is lay for him tonight near Ann's place and if he shows up there the way we figure he will, jump him and grab him, and see if we can't talk some sense into him and get him started for Mexico."

"That's exactly what I had in mind, Matt. Mexico would be the place for him, all right. The safest place. Only I don't know if he'd like it down there. That is, well enough to be willing to stay put down there."

"Way I see it, what difference does it make where he has to go long's it means saving himself from a hanging? And if he hasn't got that much sense to know what's good for him . . ."

"Trying to talk him into seeing things our way won't be easy," Bill said, interrupting him. "Man on the dodge probably figures everybody's against him. Even his own. So like Ma said, Pete's liable to act up with us, and figuring what's he got to lose by killing a couple o' more, start shooting. Ya know?"

"I know," Matt said grimly. "So it'll be up to us to see that he doesn't. Even if it means walloping him good to make him listen to what we've got to say."

"We'll be going against what the judge told us to do," Bill pointed out. "To stay put here."

"Pete isn't his brother. He's ours. So we'll do what we think we should and never mind the judge."

"What about Ma?" Bill wanted to know. "Gonna let her know what we're up to?"

"Nope," Matt said with finality. "If Ma knew, it would be something else for her to worry about and she's got enough on her mind the way it is without us adding to it."

"Just one last thing, Matt."

"Yeah?"

"When it comes time for us to get going and Ma wants to know where we're off to . . .?"

"I've got the answer for her."

"You'd better tell it to me so I'll know what to say in case she asks me."

"We've been away from our spreads since last night and while we've got good hands working for us, we still think we oughta go have a look around just to make sure that everything's all right. Then we'll come back here."

"Uh-huh," Bill said, nodding and straightening up again.

"Only once we get away from here," Matt continued, "We'll head straight for the Snow place, duck down somewhere's outta sight but close to the house and without letting anybody know we're there and wait for Pete to show up."

"Ya don't think I oughta let Ann know?"

"What for? Just to give her something to worry about? Why get her all het up over something that she mightn't even have dreamed of herself? We'll grab him and stop him from getting to her and she'll never have to know anything about it."

Scuffing, gravel-crunching bootsteps sounded in the path outside and the two brothers looked wonderingly at each other. Matt started to get up from his chair. Bill, already half-turned toward the door, stopped him with a gesture, and Matt grunted and slumped down again.

55

Bill opened the door and poked his head out; he withdrew it almost at once, looked back at Matt and said simply:

"Sam Potter."

Matt grunted again. He was holding his gaze on the open doorway when a lanky man with a lined, leathery face came up to it.

"Yeah, Sam?" Matt heard Bill say. "Want something?"

"Just come to tell you something, Bill. Went after a couple o'strays a while ago and had to chase the pesky critters clear over to your place before I caught up with them."

"Well, long's you caught up with them."

"Spotted three possemen staked out around your place," Potter continued. "One hanging around the back of the house, the other two squatting on their backsides in the brush a ways off from the the front door. Thought you might wanna know that."

"Yeah, sure," Bill responded. "Thanks for letting me know, Sam."

Potter was silent for a moment, then he said:

"Ya know, Bill, I taught Pete how to ride and shoot and handle a rope. Got to know that boy real well. I think a heap of him. What's come over him of late, I wouldn't know. Not that knowing would make any difference to me."

"What are you trying to say, Sam?"

"Just that while I hold with the law, if there's anything I can do, well, to help the boy, you just lemme know. Huh?"

"I'll do that, Sam."

"What I said goes for Spence and Willis too."

This time Potter didn't wait for Bill's reply. Matt saw him turn and trudge away. Bill followed him briefly with his eyes. Then he stepped back inside and closed

56

the door, turned slowly and backed against it.

"Looks like the law thinks the same's we do," he said, meeting Matt's eyes. "That Pete hasn't hightailed it and that he's holed up somewhere close by."

"Uh-huh."

"I wish I knew for sure what's in Weaver's mind and why he's got his men staked out around my place."

"Chances are he's got my place covered too," Matt said.

"I'll bet he hasn't."

As though he hadn't heard Bill, or pretended he hadn't, Matt went on with:

"He must figure that Pete'll be needing things before he clears out, money, grub, a rifle and a blanket, maybe a horse too, and that one of us will fix him up with whatever he needs. That's why he's got his men keepin' an eye on our places."

"No good, Matt," Bill said, shaking his head. "You can do better than that."

"What d'you mean?"

"Matt, you know as well as I do that Ma'd be the one Pete would turn to for whatever he needed. He's always been her favorite, so this is where he'd come first. To you or me only afterward. Richie knows that Pete was gunning for me before this whole lousy killing business began. So the way I see it, he figures that Pete will make one last try to get me before he heads out. That's why he's got his possemen hangin' around my place, to kill Pete, or if they're lucky, to grab him and take him in so he can stand trial and swing for killing that jailer over at Rawlins."

SEVEN

Standing at the curtained window in her room with her tightly clasped hands raised and pressed hard against her mouth to stifle the sound of her sobbing, Mary Rowan peered out at the grassy incline through tear-blurred eyes. Bathed in bright, dazzling sunshine, the thick, lush grass that carpeted the rise had never looked so brilliantly green, almost as though each blade had been handwashed, put out to dry and now reflected the sunlight. The wild flowers that dotted the incline, a riot of color normally, had never been more eye-arresting and breathtaking. Mary's gaze lifted and ranged upward and held briefly on the summit where John Rowan lay buried. How glad she was, she told herself, that the pain-wracked man who had always been so proud of his good name hadn't lived to know of the shame that one of his sons had brought upon the Rowans. Dabbing at her eyes with her balled-up handkerchief, she turned away from the window and sank down into the old rocker and lay back in it with her eyes closed. She had failed her husband and she was ashamed, and she hoped and prayed that he would never know of it.

Even though Pete and Bill were of the same age, three, when she had married their father, Bill had always been the sturdier and the more manly of the two. It was a good thing for Pete had claimed so much of her time and attention. It was as though he were even younger than his twin, and his tender years and the baby of the famiiy. So she had had to give him so much more of herself than she devoted to his brothers. But, she told herself now, and it was a thought that left her feeling miserable and unhappy, she had failed him somewhere and in failing him she had failed her husband too. For it had been into her hands that John Rowan had entrusted his sons. The time that she had devoted to young Pete . . . what had her efforts accomplished and what good had come of them if Pete were to be considered proof of her teaching and guidance?

She thought back over the years, trying to recall the little incidents in which Pete the boy had been involved, either directly or indirectly, so unimportant then save for the moment of their happening but so terribly important now in view of what Pete the man had done, in her efforts to find where she had failed him. But try as she did, nothing came to her. Perhaps, she told herself, it was because she was so tired that her memory refused to function properly for her. Perhaps after a bit, after she had rested, what she had been trying to recall would return to her. Mechanically she rocked herself. The back and forth motion dulled her senses and lulled her to sleep.

Mary's long sleep was anything but restful and refreshing. It was filled with shortlived but frightening, nightmarish dreams in which Pete was the only recognizable character. The dreams seemed to be a series of episodes in which Pete was the pursued culprit who robbed and slew with wanton recklessness and whose very appearance made people pale and flee while he proceeded to uproot each tiny town that he came to. Mary went from one dream to another with only the barest respite between them. The worst one was peopled by grotesquely formed and hideous faced characters whose voices she recognized with a start. Pete was one of them, and his voice, strangely highpitched and mocking, more like a caroming echo than an actual voice, stood out above the others.

The scene was a town square that was oddly enough studded with towering mounds of hay. At each corner of the square stood a tall pole with a jutting crosspiece from which an empty noose hung. Pete was being pursued around the square and his pursuers, obviously all of them lawmen sine their leader had Richie Weaver's voice, seemed to have been waiting for him inside the hay mounts, ready to burst out and pounce upon him. As he darted by, long arms reached out and lunged for him, missed him and were promptly withdrawn till he made another flitting circuit of the square. The nooses hung motionlessly save when Pete, skidding along as he turned, neared one of them, then it would lean toward him only to draw back again and hang quietly as he swerved away from it with is mocking, taunting laugh trailing behind him. On and on it went with Pete's laugh, now tinged with hysteria, beating against Mary's ears. When she couldn't stand it any longer, she began to squirm and twist in an effort to get away from it. With a heave of her body that almost catapulted her out of the rocker, she awoke and clinging to the armrests sat quivering for a minute or two. It took her that long to regain her composure. Then almost wide awake she wondered how long she had slept, wondered too how late it was. Half-turning and leaning toward the window, she reached out and parted the curtain and peered out. Here eyes widened with surprise. She had slept away the day. She judged it to be about five o'clock. A little stiffly she got up on her feet.

Whatever there was to be done for Pete had to be done without any further delay. There was no thought in her mind as to the right or the wrong of it. Law or no, stepson or blood son, it didn't make any difference. He needed help and that was all there was to it. John would have every right to expect her to do what she could for his son. Only one thing troubled her and she had no way of knowing that she held the same disturbing thoughts as Matt and Bill did, that Pete would risk his neck in an effort to see Ann Snow, that he would not be satisfied with simply seeing and talkig with her, and that he would want much more of her than that. Helping him to get away was one thing. But the longer she thought about Pete and Ann, the darker she frowned and the more she determined to prevent it. How to stop Pete from getting to the girl did not worry her. She knew how to handle him. He might act up with someone else. He wouldn't dare with her because she would let him know right off that she wouldn't have any of his nonsense.

How to get out of the house without Matt and Bill being aware of it posed a problem for her. Unfortunately there wre no back stairs by which she might slip out unheard and unseen. She could not go downstairs and come right out with it, tell the boys what she planned to do for they would promptly take it upon themselves to do it. And if that were to happen, and if Pete succeeded in getting past the posses that were hunting him, reached the Snow place and found his brothers there barring his way to Ann there would be trouble. In his frame of mind, Pete would not listen to reason. Anyone who stood between him and what he wanted would be an enemy. He would go for his gun and in their own defense, the boys would have to go for their guns. While she knew that neither Matt nor Bill would willingly do anything to hurt Pete, she had her doubts about Pete. Anyone who had killed another as ruthlessly as Pete had would not hesitate to kill again, particularly if he became enraged.

She tiptoed out of her room and stood for a moment in the shadowy silence of the landing. Then practically holding her breath for fear that the floorboards would creak and betray her, she made her way on tiptoe up the landing. She halted for a moment at the head of the stairs and listened head bent to the murmur of voices in the kitchen. She moved off again shortly, made her way to the front of the house. Quietly raising the window in Pete's room that looked out upon the barn, the corral and the bunkhouse, she peered out anxiously. But there was no sign of any of her men and she was disappointed. But just as she was about to withdraw her head a horseman topped the slight incline that led inland from the main road and came on toward the barn at a trot. When she saw that it was Tom Spence she leaned out of the window and waved vigorously. She was beside herself when he glanced in every direction save hers. Then just as he neared the barn and was about to wheel onto the wooden ramp, he happened to look up at the house, spotted her framed in the open window, hastily reined in and stared wonderingly at her. When she beckoned, he wheeled away from the ramp and started to ride on to the house. She gestured frantically and he pulled up again, so abruptly though that his horse snorted in protest when the iron bit cut into his jaws. Looking hard at Mary, Spence sat motionlessly for a moment, apparently trying to figure out just what she wanted him to do. Then quite suddenly it must have come to him for he swung down from his horse and hitching up his levis came plodding up to the house. Halting directly below her, he lifted his questioning gaze to her.

Leaning out as far as she could and cupping her hands around her mouth so that her voice wouldn't carry beyond him, she told him:

"There's a ladder lying in the grass around the other side of the house. Raise it to the window in Matt's room."

She pressed her finger against her lips as a sign to him

to hold his tongue.

When he nodded and started to turn away, she backed inside and closed the window. Leaving Pete's room, she tiptoed back to her own room, took a hooded cloak from the closet, donned it and went out again. Hurrying into Matt's room, she closed the door behind her, crossed the room to the window, raised it and poked her head out. Spence had propped up the ladder flush with the windowsill and was standing next to the ladder and looking up at her. It took some maneuvering on her part, the cloak making matters even more difficult for her than they might have been without it, to get herself up on the sill and across it with her legs dangling out. It was anything but a ladylike pose for one so proper and dignified, and she knew that Reverend Goslin would have been shocked into speechlessness had he been there. But she had no time to be concerned with anything other than the business of getting out of the house by means of the ladder. While Spence eyed her apprehensively, gulped and swallowed hard, painfully too, judging by the nervous jerking of his Adam's apple, she moved herself out of the window and stepped onto the ladder. Fearfully certain that something was going to happen to her, Spence kept moving about under her with his arms upraised as though he fully expected her to come tumbling down into them. Once or twice he even planted himself securely with his legs wide-spread and his whole body tensed and expectant. But his fears did not materialize. Slowly, carefully probing below her with her right foot for each successive rung, she made her way down the ladder to the ground and when she finally stood beside him, Spence breathed a deep sigh of relief.

"I'll need your horse, Tom," she told him. "Take him into the barn and then out the back door and leave him there for me."

"All right," he said.

"You used to keep a rifle in the barn. Is it still there?"

"Uh-huh," he said, nodding.

"I'll want that too."

"Anything else?"

"No."

"I dunno what you're up to, Ma'am, but whatever it is and wherever it is you're going, how about me trailing along with you? I won't get in your way. I'll just be around and handy in case you need somebody. Huh?"

"No, Tom. It's kind of you to offer and I appreciate it. But I'll be all right."

"How about tellin' me what this is all about?"

"When I get back I'll tell you. Till then though, not a word about this out of you to anyone. Is that clear?"

"Yeah, sure. Oh, that go for the boys too? Matt and Bill, I mean."

"For them too. Remember now, not a single word to anyone. As a matter of fact, you haven't even seen me, and if anyone should say I can't be found and that I seem to have disappeared, I want you to be just as surprised as everyone else."

"How long do you figger to be gone, Ma'am?"

"I don't know. It all depends."

"On what?" he pressed her.

"On what I find," she retorted. "And don't ask me any more questions. Just do as I tell you. Oh, don't leave the ladder propped up against the house. That will be a dead giveaway. Lay it in the grass."

She stepped back to give him room to handle the ladder. He lowered it, laid it in the grass just as he had found it.

"Dunno if you've heard this, Ma'am," he said, turning again to her. "But that Weaver feller's got some of his possemen posted around Matt's place, Bill's and

Pete's too. Just in case the boy shows up at any one o' them. By nightfall, I figger Weaver'll have some more o' them hanging around here too. He's sure making a good try to grab Pete."

"He's only doing his job, Tom."

"Yeah," he conceded. "Guess that's so. Only," he added wryly, "why he have to be so blamed conscientious this time?"

"We're wasting time, Tom," she said.

He grunted and trudged away.

EIGHT

It was evening. The long day, uneventful and therefore more tiring than if it had been filled with a normal workday's activity, was finally, and rapidly, drawing to a close. Outside the old house the shadows had already begun to lengthen, deepen and veil the land and everything upon it. Inside it was hushed and dark for neither Matt nor Bill Rowan who had idled away the whole day in the kitchen waiting for nightfall seemed to be aware that it was almost upon them. Slumped down on their spines in their half-turned chairs on the opposite sides of the table with their long legs thrust out before them and crossed at the ankle, and with their chins resting on their chests, both sat quietly, apparently talked out, each plainly absorbed with his own grim and disturbing thoughts. Finally though, Bill stirred and shattered their self-imposed silence. He struggled up into a sitting position, stood up and grimaced and stretched himself mightily, rising up on his toes at the height of his stretch, yawned and rubbed his nose with the back of his hand. He grimaced again and muttered:

"Been sitting so blamed long, I'm as stiff as a board."

There was no response from Matt.

Bill stamped about for a minute or two, twisting his body from side to side in an obvious effort to ease the stiffness in his back and stamped about again. He struck a match on his bootheel and made a light in the overhead lamp that hung from a ceiling crossbeam at the end of a shortcut of chain. Glancing at Matt, Bill saw him frown and hastily put up his hand to shield his eyes from the light. Quickly Bill turned it down.

"That better?" he asked.

Matt peered out between his spread fingers.

"Uh-huh," he said.

Bill seated himself again. Pushed back coffee cups that had been filled and drained a dozen times through the day and an empty cake plate that had held a coffee cake. A dozen or more buns stood between them on the table surrounding the sugar bowl and the milk pitcher.

"I'll be damned glad when this day's over and gone," Bill announced after a brief silence.

Squirming back in his chair and then a little forward again, he slumped down in it on the tail of his spine.

"You and me both," Matt said. "Day like this takes more outta me than a day's work. This layin' around and waiting gets me down."

"Won't have to lay around and wait much longer," Bill said. "Getting near that time."

"I know. I've been thinking about you, Bill, about you and Pete, and I don't think you oughta go thrugh with what we've got planned for tonight. If Pete's still got it in his mind to get you, I don't think we oughta give him the chance. So you stay put here and I'll go."

"Nope," Bill said evenly. "I said I was going with you and that's what I aim to do. I don't see any reason for backing out now."

"All right," Matt said with a lift of his broad shoulders. "If that's the way you want it. Only if you should change your mind before it gets to that time, I'll understand and I won't blame you any."

"You think Ma's all right? She's just about slept away the whole day."

"That oughta give you a pretty idea of how beat she musta been," Matt answered, sitting up. "But she oughta be coming downstairs any minute now, and one look at her'll tell you that that sleep musta been good for her."

"What about these things?" Bill asked, indicating the dishes on the table with a nod. "What do we do with them? Leave them where they are?"

"I'll take care of them," Matt said.

He got up on his feet almost as stiffly as Bill had minutes before. He made a wry face, but he voiced no complaint. Bill arose too. Together they cleared the table, putting the dishes on the wooden drainboard that emptied into the iron sink.

"Gonna wash 'em too?" Bill wanted to know.

"No," Matt replied. "Long's they're outta the way."

"Then whenever you're ready," Bill said simply.

"Still wanna go through with it, huh?"

"'Course."

Their gunbelts were hanging from the pegs that held their hats. Wordlessly they lifted them off and buckled them on around their waists. Then they clapped on their hats.

"We don't wanna make any more noise than we have to," Matt said. "The longer Ma sleeps the better for her."

"For us too," Bill added.

"Yeah. All set?"

"Yeah, sure . . . all set."

Bill was nearer the door. He turned the knob, opened the door and glided out.

"Kinda nippy out," he said low-voiced over his shoulder. Standing a step or two from the door, he saw Matt step outside, turn and quietly close the door behind him. When he heard Matt swear under his breath, Bill hissed at him: "What's the matter?"

"Got my finger caught in the door," Matt told him.

"Oh!"

"That all you can say?" Matt demanded crossly,

68

putting his bruised finger in his mouth and laving it with his tongue.

"What do you want me to say?" Bill retorted. "I'm sorry? All right, I'm sorry. Or do you want me to go call Ma so she can kiss it and make it all better?"

Matt glared at him.

"You're a real funny feller, aren't you? Come on."

With Matt a stride in the lead, they headed away from the back door. Stopping abruptly, Matt looked up at Mary's window. Bill promptly crowded into him. Matt gave him a hard look.

"Watch it, funny man," he said grumpily.

"Next time lemme know when you're gonna stop so all of a sudden," Bill answered. "There's no light up there. I had a look before you came out."

With Matt again leading the way, they rounded the house.

"The grass," he said low-voiced over his shoulder.

"Right," Bill said behind him.

The grass that flanked the path muffled their boot-steps. Presently they were past the house and heading for the barn. As they neared it a shadowy figure emerged from the darkness around it, a shadowy figure holding a half-raised rifle on them.

"All right, you two," the man behind the rifle said curtly. "You've had the air and the exercise. Now you can turn yourselves around and go on back into the house. And if you know when you're well off, you'll stay put there."

The two Rowans jerked to an awkward, uncertain and shoulder bumping halt and looked hard at the approaching figure. With his rifle held about waist-high and leveled at them, with a thin ray of moonlight suddenly touching and flashing along the length of the barrel and vanishing again in almost the same instant of its appearance, the man stepped squarely in front of

69

them, blocking their way.

"All right now," he said in the same curt tone that he had used before. "Go on back inside."

"Just a minute now, partner," Matt began. "We . . ."

His protest ended abruptly when the muzzle of the rifle collided with his belt buckle.

"Inside, I said."

Matt was jabbed a second time.

"Take it easy with that thing," he said evenly.

"Then do as you're told!"

"Don't poke me again!"

"And if I do?" the posseman taunted Matt.

"I'll take that rifle away from you and bend it over your thick skull!"

"Oh, you will, huh?" the man retorted. "You make just one move, *Mister* Rowan, and I'll blast you good. Now what do you know about that?"

Deliberately then he dug his rifle muzzle into Matt's midsection.

"I told you not to do that," Matt said quietly. "I won't tell you again."

"Now you're making sense. Now suppose you get real smart and go on back inside and stay put there like I've been telling you, huh? Buckin' the law won't get you anything 'cept trouble, and being that I represent the law . . ."

"The hell you do," Matt flung back at him scornfully. "Only thing you represent is Mike Campbell's saloon. I thought there was something familiar about you. But I wasn't sure who you were till I got a good whiff of you. Then I recognized you, Wiltse. The smell of booze stands out all over you. Richie Weaver that hard up for possemen that he had to deputize the town's leading drunk?"

Wiltse didn't answer. He drew back his rifle and

leveled it at Bill. Just as he was about to jab him with it, Bill, on the alert for it, brushed it aside with his left arm, lunged and swung with his right. The punch landed solidly, exploding in the man's face with the pulverizing force of Bill's muscular body behind it. The rifle fairly popped out of Wiltse's hands and went one way while the hapless posseman went another. Careening backward, he went sprawling in the dirt and landed on the flat of his back with his arms outflung. There was a sudden cry that made the Rowans look up, a rush of booted feet and another man, a tall, rangy man, burst out of the deep shadows beyond the bunkhouse that stood diagonally opposite the barn, and came dashing toward the Rowans.

"Hold it right there!" he yelled authoritatively.

Both Matt and Bill recognized him at once. It was Richie Weaver. He skidded to a stop half a dozen feet from them, just barely managing to stop himself and twist away from the sprawled out Wiltse when it appeared that he was going to trip and fall over him.

"What . . . what's going on here?" he panted.

"You oughta be a mite fussier, Rich, when you go rounding up a posse," Matt told him. "You that hard up for men that you had to take on that drunk?"

Ignoring Matt's comment and question, Weaver asked a question of his own.

"What happened?"

"Wiltse kept pokin' me in the belly with his rifle and even though I told him to cut it out, he kept right on doing it. When he turned to Bill and made like he was gonna poke him . . ."

"Bill upped and walloped him," Weaver said dryly.

"That's right," Bill said. "And I walloped him good."

"Guess he musta let himself get carried away when I deputized him."

"We came down from the house to get our horses outta the barn," Matt related. "I was gonna ride over to my place to sorta see that everything's the way it oughta be. And Bill was gonna cut over to his place. Then we were gonna head back here. Wiltse popped up outta the darkness and held his rifle on us and told us to go back in the house and to stay put there."

"And you didn't like the way he told you."

This time Matt ignored Weaver's remark and asked: "There a law that says we can't go?"

"No, no law, Matt," Weaver replied with an over-the-shoulder glance at Wiltse who had hauled himself to his feet and who was rocking a little, his legs a little rubbery and wobbly and apparently not yet up to supporting him. Weaver reached out and offered him a steadying hand. Wiltse clutched it with one hand and curled his other hand around the lawman's wrist and clung to him. Half-turning again to Matt, Weaver said: "Like I said, Matt, there's no law that says you can't go anywhere you like. Only I'm suggesting, and this goes for you too, Bill, that you stay put here. Least ways for the time being. Till we grab Pete or we know for sure that he's gone."

Neither Matt nor Bill answered.

"I've got your spreads covered," Weaver continued, "just in case Pete takes it into his head to show up at either place. And the men I've got posted around them might have itchy or nervous trigger fingers, and even though I've told every last one of them to make sure before he starts shooting, I'm afraid the moment they hear somebody coming, they're liable to think it's Pete coming and peg lead."

Wiltse showed that he was all right again. He stepped around the deputy, plodded over to where his rifle lay in the dirt and picked it up. Weaver looked at him.

"Long's I'm here, Wiltse," he said to the posseman,

"I might as well stay put. So you go get your horse and head back to town. Thanks for your help."

"Yeah, sure," Wiltse retorted. He halted at Weaver's side. "You might tell those two that I won't forget this and that one o' these days I'll square up with them for the walloping I got."

"Walloping?" Bill repeated. "I only hit you once."

"Ya mean each o' you hit me once. Ganged up on me."

"If both of us had hit you, you'd still be layin' there."

"Go get your horse," Weaver said a second time to Wiltse.

The latter grunted, and hoisting his rifle to his shoulder and then lowering it and cradling it in his arms, he trudged off. He disappeared into the shadowy darkness that shrouded the side of the barn.

"One thing more," Weaver said. Matt and Bill looked at him. "Figuring that Pete might make a try to see Ann before he hightails it, I had the Snows drive in to town and put up at the hotel. They're gonna stay there till I think it's safe for them to go back home. I've got four good men standing guard over them. So even if Pete should manage to find out where Ann's at, he won't stand a chance of getting to her. So don't go worrying yourself about her, Bill. She's gonna be all right."

"Hm," Bill said, but that was all.

"I suppose if Pete was my brother," the rangy lawman went on, "no matter what he'd done, I suppose I'd want to do everything I could for him. I wouldn't want to see him swing any more than you wanna see Pete swing. So putting myself in your place, I think I know how you feel and what you're thinking. I'm sorry, but you're not gonna be able to do anything for Pete. For one thing if either of you tries anything, I'll be right

73

with you every step of the way. For another, helpin'
anybody escape from the law makes you just as guilty as
the one who committed the crime. On top of that, I've
got forty men on the lookout for Pete and for anybody
who tries to help him beat the law. So what do you say
you fellers go on back to the house and stay put there?''

NINE

"Well, here we are again," Bill Rowan said as he trooped into the house at Matt's heels.

"Yep," Matt responded over his shoulder. "Right back where we started from."

Bill closed the door. They unbuckled their gunbelts and hung them up, took off their hats and slapped them up on the pegs that held their guns. Hitching up his Levis, Matt sauntered on to the table, drew out the chair that he had occupied throughout the long day, and with a wearied sigh slumped down in it. Standing a little spread-legged, with his thumbs hooked in his pants' belt, Bill was backed against the door.

"Least we know that Ann's safe," Matt said after a brief silence, raising his eyes to meet his brother's. "So that's something."

"A helluva lot, believe me."

As though he hadn't heard Bill, Matt went on with:

"So that's one worry less for us to wrack our brains trying to figure out what to do."

"Uh-huh," Bill acknowledged. "What bothers me now is this. Suppose like we figure he will, Pete does make a try to see Ann, gets to her house only to find Ann and her folks gone, figures out for himself where they must be and decides to follow them into town?"

"You oughta know the answer to that same's I do. It'll be just too bad for him."

"He won't have a chance. Weaver's men will cut down on him just like that," Bill said and he snapped his fingers.

"That's right. But what can we do about it? With Richie ridin' herd on us, seeing to it that we stay put here, we're, well, helpless and we can't do a damned thing about it."

"That's the lousy part of it. Being willing to do something and not being able to."

"'Less of course . . ."

"Yeah?" Bill pressed his older brother. "What were you gonna way? 'Less of course what?"

"I wonder if I couldn't slip away from here without Richie being any the wiser and still make it to the Snow place in time to stop Pete and head him off from going into town and like we said before get him started for the border and Mexico?"

"What's the matter with me doing it?" Bill wanted to know.

"No," Matt said with a firm shake of his head. "Not you, Bill. Me. You oughta know what chance you'd have of getting Pete to do anything you might suggest. I'll go. Only we've got to figure out a way for me to get away without Richie knowing about it."

Bill rubbed his chin with the back of his hand.

"Well, let's see now. Suppose I get him to come in say to have some hot coffee? If you slip outta here before I call him and you duck down somewhere outta sight and then skip down to the barn while he's in here with me, get your horse and start riding . . ."

"Whoa now, Bill," Matt commanded, stopping him. "Don't you think he's gonna think it kinda funny, you being here alone and no sign o' me even though he knows I was here just a while ago? We wanna play it smart, Bill, and not give him any reason to suspect anything."

Bill refused to have his suggestion beaten down.

"All right," he said calmly, "the minute he comes in here, even before he gets a chance to notice that you

76

aren't here too, I'll tell him you were so beat, you went upstairs and turned in and that it's just him and me having the coffee. How's that sound to you?''

"Sounds pretty good," Matt admitted. "Fact is, I don't see how it can miss satisfying him."

"Then just give me a couple o' minutes to fix the coffee and we'll be all set."

"I'm just thinking," Matt said.

"Yeah? Thinking about what?"

"If what you tell him doesn't satisfy him, so what? There won't be anything he can do about it because by then I'll have the jump on him. I'll be on my way and he won't know where I'm headed. And if I have any luck and I catch up with Pete and stop him from getting himself killed and I steer him off to the border, I'll call it a good night's work."

"A damned good night's work," was Bill's comment.

"And when I get back here," Matt continued, "what can Richie do? Give me a good layin' out for interfering with the law? That I can take, 'specially if I know that Pete's all right and on his way to where the law can't reach him."

"Might turn out that you get a lot worse than just a layin' out, Matt."

"Oh, you thinking about what Richie said, about helpin' a . . . a criminal escape? How that makes him, the one helping him, just as guilty of the crime that's been committed as the one who committed it?"

Bill nodded wordlessly.

"Would you let that stop you, Bill?"

"No," Bill answered bluntly.

"I'm not letting it stop me either."

There was a sudden heavy-handed knock on the door.

"Now who do you suppose that could be?" Bill asked.

"Only one way to find out," Matt said dryly.

Bill looked at him obliquely, turned and opened the door. Facing him across the threshold strip was Richie Weaver. If the deputy could see Matt Rowan from where he stood, he gave no sign of it.

"Thought I oughta pass this tip on to you, Bill," Weaver said evenly. "Just in case you or Matt have been kickin' any wild ideas around. Six men just rode out from town to give me a hand and I've got them staked out around the place. Now nobody can get in or out. So if either of you thinks he can play cute with me and thinks he can get away with it, take a tip from me and forget it. You haven't got a chance. I've got the house covered back and front and the same for the barn, so you aren't getting outta here and you aren't going anywhere, least ways not tonight."

Bill made no reply.

"I'm telling you this, Bill," Matt heard Weaver say, "because you and Matt and me have been friends for a long time, and I want to keep it that way. I don't want to see either one o' you wind up with a slug in your gut."

The lawman stepped back, turned on his heel and strode away. Slowly Bill closed the door. Slowly too he turned, backed against it as before and raised his eyes to meet Matt's.

"You heard him," he said. "Didn't you?"

"Yeah, sure," Matt said.

"What do you think? Think he's bluffing and trying to scare us into staying put?"

"No. Richie doesn't go in for bluffing. Any time he says anything, he means it, and you can count on it."

"Then for the second time we're right back where we started from and Pete's out there on his own."

"Yeah," Matt said a little heavily. "All we can do now is hope we're dead wrong and that Pete never had any idea of trying to see Ann before he cleared out."

"And that he's hightailed it," Bill added, "and that he's far away from here by now."

"Right."

Bill came back to the table and seated himself. For a time he sat quietly, grim-faced, staring off into empty space. Then he jerked his head around to Matt.

"Ma's sure doing a job of sleeping isn't she?"

Matt shrugged and said simply:

"She was tuckered out and needed the sleep."

"Never knew her to sleep this long though. Must be about twelve hours by now. Far back as I can remember, she was always the last one to turn in at night and the first one up in the morning. Used to make me wonder how she could always be so bright and chipper with so little sleep."

"She had something to do then, a family to raise and take care of. What's she got to do now 'cept to take care of herself?"

"Yeah," Bill conceded. "Guess that does make a difference."

"But if you'll feel better about it, go on upstairs and look in on her," Matt suggested. "Only be quiet about it so you don't wake her."

Bill nodded, got to his feet and left the room. Matt, slumped down again in his chair, heard him go up the stairs, heard his step on the landing above, and presently heard a door creak open. There was a brief silence, then he heard Bill's stop again overhead and shortly after that an even quicker step on the stairs. Matt twisted around and levelled a questioning look at Bill as he reentered the kitchen.

"Satisfied?" he asked.

Bill didn't answer. He came striding back to the table.

"She's all right, isn't she?" Matt asked him.

"I wouldn't know. But I sure hope so."

Matt sat up and looked hard at his brother.

"What's that supposed to mean?" he demanded.

"She isn't in her room, Matt. On top o' that, her bed's made up like it hasn't been slept in."

"Maybe she's sleeping in one of the other rooms," Matt suggested. "You shoulda looked in them, Bill. No reason for her to stay put in her own room when there are others even handier and just as comfortable. Maybe changing around does something for her. Maybe . . ."

"Matt, I looked in all of them," Bill said patiently. "But there wasn't any sign of her in any of them."

Matt stared at him for a long moment. Then he stood up. But after a bit some of the grimness went out of his face.

"Son of a gun," he said and he shook his head. "She sure put one over on us. I should have expected something like this outta her. She's always a thought and a step ahead of everybody else. While we talked about what we were gonna do and waited for it to get dark so we could go and do it, she got, and took the play right smack outta our hands. The son of a gun."

"Ya think she had the same idea we had that Pete might make a try to get to Ann?" Bill asked.

"It figures, Bill. And the way I see it, she must have decided that it would be better all the way 'round if she was the one to stop Pete, not us or even one of us, and that's where she's gone."

"I sure hope Pete doesn't act up with her."

"She'll handle him no matter what he does. The funny thing about it is that Richie was worried about us tryin' to give him the slip when all the time he should have been keepin' an eye on Ma."

"That's right. But how d'you suppose she got outta the house without us knowing she was going?" Bill wanted to know. "No back stairs here. Only one way out and that's through here even if she went out the front door instead of the back door. We still would have

80

seen and heard her."

"You wanna know something, Bill? I dunno how she did it and what's more I don't care. The point is she got out, so now all that I want is for her to come back. Like you I hope to hell she's all right and that she comes back soon so we'll know she's all right. And if she caught up with Pete and was able to drum some sense into him and got him to realize that Mexico is the safest bet for anyone on the dodge, swell. But right now I'm more concerned about Ma than I am about Pete. Sure I'd do anything to help him. But he brought this on himself, and if it comes to the worst and nobody can do anything for him, he'll hafta find some way to do it himself. Now how about that coffee you were talking about before? All of a sudden I've got a hankering for some. So what do you say?"

"I'll make it."

"I was kinda hoping you'd say that, Bill. Yours is still a mite better'n the kind I make. Oh, and make a whole potful, Bill. I don't aim to turn in till I know Ma's back. And I'm liable to need the coffee to keep me going."

The road on which Fred Snow's place fronted, a couple of miles townward from the Square-R, was gloomily dark and hushed. An arched gateway that was made of two wooden uprights and a curved stave that had once supported the canvas top of a prairie schooner, the very one in which Snow had made the overland haul from Illinois many years before, led to it. At the very top of the arch and squarely in the middle of it was a cracked and somewhat warped signboard on which Snow had painted the legend "Bar-S," his brand name. Aside from the fact that Snow was not much of a hand when it came to lettering, and that the result of his efforts was a very crude affair, time and the elements had conspired to fade the lettering. Now it was barely readable, then only in broad daylight when one stood directly in front of it and at no more than a foot or two away. For years Snow had threatened to repaint the sign. Somehow though, he had never got around to doing it. So it remained as it was.

Because the Bar-S was a comparatively small spread on which its owner did all the work, the barn was small and the house that stood a short distance beyond it was small too. It was a one story structure that had come into being as a one room cabin that had had a second added to it when Snow acquired a wife. The birth of their only child, their daughter Ann, had made it necessary to add still another room, this one for her. When Ann grew into young womanhood, Snow yielded to his wife's uncompromising insistence that every girl needed a parlor in which to entertain her friends. Ada Snow was a most practical mother. She wasn't thinking of Ann's girl friends but of the eligible young men who would call upon Ann and then take to courting her. And when the parlor was finished and furnished, Snow was pressured into giving the house a fresh coat of paint, something else that he had been threatening to do for a long time. Because Ada wasn't particularly concerned about the signboard, she did not press Snow to repaint it. It was a different story though where the house was concerned.

Ada was determined to see to it, subtly of course, that Ann made a "good" marriage. While she insisted loudly enough for everyone in and around Ryerton and even beyond it to hear that Ann alone would choose the man she wanted for her husband, she quickly showed that she had no intention of leaving everything in her inexperienced daughter's hands. Maintaining that whle she admired the ambitious and the industrious, she felt that it would be most unfair to disqualify a suitor simply because he hadn't had a hand in earning or accumulating a sizeable amount of money and property that he would soon inherit. Obviously she was thinking of the Rowans. She was all too aware of the fact that when old John Rowan who was ailing and who was said to be fading fast finally passed on, his sons' shares of what he had built and would leave behind him would be noteworthy. At first it was Pete Rowan who spent more time in the Snow parlor with Ann than any of the other young hopefuls. But then competition in the stalwart form of Bill Rowan appeared on the scene. Ada was delighted and encouraged their visits for as she saw it one Rowan was just as good as the other. She was not overly cordial to other eligible young men who while they showed promise for the future had little to offer at the time save themselves. Fortunately Ann liked both Pete and Bill. Hence there was no conflict of opinion between daughter and mother.

While few people, and they included Mary Rowan, approved of Ada Snow, practically everyone, and Mary was among them, approved wholeheartedly of sweet, pretty Ann.

A dozen feet or so from the arched gateway, a rifle-armed figure crouched behind the thin wall of brush that lined the road on Snow's side, raised up every now and then, peered over the top of the brush and swept the deserted roadway with anxious eyes. But there was no sign of anyone, no sound either, nothing but the whispered drone of the soft breeze that had whipped up with the approach of night. Once or twice the crouching figure twisted around and looked wonderingly at the house that was steeped in shadowy and at times distorting darkness. Either the Snows retired unusually early even for ranch people who were known to be dawn and sometimes pre-dawn risers, or they had gone off some-where to visit someone in town or at one of the other ranches. The watcher jerked around instantly when there was a sudden, muffled beat of hoofs somewhere off in the darkness beyond the gateway. It came closer shortly, then abruptly there was silence again. The half-raised up figure listened intently to the night sounds, trying to distinguish between them, seeking those that were man-made.

Suddenly a half-bent over figure, that of a man, appeared on the opposite side of the road, raced lightly across it and came panting up to the brush a step or two at the most from the spot from which he was being eyed. He parted the brush with his hands and stepped through it onto the Bar-S, stopped momentarily and raised his gaze to the darkened house and seemed to be staring at it, obviously disappointed. There was movement behind him. But before he could turn to meet it, a rifle muzzle dug into his back and he froze in his tracks.

TEN

"Stand where you are, Pete," the shadowy figure holding the rifle on him commanded.

He recognized the voice instantly.

"Ma!" he said in a hushed yet excited whisper over his shoulder and whirled around to her. "You nearly scared me outta my boots coming up behind me and throwin' down on me like that. But, gee, am I glad to see you, Ma! But . . . but what are you doing here?"

"Suppose you tell me what you are doing here?" Mary Rowan asked.

"I came to see somebody."

"That all you came for, Pete? Just to see her?"

"'Course."

"I don't think that just seeing her would have satisfied you."

Pete held his tongue.

"Sure you didn't have something more than that in mind?" Mary pressed him, peering hard at him. But in the darkness neither of them could see the other's face, only the other's figure. "Sure you didn't think you might be able to talk her into going away with you, that if you didn't succeed in that that you might try to make her go with you, even if you had to kidnap her?"

"Aw, come on now, Ma!" he protested. "What ever gave you such a crazy idea?"

"Anyone who will kill as cold bloodedly as you did, Pete, won't stop there. Somehow killing and kidnapping seem to go hand-in-hand, and since you've done one, why shouldn't you try the other? I knew you wouldn't go without trying to get to Ann. That's why

I'm here. To make sure you don't add to what you've done already. Why did you kill that jailer?"

"Old fool wouldn't let go o' me, Ma, and I guess I kinda lost my head."

"That was out-and-out murder, Pete, and I'm sure you know the penalty for murder." When he failed to answer, she asked: "What do you plan to do now?"

"Only one thing I can do. Get across the border into Mexico."

"And then?" she pressed him again, just as she had before.

"And then?" he repeated with a shrug. "Try to make a new life for myself down there."

"Hm," was her comment.

"The wedding still on?" he asked her.

"Yes, of course. That is, as far as I know it is."

"That's swell," he said bitterly. "Nice brother I've got. Cuts me out with my girl and now he's fixin' to marry her because he knows I can't stay around and stop him. On top o' that, it's on account of him that I have to hightail it to save my hide."

"That's a lie and you know it!" Mary flung back at him, her tone a little louder this time and sharper too, a sign of her irritation with him. "And to blame him or anyone else for that matter for what you've done is about as low as anything could be. I've told you this before, Pete Rowan, and I'll tell it to you again: Ann Snow was never your girl, except maybe in your own twisted mind. She liked you, yes, but she didn't love you. When Bill asked her if there was anything between you two, an understanding of some sort, and she said there wasn't anything at all, that you were just good friends, Bill felt that he had just as much right to see her as you did. So don't you ever tell me that again, that Bill cut you out with Ann. Because if you do, I'll tell you again that it's a lie."

"If he hadn'ta horned in on me nothing would have happened and I wouldn't be in this fix," he insisted grumblingly. "And instead of Ann marrying him, it'd be me she'd be marrying."

"For her sake and for her good, I'm glad she chose Bill instead of you," Mary retorted. "You'd have given her nothing but trouble and heartache and she doesn't need either of them. She's too fine a girl."

"All right, Ma," he said, holding up his hands. "I know where I stand with you. You're on Bill's side. So don't lets waste time arguing. That won't get anybody anywhere. If I have to play a lone hand, I'll play it. And whatever happens to me, well, you'll be rid of me and that oughta make you happy."

"Oh, Pete, Pete . . . what's happened to you? What's come over you?"

"You wouldn't know, would you? Well, never mind. It doesn't matter. Nothing does. I came here to see Ann and that's what I aim to do."

"Pete, if you really love her . . ."

"If I didn't, do you think I'd be here now when I coulda put distance between the law and me?" he demanded. "Ann's my girl, Ma, no matter what you or Bill say, and he isn't gonna take her away from me. I think you'd better go home now. It'll be better that way for you and me both."

"But not for Ann, or doesn't that matter to you?"

"I told you to go home, Ma."

"You aren't going to see Ann," Mary said quietly.

"I'm not, huh?"

"No. Turn around, Pete."

"Ma, I just told you something, didn't I?"

"And I told you something."

The rifle swept upward again, leveled and steadied with the muzzle pressed against Pete's chest.

"You're crowding me, Ma, and I don't like that.

You're gonna make me do something I don't want to do."

"You mean maybe kill me like you did that jailer? Turn around, Pete," she commanded and the rifle muzzle pressed even more firmly against his chest.

"For the last time, Ma, don't make me do something I don't want to do."

"Turn around," she repeated.

"First time I ever heard of a mother or even a stepmother takin' sides with one son against another. Children are supposed to be the same to their mother. But not with you, huh, Ma? Instead of asking me what's come over me, why don't you ask yourself what's come over you? You used to be fair and square with us when we were kids, treated us all alike. Now all of a sudden . . ."

She nudged him again with the rifle.

"I told you to turn around, Pete," she said evenly.

He turned slowly. Holding the rifle on him so that the muzzle continued to bore into his back, she shifted the rifle from her right hand to her left, reached for his gun with the right and lifted it out of his holster and quickly stepped back from him.

"Thanks for your help, Ma," he said bitterly over his shoulder. "If I ever had a chance of getting away, you sure fixed that for me. Without a gun I'm done for. But what's that to you, huh?"

Ignoring what he had said as completely as though she hadn't heard him at all, she said:

"We're going out to the road, Pete. Through the brush. We'll get my horse first, then we'll get yours."

"And then we'll head for town, right, so you can turn me over to the law?" he taunted her, again over his shoulder, hunching it up a bit though.

"No," she replied. "I'll probably regret this the rest of my life. But I'm going to see to it that you get safely away. But I'm not going to leave it to you to do it because I don't trust you. When I leave you, I'll want to be sure you've gone. I don't hold with lawlessness. But I'm willing to help you escape because I think your father would have wanted me to do what I could for you even though it means going against my principles. Walk ahead of me, Pete. But don't try any tricks. I can shoot. You know that. So don't tempt me. I might forget you're your father's son and shoot you down just as you did that jailer.''

"Where are we going after we get the horses?" he wanted to know of her.

"You'll find that out soon enough."

"Ya know something, Ma? I used to think I knew you. All of a sudden it comes to me that I don't know you at all. Can't figure you out."

"Don't try," she said curtly. "We're wasting time. Go on now."

Holding his own gun on him and maneuvering the rifle, muzzle downward, she brought up the stock and caught it under her left arm. When she poked him in the back with the Colt, he trudged forward to the brush, parted it with his hands and stepped through it, emerged in the darkened roadway and stood there mutely waiting for her.

It was Friday, two days later. Richie Weaver had just returned to the sheriff's office, leg and body sore from long hours spent in the saddle in a futile effort to find Pete Rowan. As he sank down into the armchair behind the old desk that stood in the middle of the office, the door opened. Weaver raised his tired eyes, stared a little, blinked and looked hard again at the cloaked and rifle-armed figure that was framed in the open doorway.

"Oh!" he said. "Mrs. Rowan!" With an effort and a grimace, the unspoken protest of tired, aching muscles, he hoisted himself up from his chair. "Come in, Ma'am. Come in."

She stepped inside and closed the door with one hand and held out the rifle to him with the other. He looked puzzled. His hesitant, uncertain reaction reflected it. As he came out from behind the desk, he gave her a wondering look, took the rifle from her, half-turned and laid it on the desk and turned again to her.

"You are the sheriff now, aren't you, Mr. Weaver?" she asked.

"That's right," he replied gravely and fingered the somewhat worn and tarnished star that was pinned to his shirtfront. He smiled a bit and said: "Just because I'm wearing the star doesn't mean I can't go on being Richie to you, Ma'am."

"I've come to surrender myself," she said simply.

"Huh? What . . . what've you don? You shoot somebody?"

Her thin little smile mirrored her weariness.

"No," she said. "As I understand it, the law says that anyone who aids a fugitive from the law makes his escape becomes an accessory and thereby renders himself, or in my case, herself, equally responsible for the crime committed with the one who actually committed it."

"You talking about your son, Pete, Ma'am?"

"Yes. I helped him escape to Mexico," Mary answered. "So I've come to surrender myself. I'm ready to take the consequences."

Weaver rubbed his sparsely bristled chin with his big right thumb.

"You just get back from there?" he asked.

"Yes."

"Then you must be pretty well tuckered out after all that riding," he suggested. "Going and coming, and chances are without much sleep."

90

"Yes," she admitted. "I am tired. But it doesn't matter. I'll probably get lots of time to rest."

"Judge McCreary know about this?"

"No, he doesn't. I haven't seen him. I came directly here."

Weaver moved alertly this time. He wheeled around and reached over the desk, lifted his armchair and turned with it in midair and set it down in front of her.

"I've gotta go out for a minute, Ma'am," he told her. "So supposing you set yourself down and rest till I get back? I won't be gone long."

"Thank you, Sheriff." She smiled and corrected herself. "Thank you, Richie. After two days in the saddle, the thought of sitting in a comfortable chair . . ."

"I know how you feel," he said, interrupting her, and went striding out, yanking the door shut after him.

It was five minutes later when the door opened again. But it wasn't Richie Weaver who came in. It was Judge McCreary. He came at once to Mary's side and bent over her and peered into her face.

"I've been terribly concerned about you, Mary," he said. "Are you all right?"

She managed a wan smile for him.

"Yes, of course I'm all right, Judge. A little tired. Otherwise I'm quite all right."

"Good."

"I'm sorry I caused you any worry."

"The fact that you're back and that you're none the worse for your long ride is all that matters now, Mary," he told her. Then with a smile he added: "I've been doing a bit of chasing about myself these past two days, back and forth to your place, hoping to learn that you'd returned, or that the boys might have had some word from you. While they assumed that you were with Pete, when you failed to return in a reasonable length of time, they began to worry, afraid that something might have happened to you. So they started to search for you."

"I couldn't very well let them know what I was up to for fear they would stop me and go themselves. And that wouldn't have served any good purpose. Pete wasn't in a very friendly frame of mind."

She looked around, behind her and in the direction of the door, then again at the judge.

"Looking for Richie?" he asked.

"Yes. Didn't he come back with you?"

"No. He went up to the stable to get my rig. I'm going to drive you home."

Her expression reflected her surprise.

"Isn't he going to, well, hold me, or whatever the legal term is?"

McCreary shook his head.

"No," he replied. "He's released you in my custody on my assurance that you'll be available whenever he may want you. That won't be for some weeks yet, when Judge Harmon who is currently making his circuit of the county reaches Ryerton and holds court. Then we'll have to appear before him."

"Oh," she said.

"However, I don't believe you have anything to worry about," McCreary continued. "Harmon will probably reprimand you for what you've done, and after warning you of the consequences if you again take liberties with the law, he'll put you on probation." He straightened up, walked to the door, opened it and poked his head out. Withdrawing it almost at once, he turned and said: "Come, Mary. Richie's coming with the rig."

He held the door wide, waited till she came to him, and taking her by the arm, led her outside to the curb. Moments later Richie Weaver drove up in the judge's buggy.

ELEVEN

While McCreary helped Mary mount the high step and
climb up, Weaver tied her horse to the tailgate of the
judge's buggy. Then McCreary hauled himself up too,
and wheezing a little from his efforts, took his place
next to Mary. He unwound the reins from around the
handbrake, looked at Weaver, and when the lanky
lawman nodded, released the brake, snapped the lines
and pulled away from the curb.

"Oh, hold it a minute, Judge!" Weaver called to him
and the stocky jurist pulled back on the reins, halting his
team.

Weaver wheeled around and dashed back into his
office. One of the judge's horses stood quietly and
patiently. The other one gave McCreary a questioning
look, and apparently impatient and eager to run,
snorted and pawed the trampled ground with his hoof.
Weaver reappeared at that moment with Mary's rifle,
stepped down into the rutted gutter and handed the
Winchester to the judge who took it and propped it up
against the seat between Mary and himself. Then with a
wordless nod to Weaver, he rode up the street.
Passersby glanced at the oncoming rig and its
occupants. Some of them showed no interest in either
Mary or McCreary and continued on their way. But
those who looked wonderingly at Mary, stopped, turned
their heads and followed the buggy with curious eyes. It
rumbled up the street to the corner, halted there briefly
to permit a heavily loaded farm wagon to cross in front
of it. Then it went on again and took the road that led to
the Rowan place.

Mary sat quietly with her eyes lowered and her hands clasped in her lap. She showed no desire to talk. Hence the wise old judge made no attempt to intrude upon her and her grim thoughts. He knew that when she felt the urge or the need to unburden herself she would do so without any prompting on his part. From time to time though he stole a guarded look at her. But mostly he looked straight ahead and kept his eyes fixed on the ruler-straight road that stretched away before them and lost itself in hazy distance. But he smiled a little to himself when he felt her turn to him and heard her say:

"I had quite a time of it with Pete."

"Oh?" he replied without looking at her. "Mean he wasn't particularly enthusiastic about having to take refuge in Mexico?"

"Having to live there seemed to bother him far more than simply taking refuge there. But as I pointed out to him, he hasn't any alternative."

"For his sake, Mary, and of course yours too, I hope he finds some measure of contentment there."

"I hope so too. But I'm afraid to be too hopeful."

"If he can find something to do, something to occupy his time and his thoughts . . ."

"I know. But I've been told it's an undeveloped country and that its people have a hard time of it eking out a living for themselves. So what chance would an outsider have, an intruder in their eyes? And that's what troubles me, Judge, that he won't find anything to do, he'll get bored and restless, and turn his eyes toward home. And when that happens, being restless and impulsive, he'll throw all caution to the winds and head for home."

"Hm," was McCreary's comment.

"I don't think I'll ever again have any peace of mind," Mary continued and the judge looked at her. "Something's happened to that boy and it frightens me.

He isn't the same. He doesn't think the way he used to and trying to reason with him is wasted effort."

"Mary, how close was he to John?"

"How close?" she repeated.

"Yes. I'm trying to find an explanation for the change that's come over the boy."

"Oh!" she said. "He wasn't any closer to his father than Matt and Bill were. In fact, they were even closer to John and he to them. Till Pete got to be, oh, fifteen or sixteen, he was closer to me than to anyone else, his father or his brothers. After that he seemed to veer off somewhat and appeared to be trying to follow his brothers' lead when they began to work with John and share his interests. But even then I don't think Pete ever got really close enough to his father to have John's death affect him so that it changed him. I would find that hard to believe."

"Maybe he felt more secure with his father alive?" the judge suggested. "Maybe having to stand on his own two feet and having to assume full and complete responsibility for himself, maybe it proved too much for him?"

"I wouldn't know how to answer that," Mary said. "All I know is that his brothers assumed their responsibilities quite willingly and quite capably too. And knowing them as I do, I'm sure they would have been only too glad to lend a hand if Pete had turned to them for help."

"Granted, Mary. But his pride may have made him hesitate. There are those who would rather die than ask for help from anyone. Even from their own, from their closest. To them it's a sign of weakness, of incapability, and what's even worse, a sign of . . . of inferiority, and they do everything they can to keep others from knowing what's gnawing away at them. So they suffer in silence and live bitter, resentful and lonely lives. Pete may well be one of those."

"What happens to them when their bitterness gets too much for them to bear? Does it boil over and cause them to explode in violence as Pete did?"

"I think it's logical to assume that some do."

"Hm," Mary said.

"Do you see much of Matt and Bill?" McCreary asked.

"Oh, yes! I see them practically daily. That is, I see Matt every day. He rides over to have breakfast with me. And Bill comes almost as often. Sometimes every day, sometimes every other day."

"And Pete? How much did you see of him?"

"In the beginning he came quite regularly. Sometimes with Bill, other times by himself."

"And then?"

"Then his visits began to fall off and finally they stopped altogether."

"Did the boys continue to see him?"

"In the beginning, yes, Bill more often than Matt. Then that stopped too."

"Why?" the judge wanted to know. "What happened?"

"It seems that Pete wasn't very cordial when Matt rode over to see him one day," Mary related.

"Had they quarreled?'"

Mary shook her head.

"No. I would have known about it if they had."

"What about Pete and Bill? What caused them to stop seeing each other?"

"When Bill noticed that Pete seemed to resent his calling upon Ann Snow, Bill stayed away from him. Bill felt that he was within his rights since there was no understanding between Pete and Ann, and that Pete had no right to take the attitude that Ann was his and his alone."

"That's when the trouble began."

"Yes."

"I'm glad you've been able to keep Matt and Bill close to you, Mary."

"You'll never know how glad I am. When the boys left the old house and moved into their own homes, I had prepared myself to see less and less of them as time went by. After all, I wasn't their mother, only their stepmother. So there weren't any blood ties to keep them close to me. The fact that they, Matt and Bill, have kept coming to see me as often as they have, they must feel that there is a bond between us. I'm terribly grateful for that, Judge. And I'm pleased too because they make me feel that inwardly they must look upon me as their mother and not at all like their stepmother."

He smiled at her. When he saw tears well up into her eyes, he leaned over and patted her hand, then he sat back again and drove on. Squaring even farther back in his seat he eased his hold on the reins and the horses promptly quickened their pace. Suddenly an oncoming buckboard loomed up some distance away. The judge eyed it interestedly. The distance between the two vehicles narrowed steadily.

"Looks like the Reverend Goslin coming, doesn't it?" McCreary asked when they were about a hundred feet or so apart. "I don't know of anyone else around here who wears a flat black hat like his."

"It is the Reverend," Mary said.

Both men slowed their horses as they neared each other, and halted them when they came abreast of each other.

"Hello, Reverend," the judge said pleasantly. "Isn't this somewhat off the beaten path for you?"

"No place is too remote for the word that I bring," Goslin answered, curtly though, and as he started to climb down from the buckboard Mary and McCreary

97

looked at each other, the latter arching his thick, shaggy eyebrows a bit. The reverend stepped up to the buggy on Mary's side and completely ignoring the judge, said sternly to her: "When I ordered you to appear daily in church so that you might pray and seek forgiveness for your failure to live up to your moral and religious responsibilities, you refused to obey. Do you need any further proof of the fruits of your neglect than your son who has wilfully disobeyed the Lord's commandment forbidding him to kill? Mary Rowan, before you commit your soul to eternal damnation, take advantage of this last opportunity to . . ."

"Judge," Mary said. "Please drive on."

McCreary jerked the reins and the interrupted and startled reverend had to step back hastily to avoid the grinding wheels of the rig as it rolled away. Goslin yelled something after them but it was lost upon them, the horses' thumping hoofs and the crunch of the buggy's wheels drowning out his voice.

"So you and Mr. Goslin have locked horns before this," the judge remarked in a musing tone. "And I thought I was the principal sinner in the reverend's flock. Apparently he doesn't think any more highly of you than he does of me."

"He hasn't permitted his opinion of me to interfere with his unsolicited willingness to marry me though," Mary answered.

McCreary leveled a wide-eyed, surprised look at her.

"Oh? So he's wants to marry you, does he?"

"Yes."

"Well, all I hope is that if you accept him, that you buy him a new pair of britches. I walked behind him the other day and I give you my word, Mary, I could see my reflection in the seat of his shiny pants."

"I thanked him for his most flattering offer," Mary related, "and left him standing in almost the same spot that we did just now."

"Somebody should tell him that moonlight and softly lighted parlors are the proper settings for proposals, not roadways and broad daylight. Does that mean what I hope it does, that you declined his offer?"

"Of course."

The judge breathed a deep sigh of relief.

"I must admit that for a moment there, you had me worried, Mary."

"Then I'm disappointed in you, Cornelius McCreary. After being married to a man like John Rowan, do you think I could accept a Jeremy Goslin as a fitting replacement?"

"No, 'course not," McCreary said hastily.

"Yet you thought I might."

"Not quite, Mary. But in a moment of weakness and loneliness anything or just about anything might have happened, and I was afraid he might have caught you at such a time when you weren't up to dealing with him. He's an overpowering individual. Not very many people are able to stand up to him and hold their own with him."

"Hm," she said.

"Am I forgiven?"

She smiled at him, and apparently satisfied with her unspoken answer, he turned his attention again to the horses and the road ahead. Then suddenly aware that the entrance to the Rowan place was almost at hand, the judge pulled back on the lines, slowing the horses to a mere trot. Presently they came up to the gateway. He wheeled them through it and onto the gentle incline that led to the ranch.

"Come to think of it, Mary," McCreary said, turning to her, "when we were still in town it never occurred to me to ask if you were hungry. That was pretty thoughtless of me."

"I wouldn't have wanted anything then," she replied. "So it's just as well that you didn't. Once I knew I wasn't going to be held, all I wanted to do was to go home."

He nodded and squared around again.

TWELVE

Haggard looking and unusually slow of movement, signs of little sleep and of long, uninterrupted hours in the saddle, Matt and Bill Rowan emerged from the barn and were trudging heavylegged down the ramp when Judge McCreary's buggy topped the upgrade. They stopped more or less mechanically and leveled their gaze at it.

"Hey, it's Ma!" Matt yelled, and Bill and he forgot their weariness and ran to meet the oncoming rig.

Matt's yell produced reaction in the bunkhouse too. The door was opened and a head, Tom Spence's, was poked out. He said something over his shoulder, flung the door back and came striding out. The door swung after him, and just as it was about to close someone else in the bunkhouse caught it, stayed it and opened it wide. Willis and Potter came hurrying out. They joined Spence and stood with him in front of the bunkhouse and looked on as Matt and Bill and the slowing buggy came together.

"For the love o' Mike, Ma!" they heard Matt pant as he skidded to a stop on Mary's side of the rig. Bill came crowding up alongside of him. "Where've you been all this time? You all right?"

"You sure had us worried, Ma," Bill told her. "'Course we had an idea where you'd gone. But when you didn't show back we didn't know what to make of it. Oh, hello, Judge. How are you today?"

McCreary smiled. But he made no response,

apparently unwilling to divert any attention from Mary and focus it upon himself.

"We covered just about every square foot o' ground in the county looking for you, Ma," Matt went on, still a little out of breath. "The boys and us."

"Yeah," Bill added, "and we nearly ran the legs off our horses doing it."

Spence came sauntering up to the buggy, gravely touched his hat to Mary, untied the jaded horse that he had provided for her and started to lead him up the ramp when Mary called to him. He stopped and looked back at her. When she held out the rifle to him, he left his horse standing on the ramp, retraced his steps to the rig, took the rifle, plodded back to his horse and led him into the barn.

"You look beat, Ma," Bill said. "Like you haven't had much sleep since you left here."

"More like she hasn't had any," Matt said. "Wanna tell you something, Missus Rowan. Once you get upstairs and you hit your bed, you're gonna stay put there. We'll take turns keeping you there till you get so caught up with yourself. You'll hate the sight of your bed."

"See how they bully me, Judge?" Mary said to McCreary. He smiled again, but as before he refused to voice any response. "I'm afraid you boys will have to help me get down. Somehow I don't think I can manage it myself."

Strong, eager arms reached for her when she stood up and she was lifted bodily out of the buggy.

"You can put me down now," she said.

"Nope," Matt said firmly. "We're taking you up to the house in style. Coming, Judge?"

"No, not this time, Matt," McCreary replied. "I've got to get back to town. But I'll drive out again tomorrow or the day after."

"Thank you, Judge," Mary said. "For everything."

"See that you get some rest," he answered.

"Leave that to us, Judge," Bill said. "We'll see to it."

McCreary squared back in the wide seat, wheeled his team and drove off. Tom Spence came trudging down the ramp, rejoined Willis and Potter and led the way back into the bunkhouse. With her arms curled around their necks, Matt and Bill carried Mary up the path and as they rounded the house to the back door, Bill asked:

"How come the judge brought you home, Ma? Or was he with you all the time?"

"No," Mary replied.

"Let's save all the talk for when we're inside," Matt suggested. "Got a lot o' questions I wanna ask too."

They carried Mary into the house and deposited her at the kitchen table in her own chair. She stood up once to shed her cloak. Bill held out his hand for it, took it from her, folded it carefully and laid it across the back of another chair as Mary sank down again.

"Want something, Ma?" Matt asked her, practically standing over her.

"Some hot coffee sounds awfully tempting."

"We'll all have some," Matt said.

"Yeah," Bill said. "Only I'll fix it. I don't want any more o' yours, Matt. Ma, when you feel up to it, I wish you'd show him how to make coffee. The kind he makes is awful. Tastes more like . . . like sheep dip than coffee."

Matt's ears reddened.

"You got a lot o' gall," he retorted. "You ever taste sheep dip?"

"Nope," Bill answered calmly, and a grin broke out over his face. "All you have to do is use your imagination when you look at a tub of sheep tip. If you can't imagine what anything that looks that bad must taste like . . .''

"Huh," Matt said scornfully. But he didn't pursue the matter. While Bill set about preparing a potful of coffee, Matt seated himself at the table, leaned toward Mary, smiled at her and asked: "Feel like talking, Ma, and telling us what happened? Or would you rather wait till after you've had a chance to catch up with yourself?"

"Can't you see how beat she is?" Bill protested, turning around. "So what's the point pushing her?"

"All right," Matt agreed. "Just wanna ask you one thing, Ma, and that's all. We're taking it for granted you found Pete. You did, didn't you?"

"Yes," she replied with a nod.

"He get away all right?"

Bill turned again to hear her answer.

"Yes, he got away safely."

"That's all I want to know for now," Matt said. "The rest can wait till later."

He arose and brought the sugar bowl, cups, saucers and spoons to the table, looked a little sheepishly at Mary and said:

"Haven't got anything to go with the coffee, Ma."

"Just the coffee will be fine."

He slumped down again in his chair with his gaze holding on Mary.

"I went down to the river with Pete," she said. "The Rio Grande. When he crossed over into Mexico and started inland, I started back."

There was no comment from either of her listeners.

"That day Judge McCreary was here," Mary said, "and I went upstairs to . . ."

"To rest," Matt said.

"Yes. Late that afternoon, when I was sitting at the window . . ."

"When you were supposed to be asleep in bed," Bill

interrupted wryly.

Mary smiled and said:

"Oh, I slept all right. Not in bed though. In your father's old rocker."

She told them quite simply what had decided her to do what she had done, told them too how Spence had helped her get away without anyone becoming aware of it.

"Why the old coot," Bill said as he sauntered back to the table and stood behind Mary's chair. "He never let on to us what he knew abut it. Fact is, Ma, when we told him you'd just upped and disappeared, he put on such a look of surprise . . ."

"He was following my instructions, Bill. So you mustn't feel put out with him."

"'Course you had no way of knowing it, Ma," Matt said, "but we had it figured same's you did that Pete would clear out without first making a try to see Ann. So we were gonna wait till it got dark, then we were gonna he for the Snow place and lay for Pete to show up there. Only you beat us to it by slipping away from here before Richie Weaver and some of his possemen showed up and kept us from doing anything."

"It's a good thing I got to Pete instead of you two. If you and Bill had got to him, there would have been trouble because he wasn't in the mood to be talked to or reasoned with. It's only when you're holding a gun on a man in Pete's frame of mind that he has to listen to what you've got to say whether he wants to hear it or not."

"That what happened with you and Pete?" Bill asked.

"Yes. That's how I was able to stop him from getting to Ann."

"Hate to disappoint you, Ma," Bill said, seating himself in the chair next to Matt's. "But even if you hadn't been there, he wouldn't have got to her."

"Oh?" Mary said. "You mean she wasn't at home? I thought as much because the house was dark, and since it was still rather early, too early even for early risers like Fred and Ada Snow to go to bed, I assumed they had gone off somewhere for the evening. But then I got to thinking that maybe that was what they wanted it to look like. Then maybe they hadn't gone anywhere, that they were at home, but because they feared that Pete might decide to pay them a visit that they wouldn't have welcomed, that they had darkened the house deliberately to mislead him."

"Ma, Weaver had the same idea 'bout what Pete might do that we had," Bill told her. "So he talked the Snows into moving into the hotel in town, for the time being that is, and brought in four men to stand guard over them. It didn't figure that Pete would have any way of finding out about that. But just in case he did, and he still made a try to get to Ann, Weaver was seeing to it that he couldn't get very far."

"Oh," Mary said.

"Good thing Pete didn't find out and that he didn't make a try," Matt commented. "Best he could've got out of it would've been a bellyful of lead. Richie's possemen wouldn't have given him a chance. They would have blasted him good."

"And how they would've," Bill added.

"How was he when you left him, Ma?" Matt asked.

"He was feeling pretty well broken up," Mary replied, "and sorry for himself too."

"He sorry for what he's done?" Matt wanted to know.

Mary shook her head.

"Hm," Matt said grim-faced. "That's what I was afraid of. I suppose the way Pete sees it, it was the jailer's own fault that Pete killed him."

Mary didn't answer.

"Well," Matt said, sitting back in his chair, "I'm not going to try to figure him out. I'm not smart enough for that. I'm glad he got away with a whole skin. I wouldn't have been willing to bet on him makig it, not with forty men out looking for him. So luck must've been riding with him. I hope it stays with him. How was he fixed, Ma? Have enough money on him?"

"He had some of his own and I gave him two hundred that I had brought with me."

"Hope it lasts him till he finds some way of making some more. Oh, before I forget this, Ma, you had a caller a while ago. Fact is, he was here yesterday and the day before that too. That Preacher Goslin."

"We ran into him on the road from town," Mary said.

"He tell you want he wanted?"

"He doesn't approve of me," Mary answered gravely. "As a matter of fact, he blames me for what's happened to Pete."

"Oh, yeah?"

"But despite his disapproval," Mary went on, "he is willing to marry me."

Matt stared at her. Bill did too. But then he laughed a little, pushed back from the table and got up and strode to the stove and returned with the coffeepot. Steam was belching from its spout. He filled the cups before each of them, reconsidered when he was about to put the pot on the table, returned it to the stove and came back to his chair. Matt was still staring at Mary. She smiled at him, leaned toward him and patted his big hand.

"Don't look so shocked, Matt," she said to him. "I haven't any intention of accepting Mr. Goslin's proposal. As a matter of fact, I've already told him so. I'm quite satisfied I shall never meet another man like your father. And since I don't like substitutes for the real thing, I can't possibly conceive of myself marrying

107

again."

Matt looked relieved. He reached for the sugar bowl and put it down in front of Mary.

"Ma," Bill said. "You never did get to telling us how the judge came to drive you home."

Simply she told them of her offer of surrender to Richie Weaver and of what came of it.

"So you'll have to go before Judge Harmon, huh?" Matt said musingly. Then suddenly with alarm, he added: "Hey, I hope old man McCreary knows what he's talking about."

"He usually does," Mary assured him. "And please don't refer to him again as old man McCreary. I don't like that."

"Sorry, Ma," Matt said apologetically. "I like the judge so you oughta know I didn't mean anything by that. Oh, you wanna take some sugar, Ma, and pass it?"

The sugar bowl made its way from one to the other and was then returned to its usual place in the middle of the table.

"Hey, that's pretty good coffee, Bill," Matt said after sipping his.

Bill grunted an indistinct response.

"I think it's very good coffee," Mary said.

"I make it the way you showed me," Bill answered.

"I do too," Matt said. "What gets me then is why'n blazes doesn't mine turn out like this?"

Bill caught Mary's eye and winked at her.

"Dunno, Matt," he said gravely. "'Less it's the water you use."

"The water?" Matt repeated.

"Yeah. Were do you draw it form, the sheep trough?"

Matt frowned and gave him a hard look.

"You know doggone well I don't run any sheep," he

retorted. "So I don't have a sheep trough. You wanna try again, funny feller?"

"Please," Mary said. "I don't feel up to that sort of thing just now. So if you don't mind." Matt and Bill drank their coffee in silence. "I've been thinking," she said and they lifted their eyes to her. "Something should be done about Pete's stock. I think you boys had better divide it and add it to your own. There's very little likelihood that he'll ever have any use for it."

There was no comment from either of her listeners.

"It might also be advisable," she went on, "for you two to buy him out, land, stock and everything else. You'll have to take that up with the judge and hear what he has to say about it."

Bill put down his half-drained cup.

"I don't think I can scare up enough cash to swing a deal that big," he said. He looked at Matt. "Can you? We started even, so I don't see how you can be any better fixed than I am."

Before Matt could answer, Mary said:

"Then tell the judge that I'll advance whatever cash you boys might need. I don't want you to leave yourselves short of working capital."

"How about leaving you short, Ma?" Bill asked. "That doesn't matter, huh?"

"Why don't we go talk to Joe Hazel at the bank?" Matt suggested. "Our credit oughta be good there."

"No," Mary said firmly. "I don't want you obligating yourselves to anyone. Your father didn't approve of borrowing. When he was building the Square-R, he went without things he could have put to good use many a time. The bank, Willis Caldwell was the head of it in those days, would have been glad to let him have just about any amount he might have wanted. But your father insisted upon waiting till he could pay for what he wanted. I have the money. More than I need, too. I

109

think your father arranged it that way purposely. I mean instead of willing you more than he did, he left most of his money to me. I like to think that he felt quite confident that I wouldn't refuse you any help when I considered your need reasonable and worthwhile. Since I approve of what you want the money for, you may have it and we'll say no more about it."

Matt and Bill looked at each other. Bill shrugged and smiled and sat back.

"All right, Ma," Matt said. "If that's the way you want it, that's the way it'll be. And thanks from both of us. Thanks a lot, too. We sure appreciate your help. But come to think of it, you've been doing for us for, well, for just about as far back as I can remember. We ever supposed to do something for you?"

She smiled at him and answered:

"Just by being what you are, both of you, decent and upright and . . . and industrious and worthy of the good name you bear, you're repaying me amply for anything I've ever done for you."

"What about Pete, Ma?" Bill asked her. "There any chance at all of him staying put in Mexico? I wouldn't want to give him something more to hold against me like taking his land and his stock without first asking if it's all right with him. Maybe he wouldn't want to sell out, ya know?"

"Bill, let's be practical and honest about this," Mary replied. "Pete's a fugitive from justice. As long as he stays away, he won't have any use or need for his land or his stock or for anything else. And if he returns . . ."

"Yeah?" Bill pressed her. "What then?"

"The law will take care of him," Mary went on simply, "and he won't have any use or need for anything then either."

"You're pretty sure he won't stay down in Mexico for long, huh, Ma?" Matt asked her.

"He'll be back here. How soon I don't know. But he will come back. And that worries me. Frightens me too. I have an uneasy feeling that one night, probably in the very middle of the night, there will be a knocking on the door. It'll be the judge come to tell me that Pete's returned and that he's been caught. This time they'll make sure that he doesn't escape. And you know as well as I do what they'll do to him." She sat hunched over her coffeecup, stared down into it. Suddenly she raised her head. "If you don't mind, I think I'll go upstairs now. And forgive me, Bill, for not drinking my coffee. But I don't think I want it now."

THIRTEEN

"She's all right, ya know that, Matt?" Bill stated after Mary had gone upstairs and they had heard her door close after her.

Matt didn't answer right away. He finished drinking his coffee, drained the cup of the very last drop, put it down and pushed it aside. Then he looked up and met his brother's eyes.

"Take you all these years to come to that conclusion?" he asked.

"No, 'course not," Bill said quickly. Then bristling indignantly, he retorted: "You know damned well I've always thought the world of Ma."

"You have? You've never let on, so I've never had any way of knowing. And I quit trying to read other people's minds a long, long time ago. So 'less they tell me, I never know what they're thinking."

"All right, all right;" Bill said rather grumpily. "So the way it came out wasn't the way I meant to say it. What I meant to say was that they don't come any better than her. That better?"

"Uh-huh. A lot better too, and I'll go along with you on that."

"Gee, thanks. Thanks a whole heap," Bill said dryly. He added sarcastically, "Knowing that you agree with me makes the whole world look rosy again."

Matt grinned. But he didn't say anything. Frowning and staring down into his coffeecup, Bill toyed with it for a moment or two, swishing about the bare spoonful that hugged the bottom of it, then he stopped abruptly, raised his eyes and said:

"Hey, being that Richie Weaver knows that Pete got

away so that there can't be any point going on looking for him, I wonder if he's called in his possemen?"

"Oh, he must've. Those who have jobs have to get back to them, and those who haven't, like that drunk Wiltse, must be anxious to get back to Campbell's so they don't lose their places at his bar."

"Then what's to stop us from riding out to our spread and seeing what's going on with them?"

"Nothing that I know of."

"Then why don't we?"

"I'm ready to go when you are."

"I'm ready now."

Together they pushed back from the table and got up. They took their gunbelts from the wall pegs on which they had hung them and buckled them on, clapped on their hats and headed for the door. As Bill followed Matt out of the house and half-turned to close the door, he asked, "Think we oughta leave word for Ma with one of the men so she'll know where we've gone?"

"Yeah, sure," Matt replied over his shoulder. "Besides, I want her to know I'll be back tonight to stay over. After what she said about layin' awake and listening for that knock that's liable to come any night and at any hour of the night, I'm kinda leery about leaving her here alone."

"I'm planning to come back here tonight too," Bill said, quickening his pace and stepping up alongside of Matt and rounding the house with him.

"You don't really have to, ya know, being that I'll be here. But if you wanna come back anyway, come ahead. I'd suggest that we take turns staying over. But a couple o' days more and you'll be married and you'll have a wife who'll expect you to stay home with her. Being that I haven't any ties, it'll be a lot easier for me to do the staying over."

It was late evening when they returned to the silent,

old house. Mary was sitting at the kitchen table, dozing, with her head bowed and nodding. The ceiling lamp was lit. But the wick had been turned downlos so that a thin circle of light shone down upon the table, leaving the rest of the room on every side of the table in shadows. Mary's head bobbed and jerked and she sat upright when she heard the door close after Matt, Bill having entered ahead of him.

"Oh," she said when she saw them, and added with a wry smile, "I must be getting old. Dozing off is a sure sign of advancing age." They hung up their hats and belts, and as they came sauntering up to the table, Mary said: "I didn't know you were coming back tonight."

"Ya mean Willis didn't tell you?" Matt asked as he drew out a chair, turned it around and straddled it.

"He told me where you boys had gone, and he may have said you were planning to return tonight. If he did, and he probably did because he rarely forgets anything, I must have forgotten. So don't blame him."

Bill seated himself in his usual chair, looked around the room and then up at the ceiling lamp, stood up and with a slight twist of his wrist brightened the light. When he looked at Mary, she nodded, and he sat down again.

"Have you boys had your supper?" she asked.

"Uh-huh," Bill said.

Mary turned her gaze on Matt.

"Matt?" she asked. "Have you eaten?"

"Yeah, sure, Ma," he replied. "How about you?"

"I had my supper at about seven." There was a brief silence. Then Mary said: "Maybe it's selfish of me, but I'm glad you boys came back tonight. When I came downstairs at sundown and found you'd gone, I felt terribly low and depressed. The house was dark and so quiet, it gave me an uneasy turn. But now that you're here, I feel ever so much better."

"We're staying over tonight, Ma," Matt told her. "And I'll be here every night from tonight on."

"Oh, that won't be necessary," Mary assured him. "Really, Matt. Ordinarily I don't mind being here alone. It was just tonight that I felt the way I did. You have a lot to do working your place and I don't want to make things any more difficult for you than they are. You need your rest and you won't get it riding back and forth. So I don't want you coming back here after your day's work. I want you to stay home."

"Nope," Matt said firmly. "I'm gonna do just as I said. And I'll still get my rest. Don't you worry none about that. As for you living here alone, I didn't like the idea right from the start. I went along with it because you and Bill and . . . and Pete too, were all so blamed sure it would work out fine. But ya see it hasn't and for my dough it can't and won't. So for the time being I'll stay here nights and I don't want any arguments about it." He grinned a little and said: "I'm a stubborn old cuss and once I make up my mind to something, that's it, and nothing can change it."

Mary smiled at him and said:

"All right, Matt. I won't argue with you."

"Better not. 'Cause if you do, I'm liable to get real mad. And when that happens, I get so downright mean and ornery, I even scare the pants off me."

She smiled again. But wisely, instead of continuing the discussion, she turned to Bill and said to him, "There's something I want to know of you, Bill."

"Is it about Sunday?"

"Yes."

"Dunno what I can tell you, Ma. I haven't seen Ann in . . . lemme see now . . . three, no, four days."

"Why haven't you see her?"

"Oh, with one thing and another, there just wasn't enough time for everything."

115

"Hm," Mary said.

"That's a fact, Ma. First, with Weaver and his posse-men riding herd on us and keeping us penned up in here, there wasn't anything I could do but stay put. Then when you went off and didn't show back, we broke outta here even though Weaver put up a squawked and tried to stop us, we went looking for you. 'Course we wouldn't tell him that we were looking for you and not for Pete. So he had a couple of his men trail us. Only we split up and went off in different directions and that threw them off altogether. That went on from sunup to sundown. When we got back at the end of each day, we were so beat, we just about made it up to the house and upstairs to bed. Then bright and early the next morning we'd hit the saddle and off we'd go again."

"Go on."

Bill hesitated for a moment, then he fairly blurted out, "To tell you the truth, Ma, I just didn't feel up to seeing her."

"You mean you didn't have the courage to face her, don't you, Bill?"

Crimson glowed in his cheeks, then his whole face, his ears too, reddened.

"You still love her and you still want to marry her, don't you?" Mary pressed him.

"'Course I do, Ma."

"Then why don't you go to see her?"

"I'm thinking about doing that tomorrow."

"Tomorrow?" Mary repeated. "Why tomorrow? What the matter with tonight?"

"Nothing, 'cept that it's kinda late now," Bill answered and the flush that had begun to fade deepened again over his face. "Must be after nine by now. I know that isn't late for us. But it is for them, for Ann's folks. I wouldn't want to have to wake them and get them down on me before I even get into the family."

"Hm," Mary said again, a sign that she wasn't overly impressed with his rather lame and somewhat faltered explanation.

"Take me a good fifteen minutes to get to their place," Bill continued. "And if they're still staying at the hotel and haven't moved back yet, it'd be still another fifteen minutes before I could make it to town. So I think it'll be better all around if I wait till tomorrow."

"Pete was willing to risk his neck to see Ann," Mary said quietly.

Pretending that he hadn't heard her, Bill mused aloud, "I wonder how Ann's folks feel about this business with Pete?"

"It isn't Pete whom Ann has promised to marry," Mary pointed out. "It's you, and you haven't done anything to be ashamed of."

Matt, sitting between them, shuttled his gaze from one to the other, but he held his tongue and made no attempt to inject himself in the discussion. A couple of times when Bill, seeking his support, looked at him, Matt averted his eyes or met Bill's gaze stonily and almost expressionlessly.

"Bill," Mary said. "Did I ever tell you of the time your father proposed to me?"

Bill thought about it for a moment. Then with a shake of his head, he answered:

"No, I don't think so."

"Well, I had come to Ryerton some two or three months before to teach school and . . ."

She stopped when Matt suddenly chuckled and leveled a wondering look at him.

"When Pop told me he was going to marry the school teacher," he related, "I made up my mind to run away. From what I had heard about school teachers, they were all pretty much alike, crotchety old spinsters who hated

117

everybody, 'specially kids, and boys even more than girls. But I decided I'd have a look at you before I started running. When Pop brought you here, I couldn't believe that anyone as sweet looking and with such a nice way about her could hate anybody. Then that night you fixed supper for all of us and you baked the biggest and swellest chocolate cake I'd ever seen or tasted, and you had us, all right, right where you wanted us too, right smack in the palm of your hand."

He laughed a little, and Mary smiled, and Bill forgot himself for the moment and smiled a bit too. But when Mary resumed her story of John Rowan's proposal, he was grave-faced again.

"I had met your father several times and I liked him," she continued. "Liked him well enough to go buggy riding with him a couple of times too, and no girl in my time did that unless she really liked the man. Anyway, I lived in town, in Mrs. Hamby's boarding house. Late one night, oh, long after I had gone to bed and the town was as dark and hushed as a graveyard, the idea that he wanted to marry me suddenly came to your father. Once he had made up his mind to do something, he wouldn't allow anything, time or anything else, to interfere. He came riding into town at a full gallop, rode his horse up on the wooden walkand probably would have ridden him up the steps to the veranda too save for the fact that he knew the steps were splintered and rotted. He made such a commotion, he didn't just wake Mrs. Hamby and me and the other boarders. He woke the whole town and if Mrs. Hamby hadn't hurried to unlock the front door for him, I think he would have battered it down with his bare hands. People sprang from their beds, got their guns and ran to their windows and peered out expecting to see the street filled with screaming Indians.

"That was twenty years ago. But I've never forgotten

it. In fact, I remember it as clearly as though it had just happened yesterday.'' She smiled a little wistfully. "I remember sitting on the top step of the stairway in my nightdress with a blanket thrown around me, listening to your father pleading his case to me while in the background I could hear the others grumbling. Wait a minute, Bill. I haven't finished. You want to hear the rest, don't you?''

Bill was within a step of the door. He snatched his hat off the wall peg and slapped it on his head, took his gun-belt from the peg too, slung it over his arm, and with his hand on the doorknob, looked back at Mary.

"'Fraid I haven't got time tonight, Ma,'' he said, opening the door. "Wanna see Ann.''

In another moment he was gone. The door swung behind him and slammed shut.

Matt grinned and said: "You sure lighted a fire under him, Ma.'' He climbed to his feet, yawned and stretched mightily, rising up on his toes at the height of his stretch. He swung his chair around and pushed it in close to the table. "Me for bed,'' he announced. "How about you, Ma? You're gonna turn in now too, aren't you?''

"I should say not!''

"Huh?''

"I wouldn't think of going to bed now.''

"Mean you're gonna wait up till Bill gets back?''

"Of course.''

He yawned again and covered his mouth with the back of his hand.

"Bill and Ann planning to be married in church, or are they gonna have the judge do the honors?'' he asked.

"In church,'' Mary said at once. "Every girl looks forward to being married in church. I don't think Ann's an exception to that.''

"Yeah, but how Goslin likes the idea of marrying a Rowan, being that he doesn't think too highly of us, might make them change their plans, huh?"

"I don't think he'll let his personal feelings enter into it. After all, the Snows are members of his congregation, and he can't very well overlook that. Not without offending them and probably losing them too as he has so many others."

"Uh-huh," Matt said. "Night, Ma."

"Good night, Matt."

Nearing the top of the stairs, he stopped and called: "Hope you don't have to wait up all night."

It was after midnight when Bill returned. He found Mary, head bowed and nodding, with a blanket draped around her, sitting at the table with soft, turned down lamplight playing over her and highlighting her hair. He stood in the doorway for a long moment, looking at her and shaking his head. He stepped inside, quietly closed the door, hung up his hat and belt, tiptoed across the room to Mary's side and bent over her.

"Ma," he said.

There was no response. He listened to her gentle, even breathing. He touched her arm.

"Ma," he said again.

This time she stirred, sighed and slowly raised her head. He knelt down in front of her.

"Ma."

Her lids fluttered and finally opened.

"Oh!" she said. "Bill." She pushed off the blanket, freeing her arms, leaned toward him and took his face in her hands. "Tell me."

"It's still on for Sunday, Ma," he told her with a happy smile.

"I was sure it would be, Bill," she answered, and the warm smile that she gave him matched his. "I'm so glad for you, Bill." She drew him to her and kissed him. "So very glad."

FOURTEEN

There was far, far more to wife-taking, Bill Rowan quickly discovered than merely acquiring a female companion to share his name, home and life with him. Marriage brought about drastic changes in his way of life and in his daily routine too, changes that left him continually at odds with the clock. Because Ann maintained that it was a wife's duty to see to it that her husband was well fed, arguing that no man could be expected to do his day's work properly unless he was well fed, she insisted upon preparing his breakfast and then sitting down to it with him. So Bill's usual five-thirty to six rising was changed to seven o'clock, a more reasonable getting up hour for Ann. So it was eight and more often than not far after eight by the time Bill left the house. Then having to return home for their midday meal, another hour-long affair, and again at five to wash and change for supper meant the loss of even more time.

It meant also that he was forced to forego his weekday visits to the old house. There simply wasn't enough time for everything. But because Mary was aware that Ann was filling his cup of happiness to its fullest, she refused to resent the girl. The fact that he was so happy was all that mattered to her. Then the day he learned that Ann was bearing his child, he brought the exciting news to Mary as fast as his horse could cover the distance between his place and the family home. Flinging himself off his lathered and panting horse, he bounded up the path, rounded the house in full, breathless stride and burst in upon Mary with a yell of "Hey, Ma, you're gonna be a grandma!"

Because Ann had many girl friends who like herself had recently become brides, who with their husbands took to driving out to visit the newlywed Rowans, courtesy and Ann's desire to continue those friendships demanded that Bill and she return those visits. Some evenings were pretty largely taken up with their social obligations.

Because Mary was daily louder in her insistence that it wasn't at all necessary for Matt to stay over nights, he finally yielded and abandoned the ride back to the old house when it got too dark for him to do any more work on his own place. But he continued to be her most constant visitor. Despite his report to her that his coffee making was steadily improving and that his hot cakes were beginning to look and taste more and more like hers, it was such a sinful waste, he claimed, for him to fix things for himself because there was always so much left over. So he continued breakfasting with her. Of course she was delighted and she fussed a great deal. Matt, shaking his head, would gravely remonstrate with her and tell her she was spoiling him. So Mary fussed even more, and Matt loved it even though he loudly insisted that it had to stop.

The boys had always taken it for granted that Sunday dinner was meant to be a family affair, and they continued to come regularly, with Ann perched between them on the wide seat of Bill's newly purchased buckboard. They came bright and early too, and usually long before Mary was ready for them. They sniffed loudly as they trooped into the kitchen and wondered aloud to each other as to what it could be that Mary was cooking that smelled so overpoweringly good. Of course she refused to tell them and shooed them out, that is, the boys. Ann wasn't included in that, and while the dinner

122

cooked and simmered, Mary and she sat down for their woman's talk.

When Bill got a minute or so alone with Mary, he told her, "Ya know, Ma, we're supposed to go over to the Snows once a week for supper. Of late though, Ann's taken to looking for excuses so we wouldn't have to go. Then when she's got one, she scribbles a note to her mother and I send one of the boys over with it. But when Sunday comes around, there's never any question about us coming here. I think Ann looks forward to it just about as much as I do. She's always dressed and ready and waiting for me to get done so we can get out the buckboard and go pick up Matt and haul him over here with us."

"I'm flattered, Bill."

"I think I know why Ann's always so ready to come here, Ma," he went on. "When Mrs. Snow knows we're coming, she waits for us at the front door, and the minute we pull up there, she starts talking and firing questions at Ann and she never lets up once all the time we're there. We can never get away from there soon enough, and all the way home Ann sits alongside o' me looking down at her hands and never saying a word. Ma, you don't go to work on Ann the way her mother does. You don't keep telling her that everything she does, she does wrong. Ann's a pretty smart girl, and what she doesn't know now she'll learn. And if it takes time, so what? We've got a whole lifetime ahead of us, so she can take all the time she wants learning."

"Of course," Mary agreed.

"But every day she seems to pick up something, and on her own too, Ma, and for my dough she's doing all right. Fact is, Ma, I'm doggone proud of her."

"You should be, Bill. She's a fine girl. As for Mrs. Snow, I'm sure she means well."

"That's what I keep telling Ann. Only sometimes,

'specially right after we've been to see her folks, I'm not so sure that I believe what I'm saying."

"Oh, Bill!"

"Ma, I'll bet you anything you like that Ann feels a heck of a lot freer with you than she does with her own mother and so she probably opens up to you a lot more than she does with Mrs. Snow."

One Sunday morning Matt came alone, and Mary eyed him wonderingly and a little concernedly too.

"Figured I'd come over by myself today instead of waiting around for Bill and Ann to come by and pick me up," he told her. "They went to that shindig over at Molly Wharton's last night, ya know, and probably got home so late and so beat, they'll sleep later today."

"Of course," Mary said and she sounded relieved. Her eyes brightened too as the look of concern went out of them. "I'd forgotten about Molly's party. Now that you've reminded me of it, either Ann or Bill told me they were going when they were here last Sunday."

Matt grinned and said, "Must've been Ann who told you. She's the one who makes the dates. Not Bill. He goes along because he has to."

"You were invited to the party too, weren't you? Why didn't you go?"

"Ma, the invite said to bring a girl. So without one I'd have been outta place, like a fish outta water. Now who could I have brought being that just about every girl in town who'd have been worth taking is spoken for? So I stayed home."

"We're going to do something about that. Turn your head, Matt."

"I said, turn your head."

He obeyed, and when she said, "All right. You can turn around now," he did and gave her an odd look.

"Your hair needs cutting," she told him. "But I don't mean for you to do it. There's a new barber in

124

town and I'm told he does good work. Have him cut it for you."

He grunted.

She fingered the lapel of his suit coat.

"These your best clothes?" she asked.

"S'matter with them?"

"Don't always answer a question with a question. I asked you, are these your best clothes?"

"Yeah. But why? Why do you ask?"

"I didn't like this suit on you the very first time I saw it. It didn't do a thing for you then and it does even less for you now. And since you've broadened out and put on some weight . . ."

"I know it's a mite snug on me, Ma. But that's your fault even more'n it's mine. You keep fattening me up like you're fixin' to ship me to market and pretty soon the only thing that'll fit me will be a tent."

Disregarding his remark, she said, "Tomorrow morning, the first thing mind you, I want you to ride in to town and get your hair cut. Then I want you to ask Mr. Weber to show you some of the nice new things for men he's just gotten in. I took particular notice of them yesterday when I was in the Emporium and I liked what I saw very much."

"Why's it have to be tomorrow? Where am I gonna go that I have to get myself so duded up and in such a rush?" he wanted to know. "Tomorrow's Monday, Ma, and it's a bad day for me to take off. Always seems to be more to do on Monday than on any other day."

"Aren't you at all concerned with your appearance?"

"Yeah, sure, but . . ."

"A man's appearance is the first thing a girl notices. And the first impression is always so important."

"Oho, so that's it, huh? A girl, huh? Shoulda known you were working up to something. Who is she, Ma?"

"What I said goes for any girl."

"Yeah, I suppose it does. Only you aren't making all this to-do about just any girl. There's one girl in particular that you're thinking about and don't tell me there isn't. You aren't fooling me. I know you from way back. Now who is she?"

"I ran into Mabel Hawkins yesterday and . . ."

"Oh, no, Ma!"

"Mabel isn't the girl I'm talking about."

"That's a relief, believe me. She's been looking for her third husband ever since I can remember, same as she's been forty since the first time I saw her. And that was a long, long time ago, when I was just a sprout, about knee-high to a flat rock. Bet she'll still be forty and still looking for another husband forty years from now. When she finally cashes in and they plant her, they can put something like this on her marker: 'Here lies Mabel Hawkins who sure did and who never got any older even though everybody else did,' or maybe, 'Here lies Mabel Hawkins, the only woman who was able to hold back time. When it finally broke free, it was too much for her, and it killed her.' "

"That's awful, Matt," Mary said severely. "Really now."

"Yeah, I suppose it is," he admitted. "'Specially since she never did anything to me. I'm still waiting to hear about that girl, Ma."

"She's Mabel's niece. She's here on a visit. Fact is, she just arrived in town yesterday."

"That doesn't tell me much."

"Her name is Martha. Martha Davies. She's very pretty," Mary continued, "and very nice. You'll like her, Matt."

"Uh-huh. But how about her liking me, or doesn't that matter?"

"I think she'll like you too," Mary replied. "Get your hair cut and buy yourself some new clothes tomorrow so that you'll look your best."

"And then?"

"And then you'll call on her."

"Huh, call on her?" he repeated. He looked aghast. "You mean just like that? Without being invited? Ma, I haven't got time for sparkin' a girl right now. I've still got a lot o' things to do around the house, little things, I know, but they take time, and the only chance I get to do them is at night, when it's too dark to work outside. How about some evening next week?"

"And meanwhile let some other young man get to her before you do? Oh, no, Matt Rowan! You're going to call on her tomorrow evening."

He grinned a little.

"I am?"

"Yes. As a matter of fact, she'll be expecting you."

"She will, huh?"

"At seven o'clock, and you'll be on time too. It's a woman's privilege to be late, not a man's."

"How . . . how do you know she'll be expecting me?"

Head tilted back, he eyed her obliquely.

"How do I know?" Mary repeated.

"Yeah, how?"

She smiled up at him.

"I know," she answered calmly, "because I arranged it with her for then. I suggested that since she doesn't know any of the young people around here, that you would be delighted to introduce her to them."

"Go on," he commanded.

"However," she continued, "if you're smart, you won't do anything of the kind. You'll take her riding in the buckboard and keep her to yourself."

"Ma, you son of a gun!"

"I'll have Spence or one of the other men go over the buckboard tomorrow morning and have it bright and shiny for you. You can come for it before you go calling on Martha. That will give me a chance to look you over and see what a haircut and some new clothes do for you?"

"You know something, Mary Rowan?"

"What?"

"You're a doggone schemer, that's what!"

She smiled again and said, "Every woman is, more or less. Seriously though, Matt, in this life when you want something, and you want it bad enough, you've got to go after it. No one's going to give it to you. But going after it isn't always enough. That's only part of it."

"I'm listening, Ma. What's the rest?"

"You've got to plan how you're going after what you want. You've got to know in advance what you're going to do. Then if there's competition, and there usually is for anything that's worthwhile, you've got to anticipate what your competitors will do and plan to offset it. Depend upon it, Matt, you'll have competition for Martha Davies. You know what will happen once word gets about that there's a new girl in town and that she's pretty and unattached. There will be a swarm of eligible young men and some not so eligible beating a path to her aunt's door. But you'll have an advantage over them and it will be up to you to make the most of it.

Matt Rowan met Martha Davies as Mary had arranged for him to do, and the two young people were so attracted to each other that a whirlwind courtship that lasted exactly two weeks resulted in an announced "understanding" that was followed some days later by a scheduling of their marriage for the last Sunday in the month.

It was shortly before the wedding was due to take place that Judge McCreary called to see Mary.

128

"I've been intending to drive out here for about a week," the stocky, white-haired jurist told her as he seated himself opposite her at the kitchen table. "But something's come up each time just as I was about to set out and each time I've had to postpone it. This morning though I made up my mind that nothing would be permitted to delay me any longer. So here I am." He moved in closer to the table and leaned over it on his folded arms. "How are you, Mary, and how are the boys?"

"We're quite well, thank you, Judge. The boys are busy running their properties and I manage to occupy myself too. Bill's happily married and is soon to become a father, and as you've probably heard, Matt's to be married next Sunday."

He nodded and said, "I hear Matt's bride-to-be is a very pretty girl."

"Yes, she is, and she's just as sweet as she is pretty," Mary said. "Matt brought her here Sunday to dinner. It gave us a chance to get better acquainted. You see, I'd met her before. She's very nice and I'm delighted for Matt."

McCreary nodded again.

"What about Pete, Mary?"

"What about him?"

"He still in Mexico?"

"As far as I know, Judge."

"Mean you haven't heard any word from him?"

"Nothing," she said simply.

McCreary looked surprised. However his only comment was, "Too bad it had to happen. To spoil things for you, I mean."

"Yes," Mary said heavily. "But as I told you once before, Judge, I'm glad it didn't happen while John was still alive. He was a proud man and terribly proud of his good name. This would have been a cruel blow to him.

129

So I'm grateful that he wasn't here to know of it. As for Pete, even if he should find contentment in Mexico, I'd still want to know about him fairly often, that he's well and that he's getting used to the new life he's had to adapt himself to and so on."

"But if you don't hear from him . . . ?"

"There's a way of finding out what I want to know."

"You mean by that that someone will have to go into Mexico and seek him out?"

"Yes," Mary said. "But it won't be one of the boys who will go. That would be much too risky."

"Then you'll probably have to be the one to go."

Mary nodded and said, "Yes, I guess it will be up to me."

"How will you know where to look for him?"

"I'll probably have to begin my search at the point where I saw him step ashore in Mexico."

McCreary pushed back from the table and got to his feet.

"Whatever became of Judge Harmon?" Mary asked. "I thought I would have to appear before him when he reached Ryerton?"

"You mean I never told you that I had talked with him and that he accepted my assurance that you wouldn't again do anything contrary to the law?"

"No, Judge," she answered with a grave little smile. "However, I'm glad to know that my little brush with the law has turned out all right. And since I wouldn't want to betray your confidence in me, I want to assure you that I won't ever again step outside the law."

She arose and followed him when he walked to the door.

FIFTEEN

t was six months later.

Coming from opposite directions toward the stream hat divided their properties, Matt and Bill spotted each other from a short distance off, waved and came on at a omewhat quickened pace. Pulling up almost at the very dge of the stream on their respective sides of it, they dismounted and turned their horses loose to drink of the clear, cold water. Then sauntering off, they came together shortly in the middle of the planked crossway hat spanned the stream.

"Hi," they said as one.

"Looked for you yesterday," Bill said. "Stopped by he house too. But there wasn't any sign of you, or of Martha either."

"Martha wanted some things for the house," Matt explained. "So I drove her into town to get them. You know, some more curtains and stuff."

"I went through one o' those sprucin'-up-the-house deals with Ann a couple o' weeks ago, and did I get myself into something! Had to tag along with her because she wanted my opinion on what she was gonna buy. Now I ask you, Matt, what does the average man, and that's all I am, know about curtains an' bedspreads and stuff like that? But I played it real smart. Least ways I thought I was."

"Yeah? What'd you do?"

"I watched her real close, and whatever she kinda lingered over and kept looking at, I made a to-do over, and that's what she bought. So what happened? She told me she was real pleased with me. Said I had good taste, a heap better'n most men. So the next time she needs something she's gonna leave it to me to go and pick it out for her. Now how do you like that?''

Matt grinned and said:

"Can't win, huh?"

"And how, you can't."

"Did you want something when you came looking for me?"

"Yeah. Found we'd run outta wire. So I rode over to your place to borrow some, just enough to do me till the stuff I ordered gets delivered."

"Aw, that's too bad, Bill."

"What is?"

"You having to ride over for nothing. I've got enough wire to do me for the next five years. Only we wanted to get it out of the way because we don't use much of it, so the other day we moved it outta the barn and into the tool shed."

Bill grinned and countered with:

"Well, where do you think I got it from?"

Matt who had turned his head for a glance at his horse—the animal had finished drinking and now stood backed off a dozen feet or so from the water and was eyeing Bill's horse with interest—shot a quick look at Bill, saw the grin on the latter's face and answered, "Why, you weasel . . . from the tool shed of course!"

"Hey, you ketch on quick."

"Yeah, don't I though? Look, don't bother to return the wire you took. Like I said, I've got enough of it, in fact a lot more than I know what to do with."

"Thanks."

"How are things otherwise? Ann doing all right?"

Bill grinned again.

"Getting rounder every day."

"And getting nearer her time every day too."

"'Course."

"Bill, you haven't seen Ma this week, have you?"

"Nope. Only get to see her on Sundays. Why do you ask? Something bothering you?"

"I think there is."

"Like what?"

"She isn't the same. Or maybe I should have said she isn't herself. All of a sudden she's gotten awfully quiet. She smiles a little, but kinda said—like I think, and doesn't say very much. You know how she always wants to be told everything that goes on with us. But when I'm telling her something she seems to be listening only I can see a kinda far away look in her eyes and I know damned well she hasn't heard a thing I've said."

"Hm," Bill said thoughtfully. "That doesn't sound so good."

"It's got me worried, ya know that?"

"You think it's Pete?"

"It figures, doesn't it, because what else could she have to worry about?"

"How long's it now, six months?"

"Just about."

"Well, what are we gonna do about it?"

"We," Matt replied. "We aren't gonna do anything about it."

"Ya mean just let things ride?"

"Nope. That isn't what I mean at all. You're out of it. You aren't gonna do a thing. Whatever has to be done, I'll do."

"What's the idea?"

"Bill, you haven't got any right to, well, risk your life. You've got others to think of ahead of yourself. You've got a baby coming, and it wouldn't be fair to Ann or to the baby either, 'specially when . . ."

"Hold it right there, Matt," Bill said, interrupting him. "I'm in on this just as much as you are. I'm Pete's brother same as you are, remember? So if there's anything to be done, we'll do it together and don't you go thinking otherwise. Ya hear?''

Matt grunted, and Bill who wasn't certain as to what the grunt was supposed to mean, said, "I'm telling you, Matt.''

"Suppose we wait till we come to where we have to do something before we go arguing about who's gonna do it?''

"You aren't just saying that, are you, to throw me off while you go off on your own hook and do it?''

"Hey,'' Matt protested. "You oughta know me better than that.''

"I oughta,'' Bill retorted. "But all of a sudden I'm not so sure that I do.''

"I'm not planning to do anything till after I've talked it over with you. Satisfied?''

"That a promise?''

"Yeah, it's a promise if that's what you want.''

"And meantime we'll go on as we have?''

"Uh-huh,'' Matt said.

"Doesn't make sense to me because the longer we put off doing what we know we're gonna have to do, the worse it'll be. For Ma, I mean. I think we oughta do something now.''

"Tell you what, Bill. Ride over to see Ma some time this afternoon and have a look at her for yourself.''

"All right, I'll do that.''

"Then stop by my place on your way home and lemme know what you think.''

"Right.''

They parted, returned to their horses and climbed up on them. Then just as they were about to wheel away from each other and ride off, Bill twisted around in the saddle and called across the stream, "Hey, Matt! How about you bringing Martha over to the house one night soon?''

"S'matter with you and Ann making it over to see us instead?" Matt wanted to know. "We've been over to your place three times now to your once over to see us. So how about it?"

"It's all right with me and I'm sure it'll be all right with Ann too. What nights are you people free?"

"Any night you wanna come we'll be home."

"Huh?" Bill gave his older brother a puzzled look. "Mean you're home every night? Mean you don't ever go anywhere?"

"Sure we do, that is, once in a while. But no more'n we have to. Think we're a couple o' sprouts like you and Ann? We're too old to go gallivantin' around like you two do."

Bill stared at him.

"Gallivantin' around, huh?" he said. He snorted scornfully and retorted, "All right, Grandpa. Thanks for the invite. Tell Grandma we'll make it one night real soon. And we won't stay too late. Wouldn't want you two old timers to lose any of precious sleep on account o' two night owls like us."

They rode of then.

"Hey, Grandpa!" Matt heard Bill yell, and he pulled up and looked back. Bill had reined in and had swung his horse about halfway around. "Watch it going home, ya hear? Hang on to that cayuse so he doesn't go spilling you and bustin' some o' your old bones!"

Matt didn't answer. He grinned broadly though, nudged his horse with his knees and loped away.

The rhythmic drum of an approaching horse's hoofs carried in the waning afternoon's air and brought Martha Rowan to the front door. She poked her head out and peered wonderingly in the direction of the oncoming horseman. When he came closer, Martha recognized him, and turning her head, said something over her shoulder. She opened the door wider and stood astride the threshold strip and waited. Presently Bill Rowan came clattering up to the cottage, pulled up in front of Martha, smiled and touched his hat to her, and slacking a bit in the saddle, said, "Hello, Martha. How are you?"

She smiled and responded, "Fine, thank you, Bill. And you?"

"Oh, pretty good for a . . . a sprout." He grinned and asked, "That elderly gent of yours somewhere around?"

She laughed lightly and made room for Matt who crowded up next to her in the open doorway.

"Hello, Bill. Climb down and visit."

"Can't, Matt. I've lost most of the afternoon and I've got things to do before supper. So I wanna get on home soon's I can."

Matt nodded understandingly and asked, "Ya see Ma?"

"Yeah, sure, and like you said, Matt, something's worrying her, all right. Only you don't have to be a mind reader to know what that something is."

"Pete, huh?"

"'Course. I don't think we oughta wait any longer. Ma looks bad to me. Like she doesn't eat or sleep any more."

"It's all because she doesn't know what's going on with him. So she imagines all kinds of things and all of them bad."

"You'd think he'd have managed somehow to get some word to her in all this time. He must know she'll be worrying herself sick over him. 'Less it's a case of outta sight, outta mind with him."

"Who knows what anything is with him? I don't. How soon can you be ready to go?"

"Soon's I get things set for Ann so she'll be taken care of while I'm away. Can't leave her alone, ya know, not in the condition she's in. I'll see if I can get Molly Wharton or that Emma Haines to stay with her. Either one o' them would be good company for her."

"If we could get going some time tomorrow . . ."

"Don't know why we shouldn't be able to."

"All right, Bill. I'll be here waiting for you. Soon's you get here, we'll head out."

Bill nodded, and straightening up in the saddle, said, "So long."

Matt and Martha chorused their response and Bill loped away.

Slowly Martha stepped back inside. Stepping back too, Matt closed the door and turned after Martha. She stood at the table, her back turned to him. He came up behind her.

"I haven't any alternative, Martha," he told her. "I owe Ma a lot, more than I can ever pay back, and since this means so much to her, I've got to do it for her. You can understand that, can't you?"

"Have you any idea how long you'll be gone?"

"No," he replied. "But I don't think it should take us too long. Once we know where Pete crossed the river, picking up his trail from there on shouldn't be too much of a chore. There aren't that many Americans down there and those that are there must stand out like sore thumbs."

"I've got to get things started for supper."

"That can wait a bit."

He stayed her by curling his big hands around her arms, turned her around and brought her into his arms and imprisoned her in them. She buried her face in his shirt and he pressed his lips into her hair. When she finally raised her head, he kissed her. She whispered, "Of course you must do this for Ma. I know that. It's just that I, well, I guess I resent anyone who takes you away from me for any length of time. Go when you're ready and come back as quickly as you can."

When he released her, she turned and started for the kitchen. He followed her for a moment with his eyes. Then he turned on his heel and left the house. He stood in front of it briefly, obviously debating something with himself. Then he strode briskly down to the barn and disappeared inside. Minutes later iron-shod hoofs thumped on the wooden flooring and presently Matt rode out astride his horse. He walked his horse up to the cottage, halted him at the door and called, "Martha!"

He waited patiently. The door opened shortly and Martha, wiping her hands on a dish towel, appeared in the doorway and lifted her eyes to him.

"How long before supper?" he asked her.

"About an hour," she answered.

"Gonna ride over to Ma's," he told her. "But I'll be back before the hour's up."

"Matt, will you do something for me, please?"

"'Course," he said and he eyed her wonderingly.

"Will you ride over to Bill's place too and tell Ann that I'll stay with her?"

He smiled a little, nodded and said:

"Sure," swung his horse around and rode off.

Mary Rowan was coming downstairs from her room when she heard the back door open and heard someone come in.

"Ma?"

She recognized the voice at once and answered, "Coming, Matt." When she entered the kitchen she found him standing at the table. "I didn't expect to see you today. Martha all right?"

"Yeah, sure. She's fine."

"Oh," she said and there was relief in her voice.

"Ma, whereabouts did Pete cross over into Mexico?"

His question surprised her and her expression reflected it.

"Why . . . why you ask, Matt?"

"Because Bill and I are gonna go looking for him. Then you can quit worrying because you haven't heard from him and so can we."

"I'm sorry, Matt," she said evenly. "But I can't tell you."

He smiled a little wryly.

"Can't, Ma, or do you mean you can, but won't?"

"Very well then, won't," she said, as evenly as before. "When the times comes for something to be done, I'll do it."

"Even though Mexico's no place for a woman to be travelin' through and all by herself too, and even though we could make it there and back again in half the time it'd take you to do it?"

"Yes," she said. "Even though."

"All right, Ma," he said with a lift of his shoulders.

"Matt, I want you to promise me that neither you nor Bill will go after Pete."

"Ma, you know I'd do anything in the world for you. That goes for Bill too. But this is one time when we have to go against you and what you want. If you won't tell us and make it easier for us to pick up Pete's trail, we'll have to go it blind . . . and trust to luck." He walked to the door, opened it, looked back and said, "Bye, Ma."

It was probably half an hour later when Mary heard the thump of horses' hoofs on the ramp that led to the barn and the carrying murmur of men's voices. She hurried out. Just as she reached the end of the path, Tom Spence emerged from the barn and started down the ramp.

"Tom," she called and he stopped and looked in her

direction. When she beckoned, he came trudging over to her. "Tom, I'm going to Mexico tonight. I want you to come with me."

He nodded and said:

"Just lemme know when you're ready to go, Ma'am."

"Thank you, Tom."

She turned on her heel and retraced her steps up the path, rounded the house to the rear and went inside.

SIXTEEN

Stripped to the waist, Bill Rowan had just started to wash up for supper when Ann poked her head in on him and said, "Forgot to tell you, Bill, that we had a visitor this afternoon."

"Oh?" he said as he began to soap himself. "Your mother?"

She laughed lightly and answered, "No, it wasn't mother. It was Reverend Goslin."

"What'd he want?"

"He's rather put out with us because we haven't attended Sunday services since we were married. He feels it's up to me to see to it that we remedy our ways."

Bill made no comment.

"But that wasn't his principal reason for calling," Ann went on.

Bill's head jerked around to her.

"Didn't think it was," he said, and he wiped some soap away from his mouth with the back of his hand. "Didn't think he'd ride this far out just for that. Any time he's come out after the Rowans it's been for money. He hasn't had any luck with us yet. But he keeps trying. Probably figures if he keeps after us long enough, he'll wear us down and get us to come through for him.

"He said he knows the Rowans can afford a generous contribution to the church," Ann continued, "so he intends to keep after you people till he gets it."

"Guess he doesn't realize it but he got my contribution the day we got married. "Twenty-five bucks," Bill told her. "If he thinks he's gonna get more outta me, he's got another think coming. I told you what happened between him and Pop, didn't I?"

"Yes."

"Well, if he hadn'ta been so . . . so blamed demanding with Pop and then threatening him, chances are he would have got himself a nice contribution and we would have become regular members of his church. But Pop wasn't the kind to take any nasty talk from anybody, not even from a preacher, and Goslin would up getting himself booted out. So he lost us same as he's lost so many others. But he doesn't seem to learn anything from those experiences. He goes right on loud mouthing people and antagonizing them. One o' these days he'll wind up with no congregation at all, and then I wonder who he'll blame it on? Not on himself though. That you can bet on. It'll be everybody else's fault. And he'll probably ring in the devil and blame some of it on him."

Ann smiled and withdrew her head.

Martha Rowan was in the kitchen when she heard the front door open. Half-turning her head, she called, "Matt, that you?"

"Yeah, honey. Made it back home even sooner than I expected."

The door closed. Martha heard Matt's heavy step as he crossed the dining room. Then as he appeared in the doorway between the two rooms, he sniffed loudly.

"Hm," he said. "Something smells awfully good around here."

She smiled at him and said, "Hope it tastes as good as it smells."

"It can't miss," he assured her. "Anything that smells that good has to taste good too."

He came up behind her, nuzzled her neck and walked

on to the back door to hang his hat and belt on the hooks that jutted out from the upper panel of the door.

"Did you stop at Bill's place?" she asked.

"Uh-huh," he replied. "Told Ann you'd stay with her and she was real pleased."

He came sauntering back from the door.

"We had a caller while you were out," Martha told him as she stirred something in a deep pot.

"That so?"

"It wasn't Aunt Mabel this time. It was the minister."

"Huh," Matt said. "What'd he want as though I don't know."

"Mean you were expecting him to call?"

"Yes and no."

"He scolded me because we haven't attended church since he married us," Martha related.

"Don't tell me that that was all he came out here for."

"Well, no. He wants a contribution to the church from us."

Matt frowned a bit.

"He got it the day he married us. Bill told me he gave Goslin twenty-five bucks for marryin' Ann and him. So I gave Goslin the same. But if he doesn't think that was enough, he can send it back."

"He won't like you if you take that attitude with him."

"I'll try to bear up under it. Anyway, all I care about is having you like me."

"Oh, I do," she said very gravely. "In fact, I like you a lot."

He grinned at her and said, "Thanks. Then if I want to make any contributions to anyone, I'll make 'em to you. But come to think of it, you don't need anything from me. You've got your own."

She lifted puzzled eyes to him.

"My own?" she repeated.

"Uh-huh," he said nodding. "Ya see, the day after we got married, I had the judge put everything I have in both our names instead of in just my name. So everything, the land, the house, the stock, the money in the bank, it's just as much yours as it is mine."

"Wasn't that taking an awful chance with me?"

"You took an even bigger chance with me. The way I see it, the girl takes a heck of a bigger chance with the man than he does with her."

"I wasn't taking a chance with you, Matt," she told him soberly. "I knew all along what I'd be getting if I married you and I was quite happy about it. I haven't had any regrets yet and I don't think I ever will."

He cupped her face in his big hand and kissed her on the lips.

"You wanna know something? I was crazy about you the very first time I saw you. Will you think there's something wrong with me if I tell you that I get crazier about you every doggone day?"

"No," she replied and her eyes shone. "If there's anything wrong with you, there is with me too. And I think're both afflicted with the same disease. I hope we never recover from it."

With their arms around each other, she gave as much to the kiss that followed as he did. When she drew back her head, she smiled at him and said, "Supper should be ready in a matter of minutes. Want to get cleaned up while I set the table?"

Mary Rowan, her deeply thoughtful expression a reflection of the disturbing thoughts she was thinking, was startled by a sudden heavy-handed knock on the back door. Quickly she went to the door, opened it and stepped back with it.

"Oh!" she said when she found herself confronted by Jeremy Goslin. "Reverend Goslin!"

He gave her a curt nod, stepped inside and passed her, turned and took off his hat and handed it to her, walked to the table and drew out a chair and seated himself in it. He sat stiffly, almost on the edge of the chair. She came to the table and sat down opposite him. He squirmed back a little and said, "I am more concerned about you than ever, Mary Rowan."

He rested his left arm on the table. The cuff of his shirtsleeve was frayed. She raised her eyes to his shirtcollar. It was badly frayed too.

"You should be concerned about yourself," she told him severely. "Are these things the best you have to wear?" She didn't wait for him to answer, but went on, "A man must make some kind of an appearance if he expects to command attention and respect. How can you expect anyone to respect you if you look so shabby? I want you to see Mr. Weber at the Emporium and tell him he's to fit you out from top to bottom and to send me the bill. And the sooner you do that, the better. Now don't argue with me. Just do as I've told you. If you head for town now, you can catch Mr. Weber before he closes. That's if you hurry."

She was on her feet in almost the same instant, went swiftly to the door and waited there for him with the door wide open and his hat in her hand.

"A new hat's to be included, Reverend," she told him as he came forward to the door. She pushed his hat into his hands. "This one has seen better days and it's high time you discarded it. Go on now. Hurry."

She didn't usher him out. She actually pushed him out, and when he had gone, she closed the door and lay back against it. She shook her head and murmured, "Oh, that man! That poor misguided man! And he's concerned about me!"

Then she straightened up and as she came away from the door, a look of apprehension clouded her face.

"I hope I haven't done the wrong thing," she thought to herself. "I hope this doesn't encourage him and give him ideas. Well, if it does, I'll have to set him straight and right off too."

She put him out of her mind as she set about getting together the foodstuffs that Spence and she would need when they rode southward that night.

It was night, nearly ten o'clock. Martha Rowan had turned in about half an hour before that. Matt was sitting at the table in the lamplit dining room of their cottage with his account books opened before him. As he hunched over the ledger . . .

"Matt!"

He raised his head.

"Yeah, honey?"

"What are you doing?"

"Just going over my books," he answered. "Seeing how things stand."

"Must you do that now?"

He smiled a little to himself.

"Been puttin' it off for weeks now. Then I thought I might get to it today. But I kinda ran outta time what with one thing and another and . . ."

"Can't it keep till you get back?"

"Yeah, guess so."

"Then come to bed. It's late and you must be tired."

"All right, honey," he told her. He closed the books, got up and took them into the kitchen and put them away on the top shelf of the cupboard. Returning to the dining room, he said, "Gonna lock up and put out the light and be right with you."

146

He walked to the front door a little stiffly. It had been a long day and he was tired. But it was a tiredness that did not weight him down. Every day he could see the expanding results of his labors and the satisfaction that he derived from them was more than worth his efforts. Just as he was about to bolt the door, he heard hoofbeats somewhere off in the night. Quickly he went to the window, parted the full, billowy curtain that hung over it and peered out. But the darkness that lay over the range was blanketing and veiling and he couldn't see anything. Closing the curtain he retraced his steps to the door. As he came up to it, the hoofbeats swelled and came closer. He opened the door and poked his head out.

Shadowy, unrecognizable horsemen, six, eight, ten of them, pounded up into view and swept on toward the cottage, drummed up to it in a flurry of hoofbeats and pulled up in front of it. Matt eyed them wonderingly. A lean, rangy man dismounted, rather stiffly Matt thought, holding his gaze on him, and trudged up to the door. It was Richie Weaver. Matt opened the door wider and stood straddling the threshold strip, silhouetted by the lamplight behind him.

"Sorry to bother this time o' night, Matt," Weaver began. "But it's for your own good. Word's come to me that Pete is headed this way, and we aim to get him. We don't want anybody doing anything they shouldn't, like heading him off or warning him off. I've told Bill the same thing, and just to make sure he does what I've told him and that Pete doesn't get to him, I've left some men staked out around his place. I aim to do the same thing here. Now how about it?"

"All right, Richie," Matt answered heavily. "I won't do anything. I'll stay put here."

"Thanks, Matt. That'll make it easier on all of us. Ya know, when a man runs wild, it doesn't pay to try to help him. All it does is give him more opportunity to run and more of a chance to add to what he's done already. Oh, nearly forgot this, Matt. Did you know your mother was planning to head south tonight to look Pete up?''

Matt looked hard at him.

"Judging by the look on your face," Weaver said, "I don't think you did. We stopped her in time, her and that old timer o' hers, that Tom Spence, and turned them around and made them go back home. I've got men staked out around there too. Night, Matt.''

"Night," Matt answered mechanically.

He backed inside and closed the door. There was movement just beyond him and he raised his eyes to it. Martha, with a blanket wrapped around her and the bottom of her nightdress fluttering about her slippered feet, stood at the table looking at him.

"I'm sorry, Matt," she said gently. "No matter what he is or what he's done, he's still your brother. So I know what this must mean to you."

He smiled faintly.

"I'm sorry too," he said. "Sorry for him, but a lot sorrier for Ma because none of this has been her doing. They'll get him and that'll be the end of it for him. But it won't be for her. As long as she lives she'll never forget him or what he's done and it'll stay with her, eating away at her, till she dies.''

SEVENTEEN

Sitting at the dining room window, with the curtain parted and the panels pushed aside so that he might have an unobstructed view, grim-faced Matt Rowan watched the thinning darkness disolve into nothingness and saw the dawn break. He watched the shadows lift, saw a faint, flickering light appear on the horizon, and with the birth of the new day, he climbed to his feet and stretched himself. He trudged wearily to the front door, opened it and stepped outside. There was an uncomfortable chill in the air, a dampishness too, but he knew that when the sun broke through it would burn them away. His eyes ranged about seeking a sign of the possemen whom Weaver had posted around the place. When he failed to spot any, he knew that it was over. The fact that the possemen had been withdrawn could mean only one thing, that the law had finally reclaimed Pete Rowan.

Slowly, with his normally squared shoulders rounded and sloping and his jaw muscles twitching, Matt turned and plodded back inside. He slumped down int his chair with his chin resting on his chest, his open-fingered hands hanging limply at his sides and his long legs thrust out before him. This would be it for Pete, he told himself. The end. This time Pete would be propery guarded. There would be no opportunity for escape. The law would demand and receive the right to exact the extreme penalty and Pete would die on the gallows.

Matt was still wallowing in his bitter thoughts when Bill rode up to the cottage. Matt admitted him with an admonishing "Sh" and told him in a low voice that was hardly more than a loud whisper, "Don't wanna wake Martha. She didn't get to sleep till after four. She wouldn't go back to bed after Richie left and insisted on staying up and talking with me, thinking it would be good for me to have somebody to talk to. Finally though, she couldn't keep her eyes open and dozed off in her chair. She was sleeping like a baby when I lifted her in my arms and carried her inside to bed and covered her up."

"Went through just about the same thing with Ann," Bill whispered. "You haven't heard anything, have you?"

"Nothing 'cept that shooting last night."

"It didn't last very long though, did it? No more'n, oh, about a minute. Maybe not that long. Wonder who did the shooting and what happened?"

Matt's shoulders lifted.

"Coulda been Pete or it coulda been one of Weaver's possemen," he replied. "Doing the shooting, I mean."

"Uh-huh. And if Weaver's bunch are as trigger happy as they were last time, and if it was one o' them who cut loose with is rifle, he coulda been blasting away at a shadow," Bill suggested. "That could mean that Pete mighta got away again."

"I don't think so, Bill. I don't think Richie would've pulled is men off if Pete had got away."

"No, I don't suppose so," Bill conceded. "I'll bet Ma's a wreck wondering and worrying and not knowing. She was worried enough about him before because she hadn't heard from him. Now . . ."

"I think we oughta ride over to Ma's and see what's doing over there."

"Yeah. Wanna go now?"

"Sure."

"You're not gonna wake Martha and tell her you're going, are you?"

"Nope. Gonna leave a note for her so she won't have to wonder when she wakes up and finds me gone."

"That's what I did," Bill whispered. "Left a note pinned to my pillow so that Ann'll spot it right off the moment she opens her eyes."

"Uh-huh."

"How long do you figure you'll be?"

"Oh, only a couple o' minutes. Why?"

"Suppose I go saddle up for you? That'll save some time."

"All right. You go do that, Bill. I oughta be out front by the time you bring my horse around."

Bill opened the door quiety and eased himself out. Matt closed the door after him noiselessly and tiptoed into the kitchen to tear a blank sheet of paper out of one of his account books.

The clock that stood on the scarf-draped mantle in the shadowy, heavily curtained and shade drawn closed-off parlor in the old Rowan ranch house began to boom. The deep throated, awing sound carried into the adjoining room, the kitchen, where Mary, Matt and Bill were seated at the table. An empty coffeecup that had been filled and drained three times stood in front of each of them. All three were troubled looking, Mary thoughtfully silent, the boys grimly silent. Mary sat motionlessly, staring down into her cup, with her clasped hands perched on the very edge of the table. Matt and Bill sat a little hunched over on their elbows and toyed with their cups. Only Bill showed any reaction to the clock's booming. Head tilted a bit, he was counting, and when the booming stopped, he grunted and without looking up, said, "Nine o'clock."

"Yeah," Matt said.

Bill squared back in his chair.

151

"That damned clock," he said. "When I was a kid and I'd hear it at night, it used to give me the willies. Took me the longest time to get used to it."

Matt pushed back from the table.

"I wish we'd hear something from somebody," he said, "so we'd know what's happened. This sitting and and waiting and not knowing anything . . ."

"I've been hoping the judge'd drive out," Bill said.

"Depend upon it," Mary said, raising her eyes to him. "If anyone has anything to tell us it will be the judge. And I'm quite sure he'll be here just as soon as he can get away from wherever he is."

"Go another cup o' coffee, Ma?" Matt asked her.

"No, thank you, Matt."

"Bill?" Matt asked, turning to him.

Before Bill could answer, Mary added, "The judge knows how anxious we are to know what has happened to Pete. He won't keep us waiting any longer than he has to."

"How about it, Bill?" Matt asked him. "S'more coffee?"

"No. Skip me this time. I've had three cups already, and I can feel it splashing around in my belly."

Cup in hand, Matt stood up. There were footsteps outside. Someone came up to the door and knocked. Before anyone could answer, the door opened and a pudgy, white-haired, hat-in-hand figure appeared in the doorway. It was Judge McCreary.

"Morning," he said.

There was a chorused reponse. The door closed behind McCreary. He hung his hat on an unoccupied wall peg beyond the two that held Matt's and Bill's things. Matt put down his cup and started to round the table to pull out a chair for the judge. But Bill, already up on his feet, stopped him by saying, "Never mind, Matt. I've got it."

McCreary came plodding across the room. He looked tired and older than ever. The lines in his face were deeper than usual. There were dark circles under his eyes, and the corners of his mouth drooped a little. Bill held the chair for him. The judge grunted his thanks and eased himself down in it. Matt and Bill returned to their chairs and looked at McCreary who moved in closer to the table.

"Want some coffee, Judge?" Matt asked him.

McCreary shook his head.

"We were hoping you'd come out, Judge," Bill said, "and let us know what's going on."

McCreary grunted again and said, "Pete will be brought to trial tomorrow morning."

"Then that shooting we heard last night," Matt said quickly. "He came outta that all right, huh?"

"I didn't hear it. However, I know there was some gunfire. Pete was untouched," the judge said. "When I was informed that he had returned, I wasn't particularly surprised. You were so certain, Mary, that he wouldn't stay in Mexico very long, I suppose your belief communicated itself to me. When I learned that he had been captured and that he was being taken back to Rawlins, I followed him there. I was permitted to talk briefly with him. He hopes to see you today, Mary."

"I'll be there," she said simply.

"What'd he have to say for himself?" Matt wanted to know. "What made him come back when he must've known what was waiting for him if he was caught? Even he must've known that his luck would run out on him if he kept pressing it."

McCreary didn't answer right away. Hence the Rowan's eyes held on him wonderingly.

"I think I had better tell you everything," he said finally. "It will be brought out at the trial anyway. Besides, it may answer whatever questions you may

153

have in mind to ask me." The judge paused, then he went on again. "When I confronted Pete with what I had been told, he didn't deny it, any of it. As a matter of fact, he even told me things that the prosecutor doesn't know. I'm sure he doesn't because they aren't included in the indictment already drawn up to be presented tomorrow when the court convenes."

"Tell us everything," Mary said. "Don't feel that you must spare us. We're his family. So we should know everything. Even the very worst."

"Very well, Mary. To begin with, in a small town some distance inland from the Rio Grande, Pete met and was attracted to the wife of the local cantina owner. Saloonkeeper, that is. Apparently, the woman, Pete judged her to be about thirty or thirty-five, must have been attracted to him too. Anyway, in the course of their affair, and Pete didn't deny that they had been intimate, when they were keeping a rendezvous somewhere under cover of darkness, the woman's husband appeared. There was a fight and Pete claims the man died accidentally when he stumbled and fell and impaled himself on his own knife. Deciding that that was no place for him, Pete fled for his life. A lynch mob, you know, is the same there as it is here."

Thee was no comment from anyone, only a "Hm" that could have meant just about anything from Matt.

"In another small town, Pete met and took a fancy to the pretty daughter of the bootmaker," McCreary related. "The girl was very young, probably no more than about sixteen. Pete admits he should have known that nothing good could have come of an affair with her. But he was infatuated with her and he permitted it to run the length that such sordid things usually run. When he decided that he had had enough and sought to break it off and move on, the girl ran in tears to her father. That night the father and a dozen or more male elatives of the girl, all of them armed in one way or nother, appeared at the inn where Pete was staying and lemanded that he marry the girl or suffer the onsequences."

"What . . . what happened?" Bill wanted to know. 'Did he marry the girl?"

"Yes, he married her," McCreary replied. "It was he simplest and the safest way out of the mess for Pete, o he took it. But that very night, when his bride lay isleep beside him, he arise, slipped out and fled. That vas the last he ever saw or heard of her. He laughed quite a bit when he related it to me, obviously thought it vas very funny. As though it were more of a boyish prank or a mere escapade than the serious matter that it eally was."

As before no one had any comment to offer.

"In another town, this one fairly close to the river, Pete got into a card game with a man whom Pete claims cheated him. When the man drew a knife and brandished it menacingly, Pete went for his gun and shot him. Killed him." Mary caught her breath. "The nan had friends in the place and Pete had to fight his way out. He was pursued all the way to the river. In the course of the pursuit, he shot two of the men who were after him. He got across the river quite safely though."

"Really had himself a time down there, didn't he?" Matt commented grimly.

"Then, suddenly possessed of an overpowering longing for home," the judge continued, "he cast aside all caution and headed northward. In a small border town, a place called Paradise, a deputy sheriff who apparently thought he recognized Pete from the description given of him in the wanted circulars that the Rawlins authorities had sent out to all law enforcement officers, sought to detain Pete. When he tried to disarm Pete . . ."

He paused deliberately.

"Pete pulled his gun on him," Matt said, "and sho
him."

"Yes," McCreary said heavily. "Pete killed him."

"Oh, my God!" Mary said and covered her face with
her hands.

"There's still another killing that has been laid to
Pete," the judge told them. "One of Weaver's
possemen, a newcomer to Ryerton, a man named Glenn
Harder. Pete shot him just as the posse closed in on him
and overpowered him. That must have been, in fact that
was the shooting you heard last night, Matt. Harder was
taken back to town. He died of his wounds at dawn."

"Ya say Pete only wants to see Ma?" Matt asked.

McCreary nodded.

"That's right. And she's the only who will be
permitted to see him."

Mary stood up.

"Excuse me, please," she said and all eyes held on
her. "I want to get my cloak. Bill, will you go down to
the bunkhouse, please, and have Spence hitch up the
buckboard? Oh, and tell him I want him to drive me to
Rawlins."

"Never mind, Bill," Matt said, stopping Bill who had
pushed back and who was about to get up from his
chair. "I'll hitch up and I'll drive Ma."

As Bill sank down again and Matt got up, McCreary
said, "As I told you a moment ago, Matt, you won't be
allowed to see Pete."

"That's all right," Matt said over his shoulder as he
headed for the door. "I don't have to see him.
Wouldn't know what to say to him if I could see him.
Long as Ma gets to see him." He took his hat from the
wall peg and put it on, whipped his gunbelt around his
waist and buckled it on, opened the door and looked
back. "Bill, tell Ma I'll be waiting for her out front. Oh,

156

on your way home you might stop by my place and tell Martha not to look for me till later on, probably some time this afternoon."

"Right," Bill said.

Alone for the minute with the judge, Bill turned to him and asked, "Think Pete's got any chance of beating the rope, Judge?"

"Very little chance, I'm afraid, Bill," McCreary replied. "When a man kills as indiscriminately as Pete has, he must be stopped. Society has the right to demand protection from such a man, and the laws were written and the courts created to provide that protection."

"Uh-huh," Bill said.

"But don't misunderstand, Bill. I don't want you to think I'm giving up without a fight. I'm not. I'm going to do everything I can to save him from the gallows and get him a prison sentence instead."

"Uh-huh," Bill said again. "What I don't get is what's come over Pete. He was never cruel . . . or . . . or vicious or even mean. He was like everybody else. Fair enough, friendly with people and never one to go looking for trouble. How do you explain it?"

Mary, wearing her long cloak with the deeply recessed hood hanging between her shoulders, came into the room.

"I don't think anyone can really explain it, Bill," she said. "All anyone can do is theorize. But that's all. And I have a theory of my own and it's troubling me. Somewhere along the line when I was bringing you boys up, teaching you right from wrong, I must have been negligent with Pete. I must have failed him somewhere. That's the only way I can explain it, why he's so different from you and Matt. So he alone shouldn't be standing trial. Somehow some of the blame for what he has done should be laid at my door."

157

EIGHTEEN

Rawlins was a good-sized, sprawling and still growing town with a four-block-long main street and a handful of offshoot side streets that right-angled and intersected it. They served to absorb the main street's overflow of secondary commercial establishments and sandwiched them in among their boarding houses and private homes. Only the saloons, and there were seven of them, three of which considered themselves so far above the others that they referred to their places as cafes, found it necessary to establish themselves on the main thoroughfare. Survival for them, they had learned, was dependent upon their nearness and immediate availability to those with a thirst that demanded prompt quenching. However, smaller businesses such as tailor shops, piece and dry goods stores, millineries and dressmakers and groceries found the side streets with their lower rentals amply suited to their requirements.

Because it was the county seat, a rail head and cattle shipping center, Rawlins boasted of a United States Marshal as its law enforcement officer instead of a sheriff whose authority was limited to his township and the territory immediately surrounding it. A sheriff was an elected public servant, answerable for his actions to the citizens of his community and there compelled to bow to the dictates of local politicians. Commissioned and backed by the federal government, free of local obligations and entanglements, a marshal's range of authority and activity was practically unlimited. He was permitted to cover as much territory as he deemed

158

necessary. Law breakers found that it was one thing to taunt and dare a sheriff to take action against them. It was something else, they soon discovered, when a marshal took the trail. Where the former, usually willing and more often than not most eager to overlook infractions of the law, might hesitate to take a firm stand with the culprits, the latter, taking a very dim view of any kind of lawlessness, dealt harshly with it.

There were two rather burly, stubbly-faced men, one of them mustached, wearing deputy marhsal's badges pinned to their shirtpockets, idling on the walk in front of Marshal Nate Adams' office on Rawlins' main street. When the Rowan buckboard wheeled into town and came rumbling down the street, they looked up more or less mechanically. When it pulled up at the curb in front of them and braked to a stop, they eyed it interestedly. Matt glanced at them as he whipped the reins around the handbrake, jumped down and stepped around to Mary's side of the buckboard and helped her alight.

"Now look, Ma," he said to her in a low voice, turning his back on the two deputies. "I want you to kinda prepare yourself for when you see Pete. He must have enough sense to know that this is the end of the trail for him. So you're liable to have a hard time of it with him. Just remember that all these killings and the rest of what he's been mixed up in, well, they're all his doing, not yours, Bill's or mine. Tell him for all of us that we're standing by him, that we're ready and willing to do anything and everything to help him. Only he's gotta be told, Ma, and he's gotta be made to understand that there's the law, so we can only go so far and do only just so much for him. But I don't want him or you either, Ma, to think I'm forgetting that he's my brother. Because I'm not. But . . ."

159

"I understand, Matt."

He looked relieved, managed a little smile and said, "Good, Ma. Go ahead. I'll be waiting for you right here when you come out."

She crossed the walk. The mustached deputy stepped in front of the door, barring her way to it, and looked questioningly at her.

"I'm here to see my son," she told him. "Pete Rowan."

"Oh," he said, opened the door, held it wide for her and closed it after her.

Halting a step or two inside the office, Mary waited quietly till a lean man with iron-gray hair who was seated at a desk that faced the door looked up at her from some papers that were spread out before him.

"I'm Mary Rowan," she said. "Judge McCreary told me . . ."

"I've been expecting you, Ma'am. Your son asked to see you and when the judge put it up to me, I said it would be all right." He swept together the papers that he had been studying, made a single pile of them, put them in the middle drawer, closed it, and got to his feet and came out from behind the desk to the front of it. There was a badge pinned to the front of his flannel shirt, about midway between the third button and the pocket. Across the face of the badge in raised letters was the legend "U.S. Marshal." "I knew your husband, Mrs. rowan. He was a mighty fine man. That's why I'm so blamed sorry that that young feller in there," and he jerked his head in the direction of a closed side door that Mary hadn't noticed before, "is his son."

"May I see him now, please?"

"Yeah, sure," was the prompt reply. But then as an afterthought, or so it seemed at the moment, "Kinda warm inside, Ma'm. Suppose you let me take your coat for now? I'll have it right here for you when you're

160

finished visiting with Pete."

He moved behind her so quickly, even before Mary was prepared for it, and helped her out of her cloak. He took it from her, and folded it, and turning, laid it across the desk. When she saw him run his hand over it, she said quietly, "There's a small pocket in my cloak, Marshal, just large enough for a handkerchief. But not roomy enough by any means for a gun. And I assure you I haven't a gun concealed on me anywhere else."

He turned to her again. There was a touch of crimson under his eyes.

"You . . . you wanna come this way, Ma'm?" he asked, avoiding Mary's steady eyes and leading the way to the closed door.

An iron barred door stood between Mary and Pete Rowan.

"Gee, am I glad to see you, Ma!" Pete said. She had never seen him look as he did then, dirty, unshaven, his hair rumpled and matted and badly in need of cutting, and a discolored swelling under his left eye. His shirt had been half torn off his back, revealing an undershirt that was so soiled, she wondered how long he had been wearing it. There was a huge tear in the right leg of his Levis, exposing the knee cap and some inches of his leg and thigh. She glanced critically at his boots. There were badly scuffed and so shabby-looking, the sight of them and of him too hurt her. Raising her gaze to meet is, she saw a strange burning in his eyes that frightened her. He cast a quick look around the cell room. When he saw that they had been left alone, he poked his face through the bars as far as they permitted, and asked in an eager whisper: "Where is it, Ma? Where've you got it?"

She looked at him blankly.

"Where have I got what?"

"The gun. You brought me a gun, didn't you?"

She stared at him.

"A gun?" she repeated.

"'Course! What'd you think I wanted to see you for? I figured it would be easier for you to hide one on you than for Matt or Bill. I knew nobody would make a try to search you and I know doggone well they wouldn't let one o' the boys in here without shaking him down good."

She didn't answer.

"Now look, Ma, this is what I want you to do. First, you hustle yourself outta here and bring me back something to eat. While you're out, get hold of a gun and hide it on you somewhere. Where you get it or even how, I don't care, long's you get it for me. Then you head back to Ryerton and get me some dough. A couple o' hundred'll do me. No, maybe you'd better make it five hundred. That'll give me enough to operate with till I get word to you where I am so you can send me more. Matt can bring the dough with him tonight along with a good, fast horse that I'll want waiting for me somewhere outside but close by, so the minute I hit the street, I can get going. Bill will hafta come with Matt and they'll hafta have their rifles with them so they can hold off anybody who tries to come after me. Guess that's it, Ma. Oh, nearly forgot this. I wanna make my break outta here at midnight. Be sure and tell that to the boys so they'll be all set for that time. I think that about covers everything."

Mary was speechless. She wanted to answer him. But something had happened to her. She tried to speak. But she couldn't. Only a gurgling, choking sound came from her, from deep down in her throat. But he didn't seem to notice it.

"Ya know where I'm heading for when I get outta here, Ma?" she heard him ask. "California. That's

ght, Ma. Feller I ran into in Mexico told me he'd been
ut there, and he raved about it. Just about the most
eautiful country anywhere according to him. He got
.e so excited about it, I know I won't be satisfied till I
et out there too and see it for myself. And when . . ."

He stopped for she had half-turned away from him.

"Wait a minute, Ma," he said. "I'm not finished yet.
o where you going?"

She looked back at him over her shoulder.

"Out of here, Pete," she replied. "I've got to. I can't
tand it in here any longer."

"You gonna do what I asked you? You gonna get me
vhat I want?"

"No, Pete," she said evenly.

"Huh?" He stared hard at her. "Ya mean you aren't
;onna help me get outta here? You're gonna let them
aang me just like that without you lifting a hand to save
ne?"

"That's right."

"I . . . I don't believe it!" he cried a little wildly.

"You'd better believe it, Pete."

She retraced her steps to the barred door and faced
aim again, squarely too. His eyes were wide and fixed
on her, his mouth opened a bit too.

"Pete, I'm going to tell you something and I want
vou to listen to me and listen good for it may be the last
ime you'll ever see me or hear me," she began. "I came
aere hoping to here you say something about how sorry
ou are for what you've done. But you haven't said any-
hing of the kind because you aren't at all sorry. Instead
vou want us to help you get out of here even though it
would probably mean killing those who might stand in
your way. We won't do it, Pete. We won't let you make
us a party to any killings. A man who has killed as ruthlessly as you have and who will go on killing till he is
stopped, must be stopped and brought to task. The law

163

has finally done that. It has finally caught up with you. Now you're to be punished for what you have done. haven't any quarrel with that. I think you should be punished. Maybe you don't realize what you have done. Maybe you haven't the capacity for understanding. I don't know. I can't see inside of you. But if you can't distinguish between right and wrong, and it's quite obvious that you can't, I'm sorry for you because there isn't any place for a man like you among decent, law-abiding people."

She turned away from him again, suddenly flung a "Good-bye, Pete" over her shoulder and hurried to the door. But the tears that suddenly welled up into her eyes blinded her and she had to grope for the door with out-thrust hands. Just as she neared it, it opened, and the mustached deputy came in. He stopped abruptly when he saw Mary with tears coursing down her cheeks, hastily backed out and held the door for her. With a cry she fled past him. But through the closing door she heard Pete's voice. It cut into her like a knife-thrust.

"Ma! Don't go! Don't leave me, Ma!"

Matt had been pacing up and down along the curb, stopping every now and then to level a look at the marshal's door. Pacing again, when he heard it open, he whirled around. When he saw Mary emerge, saw her tear-streaked face, and her balled-up handkerchief clutched so tightly in her hand, he started toward her only to stop when she looked up and shook her head. Slowly he backed off and stood at the right front wheel of the buckboard and watched her come across the walk.

"You all right, Ma?" he asked her anxiously as she rejoined him.

"Yes, I'm all right now, Matt," she replied. "But

don't ask me anything else now. Wait till we've gotten away from here."

"Yeah, sure, Ma."

He helped her climb up, watched her settle herself on the wide seat and tuck in her long, full skirt under her legs, then he stepped down into the gutter, passed in front of the idling horses and climbed up next to her. As he unwound the reins and released the handbrake, the door to the office opened again and a tall figure of a man, Nate Adams, appeared in the doorway. Their eyes met and held for a brief moment. Then the buckboard pulled away from the curb, wheeled around and headed upstreet. Passersby raised their eyes mechanically to the oncoming vehicle and its occupants. Matt stared back at them. Mary lowered her eyes and kept looking down at her clasped hands. Matt glanced at her. But mindful of her request to save his questions for later on, he made no attempt to press her to talk. He kept his gaze fixed on the intersection that they were approaching and on the open roadway beyond it and ahead of them. He slowed the team as they neared the intersection to permit a farm wagon to pass. Then they were across it and Rawlins was behind them.

Mary raised her head and said dully, "He had asked to see me for two reasons. First, he thought I would understand that he wanted a gun and that I would bring one. And secondly . . ."

Matt's head jerked around to her.

"A gun?" he repeated. "What for? Ya mean he hasn't had his fill of killings yet and that he wants to kill s'more?"

"That it would be safe for me to conceal a gun on me because he didn't think that anyone would insist upon searching me."

She told Matt everything that Pete had said and related what she had replied. He listened attentively and

165

without interrupting her, and when she had finished, he shook his head and said bitterly, "So that's all he thinks of us. A means for him to break out of jail so he can go on killing. Ma, he must be crazy. He must be to think the way he does."

Mary made no response.

"He say anything about that Mexican girl?" Matt asked.

"No, and I didn't mention her either."

"Ya think he thinks we're still gonna do what he wants?"

"I told him we wouldn't. But there's no telling with that boy, Matt. There's no way of knowing what he thinks."

"When they take him outside and loop the rope around his neck, then he'll know for sure that you meant what you said."

"That awful look in his eyes. I'd never seen it there before. It really frightened me."

"Wild-like, huh?"

"Yes. Matt, I think he's terribly sick. Mentally, that is."

"He must be," Matt agreed. "But don't you go looking for the law to let him off on account of that. Because it won't. I don't know how the judge feels about this. But for my dough, Ma . . ."

She lifted her eyes to him.

"For my dough," he repeated, "I don't believe Pete stands even a ghost of a chance of beating the rope."

She had no answer for him.

NINETEEN

Neither Mary nor Matt had anything more to say the rest of the way to Ryerton. The horses, loping and prancing at first, finally settled down and drummed over the road at a fairly steady pace. As they neared Ryerton, Mary looked up and said, "I'd like to see the judge, Matt, before we go on home."

He nodded and said, "Sure, Ma. We'll stop by his office and see if he's in. Seems to me though he's always on the go. For an old feller, he sure does plenty of chasing around."

Fortunately the judge was not on the go this time. He was in his office when the Rowans arrived.

"Well, Mary?" he asked after insisting that she sit in the big, comfortable chair behind his desk. "Did you see Pete?"

"Yes, I saw him," she replied. "But that's about all I can tell you, Judge. Now I'd like you to tell me something, if you will, please."

"If I can," McCreary said with a little smile.

"Judge, I think Pete is a sick boy. Mentally sick."

"I think he is too. I'm basing my plea for him on that."

"Will the court take that into consideration?"

"Frankly, I don't know. It depends entirely upon the judge before whom Pete will be brought. Since the law, written so many years ago, makes no distinction between the mentally ill offender and the usual run of law breaker, there are those of us who interpret the law as it is written and refuse to recognize the fact it is now antiquated and that it should be tempered with reason and judgment. If I am successful in my pleading, I'll get Pete off with a prison sentence. If I fail, if the court refuses to go along with me . . ."

"Yes?"

"Then the law will be followed to the letter."

"But . . . but I can't believe that the court will sentence a mentally sick man to the gallows, a man who isn't responsible for his acts as it would a man possessed of all his faculties," Mary protested.

"Well, what would you have the court do with Pete? Free him and turn him loose on society?"

"No, of course not. I think something should be done for him. Some kind of medical treatment. Something that would help restore his . . . his mental balance."

"We have no institutions to which we may commit the insane or even those only mentally disturbed. Only our prisons were all inmates receive the same treatment as prescribed by law for those who break it regardless of their reasons or their mental responsibility."

"If what I have heard about our prisons is true, then those committed to them are mistreated rather than treated," Mary retorted.

McCreary shrugged and said, "There are a couple of privately maintained institutions for the mentally ill in Philadelphia and Boston. But more instances of brutality and inhumane treatment have been reported from those places than from our prisons. It is unfortunate, Mary, that while our civilization and medicine continue to progress, neither of them has reached the point where it recognizes the need for special consideration for the mentally ill. So until they do and provision is made for them, the mentally ill will continue to be treated as common criminals rather than ailing people sorely in need of understanding and help. I'm sorry,

Mary. But there it is. And there isn't anything that you or I can do about it."

The following day when Pete Rowan was put on trial for his life, his brothers Matt and Bill were in attendance. Mary had intended being present too, maintaining that it was her place to be there. But the boys' argument that it couldn't possibly do Pete any good and that their presence would assure him that he hadn't been abandoned prevailed and Mary yielded and stayed at home.

It was the middle of the afternoon when the boys returned from Rawlins. They found Mary sitting motionlessly at the kitchen table. She raised her head and looked at them, watching them hang up their hats, and held her gaze on them as they came to the table and slumped down in the chairs that they usually occupied. There was a brief silence. Then unable to restrain herself any longer, Mary asked, "Well? Aren't you going to tell me what happened?"

"'Course, Ma," Matt replied. "We saw Pete, all right. But from a distance. They wouldn't let us or anybody else get close to him, much less talk to him."

"Bet that was just about the quickest and the shortest trial they ever held there," Bill said, and Mary's shuttling gaze focused on him.

Her face paled and falteringly she asked, "You mean . . . it's over . . . already?"

"That's right, Ma," Matt said, drawing a deep breath, and she looked hard at him. "It's all over."

"They had him dead to rights, Ma," Bill told her. "One witness after another got up and spoke his piece and when the judge, man named Ferris, a thin-faced feller of about sixty or so, with cold eyes and thin lips, had heard enough, that was it.''

"Never heard of that Ferris before," Matt added."Somebody sitting behind me said that Judge Harmon's laid up with something or other and that they brought in Ferris to spell him.''

"McCreary did all he could for Pete," Bill said. "But Ferris wouldn't go along with him on the idea that something had happened to Pete to turn him into a killer and that he shouldn't be held responsible for the things he'd done. Far as Ferris was concerned, Pete was an out-and-out killer, and nothing that anybody could say would make him think otherwise.''

"That's it, Ma," Matt said. "That's the whole story of what happened.''

"When . . . when will they do it?''

Matt moistened his lips with the tip of his tongue before he answered.

"Tomorrow morning at eight.''

"Then the law will be satisfied," Bill added, "and society, according to Ferris, will be able to breathe easy again. It won't have anything more to fear from Pete Rowan.''

With head bent and the back of her hand pressed hard against her lips, Mary sobbed quietly. Matt motioned to Bill not to say anything more, but Bill with a reassuring gesture of his own said, "I got to the marshal after they'd locked Pete up again, Ma, and he said he'd give us a couple o' minutes with Pete just before they take him out tomorrow morning.''

They sat in silence after that till Mary seemed to have regained her composure. Then Matt, leaning over and covering her hand with his, asked, "Ma, think you'll be all right by yourself for a while?''

She nodded wordlessly in between dabs at her eyes with her handkerchief.

"I'll be back later on though," Matt told her, "and

'll bring Martha with me.''

"I'll be back later too," Bill said.

Mary lifted her tear-streaked face to him.

"I don't think you should, Bill," she said. "I don't think you should leave Ann alone at this time any longer than you have to. And I certainly don't think you should bring her here tonight.''

"If I know Ann, she'll insist on coming," Bill replied. "She'll feel that we all should be here with you tonight.''

"I think Ma's right, Bill," Matt said, turning to him. "Martha and I will be here and we'll stay over. So there won't be need for you and Ann to be here too.''

Bill rubbed his chin with the back of his hand.

"Well, all right, if you say so. Oh, what about tomorrow, Matt?''

"Want me to stop by your place and pick you up, or do you wanna . . . ?''

"You stop by for me.''

Matt nodded and asked, "Say around six-thirty or so?''

"I'll be ready to go whatever time you get there," Bill answered. Then turning again to Mary he said, "Ma, I hope you aren't planning to go to Rawlins tomorrow. No point to it, ya know?''

"That's right, Ma," Matt said. "We'll take care of everything.''

"You boys will let me decide that for myself, won't you?" Mary asked.

"'Course," Matt and Bill said together.

Matt got up, bent over Mary, kissed her cheek and squeezed her hand, and straightening up again, turned and walked off. Bill knelt down in front of her and she put her arms around him, held him tight against her for a moment and released him. When he came across the room to the door, Matt handed him his hat and followed him out of the house.

Having arranged with the Rawlins undertaker for him to claim Pete's body after the execution, prepare it for burial and deliver it to the family home, Matt and Bill stepped out into the sun drenched street.

"What a day," Bill said with a shake of his head. "Ever see one like this before? Ever see one so beautiful?"

"Made for living," Matt commented glumly. "Not for what they're gonna to do Pete."

Unhurriedly because it was only about seven o'clock, they strolled up the street. They were surprised to see so many people up and about at such an early hour. Passersby glanced at them, and apparently recognizing them, followed them with their eyes. The brother pretended not to notice the stares, gave no outward sign that they were aware of eyes on them. When they came opposite the marshal's office, they crossed the street and went in. There were four armed men standing about in the office, the two deputies whom Matt had seen twice before and two other men who were also wearing deputy's badges. Nate Adams came out of the cell room followed by a tall well groomed man. The Rowans stared at the latter. It was the Reverend Jeremy Goslin. They stared because they were so surprised to see him there and because of the eye-catching transformation from shabbiness to gentility that couldn't help but command respect for him. His hair had been trimmed and was neatly combed, providing a becoming frame for his normally thin face. Even his eyes had undergone change. Somehow the fierce burning had gone out of them.

"I took the liberty of coming here, hoping to be able to talk with your brother," he told them quietly instead of in his usual booming voice, "and perhaps prepare him for what is to come. I left him eating his breakfast. I shall return to him again shortly and stay with him till it is over."

With a nod, he turned and went out. The Rowans looked at each other and shook their heads.

"You said we could see Pete," Bill said to Adams.

"That's right," the marshall answered. "Make it back here in about forty-five minutes. That'll give you five minutes with him before we take him out."

Bill nodded and said, "We'll be back."

Matt trooped out after him. They stood for a while on the walk in front of Adams' office. But when more and more people began to gather across the street, Bill, eyeing them with a frown, muttered, "Look at them over there. Just as many women and kids as there are men. And all come to see a man get hanged."

"And they're all spruced up too," Matt added bitterly. "Like it was a holiday or something. Come on, Bill. Let's walk. I don't like standing here for them to gape at."

They walked down the street.

"How do you like that Goslin showing up here?" Bill asked. "I can't get over that."

"Damned nice of him, ya know that? And he was so slicked up, I had to look twice at him to make sure it was him."

"Musta struck gold some place."

"Well, wherever he got the dough it took to buy him that outfit he's wearing, he really looks like something now. Kinda think we're gonna owe him something for this, Bill."

"Yeah."

"When Ma hears about this she'll be pleased."

"A little later on, when we get back to things the way they were there for a while, we can get together with Ma and decide what we wanna do about Goslin."

They halted at the first intersection. Just as Bill was about to step off the curb to cross the street, Matt put out a restraining hand, stopping him. Bill looked at him.

"S'matter?" he asked.

"That buckboard over there," Matt said, pointing to a buckboard that was drawn up against the curb a dozen feet or so from the corner. "That's ours, Ma's, isn't it, or are my eyes playing tricks on me?"

Bill's eyes followed his brother's pointing finger.

"Yeah, it's ours, all right," he said. "Recognize it from the red trim around the wheels. But what do you suppose it's doing here?"

"I wouldn't know."

"Didn't you say you looked in on Ma before you left the house this morning and that she was asleep?"

"That's right. That's what I said."

"That's what I thought you said. If that's Ma's rig, then she must have driven it over. What I'd like to know now is where is she."

"You and me both, Bill. I just hope she isn't up to something."

"Like what?"

There was a sudden, startling burst of gunfire somewhere behind them. Instantly they spun around and looked upstreet anxiously in the direction of the marshal's office. They saw the crowd opposite it scatter, saw people collide and trample one another in their frenzied, panic-stricken haste to get under cover. Children were bowled over and women screamed and clawed at men who bumped into them. Then everyone was running, some one way, others the other way. Suddenly though the street was emptied and hushed. The door to the marshal's office was flung open and a man in a badly torn short and Levis that were ripped at one knee came bounding out. It was Pete Rowan. He had a gun clutched in his hand. He looked about him quickly, spotted a horse tied up at a hitchrail a couple of doors up the street from Adams' office, and ran to it.

But then, as Matt and Bill, rooted to the walk, watched with wide eyes, just as Pete reached the horse, a slight, cloaked figure of a woman with a half raised rifle in her hands stepped out of a nearby alley.

"It . . . it's Ma!" Bill gasped.

"Yeah! Come on!"

They dashed up the street. They were too far away for them to hear what Mary said to Pete who had already untied the horse and had just swung himself up on the animal's back. Adams' door opened a second time, and a tall, rangy man with a bloodied face, lurched out on the walk. It was the marshal himself. Pete spotted him, backed the horse away from the rail and into the middle of the street, wheeled him, and raised his gun for a shot at the marshal. As he leveled his gun, Adams stumbled out to the curb and swayed over it. A rifle cracked spitefully. Pete's gun fell from his hand. He sagged brokenly, head bent, and toppled sideways out of the saddle. He fell limply in the gutter, struck on his shoulder and slumped over on his face.

Adams' deputies with their guns in their hands burst out of the office. Two of them ran to the marshal while the other two bounded past him to bend over Pete. One of them kicked Pete's gun viciously, sent it slithering away. It caromed off the curb and lay still a foot or so from it with dust boiling up around it. The other man dragged Pete over on his back. As he bent over him again, Adams, flanked by his other two deputies, stepped down in the gutter and joined the two standing over Pete.

Matt and Bill came panting up to Mary. She handed the rifle to Matt.

"I had to do it," she told him tearfully. "I was afraid he would get his hands on a gun somehow, and you see he did. If I hadn't stopped him, he would have killed the marshal, and if he had managed to get away from here, he would have gone on killing. Since no one else was able to stop him, it had to be one of his own who did it. Maybe now that he's been stopped we can go back to living our lives as Rowans should. Take me home, please! Take me home!"

REAL WEST

The true life adventures of America's greatest frontiersmen.

THE LIFE OF KIT CARSON by John S.C. Abbott. Christopher "Kit" Carson could shoot a man at twenty paces, trap and hunt better than the most skilled Indian, and follow any trail — even in the dead of winter. His courage and strength as an Indian fighter earned him the rank of brigadier general of the U.S. Army. This is the true story of his remarkable life.

__2968-5 $2.95

THE LIFE OF BUFFALO BILL by William Cody. Strong, proud and courageous, Buffalo Bill Cody helped shape the history of the United States. Told in his own words, the real story of his life and adventures on the untamed frontier is as wild and unforgettable as any tall tale ever written about him.

__2981-2 $2.95

DOUBLE-BARREL WESTERNS

Twice the Action —
Twice the Adventure —
Only a Fraction of the Price!

Two complete and unabridged novels in each book!

Hell to Hallelujah and **Ride to the Gun**
by Ray Hogan.

___2917-0 $3.95

Hangman's Range and **Saddle Pals**
by Lee Floren.

___2913-8 $3.95

Vengeance Valley and **Wildhorse Range**
by Allan K. Echols.

___2928-6 $3.95

Young guns, old-time action!

CHET CUNNINGHAM

The Willy Boy Gang was made up of the youngest lawbreakers on the frontier, but each was ten times as deadly as any man twice his age. All six had a vendetta to settle, and they vowed to ride until every one of them had tasted revenge.

#4: AVENGERS. Headed for Denver, where the Professor had more than one score to even, the Willy Boy Gang planned to drain every cent from the Denver First Colorado Bank and murder any one who stood in their way.

__2896-4 $2.95

#5: RIO GRANDE REVENGE. Deadly *federales* had taken Juan Romero's wife and son hostage. But Romero and the gang would free them — even if they had to drown the corrupt officers in pools of their own blood.

__2967-7 $2.95

#6: FLAGSTAFF SHOWDOWN. In Arizona to save Gunner Johnson's mother from an embezzler, the gang had more than their share of trouble. For the swindler was desperate enough to kill them all — and crazy enough to succeed.

__3154-X $2.95 US/$3.95 CAN

LEISURE BOOKS
ATTN: Order Department
276 5th Avenue, New York, NY 10001

Please add $1.50 for shipping and handling for the first book and $.35 for each book thereafter. N.Y.S. and N.Y.C. residents, please add appropriate sales tax. No cash, stamps, or C.O.D.s. All orders shipped within 6 weeks via postal service book rate. Canadian orders require $2.00 extra postage. It must also be paid in U.S. dollars through a U.S. banking facility.

Name _____

Address _____

City _____ State _____ Zip _____

I have enclosed $_____ in payment for the checked book(s). Payment <u>must</u> accompany all orders.□ Please send a free catalog.